SCATTERPATH

Also by Maralys Wills

Manbirds: Hang Gliders and Hang Gliding
Higher than Eagles

SCATTERPATH

a novel by
MARALYS WILLS

LYFORD
Books

The characters in this novel are fictitious. Any characters resembling actual persons, living or dead, are purely coincidental. The names (except of historical figures), dialogue, incidents, and opinions expressed in this novel are products of the author's imagination and creativity. They should not be construed as real. This work is not intended, and should not be interpreted, as expressing the views of any department or agency of the United States government.

LYFORD Books
Published by Presidio Press
505 B San Marin Dr., Suite 300
Novato, CA 94945-1340

Library of Congress Cataloging-in-Publication Data

Wills, Maralys.
    Scatterpath : a novel / Maralys Wills.
      p.   cm.
    ISBN 0-89141-487-8
    I. Title.
PS3573.I456722S3   1992   92-39138
813'.54—dc20   CIP

Typography by ProImage
Printed in the United States of America

Dedicated to Jeff Rich, N.T.S.B. field investigator, whose help went far beyond "technical advice"—without whom this book could not have been produced.

Jeff is, in spirit, Alan Wilcox.

My deepest thanks.

Acknowledgments

Special thanks to John Wallace, whose painstaking analysis of the manuscript provided insights that were sorely needed.

Thanks also to Stu Borden, who helped work out some problems with the characters. And to my critique group, The Literary Elite, for week-by-week review and consistent help. And to my editor, Joan Griffin, for her unfailing graciousness and willingness to let me tackle problem areas in my own way. And to my agent, Pat Teal, for her abundance of ideas. And most of all to R.V.W.—for everything!

Prologue

James Higgins was suddenly fed up with disasters. Eleven consecutive months of viewing charred bodies and reconstructing the mangled chunks of jet engines had left him drained and ready to hang up his job. But when he asked for leave from the National Transportation Safety Board in Washington, D.C., his boss asked where he was going.

"Fishing, Stan, fishing," he said wearily. "Miles from here to some shining loch in the Trossachs." *Where I can sit on the bank and purge my mind and forget that I deal in airplane crashes.*

His boss nodded. "Scotland, isn't it? Perfect, Jim." He clapped the other on the shoulder. "Alan Wilcox has turned down the follow-up trip to Locherbie, and you were his choice as a replacement. So while you're there . . ."

Which meant his transportation was free, but his time wasn't.

As Higgins stepped off the people-mover to board an Airtech Aviation 323 out of Dulles, he happened to look back. He'd thought he was the last one off, but apparently not. A slight man, curly-haired with noticeably large eyes, stood in the aisle with ticket in hand—a curious thing, because when the driver gestured impatiently toward the plane, the man merely smiled and limped back toward a seat. A weirdo, thought Higgins. Not what you want at an airport.

Some time later, sitting in the cockpit jump seat just behind the captain, Higgins checked his watch. It was one in the morning, almost an hour since he and the two pilots had run out of conversation and he'd drifted into a nap. Now, looking out the side window into frozen blackness, he was grateful for empty time to search out familiar stars and think about his vacation. As soon as the stint in Locherbie was over, he'd be fishing in the Trossachs near Kilmahog with his jacket collar turned up around his ears—to the locals a damn fool activity for the cold month of March. But cold was relative. Outside the aircraft the temperature at forty-one thousand feet was minus fifty-four. *That* was cold!

His mind drifted to the incongruity of his present situation. Three of them in that small cocoon, dimly lit with an array of blue, green, and red lights from the cathode ray tube displays plus the various system status lights and circuit breaker panels—the small space aglow with light no brighter than a lighted Christmas tree in a dark room . . . both the captain and copilot with their seats reclined and the copilot's right foot propped against the bottom of the instrument panel. In here, warmth and comfort and the muted noise of engines; out there on the other side of the aluminum skin, mere inches away, a black sky and a howling wind and 20 percent of the normal oxygen—in an atmosphere so lacking in pressure that if you tried to breathe it for ten seconds, reverse osmosis would carry most of the oxygen out of your body.

The window blows out and you're dead. Not an idea he wanted to dwell on long.

For a while he watched what the crew was watching, the progress of their flight on the navigation display CRT, which showed the airplane crawling along a magenta line from reporting point to reporting point. They'd already made four en route position reports, already noted that the inertial navigation system displays were showing freakish and unusually strong headwinds "on the nose" from about 040 degrees at 130 knots. The captain, old school and due to retire in four years, had made it clear what he thought about computers: "I trust these whiz-chip control systems about as far as I'd trust Saddam Hussein. You may *think* you know what's going on, but try turning your back and you'll get bushwhacked."

The captain's voice broke into Higgins's reverie. "Bob, switch the INS to current position to verify the automatic flight control system."

The copilot looked at his captain questioningly and started to say something, but changed his mind and pulled his foot off the panel to work the switches of the INS unit on the lower console beneath the throttle levers. After a brief scan of displayed numbers, he pulled out the en route airway chart stuffed into a space beside his seat. His finger traced a printed line. "There's something wrong here . . ."

Higgins sat up straighter.

The captain turned to look at his copilot. "What did you say?"

"I've checked the INS reading twice, and if it's correct, we're nowhere near our assigned track."

Even as he was speaking, the captain moved his chair forward and in one motion switched the two backup INS displays to present position. Under his breath he said, "All the numbers are within a tenth of a minute of each other."

Like the two pilots, Higgins stared fixedly at the navigation CRT display. The plane seemed to be moving ahead as normal, still on its assigned track. The captain grabbed the chart out of the copilot's hand. "Christ!" he said seconds later, "what the damned hell is going on here? We're near a hundred miles south of track!"

"It can't be . . ." The copilot looked horrified.

"Damned piss-ass computers'll do it to you every time!" The pilot's eyes darted between monitors as he flung words at his copilot. "Get on the damned radio fast and let ATC know where we are before another aircraft T-bones us . . ."

As the copilot began speaking into the microphone, his words drifted back to Jim Higgins like fragments heard on cockpit voice recorders from bygone wrecks: ". . . south of course about a hundred miles . . . something wrong with our navigational computers . . ." Then no more, because suddenly everything went wrong at once.

It began as a low, rumbling vibration throughout the airframe. On the middle right EICAS cathode ray tube the flight control position display showed all the flight spoilers rising out on the wings. Seconds later the attitude indicators on the flight instrument displays depicted a sudden roll to the left past the ninety-degree point as the spoilers on the right wing suddenly went down again. The aircraft symbol on the attitude indicator moved rapidly toward the inverted position while the captain grabbed the controls and tried repeatedly to disconnect the AFCS and the autopilot.

Higgins sat frozen in his seat; he knew instinctively the computers wouldn't disconnect. And they didn't.

The aircraft nose pitched down and all the screens went blank.

In the absolute blackness of night, flying without indicators, the pilot had no way of knowing the attitude of the aircraft. Wind began to scream past the nose as the craft accelerated earthward.

G-forces pinned Higgins against his seat, and dimly he heard the captain spewing out a fresh vilification of computers. Dimly, too, he caught glimpses of the man moving the controls through every possible parameter

—all futile. Without the flight instruments he didn't even know which way was up.

Higgins's mind raced through a series of emotions. Helplessness. Profound fear. Rage. For a moment he fought furiously against the violent force that jammed him against his seat, and at last felt resignation. *So it's happening to me.* Who would tell his niece there'd be no Scottish doll? And then his mind turned cold and calculating. From forty-one thousand feet it would take approximately two minutes to reach the ocean.

He glanced up at the overhead panel where the cockpit voice recorder microphone was located, and suddenly, spontaneously, he began speaking, following the course of action he'd decided on years ago if this very thing ever happened. "This is Jim Higgins," he said, loud enough for the microphone to pick him up over the sounds of howling wind and pilot voices. "We've got something bizarre going on . . ."

In sixty seconds he'd said everything he needed to, and now he could feel the hairs on the back of his neck. *We're going in.*

A part of him rose out of the disaster and left behind the garbled voices of the two pilots, and he was back in his office hearing it discussed. "It took the big high dive." "A smoking hole in mid-Atlantic." "Two hundred and seventy-one SOBs."

An explosion shook the plane. Immediately the angle of attack worsened and the plane nosed vertical. Blood drained from Higgins's head and his awareness dimmed. Look for me, Alan, he thought irrationally. It won't be easy, old friend, but keep looking. I'm one of the Souls on Board.

Chapter One

Alan Wilcox sat in his tiny, cluttered office at the National Transportation Safety Board in Lawndale, California, staring at the daily he'd just plucked off the bulletin board. "Trans America flight 160, down over the Atlantic." *His* flight, or it would have been if he hadn't given it to Jim Higgins. So now his good friend Jim was at the bottom of the Atlantic, and he was sitting safe in his office and so damned angry he couldn't speak.

Nobody would believe there was a conspiracy against an airplane manufacturer.

A few months earlier Wilcox wouldn't have believed it himself, and even now all he had was a lot of useless gut-level instinct that could never pass as proof.

Conspiracy. Sabotage. As an investigator for the NTSB he couldn't even use those words without looking the fool, which was why he'd suppressed his suspicions until today and quietly kept searching. But today he *knew*. From the minute he picked up the daily and learned where the plane went down, he knew with sudden, cold certainty that this latest accident wasn't accidental. His jaw tightened. *A deliberate act. But nobody else will believe it.*

Rereading the sheet for the tenth time, Wilcox asked himself stubbornly, When have my instincts ever failed me? Yet what good were they by themselves? Even Jim Higgins, trapped in the downed jet or wherever he was, would scorn any effort mounted on pure intuition.

Okay, then, so they had to find the damned plane! And he had to start raising enough hell so they'd get the help they needed—from the Air Force's AWACS planes, if need be, whose radar monitored the mid-ocean wastelands, or the CIA's intelligence satellites, which could pick up the mustache on a Russian walking across Red Square. *Somebody* knew *something* about that plane!

In their Lemon Heights home, Alan Wilcox's wife drank her second cup of coffee and watched one last interview on the small TV above the kitchen table. Only casually interested in the celebrity, Ellie forced herself to pay attention so she'd have something to think about besides Alan; she simply couldn't worry nonstop about what was going wrong with her husband.

For months she'd been telling herself things would soon get better, that Alan was essentially a balanced, reasonable man and the long view was that such people could get a little lopsided without becoming permanently distorted. One had to wait, that's all, let the aberration run its course.

Suddenly aware she'd left herself too little time to dress for her job, she jumped up and pushed back her chair. As she reached for the television knob, a bulletin superimposed itself on the talk show, and Ellie froze. Not again! she thought, as words rolled across the bottom of the screen.

She read rapidly, dreading what she'd see. Come on, now, she thought, Let's not be an Airtech! . . . We don't need one more straw on Alan's back. But the news mentioned only Trans America Fleet, and she turned it off, wondering dimly what kind of person she'd become—thinking only about Alan and not all the people who'd lost their lives.

Shaken, Ellie rushed to her bedroom and threw open her closet door. She stood in front of her clothes as though expecting the decision to be made for her. But she couldn't concentrate and her thoughts whirled in circles. Alan was so abstracted now, he was hardly with her even when he was home. *If that plane was an Airtech, we'll both be in trouble.*

The rigger was driving west on Interstate 8 in San Diego when the news came over the radio: "A bulletin just into our newsroom. Trans America flight 160 carrying two hundred and seventy passengers is reported missing somewhere over the Atlantic. There are no details yet, but we'll bring you an update as soon as we have it."

As the voice dropped away, the rigger's hand shot out, and he punched the buttons on his radio one after the other, listening to each station a split second before going on. Nothing. The rest hadn't picked it up yet, which confirmed what he believed about radio stations and news gathering: the whole pack were a bunch of incompetents who dispensed news only as they were hit over the head with it. Idiots.

His mind went back to the downed aircraft. *Where* in the Atlantic? he wondered. At what time? How in hell would anyone know?

At St. Joseph's Hospital in Orange, California, the news flashed on the wall-hung television screen just as Miles Kimball was handing his wife, Sondra, a cup of coffee from her hospital tray. Miles's hand stopped suddenly and warm, dark coffee sloshed out of the cup and onto her white blanket cover. She didn't notice. Her eyes were on the screen, and her hand, in a series of spasmodic movements, went to her mouth. "Oh, tha's terrible!" she slurred.

Miles said nothing. His stomach lurched and he thought he was going to be sick. "Approximately two hundred and seventy people on board," the announcer was saying, reading gravely from a sheet of paper, "an Airtech Aviation 323. Prestwick, Scotland, reports the plane three hours overdue."

"Th-those poor people," Sondra stammered, and Miles reached for her bedside control and pushed the button until the screen went blank. "Arentshu glad . . . 's not one of your Shhirlings . . . ?" she said.

He looked at her contemptuously and hated her for thinking that way. "It doesn't matter one damn whose plane it is, they're still dead."

Sondra looked shocked.

"Drink your coffee," he said, and went into the small bathroom and closed the door. He caught a glimpse of himself in the mirror. Holy Mary, he'd aged ten years! His eyes were so sleep-robbed they'd turned dark and puffy, and his skin had begun to hang loose around his chin. Only fifty-three. He looked closer to sixty. He sat down on the toilet and dropped his head into his hands. *What have I done? My God, how did it come to this?*

Who am I?

In the beginning, he'd never contemplated anyone dying, not for a single moment, and even now he wasn't sure this had anything to do with him, but whether it did or it didn't, he felt himself coming apart. Too much stress. Mary Helen pressing him all the time, now, and his conscience already so full of self-condemnation he couldn't sleep nights. Lord, he thought, squeezing his head between his hands, what he wouldn't give to go back to the beginning and play it all another way.

Chapter Two

The freakish occurrences and near misses had all started innocently enough, eight months earlier. For Alan Wilcox they seemed to originate with his virgin experience with the new fly-by-wire planes, an ominous moment that never reached the media, but it had triggered something in his mind, and triggering was where good investigation began.

He remembered the day perfectly. It happened to be his twenty-fifth wedding anniversary—the day he received a call from the senior senator from California—but also the day he first suspected things weren't right with Ellie. While his wife slept that morning, Alan lay propped on an elbow beside her, thinking . . . hearing the gentle, rhythmic sounds of her breathing, a comforting whisper that filled his subconscious on the nights he was home.

Married twenty-five years! A record for men in his profession. And all Ellie's doing, a result of her patience and her willingness to put up with his god-awful life-style—a way of life he'd long since accepted and wouldn't change if he could. He should find some unique way to thank her.

He looked down and saw Ellie's smooth white shoulders, the light brown hair that curled softly around her patrician features, and knew she appealed to him as much now as she had when they'd first met. Impatient for her, he began stroking her thigh.

Abruptly she awoke. "Oh . . . Alan!" she said with a sleepy frown. She rolled over. "Isn't it our anniversary? If it is, I must be imagining you're home." Then she smiled. "But the day isn't over yet, is it?"

He forgot his speech. "I was waiting for you to wake up so we—," he broke off and shook his head as the phone rang. "Don't answer it."

She was already out of bed, looking back at him. "You have your pager, I have the phone."

Seconds later a look of astonishment came over her features and she said, "He's right here," and handed him the instrument.

Someone asked if he was Alan Wilcox, and then the speaker identified himself as Senator Connor Fairchild.

Surprised, Alan found himself listening to a voice he'd heard only on television. He forced himself to stay calm. "Well. That's an honor, sir. Thank you. Yes, I'll think it over. I respect your opinion. You're welcome."

When the call ended abruptly, Ellie still stood there, having hardly blinked during the whole two minutes. "Well?" she asked.

He tried to make light of it. "Just one of your everyday Saturday calls." His pulse belied his words.

"Alan! Be serious! What did he *say?*"

He shook his head, trying to remember Fairchild's exact words. It was useless; the wording escaped him. "It boils down to Fairchild asking me to apply for director of the Bureau of Accident Investigation. In Washington." He searched his memory. "Strange, isn't it? I don't know another field investigator who's gotten that kind of call."

"Alan . . ." Ellie stood near the bed in her shortie nightgown that stopped just above her knees. "Alan, *I'm* not that bowled over." She gave him a rare, proud smile of ownership and sat down to rub his back. It was still a youthful back, lean and strong, belying the gray that edged his dark hair. After a moment she turned his face to meet hers, "Why are you so surprised, you idiot? You're not *like* everyone else! There's only one of you in the world!"

She exaggerated, of course, but it pleased him.

"Well . . . will you apply?" Her fingers stopped. She seemed to be on some kind of breathless hold.

"What do you think? It's twice as much money and all kinds of prestige. Only a fool would turn it down."

"But will you apply?" she said, because she knew him.

"I don't know," he said, and the implications of the job whirled through his mind: Washington. The Crystal Palace. Incessant politics. But more than that, the life he'd be giving up: no more shouldering the small accidents, where he handled the case from start to finish . . . no more "fire horse" response, which was both the excitement and curse of the job . . . no more working alone off instinct and those sudden, exhilarating flashes of insight that came out of nowhere.

"I'll have to think it over, Ellie."

She looked at him, carefully expressionless.

But he *knew*. For a fleeting instant he felt a presence in the room, something that hadn't been there before. *What else haven't you been saying, Ellie?*

When it passed, he imagined it hadn't happened. California was where he wanted to live. Air Safety Investigator, Field, was what he wanted to be. Freedom and autonomy were what he needed for happiness. If you like what you've got, he thought, why change horses?

It was the pager that dictated Wilcox's afternoon—a small piece of electronics with which he had a slave-master relationship.

When he was at his office, Alan was governed by the phone. Everywhere else, he was slave to his pager. It went with him to restaurants, to the theater, to parties, and at night hovered by his bed like a watchful spirit that never sleeps. He'd come to think of it as a kind of tether that linked him to every pilot who flew through his region. One mistake by any of them and the tether jerked tight and dragged him away. Somehow the pager had come to represent the source of his enslavement, more than the Safety Board itself.

It was mid-afternoon when Alan and Ellie started down the walkway of their hilltop home in Lemon Heights, near the city of Santa Ana—headed for the caterer who would do their daughter's wedding and then out for a private anniversary dinner. He'd just reached for the car door when the pager went off.

Ellie turned toward him questioningly, though she knew what she'd find: gray-blue eyes lost in thought, already focused elsewhere.

He stopped walking and looked back at her. The pager meant *now*. Stop everything. Find a phone. Go.

Ellie started to say something, then shrugged. "I'll go by myself." He could almost feel her shoulders straighten as he said, "Sorry, Ellie. Whatever you and Jamie decide about the caterer is okay."

Minutes later he was on the phone. "Tahoe? I see. Four passengers?" From the corner of his eye he saw Ellie hovering near the front door, and he said, "Wait a minute," and put his hand over the receiver.

"I'll change our dinner reservations," she said. "How about tomorrow night?"

He shook his head no.

He could see her mind changing gears. "Then Jamie and I will have dinner. You and I . . . well, later." As he nodded and turned away from her, she came back and whispered in his ear, "Have a good anniversary, Alan." And she was gone.

He'd told her when he got the job, "They say being an investigator for the National Transportation Safety Board is hell on relationships." She'd said, "Take it, Alan. We'll be okay." And they had been. Most of the time. But suddenly he wasn't sure.

A speech for their twenty-fifth? Hell, he owed her more than a speech. He owed her . . . everything. But he'd have to find some time.

FSDO—Flight Standards District Office—set up a party line with the Washoe County sheriff's dispatcher and the Reno Flight Service Station. Between them, they gave Wilcox some of what he needed to know: the plane was a Cessna cabin class twin, eight-seater, down in a valley south of Lake Tahoe, a thickly forested area. There were four people. Everyone dead. Probably happened around 11:00 A.M. Oh, and some were children.

Children, Wilcox thought. Damn. He'd never gotten used to dealing with kids.

"What do you want us to do next?" asked the sheriff's dispatcher.

He gave his standard answer. "Radio the ground crew to secure the wreck until I get there tomorrow morning. Two men will be enough. If there are more than two, the rest can leave." It wouldn't be pleasant duty, spending a chilly October night in the mountains guarding wreckage. Search and Rescue generally consisted of volunteers. You tried not to abuse them.

The dispatcher added, "They said it's rough terrain, a helluva hike. And so many trees you can't see it from the air. And cold at night. Below freezing."

Was the man asking him to let *everyone* leave? He found himself shaking his head. Even in the deepest forest under the worst conditions, the hardy curious had a way of getting in and messing up evidence. He said, "My team will get there as fast as we can. Please have a helicopter standing by tomorrow morning at five."

The dispatcher signed off to radio the ground crew and Alan asked the Flight Service Station, "What was the weather picture up there this morning?" As his informant kept him waiting momentarily, he recalled the days before computerization when weather information for a given day remained available on hard copy indefinitely. Now, as with re-

recorded videotapes, new information erased the old, and the old could only be retrieved from the National Oceanographic and Atmospheric Administration in North Carolina. Because weather was critical to his investigation, it had to be secured immediately.

The man came back. "Scattered clouds with variable bases in the early morning . . . rapidly changing conditions to mountain obscurement, rain and turbulence with occasional thundershowers . . . a frontal system that moved more rapidly than forecast."

Midway, Alan could have finished the recitation. "Rapidly changing." "More rapidly than forecast." Words that ought to be tattooed on pilots' forearms. Or drummed into their heads until they could recite them like the Pledge of Allegiance. Weather was *always* rapidly changing. To forget it was tantamount to putting a down payment on a funeral.

"And tomorrow?"

"Cold. About twenty-eight. No clouds, as of now."

He asked for the Cessna's flight plan.

"Filed his flight plan with Hawthorne early in the morning. Came up from the Los Angeles area. Four SOBs. Man signed in was a doctor. Dave Hawkins."

"Dave Hawkins?" Wilcox repeated the name, stunned.

The sheriff's dispatcher came back on. "The ground crew has your message. Oh, and they've found some I.D. The pilot had two kids."

Wilcox wanted to shout, "I *know* how many kids he has." Instead he asked, hanging on to himself, "The fourth was the man's wife?"

"That's right, sir. If that's all, I'll sign off."

When Alan said nothing more, fighting a leaden feeling in the pit of his stomach, the man from the Flight Service Station asked, "Everything all right?"

"I know them," Wilcox said dully.

"I'm sorry."

"It's bound to happen . . . only a question of time. I've known others."

"I'm sorry," the man said again. The silence grew awkward. Wilcox finally remembered to thank him and signed off. He told FSDO he had what he needed and hung up.

Sitting at his kitchen table, Wilcox momentarily closed his eyes. Dave Hawkins. Young Dave Hawkins. Which was the way Alan remembered him. A kid, just eighteen, hanging around the airport the way flying-mad boys often did. And then taking all those lessons from Alan—more than he needed because lessons were a way of getting in the air. They'd liked each other and kept in touch, even after Hawkins finally got into medical school. In later years the contact became sporadic—Christmas cards and not much else. He'd known about Dave's two kids, though. And that his wife's name was Sara.

For the briefest moment he considered giving up on field investigation. Forever. The job in Washington would be altogether different: coordinating, organizing the big investigations for the major airline crashes. Dealing with foreign governments. As director of the Bureau of Accident Investigation he wouldn't be on some goddamned mountaintop looking at the smashed face of his old friend Dave Hawkins.

For a long time he sat in the kitchen trying not to think.

The heaviness passed. Eventually another set of feelings took its place. Unconsciously he sat up straighter and began thinking clearly again. He'd get on with the job as he'd intended. In fact, he would do it now *because* he knew Dave, and because he wouldn't trust anyone else. He was a good investigator. The best. And he knew it without conceit. It was a wholly impersonal fact, like knowing what state he lived in.

He stood up and stretched. And once again reached for the phone. *Dave, I'd rather do this with you than for you. But I don't have a choice, do I?*

When Wilcox tried to reach Cessna Aircraft in Wichita, Kansas, the office was closed. From his private list of phone numbers gathered over the years, he called their chief accident investigator, Sam Orkney, at home. Sam suggested they meet in Reno, at the plush Harrah's. Wilcox had long since stopped arguing with everyone about saving Board money and opting for cheaper accommodations; in the beginning that attitude had brought him no praise and a lot of flak: "*You* stay in the fleabags, Wilcox. If I'm going to be miserable hiking over the landscape, I'm bedding down in a nice hotel with good food." Alone, he stayed where he wanted, as a matter of principle.

He told Orkney they'd rent a car and drive together to the sheriff's office.

Wilcox's next-to-last call was to the Reno area coroner's office. He alerted them to the need for toxicology samples and a look at the pilot's coronary system after Search and Rescue brought out the bodies. *But you won't find anything. Not with this one.*

Before his last call, he quickly scanned the *Official Airline Guide*

to check airline schedules and the kind of plane he wanted. He decided on Trans America Fleet's Airtech Aviation 123—the short-range
version of Airtech's new 323. A fly-by-wire. Mostly new to him, and
he was curious about it. From the cockpit's jump seat he'd get a pretty
good look at the way it operated. Unfortunately it was due to leave
John Wayne Airport in forty-three minutes.

Using a restricted number to reach the dispatcher at John Wayne,
he said, "Alan Wilcox, NT—"

Before he could finish, a hearty voice said, "Hey, Wilcox, how you
doing? Where did the accident happen this time?"

Lay off, he thought. *Okay?* "Tahoe," he said tightly. "I see we don't
have a direct to Reno." He named the flight he wanted to San Francisco and asked if the jump seat was open.

The dispatcher asked, "How fast can you make it?"

"Fast enough."

"You've got it. We'll notify the pilot. Buy you five extra minutes."

"Thanks." As Alan hung up and grabbed his heaviest mountain jacket
off a hanger and threw his mountain boots into a bag, he was thinking that speed-packing had become one of the challenges of the job.
Today he had twelve minutes. But with the bulk of what he needed
already in a case, he could have done it in five.

Driving was another matter. It seemed he was always racing to
airports—with traffic unpredictable. When his own number came up,
he'd decided long since, it wouldn't be in a plane. He'd get it in a car.

He couldn't know that the plane that waited for him at John Wayne
had already scared one crew into swearing off fly-by-wires for the rest
of their careers.

Chapter Three

Running for planes was hell on your clothes. It could take an hour to get dry again, and by then he'd be cold. With scant minutes to make Operations and board his jet, Alan Wilcox tossed his carry-on bag on the conveyor belt and strode rapidly through the magnetometer—only to stop short as a loud buzzer went off. *The badge,* he thought, and pulled it out of his pocket. "Sorry," he said to the female security guard.

"Are you armed?" she asked, thinking she'd seen a police shield.

"I'm not armed," he said, but she made him go back through anyway.

"Operations" at John Wayne Airport consisted of a series of small rooms, one for each airline plus a lounge for pilots and flight attendants. Trans America Fleet operated out of a room about twelve by fourteen in an atmosphere of calm that Alan knew was deceptive. Under an external sense of order was perpetual quiet activity that reminded him of a beehive about to erupt.

A glance at the hanging TV monitor showed his flight was delayed, so he paused at the Operations desk and checked the weather maps on the counter. The 500- and 200-millibar charts gave him the air patterns at eighteen thousand and thirty-five thousand feet. At the moment nothing unusual at either altitude. He nodded to the dispatcher behind the desk, whose arms were going like an octopus as he listened to a squawking radio. Every inbound pilot had some request or other—for fresh water, a wheelchair, repair of a malfunctioning cabin light—and the dispatcher had to sort through them all and see that the myriad requests were filled. Wilcox wouldn't have that man's job for anything.

He found a chair and sat down. The badge was still in his hand. For a moment he sat studying the gold, roughly heart-shaped piece, larger than a sheriff's badge and mounted in a black leather folder. The top of the badge was an eagle with spread wings, across its talons the embossed words "United States of America." A coinlike circle in the center was inscribed "National Transportation Safety Board," and a larger word, "Investigator," crossed underneath. Below was his number in black, 211.

He weighed it in his hand and thought of the standard joke that the shield's usefulness was limited to impressing county sheriffs and setting off metal detectors. In fact it meant much more to him, though he would have admitted so reluctantly. Whereas his pager symbolized duty and absolute obedience, his badge represented authority and power—even freedom. With the badge he could demand and get entrée almost anywhere.

Autonomy, power, and freedom. If anyone had asked what drew him to the job, those words would sum it up about as well as any. He tucked the badge back in his pocket. His Aladdin's lamp, his genie. Except you didn't have to rub it—just show it.

Twenty minutes later he was sitting in the left-hand jump seat behind the pilot of an Airtech 123, curious as hell about their new fly-by-wires. How long had *he* been a pilot . . . twenty-eight years? . . . twenty-nine? Since before his nineteenth birthday, anyway, which was a good chunk of time to sustain enthusiasm for one activity. Yet he felt a kind of prickly anticipation knowing he was about to experience something new in aviation.

He looked over the pilot's shoulder at the monitors, a series of screens that were, from his reading of *Aviation Week* and his conversations with pilots, about what he'd expected. It struck him that the newer cockpits were literally wall-to-wall TV tubes, run by computers. Control of the plane was altogether different from that in conventional aircraft. Whereas pilot input on the wheel, the throttle, and the pedals once translated mechanically through cables to various surfaces on the plane, in this fly-by-wire four computers were in charge and control passed through a series of wires and fuses to the hydraulic actuators and thus to the plane's surfaces. When the computers disagreed, the majority ruled.

Before the plane began taxiing, Alan and the two pilots exchanged a few words, but once the craft was ready to move, Wilcox automatically observed the rule for a "sterile cockpit," which meant no extraneous conversation below ten thousand feet. He listened with interest as the copilot recited the checklist to the pilot while the plane slowly moved into takeoff position. "Transponder on . . . fifteen, fifteen and green . . . master caution . . ." with his hand pushing the light on the master panel, which in turn lit all the caution lights. Wilcox was relieved that even in this fully computerized plane, human input was considered part of the package.

After the plane reached cruising altitude—thirty-three thousand feet—Wilcox loosened his lap belt and leaned forward in his seat. "How do you like flying these things, Steve?"

The pilot looked over his shoulder briefly. "It'll take some getting used to—learning to trust a computer board when my gut tells me something else. But hey—you gotta admire a machine that can land a plane better than you can. I don't know . . ." the pilot's shoulders rose in a shrug, "sometimes you get strange glitches . . ."

"Oh?" Alan sat up straighter. "Like what?"

"Small things. Nothing reportable. I can't remember any offhand. Stuff that happens for a split second and then corrects itself. A quick thrill. But you can't fight progress. They'll all be computerized one of these days and we'll sit here and read magazines." He laughed. "I don't want to be flying planes when the time comes we have absolutely nothing to do. It'll be dangerous. Pilots will get too rusty to function."

"I hear you," said Wilcox.

About a hundred miles out of San Francisco they began losing altitude to twenty-four thousand, and Alan put his earphones on. Oakland center reported, "Cleared for profile descent," and the pilot muttered, "Time to pull the plug." Wilcox could see him easing the throttles back to idle.

The atmosphere in the cockpit changed abruptly: the casualness of a moment before was gone. The two pilots moved their seats forward, and their seat backs came up as they began going over the descent checklist.

The copilot dialed Automatic Terminal Information Services in San Francisco for the current weather. Wilcox listened to the report. "San Francisco International Airport information OSCAR, the 0046

Greenwich observation, sky obscured, visibility one-eighth mile in fog, temperature fifty-seven, dew point fifty-seven, winds calm, altimeter two niner eight three, runway twenty-nine, visual range eight hundred feet. Arriving aircraft, indicate that you have information OSCAR."

The two pilots scanned the approach charts to San Francisco, which hung off a clipboard on the wheel. Leaning forward, Wilcox tried to read the figures. Too far away. But suddenly he didn't need to see. He saw instead the two men exchange looks, saw the pilot frown, heard the copilot say, "Shit, we're down to minimums."

They were flying into fog.

Alan stiffened in his chair. It was going to be a category 3 landing—zero ceiling and runway visibility range six to seven hundred feet. Conditions any fly-by-wire could theoretically handle and any pilot would automatically detest . . . or fear, except pilots never used such words.

The minutes disappeared silently. With three jabs on an overhead button, the copilot activated the cabin bell, signaling the crew to take their seats. He threw the pilot an anxious look but said nothing.

Feeling sweat drench his armpits, Alan stared out the big side window into a swirling wall of white. Amen to all the swear words he'd heard on cockpit voice recorders, he thought. The stuff seemed to be coming right in the damned windows. He stared at the instrument panel, watching the altitude indicator in the left-hand CRT that showed the plane symbol above the horizon. His eyes shifted to the power lever, waiting for it to start moving backwards. Hey, he thought, this is automated, start working, baby, start moving.

And then his eyes were back on the instruments and scanning rapidly—from the cross hairs of the course-deviation indicator to the radar altimeter and back again. A hundred and ten feet . . . a hundred . . . ninety . . . Flare! he thought. Goddammit, START FLARING!

Nothing happened. The two pilots were bug-eyed, and he could feel their waiting like a tangible force in the cockpit. Still the power lever remained fixed.

Suddenly, at sixty feet above the runway, too low to go around, the master caution light went on and simultaneously a horn sounded. Red words flashed on the instrument panel. The annunciator light came on and Alan heard the cold, calm voice of a computer: "Autopilot disconnect." "Computer disagree." "Logic disagree."

God no! he thought.

The pilot muttered "Jesus!" and tightened his fingers around the sidestick controls. Alan knew he'd be flaring the plane without computer help and with no visibility.

The first dash light appeared on the pavement below, and he sat like a brick, trying not to see the panel and seeing it anyway, waiting for the thump of wheels on pavement—or worse. Hoping for the best.

Hoping for the best! God almighty, what a way to land a plane!

The wheels banged down hard. And up again. And down again. Into that white muck the plane rushed forward at a hundred knots, then ninety, then eighty with the engines reversed.

Eventually a small clearing in the white revealed they were traveling at land speeds of sixty, fifty, finally twenty. It was now an incident, not an accident. No harm done, if you didn't mind seeing the leering face of death.

At the end of the runway they turned and taxied toward the terminal. And stopped.

The pilot shut it down and turned around. "Well, Wilcox—we got our money's worth today, huh? Working blind. Like trying to fly it through Space Mountain. This is the second time an autopilot has done this." He smiled grimly. "It all came back to me. Maybe it was this plane, who knows? The pilot who told me said that was *it* with fly-by-wires."

The copilot spoke up. "Last week I was flying one when all the warning lights lit up. But we couldn't find a damned thing wrong and ended up going back for nothing."

Wilcox rummaged through his damp shirt pocket for business cards. "Do me a favor, you two. That landing's given me a sudden interest in computer glitches." He handed them each a card. "Give me a call the next time you get one of these nonreportable incidents. I'm going to start keeping track of how often this happens."

Wilcox ran into the Cessna rep, Sam Orkney, in the lobby of Harrah's in Reno. "Sam!" he thrust out a hand and looked the man up and down. "You must be playing billy goat in every mountain in the U.S. You're down what—thirty pounds?" And minus some hair, too, he thought. The net effect was good; Sam Orkney looked younger than Wilcox remembered.

Orkney grinned self-consciously. "It's my new wife—and a lot of time at the gym. Sally said if she ever married again she was going to have twice as much jewelry and half as much husband. The jewelry part was easy."

The two strolled toward the reception desk and later, after one drink and dinner at the buffet—and Wilcox's graphic story of how lucky he was to be there—they agreed to meet in the lobby at four the next morning.

When the alarm went off in total blackness, Wilcox asked himself, as he'd done before, if the job was worth it. But the familiar rite of pulling on jeans and heavy mountain boots brought back his sense of professionalism. He might be dressing like a deer hunter, but the prey he sought was something more elusive, less easy to track down.

Somewhere on that mountain causation mingled with the debris, hidden to all but the skilled and perceptive. Others would walk through the rubble and see nothing. But he would read the fragments as some people read words, and bit by bit a story would emerge.

Though he would never say it to anyone, he was always aware that the job took skills few people had and most couldn't learn.

The outsized lobby was deserted except for a wandering drunk and a man in coveralls pushing a vacuum cleaner. Sam Orkney, wearing a lumberman's jacket, stood near the glass doors waiting. "My car's close," he said as Alan approached. "Had breakfast?"

"Coffee in the room," Alan said. Outside, the Sierra Nevada Range loomed above the valley to the west, mammoth black cutouts pasted against a dark gray sky.

Talking little, they drove down Highway 89, stopping twenty minutes for breakfast at an all-night cafe, then reaching the sheriff substation in El Dorado County just as the sky lightened noticeably. A jet-ranger helicopter waited near the small building.

Inside, a slight, diffident man said, "Name's Bloomer," and handed Wilcox a preliminary report. "I'm holding down the fort. Our sheriff thought he should go up there himself. He left Deputy Johnson, here, to show you the way. Johnson was on the site yesterday." Johnson, wearing a Dodger baseball cap and sporting exaggerated muscles, acknowledged them with a nod.

"Sun's up," Wilcox said. "Better get going."

Inside the helicopter, Wilcox pushed his backpack under one of the benchlike seats and leaned into the cockpit for a word with the pilot.

"I can't get you as close as I'd like," said the curly-haired pilot, adjusting his earphones. "There's a lot of forest up there. Our best opening is some two miles down the mountain. We'll be airborne about twenty minutes."

They lifted off with a surge of power Wilcox could feel through the seat. The sun was a beam of light above the far horizon. Since conversation was impossible above the rotor noise, the three men looked out different windows. Through the cockpit, Wilcox saw the steep rise of the mountain and the tops of pine trees spotlighted by the rising sun. Early morning in the high country always gave him a sense of things freshly washed and starkly visible.

Eventually the helicopter hovered over a bald spot that seemed impossibly small, and with uncanny precision put down in its center.

The pilot turned around. "You want me to wait, Mr. Wilcox?"

Alan shook his head. "Meet us back here about six. Sundown's at seven."

And then he was ducking under whirling blades, running toward the edge of the clearing, where he crouched with arms over his head, prepared for a tornado of swirling dirt. The helicopter revved for liftoff. Suddenly he heard Johnson yell, "Shit!" and peeking sideways saw the man on his feet running after his flying baseball cap.

"DOWN!" Wilcox bellowed. His eyes filled with dust. Blinded, he couldn't see what happened next. The sound of the helicopter faded and Wilcox scrubbed particles from his eyes. Close by, Orkney said dryly, "Missed him."

Deputy Johnson stood there holding his baseball cap and looking sheepish.

Wilcox said, "You're lucky you still have a head to put under it."

Backpacks in place, the three began climbing. It wasn't an easy hike. Following Johnson on a steady uphill course, they climbed over fallen logs, shrugged past clinging shrubs, slipped on rolling pinecones. Johnson kept to a consistent angle, west and a little south. After two hours of steady slogging, he stopped. Wilcox saw the confusion in his eyes. The man was lost.

Orkney and Wilcox exchanged glances. "You didn't take a compass reading?" Wilcox asked.

"Thought I'd know after being here yesterday." He looked confused. "We must have passed it. Yesterday we got there in an hour and a half."

Sam said patiently, "Why didn't you stop us sooner?"

Johnson didn't have an answer.

Wilcox stared down at the sun-mottled slope dropping away sharply, angry that he'd taken so many arduous uphill steps for nothing. But he tried to be decent. "You may have the angle slightly off. If you're sure about that hour and a half, we'll retrace for ten minutes and cut sideways. We should come across signs of wreckage within the next half hour." Making a mental note of the time, he took the lead, sliding and stumbling downhill over already-broken twigs and flattened grass.

Just as Wilcox started across a fallen tree trunk, something made him look up. Across a small clearing stood a black bear with a cub almost hidden behind it. Eyes staring, it dared him to come closer. Wilcox froze. Then he slowly felt for the gun he remembered he didn't have. With no way to scare her off, he fixed his gaze on the bear's small marble eyes, trying to give the impression of calm. *Hey, girl, cut us a little slack.*

All sounds stopped—not a rustle, not a breath. The bear took a lumbering step toward him, and Wilcox considered racing for the nearest tree. Then he remembered the woman in Lake Louise, chased out of a cabin and onto a rooftop by a black bear. And eaten. *My God. Even a tree won't help.* He hoped the animal couldn't smell his fear.

The bear took another waddling step. Wilcox stopped breathing.

Suddenly a commotion started—Johnson, pulling around him, arms waving in what Wilcox could only interpret as a teacherly admonition. "Git!" yelled Johnson, gesturing toward the mother bear, "Get going! Get lost!"

The bear stood her ground. *He's an idiot,* thought Wilcox, searching the ground for a stick, for anything.

Johnson foolishly kept going. "Scat!" he ordered. "Go on, now! Go!"

Briefly the animal stood unblinking, but before the idiot could invade her territory, she abruptly turned her enormous rear end to them and led her cub away.

Wilcox let out a long breath as Deputy Johnson came back and sat down on the log. "That wasn't too smart," he said. "What made you think you could outbluff a female with her cub standing right there?"

Johnson grinned sheepishly. "Shit, I didn't see the cub until I was almost on top of them. By then I was more or less into it, so I thought, What the hell . . ."

It was easy to laugh now that the two were gone. As Sam Orkney took the lead, cutting sideways at an angle across the mountain, Wilcox mused aloud. "When I took this job I *expected* to learn about fracture lines and metal fatigue. It came as a surprise that I also had to know something about bears."

Orkney didn't answer. Instead, he stopped abruptly and reached toward the ground. When he straightened he was holding a human foot.

Chapter Four

Tim Johnson took one look and said, "Jesus!" He pulled away. "Shit, it's gruesome . . . how can you *touch* it?"

Wilcox glanced at the adult male foot—mangled and gory where it tore from the leg—and wished he felt more than he did. "Let's have a look," he said, reaching out a hand.

Holding the object by the toe, Orkney handed it over.

Tim stared at him. "Makes me want to puke."

Wilcox said, "Then look somewhere else. It's not your concern." He decided to spare Johnson the standard NTSB quip about mixed human and mechanical debris: *Parts is parts.* He regarded this evidence of death impersonally, as little more than tangible proof that the wreckage was somewhere close.

But Johnson wasn't finished. "You don't even *care*—do you?"

Wilcox pinned him with a hard look. "This accident happened to a friend of mine, Johnson, so yes, I do care—about him. But the man I knew is gone. This is just a foot. And there may be more, worse than this. Feel free to hike back."

"If you're saying I'm a pansy," Johnson said, "I'm not. *Anyone* would say that's creepy. And I'm coming," he added, and stood back, waiting.

With a shrug, Wilcox resumed walking.

Occasionally, as now, Wilcox wondered if he'd become dehumanized. Sometimes he felt he must explain; he longed to react visibly as he once had, if only to prove he was normal. Prick me. I bleed. Yet inevitably he'd become as inured to death as a mortician, a protec-

tive mind-set common to field investigators. It was the only way he—
or any of them—could do their jobs.

He looked at the foot again. What was it doing so far from the wreck?
And then his practiced eye caught the gleam of plastic. He probed a
bush and picked up the filmy bag from which it had slipped. Somebody's
carelessness.

The foot re-wrapped, he dropped it into his backpack. In all prob-
ability that one part was all that remained after Search and Rescue
took out the bodies.

Sam made a face and, as though reading Wilcox's mind, said, "I
wouldn't want to be a mortician, either."

Farther along, Wilcox picked up a rounded piece of white aluminum with part of a seven printed in black across the white. He slid a
finger thoughtfully over what had once been the finely contoured leading
edge of a wing. "A part of the left wingtip," he said for Johnson's
benefit. "You weren't as far off course as we thought."

He examined it for detail. Brownish green material transfer and the
semicircular imprint were unmistakable signatures of a tree strike, probably near the top, judging from the diameter of the imprint. Taking a
reading of the pines overhead, he carefully searched their tops for disturbed branches that would give away the initial impact point.

All eyes craned upward. And then Wilcox spotted the fresh scar on
the bark of a pine not far from the top. "There," he said, pointing.
With a practiced eye he surveyed the surrounding trees and arrived at
the probable direction from which the aircraft had come. "The rest of
the wreckage should be distributed along this bearing," he told them,
pointing again.

Johnson said sullenly, "I don't see how you know which way it came
in."

Okay, thought Wilcox, maybe I was too hard on him. Summoning
new patience, he held up the piece and explained that the orientation of the imprint to the original contour of the wing meant the aircraft
was in a five- to ten-degree climb when it hit the tree. Since the only
trees lower than that one lay along a bearing of about 110 degrees,
the rest of the aircraft had to be distributed along the reciprocal.

"We'd better move off," he said, and led them on a downward course
angled to form a V with the heading they'd been on earlier. Wilcox
took out his miniature tape recorder and began dictating. "The initial
impact point was identified . . ."

Anticipating more wreckage momentarily, his outlook changed. This was no longer a hike that was wearing and tedious. It was a mission of discovery, a leading back into events of the day before—a reliving of the last moments of four people's lives. He was their record book, their diary—their explanation to the outside of what they'd experienced. His voice would spell out the details of what had gone wrong. Before he was through, he'd have experienced the disaster himself. Weeks later it would be down on paper for all to see.

At that moment he slid into his role of consummate professional.

He stopped. Another piece of mangled aluminum, as expected.

Within a few hundred yards, they found ever larger pieces of wreckage scattered along the forest floor and, mixed with the metal, ripped branches of trees. Overhead, Wilcox saw a familiar pattern—fresh tree trunk scars in a descending arc. As he examined and identified each new piece of crumpled metal, he photographed it and summarized his exam into the tape recorder—much like an autopsy surgeon. Long ago he'd noted the ironic similarity between the professions, and it occurred to him that he was, in a way, a pathologist for airplanes.

They'd hiked only five minutes more when a glint of white appeared through the trees, and they scrambled around a boulder to find a large chunk of the Cessna's cabin section lying on the ground inverted. With its underside intact, it rested incongruously atop a cluster of seedling pines, inches off the ground. Beyond the wreckage three men sat on a log talking.

"Wilcox!" A chunky man with a drooping shoulder rose wearily and came around the broken cabin, holding out a hand. "Glad to see you, Alan. It's been a long night." To Sam Orkney, "I'm Jones—Greg Jones. Sheriff." Twenty pounds overweight, noticeably around his middle, he was round-faced and florid. He gestured backwards. "This is my deputy, Ned. And Bill Howard from the FAA."

Ned, a lanky six-four, appeared excessively tired. As Wilcox shook hands with him, he tried—and failed—to suppress a yawn.

For the next few minutes Wilcox questioned them about parts of the aircraft that might have been disturbed during the recovery of bodies. In answer, Jones led the group around the cabin wreckage, pointing to moved components and indicating their original positions.

Nodding toward the blood-soaked cockpit area, Jones said, "You can see what's left in there," and with the rest of the group he turned away. Seeing what Jones saw, Wilcox sympathized with his revulsion.

Brain matter was smeared across the gyros, and teeth and jaw fragments had fallen from the inverted instrument panel to the ceiling. Worse
was the strange, bittersweet odor, a mixture of body fluids and oil—
as though the humans and the plane had bled equally.

Once smelled, never forgotten, he thought. He didn't realize anyone was nearby until he heard Johnson's voice, soft and accusing and
near his elbow, "You *knew* what you'd see here—someone's brains
splattered all over. Why do you *do* this job?" Getting no answer he
said, "You've gotta be weird. Nobody normal would want it." He was
looking into space with a mix of horror and contempt.

"Look, Johnson," Wilcox answered quietly, "if you don't understand
what's involved here, watch and learn—or don't watch, I don't care—
but keep your thoughts to yourself. I don't have time to defend the
process." With that, he walked off to rejoin the others.

The group had assembled in a loose, silent circle. Wilcox heard a
blue jay squawk, and high in the trees a rush of wind moved like a
violin bow across the pine needles, drawing out a gentle, high-pitched
tone. A requiem to the Hawkins family, he thought.

Jones got down to business. "We had some extra men up here late
yesterday, and they hiked the bodies down to the helicopter landing
zone. Took 'em to the morgue in Tahoe City. There are still two hands
and a foot missing that we need to find. So it's your show now. What
do you want us to do?"

Opening his backpack, Wilcox took out the foot. "Here's part of
what's missing." Pulling out an assortment of wrenches and screw-
drivers, he indicated the FAA man. "You're an airworthiness inspector, aren't you, Bill? Why don't you go pull the spark plugs and rocker
box covers from both engines? I want you to get a drive and valve
train continuity, then check the fuel system and magnetos."

He looked at Orkney. "We need a good examination of the aircraft
control system, Sam, and documentation of the flap and trim tab positions." Once more he reached into his backpack and this time pulled
out a compass, pencil, lightweight ruler, a steno tablet, and a wad of
small, numbered tags. "Ned, can you do the wreckage distribution chart?
Tag each piece with a number, then mark it on the chart with the bearing
and distance from the cabin section, so we can reconstruct this mess
later."

He looked around. Sam Orkney had already started pulling off the
inspection panels on the fuselage in order to trace the control cables.

To Deputy Johnson Wilcox said, "If you feel like helping, take a walk back beyond that first tree strike and look for any other aircraft components or disturbed trees. Then come back and help Ned with the wreckage chart." To his surprise, Johnson went.

Wilcox moved away and took a deep breath. For the rest of the day he'd be in high gear. Though NTSB investigators readily used the expertise of such people as representatives of the airplane manufacturers, it was his job to make sure nothing slipped between the cracks—unintentionally or otherwise.

For the next hour he went from person to person, using his Olympus 35mm camera to photograph components, then narrating descriptions into his recorder. "Right engine lying approximately eleven yards north of cabin section . . . left engine adjacent to cabin . . . largest tail segment lying downslope thirty yards from cabin . . ." He never moved on before he'd satisfied himself about the larger picture in each spot, never studied one area without feeling he should be somewhere else.

Satisfied that everyone was making progress, Wilcox worked his way back to the initial tree strike, taking additional time with the components scattered along the way. At the point of first impact, he snapped on a telephoto lens and examined the treetop, photographing it in detail. Searching the ground below, he discovered red lens fragments, once part of the navigation light on the left wing—which confirmed his earlier assessment of which wingtip hit the tree. For a short time he stood at the base of the pine looking back along the scatterpath.

The *scatterpath* . . . a cruelly impersonal word, he thought, for the plane and all its parts strewn across the landscape. He might have defined it as a planeprint. A dead planeprint, and a sight that disturbed him beyond a sense of loss for the people who had gone down with it. To him, to anyone who loved aviation, a plane was a bird and in some sense alive. For surely only a living thing could perceive and use the wind for its own purposes, shaping the air around it to achieve lift in a way that defied gravity, seeking its own path through three dimensions—which man alone could never do. In the course of their building, airplanes managed to achieve autonomy, and he marveled that men claimed all the credit. And so he always thought of the scatterpath as being the final configuration of the plane where it fell and died.

He abandoned his reverie and from that point of first impact followed the descending path of the craft down through the trees, marked by wreckage in ever larger quantities.

He was back near the cockpit when he found something that stopped him short: one of the missing hands. Using a clean cloth, he picked it up, looking automatically at the thumb. His eyes widened, and he turned the hand over carefully, surprised at what it implied. But no, he reasoned, it must be a coincidence. The find started a new, unexpected train of thought. He began searching the ground minutely, pawing through disturbed leaves, pushing aside branches for what he guessed should be somewhere close.

Half-buried under a tree branch, he found it, the second missing hand. He stared at the thumb in disbelief. "I'll be damned," he muttered to himself.

Some distance from the cabin, the right engine lay on a bed of pine needles. As Wilcox approached, Bill Howard was on his haunches using a screwdriver to turn the crankshaft.

Camera in hand, Wilcox bent to examine it closer. A classic sine wave pattern marked the propeller blades—a polishing effect, with the paint stripped off and chipped pieces of the tree wedged between the blades. The limb segments were all cut at the same relative angles. Bill had gathered the cut branches from the vicinity, and Wilcox reconstructed the branches, then measured the distances between the cuts. Using a long-ago memorized formula, he plugged in the probable speed of the aircraft, based on the amount of structural deformation. After a few moments, he came up with the RPM at which both engines were turning when they sliced through the trees—near their normal high power range.

Bill had taken apart the fuel pumps from both engines, and Wilcox looked inside at the rotors and veins, which resembled outsized fans. During an impact sequence, the outside of the pump usually got squeezed, and when that happened—if the rotors and veins were turning—they were going to score the hell out of the inside of the housing. He took another, closer shot of the housing's interior. It was scored, all right. Which was evidence enough that the pump had been working as the crash sequence began.

After a while Sam Orkney walked up shaking his head, ready to begin their rap meeting. "Nothing abnormal about the control systems that I can find. Here are the trim tab and flapjack screw measurements and the positions they correspond to. My examination says everything was working at the end. I had a look at the autopilot system—it seemed normal, though I doubt it was being used in the mountains."

Wilcox nodded his agreement. Everyone might have been better off with the autopilot in use.

Howard got to his feet with a weary sigh. "I've looked over that engine pretty good. I don't see anything wrong with it—but I don't pretend to be an expert."

Seeing the group starting to congregate, young Ned came up with his clipboard and handed it to Wilcox. "Here's most of it—all the biggest pieces, anyway." He jerked a thumb toward a thick stand of trees. "Johnson went that way, looking for stuff that might have gone flinging off somewhere else." He sat down on the ground. "I'm bushed."

With a glance at his watch, Sheriff Jones said, "We'll have to shove off before long. We're forty minutes from that clearing."

Wilcox gathered everyone together and listened as each gave a summary of the findings on whatever portion of the wreck he had examined. To each of them Alan addressed detailed questions about their negative finds. The group consensus was that no pre-impact malfunctions had existed, and that the aircraft was performing normally before its treetop collision.

He wasn't happy. He'd hoped to find that something had gone wrong with the plane . . . and not with the decision-making process of the pilot. "Take a break, men. I want to take one more look and do some stumping."

When Ned looked puzzled, he said, "Find a stump somewhere and sit down and think."

Once again Wilcox went off by himself, snapping the last of his pictures of the overall lay of the plane. When his four rolls of film were exposed, he walked to the highest point of scattered debris—the endpoint—and sat down on a log to think. "Stumping" was a way of imprinting the accident in his mind, both a noting of where the plane and its parts came to rest and a mental re-creation of the path it took to get there. He looked back and in his mind's eye saw the final moments of flight, the plane coming in low—too low—clipping a wingtip on the first tree, rolling off center as it struck a second, losing pieces, then straightening momentarily, only to fall again and bash itself against other trees. He saw the fir that probably turned the cabin onto its back so that what was left of it landed upside down.

No still photos, no tape-recorded descriptions could substitute for a mental image of sequences deliberately implanted in the human mind.

All he needed now was causation.

As he sat on his log he tried not to draw the speediest, most obvious conclusion. There'd been no prior damage to fuel, engine, or control systems—none that any of them could find. If, on later laboratory examination of parts this was confirmed, the cause could only be pilot error.

He began to rethink the weather report given him by the Flight Service Station the day before. "Rapidly changing conditions to mountain obscurement . . . a frontal system that moved more rapidly than forecast." The family had probably left Los Angeles confident that there would be unobstructed skies all the way to Lake Tahoe. But the skies hadn't stayed clear; that much he knew.

Were they caught unawares by a sudden front that obscured the mountain only minutes before the landing in Tahoe? Did the pilot not see it in time to reverse course, or had a terrible chance been taken, an assumption made that the front was higher than it was? Was the plane, at the end, funneled by a box canyon down into a narrow slot between the clouds and the trees?

Goddammit, did you just screw up?

He stood up wearily. A classic scenario. And the likeliest cause of the accident.

Human error—what they called in the bureau "a problem in the headphone separators"—would exist as long as pilot input was one of the variables in the control of aircraft. All the investigators knew it, and imagined if they wrote enough reports and made enough recommendations "screwing up" would somehow be eliminated.

Before he rejoined the others for the hike down the mountain, Wilcox strolled into the woods to relieve himself. On his way back something white and fuzzy caught his attention. He walked over to pick it up. A teddy bear.

He stood silently holding the bear—the worst moment he'd experienced in the entire investigation. He'd never gotten used to finding toys. As he stood in the forest holding the bear and hearing the wind, now moaning softly through the pines, he saw the silent face of the child who'd once held it—Dave's kid.

For the first time that day he exploded in anger. "Goddammit to hell!" he said, and threw the bear down and pounded his way between trees, walking *away* from the crash. It was ten minutes before he could make himself turn around and go back.

Exhausted, he led the group down the mountain to the waiting helicopter. As Tim Johnson started toward the whirling blades, Wilcox grabbed his shoulder. "This time keep your head down."

"Why? What do you care?" Johnson shouted, not bothering to turn.

Forcing the muscled shoulders toward the ground, Wilcox shouted back, "It's the living I worry about."

As the helicopter rose with a whir and rumble, Wilcox looked out his side window, seeing not the trees dropping away below, nor the darkening sky ahead, but only what he'd found under a branch, what he'd seen on one hand and then the other. He shook his head, perplexed. *I know even less about the Hawkins family than when I started.*

Chapter Five

The morning hadn't started well. Miles Kimball, vice president, sales, for Stirling Industries Inc., sat at his place in the company's boardroom in Irvine, California, staring at what was probably the lousiest breakfast they'd served in a string of bad breakfasts. Dry scrambled eggs. Shriveled sausages clearly too hard to bite. White toast, soggy in the middle but burned around the edges. He guessed the meal would be a fitting complement to what was coming at the management meeting because, for some time now, currents of desperation had been flowing through the executive halls of the airplane manufacturing company.

Before Kimball had a chance to do more than play with his food, the board chairman rose with a few introductory remarks, and then CEO Lloyd Holloway, looking grim, walked to the head of the table. In that moment before everyone settled into respectful silence, Miles idly contemplated the man standing under his logo. The Stirling Industries trademark was a stylized cutout of a plane and hung—in sterling silver, of course—on the wall above Holloway's head. Like the logo, Holloway was polished and expensive. An impeccably tailored gray suit made his lean body seem leaner still, and his dark, silver-touched hair, cut by his barber to a deliberately leonine length, added an air of authority. As he stood at the head of the table he loomed above them all—literally and figuratively.

A quintessential leader, thought Kimball, who both admired and was irritated by his chief executive officer.

He was braced for the man's reaction to the news he was about to deliver. Nobody loved the bearer of ill tidings—but Lloyd Holloway was driven by unpredictable moods that kept the men farther down the organizational chart in a constant state of wariness.

And then Holloway began speaking, his words punctuated by distant, staccato bursts from Tail Assembly in Building 24, with which they shared a common wall. Lost in a moment's thought, Kimball suddenly realized that Holloway was saying, ". . . not to go outside this room."

He began listening intently.

". . . so the Pentagon is making inquiries into our recent price increases. Some smart ass in Washington got wind of the cost of a few components and began playing big shot, and now they're questioning our whole price structure. They're threatening to dump that last order of F-121s. Seventy-five fighter and reconnaissance planes. Bingo, like that."

A thick silence dropped down and blanketed them all.

Kimball noticed abstractedly that Holloway looked weary.

Holloway glanced at each man in turn. "We could be looking at frozen government payments. If word gets out that the military is considering off-loading us, our bank will call its credit line. Big trouble, gentlemen. Headline-making trouble."

Kimball's heart rate increased, and he wondered vaguely if fifty-three was old enough to have a heart attack. A cascade of implications rained down on him, and they all added up to one thing: personal financial disaster.

Max Topping, vice president in charge of purchasing, held up an authoritative hand. With a short military haircut, a hard, flat stomach, and a Marine officer's bearing, Topping had self-discipline stamped all over him. In his spare time he ran marathons.

"Something has already leaked, Lloyd," Topping said. "Saticoy Aluminum is pressing us for acceleration of payments before the next delivery of landing gear castings. They're asking for a hundred and twenty days."

Holloway fixed him with a hard stare. "You don't mean a hundred and twenty days. You mean six months."

Topping sent the look right back. "I meant it the way I said it, Lloyd."

"That's bullshit. Everyone knows the airframe business isn't run that way."

"What I told *them*. I spoke directly with their president. Said he'd talk to his people and get back to me. But he was playing duck and dodge, not leveling with me. It's anyone's guess what's happening over there."

Holloway's eyes narrowed. "Who the hell leaked this Pentagon garbage to Saticoy? *I* only heard about it two days ago! Listen, Max, you tell them this is a message from Holloway. We don't pay early. Period."

Unless, thought Kimball, it's Saticoy Aluminum, who just happened to have them by the short hairs. Who else in the industry was big enough to do major aluminum castings?

"Right," said Topping. "Consider the message delivered." And then offhandedly, with an ironic smile, "I'll tell them we may shop around."

It didn't go over. Holloway ignored him.

Suddenly Kimball was aware that Holloway's accusatory finger was pointed at him. "So, Miles! Have you brought the information from your meeting with Trans America?"

Along both sides of the oak conference table, other executives turned his way—all looking at him intently, all hoping to keep the heat off themselves.

"As much as they would tell me." Kimball pulled papers out of a flat vinyl case. The top sheet was printed in twenty-point caps: TRANS AMERICA FLEET. PROJECTED NEEDS. He turned it over and cleared his throat. "As you know, TAF's going to retire its entire fleet of 727s— all hundred and fifty of them, and replace them on a one-for-one basis. They're doing it in lots, fifty jets to start, with first delivery in late spring of '93, thirty short-range, twenty long. But they hinted they might turn back the twenty planes they've already leased from Stirling and let their option deposits go on the fifty additional."

"They might *what?*" Holloway's eyes flashed his anger. "Am I hearing you correctly?"

Kimball said pointedly, "I'm guessing they're not interested in derivative aircraft."

Holloway's voice turned icy. "You're *guessing,* Kimball?"

God, how Miles hated these public interrogations—Holloway playing the inquisitor, putting him on trial. "Their evaluation committee can't give me anything definite. They'll look at proposals early next year, probably late January, and after the board makes its decision a letter of intent will be signed in May. We've had their people watching our production for the last few months, and they've been asking detailed questions about our updates. Unfortunately, I believe they're leaning toward Airtech Aviation's fly-by-wires. But I spoke to Harry Majors, yesterday—"

"What in hell changed their minds?"

"Lloyd, you know they leased thirty new Airtechs the same time they leased ours."

"So?" Holloway's eyes bored into his.

"Right now they think they're saving money. On better fuel efficiency and the new two-man cockpit. And with the tightening of standards for ground noise around most of the airports . . ."

"Retrofitting with hush kits is a damned sight cheaper than buying new planes!" Holloway slapped the table. "So for that they're willing to take a chance on predictability! With a lot of computer boards that won't be any more reliable than the Bay Area Rapid Transit system when they first fired it up. Swell! And what was your answer to all that, Miles?"

"I said about the same things you're saying."

Holloway looked around the room. "Any more bad news to report?" When nobody spoke, he cleared his throat and began a monologue that seemed little more than his own justification for their existence.

As Holloway ranted about the proven virtues of Stirling aircraft over all others, Miles remembered he hadn't finished his sentence. Harry Majors wanted a concession that the board ought to know about—cost-plus-ten on hush kits. But Lloyd Holloway was a hard man to interrupt. Though he, Kimball, had the title vice president, it meant little. Like everyone else, he was Holloway's flunky. Holloway was a despot, and if you didn't like it you could get out. Once he'd minded very much, but now he no longer cared. He just wanted the company to stay viable long enough so he could exercise his stock options and get well financially.

"In January," Holloway suddenly pointed at him, "I expect you to take Trans America the kind of proposal that will make them change their minds. We'll give twenty percent on the front end if we have to. Just our standard equipment without customizing to TAF's usual seating configuration, so the price is going to look so damned competitive Airtech'll be peeing their pants."

"Harry Majors . . ." Kimball began.

"We'll handle the interior as BFE—Buyer Furnished Equipment—," Holloway said, ignoring him.

"So do they get engines?" Kimball asked the question under his breath, dryly, and was gratified to hear stifled laughter. He could afford some irreverence; Holloway needed him.

Holloway went on, "I'm looking for that contract, Miles, whatever it takes."

"Right," Kimball said, and Holloway picked up a loose sheet of paper and began reading figures.

Just then Kimball's secretary tiptoed into the room. She came directly to Miles and handed him a note. Before Linda slid inconspicuously out through the door, Kimball read the note, swallowed hard, and tried to mask his feelings. He couldn't sit through the rest of the meeting.

Without further thought, he stood up in the middle of Holloway's financial summary. The CEO stopped talking and looked at him.

"You'll have to excuse me," Kimball said. "My wife's been taken to the hospital." Subliminally aware of sympathetic nods, he walked out of the room. *Damn it, Sondra, you didn't look that sick. How could a little weakness send you to the hospital?*

Chapter Six

The rigger had never met anyone he wanted to eat lunch with, not at the factory, anyway. To a man the workers at Airtech Aviation bored and irritated him, so he invariably chose to sit alone in the cafeteria, reading one of his technical books. But today was his birthday. He felt compelled to do something different, telling himself he might otherwise forget what day it was. Holding his lunch tray, he studied the tables. The truth was, he never forgot anything. The other truth was, if he didn't mark the day, nobody else would.

Eventually he spotted someone he knew only by reputation—Bennett Bergman, the company's senior software designer. For once Bergman was by himself; he couldn't believe his luck. Walking slowly to compensate for his uneven gait, the rigger approached the man's table. When Bergman paid no attention, he said politely, "I noticed you eating by yourself. Mind if I join you?"

Bergman shrugged. "Have a seat." He had a thin, ascetic face widened somewhat by rimless glasses, and sparse, graying hair, short and combed flat. He went on eating as though he were still alone.

Carefully transferring dishes to the table, the rigger asked, "Where do you work?" and when the other told him, not bothering to look up, the rigger said, "Quite a coincidence. I was just thinking about that department today—how it impacts on everything we do." He sat down and smiled across the table. "There must be considerable brainpower over there. You can see it incorporated in all the structures, funneling right down to our work."

"Oh?" said Bergman, really looking at him for the first time. "What's your job?"

"Controls. I'm a rigger. But my main interest is computers. So I admire talent when I see it."

Bergman studied him thoughtfully. "What's your computer background?"

"Well—I used to work at Navtronics as a programmer, and I—"

"Is that so?"

"And I own a fair number of computers myself. I've been adding equipment over the last ten years, designing my own programs for games, that kind of thing." He smiled, his pleasure in his accomplishments spilling out before he could stop it. "Sorry. I didn't mean to bore you with all this."

"You're in my field," said Bergman. "It's never boring."

The rigger played with his fork. "Computers can grab hold of you, can't they? I always read the in-house bulletins, particularly the part about software design. No wonder Airtech's the leading manufacturer of fly-by-wires." He fixed his blue eyes on Bergman's face and asked tentatively, "What's your position in the department?"

"I'm senior software designer."

"Really?" *He's not as hard-nosed as they say.* "Then you're the man who gets most of the credit."

"Hardly," said Bergman, but he was pleased nevertheless. He pushed his chair back and looked across the table intently. "Have you ever considered getting back into design?"

The rigger paused to think about it. *Just as I thought; they're short-handed.* "Well . . . I like what I'm doing now."

"But would you consider a change?"

"I don't know . . ." He shrugged. "Maybe I would."

"Look," said Bergman, stacking his empty dishes neatly. "You said your name is . . ."

"Malec. Rudy Malec."

Bergman stood up. "I'll keep your name in mind, Rudy."

Malec rose too. "Thanks," he said, and shook Bergman's hand. "No rush, though. As I said, I'm happy where I am."

Bergman made a point of seeking out Malec's boss, Nick Lewand, on his way back to work. Because he was in a hurry, he summarized some of what he'd discussed with Malec, though his intention was mainly to get Lewand's impression of the man.

Lewand—short, barrel-chested with a Mediterranean complexion—
hesitated before he said, "He'd probably get along fine in your department, Bennett."

Bergman regarded the other over the top of his glasses. "Does that
mean he doesn't get along well in yours?"

"He's good at what he does. Capable. I don't doubt his intelligence."

"But—," said Bergman.

"We've had problems here. A couple of his co-workers don't like
him. As for me . . ." Lewand hiked up his pants toward his expansive
upper half, "to me, he's polite. I have no quarrel with him personally. If you want him, go ahead."

"I don't know," said Bergman. "We'll see."

When he walked on, Bergman knew Malec would be staying where
he was. If more than one fellow worker had a problem with Malec, he
couldn't be transferred into a department as sensitive as software design.

Back at his station near the cockpit, Malec felt his face redden as
the hydraulic specialist down in the tail barked into his headphones,
"Damn it, Malec, you've got the elevator cables so loose this ship isn't
gonna rotate on takeoff. Get the tensiometer, and recheck the tension
so I can get on with what I'm doing."

Malec mouthed to himself, "Fuck you, Hank!" and pulled off his
headphones. With slow, deliberate steps he climbed down out of his
area onto a raised platform and from there down a metal staircase to
the cement floor. Everywhere he looked, hulls of airplanes lolled under
the fifty-foot-high steel structure like beached whales. Managing his
deformed hip with grace, he zigzagged among the whales until he'd
worked his way to his locker, where he produced an article on computerized aircraft glitches and retreated to a stall in the men's room.

Wholly absorbed, he sat reading until it occurred to him to look at
his watch. Thirty minutes had passed!

In a panic, he struggled back to his station with a gait that disinte-
grated into stumbling awkwardness.

Nick Lewand was waiting for him, arms folded across his brawny
chest. "Well, Rudy, where have you been?"

"Been?" asked Malec, eyes widening in surprise. *You bastard.* "I
took a break, of course. Hank will tell you, I told him we both needed
a few minutes off, we—"

Lewand drew in a deep breath. "Hank tells me you held him up half an hour!"

Malec smiled and said softly, "Nick, he and I have been working three hours solid. We *had* to clear our heads. It's sensitive work, there's no way I'd let one of us mess up." He looked around. "Where is he? I told him we'd meet back here in ten minutes." An apologetic grin. "I guess he took a couple extra minutes, huh?"

Lewand stood looking at him without answering.

"He must have misunderstood." Cheerfully, "Well, back to work. Don't worry, he'll show up in a minute."

Lewand walked away. Out of sight of Rudy Malec, he shook his head. Which one of them was lying? For the next hour Nick recorded data in his private office. But he couldn't get Malec out of his head. There was something about the man's expression . . . a veiled, momentary flicker of . . . what? then his look of sincerity, his openness. He never dodged or denied. He explained. And it always played so damned well. He decided to haul the fellow into his office for a chat.

When Rudy Malec got there, Lewand was struck once again by the man's youthfulness. Though he walked with a limp, the rigger swung himself along gracefully in a way that made his problem barely noticeable, and moving the chair so it faced the desk, he sat down. He held a small cloth case on his lap.

Lewand nodded, studying him. Malec was a slight man, narrow-shouldered, thin-faced, with prominent cheekbones and tight curly hair. But it was Malec's eyes you noticed first—deeply blue and always wide open, conveying childish innocence, though Lewand had the feeling sometimes the innocence was feigned.

Malec was staring at him openly and, as often happened, Lewand felt strangely uncomfortable. Without preamble, Lewand began, "Why does trouble seem to follow you around, Rudy? In this department, every controversy leads sooner or later to you."

"What do you mean?" A soft, questioning smile.

"I mean the problem with Hank today. And Jim Noland last week. And Bill, who asked to be transferred."

"Ah. So that's it. A couple months ago, you see, I screwed up—made the flyers for the intercompany softball match and got the time wrong. My players showed up late and were defaulted. I felt rotten about it, Nick. The guys haven't been with me since."

A colorful story, thought Lewand. He waited to see what would come next.

"Problem was, I couldn't read my own handwriting." The eyes again—watching. "It's my birthday," offered Malec.

"Well . . . Congratulations! Hope it's a good one."

"I'll try to make it up to the guys, Nick. I know company harmony is important."

Lewand nodded.

"Anything else?"

"No. As long as you understand that our work groups have to get along."

Malec dropped his eyes. "I'll go back now." On his way out the door, he paused. "Bennett Bergman shared my birthday lunch. Did he happen to speak to you?"

"Yes."

"Thought he might. But I told him I like this department. I won't leave unless they really need me over there."

"Good of you," said Lewand. Through his glass partition, he saw Malec swinging along gripping his case. He thought, *Something doesn't add up.*

Ellie Wilcox hadn't been looking for trouble. In fact that morning, with Alan out of town and her youngest son, Todd, fifteen, at early morning swim workout, she'd had time to take her coffee to the dinette window and stand there savoring the silence and the spectacular view of Orange County stretching away twenty miles to the ocean. *Alone in my own house again; I hardly remember how it feels.*

After years of being a school psychologist and a sometimes-harried mother, she hadn't minded when her only daughter, Jamie, twenty-three, had finally passed her court reporter's exam and found a job and an apartment. With her son Doug, twenty, away at Stanford, she could enjoy Todd like an only child. Except he was seldom there to enjoy. Swimming at the high school eight thousand yards a day morning and afternoon left few waking hours at home, and she jokingly told her friends Todd didn't have the energy to be a teenage rebel.

Now, heading to her bedroom to dress for work, she detoured into Todd's bedroom with a pair of his shoes. That's when she saw the slip of paper on his desk, largely hidden under a spiral notebook. Something about the way it was tucked away told her to look at it.

She pulled it out and stopped breathing: Todd was flunking two courses.

Stunned, she reread the form letter signed by the principal. "We regret to inform you" led straight to the grim fact that Todd's current grades in Spanish and chemistry were *D* minus and *F*.

Failing! Reading the letter once more, she could hardly believe it referred to her youngest child. With all the similar notices she'd seen in the files of her junior high school students, she'd somehow never expected to find one in her own house. She felt defeated, like a failure herself. And sick to her stomach.

Suddenly she was on the other side of her own desk. No longer the professional offering calm, rational advice, she'd become a chagrined parent—the archetypal mother with a head full of excuses but anguish in her heart.

Was the distinction between bad news and terrible news simply a matter of whose problem it was?

She dropped the letter onto Todd's desk, and his digital clock caught her eye. "Oh, damn!" she muttered aloud. She'd forgotten all about Todd's dentist appointment. Minutes later she was in the car heading around the curves toward Foothill High School.

Todd never gave a thought to his morning appointment.

He didn't like swim team anymore; it was too much work. When his friend Boomer gave him the high sign, he told the coach he had a stomach ache, and Boomer told the coach something else, he didn't know what, and after they dressed they sneaked off to the football field and crouched behind the bleachers sharing a joint.

Then Todd happened to look up and see his mom's car pulling into the parking lot. For a minute he didn't know why she was there. Then he remembered and practically panicked. "Geez, Boomer, what'll we do? She's gonna smell this stuff, she has a nose like a rat."

"You shoulda said something," said Boomer. "What's she doing here?"

"Dentist appointment. I forgot all about it."

"Well take some of this, it's what I use before I go into class." He pulled a spray bottle out of his pocket and turned it in the direction of Todd's face, spraying his friend liberally. "Open your mouth," he ordered.

Todd turned his face away. "Lay off, Boomer, I stink like a perfume factory already."

Boomer laughed. "Better'n how you smelled before."

Casually Todd strolled out to intercept his mother as she got out
and slammed her car door.

She looked at him coldly—her failing son—and couldn't keep the
ice out of her tone. "So you're here. Get in the car, we're late." Instead of driving fast to make up the time, she forgot about the dentist, almost forgot she was driving. *Well, here's your first real test—
let's see how you do psychology on your home turf.* "I found the notice
from the principal," she began calmly, "hiding under a notebook. Why
didn't you give it to me?"

From her peripheral vision she sensed that Todd had turned deliberately to look out the window. And wasn't going to answer.

"What's been going on in those classes, Todd? You've never had
anything lower than a *B* before. Is there something you need to tell
me?"

When he still said nothing, she felt her face redden, her pulse quicken
with frustration. *Stay calm. Be professional.* But when she turned to
look at him and saw only the back of his head, heard only the silence,
she raised her voice. "I SAID . . . WHY DIDN'T YOU GIVE ME THAT
NOTICE?"

He shrugged. "Why should I? What good's it going to do?"

"So you were going to let us just *find out,* is that it? After the se-
mester was over and the *F*'s became permanent, Dad and I were going to have a big surprise?" She wrinkled her nose in disgust. "And
what's that stuff you're wearing; it's a god-awful smell! I can hardly
breathe!"

He decided the fewer words the better.

She turned back to the road. *Well, I've blown it, just like every other
parent. I'm shouting and he's clamming up. So now he's out of reach.
A wonderful start.* And then she wondered vaguely why he'd doused
himself so heavily in after-shave . . .

Her awareness sharpened and the heavy smell seemed to surround
her. Oh God, she thought suddenly, not pot too! Sickened, she bit back
an impulse to start afresh, climb all over him. This time she didn't.
Instead, as he got out of the car she said quietly, "That better not be
marijuana I smell."

"It isn't," he said, and didn't turn around. She watched him walk
away, the easygoing kid who'd never given her any trouble. For a moment
she believed him, felt in her heart he'd told her the truth. But then

she thought about his grades. When the schoolwork of otherwise normal kids took a sudden nosedive, the reason was usually drugs.

She had to talk to Alan at once. *We're going to crack down on you, kid.*

Anger burned a track in the rigger's mind, undiminished by the miles that passed between Airtech and his apartment. The words between him and Hank outside the plant, spewed out near a tan stuccoed wall, still rang in his ears. Hank had backed him up to the wall and actually taken his arm. "That was a lie you told Lewand! *We* didn't take a break, *you* did. You walked off the goddamn job and left me sitting back there until I had to go looking for you. You—"

His vision swimming with rage, Malec ripped away the other's hand and twisted the wrist until Hank brought his free fist down on Malec's arm, breaking the frenzied grip.

"You're SICK!" Hank spat at him, trying not to attract attention from passersby as he massaged his burning wrist. "No wonder no one wants to work with you."

"Don't ever touch me," Malec said in a voice vibrating with menace. "Keep your hands off my skin, or I'll—"

"I won't come near you again," Hank said and walked off. And over his shoulder, "I'm transferring out." As an afterthought, he walked back into Malec's range. "You do one more thing to me, and I'll blow your job wide open. *Everyone* will know you're a psycho."

Now Malec unlocked his apartment door, mouthing Hank's name. Once inside, he fingered the sign of the devil, calling up Lewand's name, too. Lewand—whose big round chest reminded him of his own thieving father. They should both burn in hell!

He went straight to his study, a plain white room that was a virtual computer warehouse, filled with tables on which sat monitors, boxes, and keyboards. The sight of them had a calming effect. Still breathing hard, he walked over and ran his fingers across his latest acquisition, a used VAX minicomputer almost three feet tall that enabled him to design programs capable of orchestrating a moon shot.

Aware that his anger was only partially submerged, and also worried that Hank might make trouble with his boss, he sat down and tried to control his rampaging thoughts; he would be physically ill if he didn't. After a time the white room, the friendly computers, the silence, brought him back to near normal. He wondered abstractly how long he could keep squeezing things back, how much longer the computers would save him.

He looked around the room, his eyes resting on each piece of equipment in turn—his friends, his allies.

So far he'd used his computers mainly for complicated games, all of which he designed himself. Like other computer games, they were plotted for a solo player, self-initiated, self-competing. Sometimes he surprised himself by designing games so complex that the computer usually won, and these he played over and over.

But he also used his equipment for lists, for keeping track of things: inventions (like MRI and the newest pacemakers) that came about because of computer enhancement; the extremes and averages of weather in countries around the world; major natural disasters by state and month; notorious drug deaths and their symptoms; the airline, product type, and numbers of dead for every plane crash in the world; serial killers; days and times when he felt the urge to masturbate.

Frowning, he sat down in front of a console and turned it on. For an hour he typed energetically, thinking. When he was through, he'd finished constructing a game he'd been working on a week, perhaps the most complicated game of all, a kind of duel in which the loser suffered one-at-a-time castration. It was sinister and difficult, and he began to play it. In his mind his opponent was Nick Lewand.

Midway through a complicated move he stood up, clenching and reclenching his fists. *A game's not enough.* In his mind's eye the face of Lewand had vanished, and the face he saw instead was his father's. Heart pounding, he rushed to his bedroom and seized a pillow. Taking the two ends in his hands, he twisted in opposing directions until the cloth split and the contents spilled onto the floor—and even when the cloth became tatters and almost nothing remained in his hands, he continued to twist. *I wouldn't* want *you remembering my birthday.*

Chapter Seven

Alan Wilcox's boss at the NTSB, Mark Brody, paused in the doorway to Wilcox's office and wondered fleetingly if the man he expected to see sitting in the chair might have thrown up his hands and decided to walk away. Ironic, he thought, that someone with such incredible responsibilities would be trying to operate *here,* in a space inadequate for a beginning clerk typist. There were five field investigators in the whole Western Region, with responsibility for all the aircraft accidents in California, Arizona, Hawaii, and the U.S. Pacific islands, and all five sat in offices like this—mere cubicles. His glance ranged over the desk, the two filing cabinets, the small table, and the floor. Every surface was buried under reports, tapes, thick files, and airplane parts, leaving no place to set anything down. Whatever Wilcox brought into the office had to be piled on top of something else.

Brody could imagine what the president of even a medium-size corporation would say if told he must work in a ten-by-ten room that contained all the records and physical evidence for every transaction he'd ever been involved in.

It was ludicrous, thought Brody, that the economy-minded National Transportation Safety Board allotted so little money to the backbone of its operation. But Alan had never complained, nor had the others. In fact, listening to their banter he detected a certain pride among the five, a cheery knowledge that what they were doing was so important it *transcended* physical impediments. Or even more—that their

ridiculous offices were one more challenge and tangible proof that
they were, in some ways, a level above mortal.

Alan suddenly appeared at the end of the hall. Brody called out, "I
hear you got a call from Senator Fairchild last week."

Wilcox smiled. "How'd you hear that?" Before Brody could answer
he added, "I know. The leaky grapevine."

"So what did you think?" Brody gestured toward the conference room.
"Got you a Diet Coke to celebrate. Let's talk." Both of them knew
there was no place to sit in Alan's office. The one extra chair already
had an occupant—an orange crate containing a plane's carburetor.

The conference room was triple the size of Wilcox's office and furnished
with a few file cabinets and four lunchroom tables and some straight-
backed chairs. On a wall covered with a simulated-wood wallpaper
hung the NTSB seal, while randomly placed pictures of airplane wreckage
provided the final decorative touches.

Brody and Wilcox sat down across from each other. Between sips
Brody said, "The Senator Fairchild call isn't exactly a surprise. I rec-
ommended you."

"Why?" Wilcox set his Coke down and looked hard at his boss: alert
hazel eyes, graying hair, unusually strong chin in a full face. A few
pounds overweight. "Are you trying to get rid of me?"

"Alan, you can't be climbing around these mountains like a billy
goat forever. When you've had enough, you should get the big job.
The big pay. Maybe you aren't ready for it yet, but unfortunately the
job's about ready for you. Nick Lexis is thinking of retiring." At Wilcox's
look of surprise, he shrugged. "The grapevine."

"I like it here," said Alan.

"Yeah." Brody let out a breath. "That's what I expected to hear.
But have you looked at all the angles?"

"I said I would. And I did." Wilcox grinned. "For about five seconds. By the way, something pretty strange happened on yesterday's
trip, a fly-by-wire ride to Frisco."

"You are incredibly stubborn, Wilcox. What about your wife and
kids? Jesus, this field work is a family-wrecker. I was thirty when I
managed to find the kind of woman I didn't think existed, not for me,
anyway. You never met her. She was smart, beautiful, and warm. She
even tried to be understanding. But our marriage didn't last three years."

Wilcox said, "Come on, Mark, two of my kids are grown. Only Todd's
around now. And Ellie . . . if she was going to give up on me, she'd

have done it long ago. I *like* what I do, and not a hell of a lot of men can say that."

Brody brought his hands to his face pensively. "So what about your trip to Tahoe? Have they found the next of kin yet?"

"Not as far as I know. Anyway, let me tell you about that fly-by-wire. I was in the jump seat on an Airtech 123 . . ." Wilcox thought back, feeling again his sense of being doomed, of having strayed into a fatal web, as he told Brody the whole story. "We were lucky. It was much too close."

"Did you file a report?"

"A couple of nights ago, from Reno. With TAF. It started me thinking about the new fly-by-wires. Both pilots reported computer glitches on other planes. I'm thinking of keeping a file on these whifferdills, on whatever odd stuff I hear about. I'll ask for input from pilots."

Brody laughed. "You got that kind of time? We must not be giving you enough to do." He stood and pushed in his chair.

Wilcox got to his feet. *You think this is a waste of time.* Well, he meant to do it anyway.

They walked out together. And then something occurred to Alan. "Why Senator Fairchild? That's not normal channels."

Brody shrugged. "Somebody mentioned you might listen to a senator over some ordinary human."

"Hmmm," said Wilcox. "It figures."

That afternoon Wilcox stuck labels on an oversize accordion file. When the mail brought the report on TAF's Airtech 123—maintenance had pulled all the autopilot boxes and put them on the test bench and nothing unusual showed up—he filed copies of the report in two slots, by date and airplane type. He shoved his file into a bottom drawer. So far one unexplained incident: the first computer whifferdill.

Okay, Brody, he thought, as he pushed the heavy drawer closed, I won't give this a lot of time. But as incidents come to me, I'll—

Sensing someone nearby, he looked up. Mark Brody was standing in his doorway with a twisted expression—a mix of stress and extreme weariness, a look Wilcox had never seen there before. And his color was bad, his face the grayish hue of a rotten peach. Brody said without preamble, "The Tahoe crash. They found the next of kin."

"Oh?" said Wilcox. Knowing instinctively he'd better feel his way, he groped for words. "Is it . . . is it someone you know?"

"Yes," said Brody in a defiant manner. "Me."

Wilcox jumped to his feet. "Mark! My God!" Unsure what to say next, he reached out and put his hand on his boss's shoulder. "I'm sorry." As though comforting a child, he gave Brody a few awkward pats. He didn't know what else to do.

Brody sighed. "The woman . . . Sara. She's my niece. My older sister's only child. A late child, no parents anymore. That's why they took so long finding someone to notify. They just reached me, this minute." He ducked his head. "Goddammit! I loved that girl!"

Brody's explosive remark brought strained silence. Wilcox tried to think of something helpful. Eventually he said, "Dave was a fine man. I knew him well when he was younger—before he went to medical school. I knew *about* Sara. In fact—," he broke off, reconsidering. Brody wouldn't want to hear he'd taught Dave to fly.

"In fact," Brody finished bitterly, "the son-of-a-bitch killed her! It *was* pilot error, wasn't it? Isn't that what you concluded?

"Yes." Wilcox felt his face heating up.

"So the careless bastard wiped her out and wiped out the children, too. I don't care *what* he did for money, how much doctoring he did or how much everyone loved him, when you get down to what's important, he blew his family into the ground. He *killed* them! Right?"

Before he could stop himself, Wilcox blurted out, "Wrong."

Brody stared at him, furious. Wilcox knew he was trapped and had to finish. As gently as he could, he said, "I'm sorry, Mark. *She* was flying the plane."

Brody had been about to speak, but now his mouth closed suddenly. Wilcox turned away, embarrassed by the look on his boss's face. Unearthing the truth—and telling it—was sometimes a rotten task, he thought distantly; the job had a few. He was aware that Brody had slumped against the door frame. No, not slumped exactly, because some part of Brody was furious and disbelieving.

Eventually Brody asked, "What's your proof?"

"The thumbs, Mark. I found the . . . evidence . . . myself. They were clearly a woman's hands. Both thumbs were broken."

Brody winced. "What else?"

"Nothing yet. The coroner's report is still out."

"Then you don't *know*."

Wilcox did know—there'd be other telltale fractures—but it was the wrong time to argue. Brody had lost his objectivity . . . but who wouldn't? he thought, wishing fervently he'd never found those hands. Who wouldn't? No decent human being ever got *that* objective.

"When the coroner's reports come in," Brody said roughly, "I want to see them. Every one."

"Mark, do you think that's a good idea? Shouldn't I—"

"Screen them?" Brody asked. "No. I'm going to know the whole story about Sara. Everything. And frankly, Alan, I think you'll be surprised. You based too much on those thumbs." He walked out with anger stiffening his back.

Poor man, thought Wilcox. *I'm glad I've got kids.*

Rudy Malec waited until the shift was almost over before he spoke to her. It had taken quite a few questions to find out who was in charge of personnel files, three buildings away—and excellent timing to catch her just as the shift was changing.

When he came up behind her and said, "Hi, Sandy," in a soft voice, she jumped and whirled around. "How did you know my name?" She was overweight, with breasts that were formless and mushy, filling her pink blouse like an oversize pillow. He smiled. "You make it a point to find out names when you're . . . interested."

She was suspicious. "I haven't seen you in this area."

"I'm in and out. A troubleshooter." He looked right at her, holding her gaze. "Lately, I've tried to be more in than out. But you didn't notice, so I . . ." he looked away, giving the impression he was fumbling for words.

When the silence went on she prompted, "So you . . ."

"I decided I'd just go for it, start talking to you." He was looking at her again, grinning self-consciously. "I found out your name's Sandy. So . . . Hi again, Sandy."

She laughed.

"Want a Coke?" he asked. "I mean, have you got time?"

"Sure. I can stay long enough for that."

He led her to the nearest vending machine, pushed in six quarters, and suggested they sit outside to drink.

The shift changed and Sandy Wallis lingered with him an extra twenty minutes.

For the next three days he came just before three, buying her Cokes and cajoling her into talking about herself. She was unmarried and glad to have someone who was interested in her former life as a newspaper feature writer. He was the only man she'd ever met who found real estate stories fascinating.

When he asked her on the fourth day if she'd let him take a look at his file, she hesitated. It was strictly against company policy. He touched her hand. "What can it hurt? Nobody's going to know."

A warning rang in her head. *Is he wooing me for this?* She glanced over at him and saw the look in his eyes. God, those eyes were blue, and so . . . gentle. He seemed almost vulnerable.

Then he said, "Look, Sandy, forget it. It's not worth getting you in trouble. Let's go out to dinner, instead. I'll go home and change and call you sometime later this evening." He stood up to leave.

She panicked. "Oh come on," she said. "But don't tell anyone."

"You know I won't."

As soon as he saw the notation, stuck into his file at one end, he guessed why Bergman had never tried to reach him. Lewand had written,

> Interviewed Malec today. Possibly a troublemaker—also possibly trying to pull something. He thinks he's got me fooled. He'll bear watching. May have to be terminated.

Malec went into an immediate rage, shoving his file at Sandy Wallis with such ferocity she stumbled backwards into the wall.

When he stormed away, she knew she'd never see him again. She also knew she couldn't tell anyone what had happened.

Chapter Eight

A half hour before he was due at a board meeting, Miles Kimball waited anxiously for the man at Trans America Fleet to return his call. When at last his desk phone rang, he crossed his knees and took a deep breath before he answered. "Kimball here."

"Swenson returning your call," the other said. "Phil Swenson. I'm not sure who I've reached. Have we met?"

So he didn't remember. "Yes, once. A year or so ago when you came out to tour the plant. Stirling?" he prompted, wondering if Swenson had any inkling whom he was talking to. But why *would* Swenson remember him? As Trans America Fleet's head of Flight Operations— a senior pilot—his expertise was airplanes; he'd have scant reason to remember a VP in charge of sales.

"Oh, yes. Yes," said Swenson. "I recall the tour, anyway. September '87." Abruptly he stopped talking.

Beginning to feel foolish, Kimball could do nothing except plunge ahead. "Orange County has a fine restaurant, Maison Chic, I was wondering if we could set up a dinner sometime—perhaps next week? I thought—"

"Why?" A long pause and then, "I'm sorry, I didn't get your title."

"VP-Sales," Kimball said hurriedly, "but the dinner would be strictly social, a chance for the two of us—"

"Social? Then why me, particularly?"

Kimball felt himself grinding to a halt. *This is a terrible idea; I'm making an ass of myself.* "Well—" Suddenly he could think of no plausible excuse. His intentions weren't social at all; why had he made such a ridiculous statement? He shrugged. "Hell, you've figured out the reason, Swenson. I need to sell you a hundred and fifty airplanes." He waited for Swenson to say no.

To his surprise, the man laughed. "As a matter of fact, I do have some questions about Stirling aircraft. Maison Chic, was it?"

Afterwards, Kimball could not imagine why the man had said yes.

At his small private sink, Kimball prepared for the board meeting by washing his hands and brushing back his graying hair, looking to see if his face showed new signs of stress. God knows he needed a relief from bad news. It had been six months since he'd learned that his investment in hillside ocean-front building sites had been the most reckless move of his life. Only weeks after he'd signed the deed, local geologists revealed that the earth was slipping and that no homes— or anything else—could be built on that land. Immediately he went to his attorney to file a lawsuit, but the group who'd sold him the properties had disappeared. Knowing he'd been taken by experts, Kimball stuck his worthless, rubber-banded documents in the garage. His only remaining investment was undeveloped desert land, waiting miles away for civilization to arrive. What he had left in his bank account wouldn't keep him six months.

With Sondra already worried about her undiagnosed muscle weakness and constant fatigue, he hadn't the heart to tell her that their retirement money was gone.

And then came the bombshell from the Pentagon.

The last week had brought no relief. Rumors, largely unfounded, had swept through the company until everyone was on edge and waiting for the second shoe—or whatever else might fall—to fall. He wondered privately if a year from now they'd still be in business.

The scheduled board meeting began in a rare atmosphere of hushed tension. Nobody spoke. Nobody looked at anyone else. Most didn't even look at Holloway, who for once addressed them without standing. "I'm sure you've all heard the news," he began.

Kimball hadn't. Just the rumors.

"The Pentagon has definitely canceled that order of F-121s. I don't expect they'll reinstate it, because a good many senators are angry and showboating for the benefit of their constituents. With the country watching, they can't back down. Which would be bad enough. But that asshole Billy Walliford stood up in the Chamber today and demanded that we pay exorbitant fines for past sales. Past sins, he's calling it. *That* hasn't made the news yet. It will this evening. I got three calls this afternoon from Washington." Holloway ran a hand wearily across his forehead, and for the first time Kimball noticed the grayish pallor of Holloway's face . . . which fit all too well with the dark, half-open spaces that passed for eyes.

When Holloway stopped talking, nobody tried to fill the void. In the quiet room small noises seemed inordinately loud: cloth on cloth as someone uncrossed his legs; a water glass clinking down on the table. Across from Miles, Max Topping stroked his lighter into life and it was like the sudden flaming of a blowtorch.

In ritualistic fashion, Topping ran his finger back and forth through the flame—a signal that he was fighting an urge to smoke. He said, "I talked Saticoy out of their hard-nosed demand for a hundred and twenty days."

Kimball thought, *Nobody's going to cheer about that.*

Silence. Holloway's frown suggested he found Topping's announcement too insignificant for comment.

The silence turned awkward. Kimball stared at his hands. The quiet was so embarrassing it was almost humorous. Just as he feared he might make some kind of irreverent crack, Holloway said, "I'm waiting for ideas."

Someone said, "We don't have to sit here and let them clobber us. Why don't you go to Washington, Lloyd, and face the Senate head on? Take our numbers on the cost of manufacturing military aircraft and—"

Holloway interrupted, snorting sourly. "All I'd get out of that is a badge for courage. Where the hell do you think we've been getting our excess profits? Christ, we've had two Pentagon men up to their asses in Stirling production for the last five years, both assuring us nobody in that whole goddam maze pays any attention to the cost of anything—until someone like Walliford gets interested. Which happens about as often as an eclipse of the sun."

Kimball asked, "Could Trans America Fleet bail us out?"

"A hundred and fifty planes? What do you think?" And then Holloway added, "The Pentagon fiasco isn't enough, of course. Our union contracts are coming up for renewal next month."

"Great!" said a voice. And another, "They'll get the picture fast enough. There's no blood in a turnip."

Topping said, "Unfortunately, unions don't think that way."

So there goes the Stirling stock, too, thought Miles, staring dully at his hands. Everything I own. For a second he wondered idly if a company's health insurance would live on after its death—like a kidney transplanted from a dead body into someone living.

He made a mental note to find out.

"Lloyd, I think our first move is obvious." It was Max Topping, thoughtfully turning his lighter in his fingers. "We on the board all take pay cuts. Not only a considerable saving to the company, but also a demonstration to the politicians that we mean right."

"Or we could all offer our firstborn child," said Kimball dryly.

Somebody actually laughed. Which relieved the tension so that others followed, until the room was filled with guffaws. *Why am I laughing?* Kimball thought, and laughed harder.

Holloway stood up. "I'll be available for anyone who has an idea, however irrelevant it may seem. Right now that's all I have to say."

His departure left the others still sitting, once more in grim silence. Kimball was the first among them to stand. "So how do we convince the IRS that fines are a deductible expense?"

Alan Wilcox sat at his desk holding a red accordion file whose tab was labeled "LAX-89 FA-019," meaning this was the nineteenth aviation accident in fiscal 1989, which began October first. The tab also contained the words Tahoe City . . . October 14, 1988 . . . Aircraft Lic. # N-33-DH . . . Cessna 421 C . . . Hawkins.

He'd been sitting in that same position for the last ten minutes, thinking. One small downed plane: two personal losses, right in their office. It was bad enough that he was forced to deal with the death of a former student—a friend—but here was Brody, kicked in the gut by the loss of a surrogate child. "Goddammit," Brody had said before he went home for the day, "Sara had me to dinner almost every Sunday. While she cooked, I wrestled with the kids." And then bleakly, "Next Sunday, where am I going to go?"

For a while Brody had drifted through the office looking disconnected and then left. When he came back the next day, Brody's mood had changed. He was angry.

Now Wilcox realized they were both taking it hard.

Death. It was always expected, he thought, routine to anyone doing his kind of investigation. In the last fourteen years he'd touched, photographed, moved, and cleaned up after it, and he'd been privy to all the sudden, terrible ways that people could spend their final minutes. He was inured to death.

Or so he thought.

He told himself to get going—and didn't. As he rifled through his preliminary report, it occurred to him for the first time that the material was vaguely repugnant: the word *bodies* used as though they'd never been anything more, the tone of absolute impersonality that accompanied all the data.

In this one, *nothing* was routine. Since the accident he'd awakened twice in the middle of the night thinking he and Dave were back in the cockpit of a Cessna 150 trainer, with Dave talking about how he was going to pilot a medical rescue plane someday, and joking that since he needed practice landing on rough terrain Alan was not to worry that he'd just put the plane down accidentally in a tomato field.

It had been night-fiction, of course. Dave had never landed anywhere except the landing strip, but it would have been like him—his cockiness and sense of humor.

He found himself thinking about Dave's kids and wondering how Brody was going to handle it when he finally realized he'd lost them all. Odd, he thought, that all these years he'd heard Brody mention his sister's child, heard her called his "adopted family" without ever knowing the Sara he meant was Dave's Sara. Death was an artist that made even indistinct lives stand out in bas relief.

His hand was near the telephone pushbuttons, ready to dial the Reno area coroner's office for the toxicology report.

Instead his line lit up. He listened for a moment and quietly put the FA-019 file on top of three others on a far corner of the desk.

The next moment he was saying, "Sure I remember you, Steve." A forced smile. "Orange County to San Francisco. A few days ago. The 'E ticket' ride on an Airtech 123. What's up?"

He made himself concentrate as Steve told him about the plane he'd piloted the day before which, over Kansas, went into a holding pattern for no good reason and then, just as unexpectedly, "let go."

"Like having a ghost grab hold of your controls," Steve added. "A ghost with a sense of humor."

Wilcox began scribbling notes on airline, flight number, aircraft type, point of origin, routing, final destination, and the date.

Steve hesitated. "I wasn't sure I should bother you. Nothing much happened, beyond losing a couple of minutes. I doubt the passengers even knew. In fact I put off calling you because I figured you were looking for real problems."

"It's no bother, Steve, this is what I'm here for. Call me any time. You'd be surprised where this may lead."

He was overstating his case. Yet part of him said he wasn't. As he'd done in the past, he was going forward on hunches. Intuition. All the intangibles that never found their way into NTSB accident reports.

As he laid the phone down he admitted the truth about himself: *Your instincts are what make you good.*

That evening Alan and Ellie sat in their family room having a glass of wine, the first free night they'd had together since the Tahoe trip. With Todd in bed, it felt like a date. Alan pushed his chair back and a platform came up for his feet. The chair was at an oblique angle to the television, but within his vision was most of Orange County—a gaudy, overdone panorama of lights in yellows, oranges, and reds. He never tired of it.

"We don't sit here often enough," he said.

Ellie nodded. And did not say, Because you're always gone. Instead, reaching for a book that sat beside the couch, she opened it, extracted a piece of paper, and forced herself to say casually, "We got this notice from school a few days ago, while you were out of town. Todd is doing badly in two subjects—Spanish and chemistry. He apparently didn't want us to know, because he intercepted it on a Saturday. I just happened to find it in his room."

"*How* badly?"

"Failing," she said.

He read the paper and folded it up slowly. Todd, he thought. *It must be a mistake.* "How are you handling this, Ellie?"

"I've spoken to his teachers and briefly to him. The rest had to wait until *we* talked—to present a unified front."

"Our first kid-failure," he murmured and looked at her, baffled. "What do we do? You're the school psychologist."

"I know. I'm supposed to have all the answers . . ." She sighed. "It's so obvious until it's *your* child, and then nothing is obvious at all. And there's more, Alan. I think he's using drugs."

Alan brought his chair upright with a thump. "*Drugs!* For God's sake, Ellie, what makes you think so?"

"Last week he drowned himself in after-shave, for no reason I could think of. I picked him up for the dentist and he reeked like he'd been dipped in a vat of perfume—which isn't like him. Underneath, some-where, I thought I detected marijuana."

"Oh boy." He felt like he'd taken a blow to the gut. At that mo-ment it occurred to him that his home had become the mirror image of his job—that here, as there, he was faced with trying to get to the bottom of problems that had no obvious answers. He said, "Why not *ask* him?"

She smiled sadly. "I did. He denied it, of course. Kids on drugs always do."

Silence filled the room like a ghostly presence. Far below them, Alan saw a flashing red light moving along a distant street, a rescue vehicle of some sort on its way to a disaster. Vaguely he wondered if the thing might end up at their front door.

He asked, "What do you tell other parents?"

Mechanically she spouted the words that came so easily when the kid wasn't theirs. "But I look at Todd and none of it applies. How do you take away privileges from a kid who's in school and swimming four hours a day? He hasn't *got* any privileges."

"Maybe you're wrong about the pot."

"I don't know. Look at his grades."

He smiled. "I can think of ten reasons, besides pot, for lousy marks. Maybe he's tired. Or bored with the subject. Talks too much in class. Lazy. Come on, Ellie, it could be anything. I'd be out of business if I jumped to conclusions like that. Let's dig down and find the real reason."

She said quietly, "Alan, you don't *want* to think Todd could be smoking pot, you—"

"That's right. But I also don't believe it. We're not neglectful par-ents, Ellie, we aren't rushing around being upwardly mobile while our kids are left to drift. We've been with them all the way." He smiled. "At least you have."

He thought about it some more. "When I'm here, *I'm really here*."

She sighed. "Sometimes you do everything right and it's not enough. Down on Waverly Street there's a family with four grown sons. They were model parents—the mother stayed home and the father took his kids everywhere, that supposedly ideal combination of discipline and love. But even they produced a flawed stone. They've got two lawyers and a doctor, then the youngest, an out-and-out drug dealer." Her palms went up in a gesture of futility. "It can happen to anyone."

"You've made your point, Ellie. You think Todd smokes stuff, I say he doesn't. Our only real evidence is the rotten grades. Let's try my approach. I'll ask Todd what's happening in school. Press him a little about the pot. See what he says."

"*Asking* won't do any good!"

Suddenly he was angry. "Then hire a detective. Follow him around. Tap his phone."

She glared at him.

"All right, *you* come up with something."

"Assume he's on drugs, Alan. You're the authority figure. Lay down the law."

He stood up. "I'm not threatening my son. I trust him. And that's that."

He went off to the bedroom and she watched his stubborn back as long as she could see it. Obdurate. As immovable as the pyramids. *I've put up with our difficult life-style,* she thought, *even lately, when it's gotten to me, I've tried to make it work. But I won't put up with this.*

Chapter Nine

Maison Chic restaurant—pronounced "Mazone She" by its regular clientele—was probably overkill for this mission, but Kimball was stuck with his hasty choice. A glance at his watch told him he'd arrived much too early—foiled by an unexpected dearth of traffic, he thought, as he clumsily boosted himself out of his Sedan de Ville. Deciding to wait outside instead of sitting at the bar, he had ample opportunity to watch while the callow kid who took his car accelerated twenty yards before aiming it like a missile into a slot that allowed no leeway for mistakes.

He wondered if Phil Swenson would even like the place. Though he knew very little about the man, that brief conversation should have made him wary about the pilot's no-nonsense bent. He glanced around at the awnings and doormen—probably a mistake. Likewise the prices: thirty-six dollars for a steak lying naked on the plate. Pretty rash for someone with neither expense account nor a secure salary.

Increasingly apprehensive, Kimball watched the parking lot for a man seen only once and fairly long ago. Eventually he decided to let Swenson find him and went inside and asked for his table.

Seated in a plush blue chair with an excessively high back to create the illusion of a private dining area, he ordered a glass of chardonnay. After a time he began to wonder if Swenson might have gotten the date wrong; he was now twenty minutes late.

Craning toward the entrance, he watched a striking woman enter the foyer—or rather he saw the body of a woman, since all else was obliterated by her breasts, which pointed straight ahead and preceded the rest of her by a considerable number of inches. Her choice of a bright green, laminated dress suggested a certain willingness to display her endowments. Amused, Kimball glanced at the nearby patrons. Judging by their covert smiles, there was a consensus that nature alone could not have produced such a miracle.

That was when he noticed the man standing just behind her. A short bulldog of a person—round face, stubby legs, not much neck, wearing a sport coat and no tie—he searched the room table by table. Kimball dismissed him at once; he couldn't be a captain for a major airline.

But then the woman turned toward the cocktail lounge and the man walked purposefully toward his table.

Kimball rose. "Could you be . . . are you Phil Swenson?"

"Sure am," the other said jovially, putting out his hand. "Thought you must be Kimball. Wasn't sure, though, after all this time. I just remembered you as dignified." He looked around appraisingly. "Not a bad place. Should have worn a tie."

Kimball smiled. "Stuffiness has its advantages—they'll pretend not to notice. What'll you drink?"

Minutes later Swenson ordered a double martini, explaining he couldn't afford to get behind.

As Swenson downed the drink in a few swallows, Kimball began to wonder about him. The vice president of flight operations for a major airline was usually a pilot, and an influential one at that; his input on the evaluating committee would be major, passing right through to the board—because whatever planes the evaluating committee chose, the board would usually buy.

Watching the man swig his martini, Kimball wondered what other surprises were coming.

As it turned out, quite a few. Over steaks and lobster, Swenson asked, "Did you happen to notice the babe in green?"

Kimball laughed. "Hard not to. Every red-blooded man in the place noticed."

"She's having hers in the bar—waiting for me. Found her crying out in the parking lot because some rat fink stood her up. So, his loss . . ." He shrugged. "Some knockers, eh? Couple hours from now I'm gettin' lost in 'em. Took tipping out my pockets to make her see it my way." He glanced at his steak. "Big bucks, though. Shoulda sent her to Denny's."

Kimball smiled politely.

"Best thing my wife ever did was cut out, crying all the way about too much competition. But hell—we only go around once, right? I said to her, 'This is *it?* Just *you?*' Well, Christ, I was honest with her, she coulda stayed."

Luckily, he seemed to need no response. Kimball was beginning to feel they'd come from different planets.

One of the penguin waiters slowed at their table with the dessert trolley, but Swenson arbitrarily waved him away. Kimball cleared his throat. "I hear Trans America Fleet is considering replacing their whole fleet of 727s with Airtechs."

The smile on Swenson's round face abruptly disappeared. "That's one of the possibilities."

"At the same time giving up their options on Stirling aircraft. All of them."

"Nothing has been finalized. We're running our numbers, and that's all I can say."

Taking a deep breath, Kimball forced himself to continue. "Could it be you haven't decided because your pilots are having problems with automation they hadn't counted on?"

Swenson eyed him thoughtfully. "Not that I know of."

"You must not be hearing what I'm hearing, then."

"What *are* you hearing?"

"That there hasn't been a computer designed you could trust unequivocally. Our engineers maintain—"

Swenson broke in. "Are you suggesting Airtechs are defective?"

"No. Of course not. What I'm suggesting is, computerized control isn't foolproof. The possibilities for glitches are endless. And we're talking major bucks—hell, you're running the numbers—on what big-school engineering considers a gamble." He caught and held Swenson's gaze. "I'm suggesting you think twice before dumping Stirling. We're established. Reliable. With plenty of updating. Take the new wings, for instance—big increase in aerodynamic efficiency—you'd save plenty on fuel consumption. And new generation engines to meet the stage-three noise standards."

Phil Swenson ordered another martini, this time a single, and looked at Kimball without expression. "I hear you. But cockpit automation is a whole new concept, and you can't fight it. It'll become the norm because it's the only way to stay competitive. How soon, I—"

"Even if you lose a few planes?" The minute the words were out, Kimball regretted them.

Swenson put down his glass. "I'm *on* that committee, Miles. I fly those planes."

Kimball felt his face redden; recklessness wasn't his style. His eyes swept the room. Nor was any of this—the foppery, the decadence. When you had a good product and weren't desperate, it shouldn't be necessary to fall back on sleaze.

But then his mouth was open again and words rolled out over which he seemed to have no control—as though once embarked on a foolhardy course he was somehow committed. Offering a bribe didn't even phase him. "I have a desert property," he said, "which may be worth millions someday. I'd be willing to sell it to you for a few thousand, but you'd have to wait—"

"It's time to go," said Swenson, standing abruptly. Without another word he started for the exit, but then he turned back. "Don't ever say another word about that property in the desert. In fact," he said, giving Kimball a long, hard appraisal, "forget you know where I work."

Kimball watched him leave with respect he hadn't felt earlier.

Saturday morning Miles Kimball was at his wife's bedside when her breakfast tray was brought in. The nurse set it on Sondra's nightstand with a questioning look at Miles.

"I'll handle it," he said. "I'll help her." Careful to place the tray so she couldn't tip it sideways, Miles handed her one dish at a time, watching in discouragement as she ate only a few bites of scrambled egg, a couple of teaspoons of oatmeal. Once she smiled at him, but her head bobbed weakly. Muscles going fast, he thought, trying to be patient.

As he managed her breakfast, Miles tried not to look at Sondra's face, tried not to see her thin cheeks and the sagging skin around her jaw. The older-woman look of her wasn't Sondra, but a manifestation of illness finally diagnosed: Lou Gehrig's disease. Just in the past few weeks she'd changed drastically. She was flat now, uncommunicative. She simply didn't have the energy to talk.

"Good stuff, huh?" Miles said, and immediately chastised himself for discussing *oatmeal,* for God's sake! Sondra's mind deserved better.

He tried again. "I see Bush took a little drop in the polls this week. But he says he's not worried. His henchmen are doing a pretty good job making sure Quayle never has to spell anything in public. In case it's something easier than potato." He smiled, and now a twisted expression on Sondra's face suggested she might be trying to laugh. It wasn't enough.

Eventually Sondra ate small bits of everything on her tray, and Miles sat on her bed a few minutes longer monologuing the news. Though he knew she heard—she managed a few fragmented sentences—he couldn't rate it as conversation. The process—the reaching out to her, her pathetic attempts at response, his knowing how she felt with her alert mind trapped in a disintegrating body—brought him despair. He wanted to escape.

He left her to get a snack in the cafeteria.

With no appetite for breakfast, he grabbed a sweet roll and coffee and sat down by himself. At half past nine the place was deserted. He wished to God he had someone to talk to.

For minutes he swallowed without tasting. And then, as though his unspoken wish had been granted, a familiar face suddenly appeared in the doorway. "Miles!" she called out.

"Well—Mary Helen!" He rose and smiled, watching her approach. Though he'd seen her only once since her husband died, some four years earlier, he noted she hadn't changed. His impression was the same as it had been then: she was just short of beautiful.

"Sondra thought you'd be here," she said, taking his hand as they both sat down again. Her eyes were deep blue, her cheeks attractively rounded. "I saw Sondra . . . well, that's obvious, isn't it?" She smiled nervously. "Sondra looks . . . of course, I only stayed a minute, so we didn't talk about the illness . . ." She broke off and looked at him helplessly.

He saw her confused expression. "What you mean is, she looks terrible. Isn't that what you're trying to say?"

"Oh, no! Not terrible." She shook her head vigorously. Her eyes met his and she looked away, letting the head-shaking taper off. "She wasn't that bad, the light was poor, I couldn't see her very well. Why, only a month ago we had lunch together, we—"

"She told me."

"She was okay *then*." She looked down at her hands, and when he let the silence grow and become awkward, she blurted out, "She's *not* okay, is she? Oh Miles, how did it happen so fast?"

"Mary Helen, I know nothing about Lou Gehrig's disease. Except what I see happening to my wife. People have told me it's slow, often goes on for years, but this has been fast. Goddam fast. She looks worse every time I see her."

Mary Helen said softly, "You poor man. You must have had a rotten month." She waited, her eyes full of sympathy.

With that he opened up, telling her what it was like, trying not to make a maudlin story out of what was the worst damned situation he'd ever lived through—a woman he loved, had loved for thirty-seven years, rapidly reduced to a thin, sagging face and a few sentences that didn't communicate.

He tried not to sound bitter. But he was bitter nevertheless, and he supposed it showed.

She said, "It's funny, I never knew how deep—how very sensitive you are." She smiled. "Come to think of it, I hardly knew you, period. I wish you and Bill had been better friends."

"We could have been. Except I hardly knew Bill—he didn't work anywhere near me. At Stirling the wives always knew each other better than the husbands."

"Strange company." She stood. "I don't know what to say, but . . . my prayers are with you." She gathered up her purse.

Surprised that her sympathy had so overtaken his normal reticence, he felt embarrassed. She was only an acquaintance, after all. Why had he spilled his guts like that? She must think him a fool.

She pulled a pencil out of her purse and scribbled on a napkin. "If you ever want to call me . . . I mean, just to *talk* . . ." She handed him the napkin and smiled and gave him a wave.

He watched her leave and thought, *You'll have to understand. I can't call you.*

"These are preliminary findings, Alan," said the coroner at Tahoe City, "but I thought you'd want to know. The adult female has fractures of both ulnas, both radiuses, both tibias, both fibulas, and most of the bones in both ankles."

"Thank you," Wilcox said.

"The written report will be out in three or four weeks."

"Fine."

Wilcox hung up the phone and picked up a pen. No surprise there. The two broken thumbs had already told him she was the pilot. *But what in hell am I going to do about Brody?*

Chapter Ten

The company was mortally ill. Though Congress, moving at glacial speed, had temporarily dropped Stirling as a hot political issue, the damage was done. The Pentagon would not reinstate its order for jet fighters.

Knowing he'd better shore up his own finances, Kimball brought a bundle of papers to the office. Packet in hand, he stood in the doorway to Topping's rich pecan-wooded office, furnished largely out of the VP's own pocket. "Max. Isn't your wife in real estate?"

Topping smiled. "Come in. What do you have there, a deed to Southcoast Plaza? Annie dabbles in real estate, yes. I made the mistake of calling it 'Annie's hobby' once; she was furious. Since then I've avoided mentioning her dubious monetary triumphs in the same breath as mine."

Kimball dropped his hand and started to edge away. *I don't know Max as well as I thought I did.* "This is a small-potatoes property I was hoping to sell. Desert land. She probably wouldn't be—"

Topping held out his hand. "On the contrary, she'll be pleasantly surprised that I'm showing an interest. Is this the description? I'll take it home, see what she says." Before Kimball could comment further, he realized Topping was back at work and he'd been dismissed.

As a second week passed without word on his property, Kimball found himself constantly on the verge of buttonholing his associate; only fear of revealing his desperation kept him silent.

In the middle of week three he finally blurted without thinking, "What's the verdict on that desert land, Max? Has Annie had a chance to show it?"

Topping slapped his thigh. "Son of a gun, Miles, I'm glad you asked! The papers got buried on my desk. Let's go get 'em."

Exactly what I expected, Kimball told himself as he followed his colleague down the hall. But that wasn't the case, not at all. What he'd expected was fifty thousand dollars.

Out of a paper pyramid came the packet. Max smiled. "Annie says it's too far away. She could sell it for a song, but you wouldn't want that, she says. Wait ten years. It'll be worth a fortune."

In ten years I'll be sixty-three.

Topping must have caught his fleeting look of despair. He said quietly, "Miles, I've got a long term CD coming due next week, twenty-five thousand. How about I reinvest with you, same interest?"

Shaking his head, Kimball turned to go. "That's generous, Max, but I'm in good shape—doing fine. Just thought this might be a good time to cash out some land. Obviously it isn't."

That night Sondra was no worse, but Kimball's tolerance was less. He sat by her bed holding her hand while they watched the evening news. Except for the feel of her dry, cold hand in his, it was like watching alone. During the commercials he made comments, but all he got in reply was a whispery sound he could hardly understand.

After a while he went out into the hall to talk to the nurse. She wasn't around.

That was when he spotted the pay phone. I'll call *her,* he thought, just to talk. But he didn't have her number, he realized. Which was just as well.

When he got back to his wife's room, Sondra was asleep. So Miles went home.

It was early evening, and Miles wandered through his empty house looking at pictures of the two of them on recent vacations, which he'd hung on their hall walls, and pictures of Sondra—much younger, always smiling, with wispy hair framing her piquant face.

The bedroom was deserted, echoing. The king-size bed looked like a football field, the strongest reminder yet of what it meant to be alone, because the one thing Sondra had always insisted on was going to bed together. "It's the only thing you do with each other that you don't do with anyone else."

The napkin was on his bureau. He looked at it, put it down, and walked into the kitchen.

When at last he called Mary Helen, she said, "Oh, Miles. I wondered if I'd ever hear from you. Can we meet for coffee?"

"Meet?" he asked blankly.

"Yes. Will that hurt anything?"

"No. I—well, where?"

And she told him.

Later that night they sat in a booth at Marie Callender's, noted for pie, though neither had any, and only he had coffee. Mary Helen had a cup of tea, which she drank in small sips, holding the cup in front of her face so all he saw were her blue eyes watching him over the rim.

She's close to beautiful, he thought. When she smiled he imagined she once might have had men lining up at her door. It was a quality she exuded, a warmth, her lacking any awareness at all of the effect she created. And she constantly listened—listened responsively, so he was in danger once more of saying too much. He noticed after a while that one of her teeth was a little crooked, that it puffed out her upper lip. For some reason it only made her more attractive.

They didn't touch, they didn't say anything intimate; but afterwards he felt they'd been intimate nevertheless.

Alan Wilcox heard the toxicology report called in by a woman from the U.S. Armed Forces Institute of Pathology, and his fingers recorded data that his mind had trouble believing. "Adult male blood sample normal. Female blood sample contained the drug hydrocodone bitartrate at a level of 23.6 nanograms per milliliter, plus acetaminophen at levels of 17 nanograms per milliliter. Additionally, heavy concentrations in the liver, brain, and vitreous. Combination highly suggestive of Vicodin."

Vicodin. Shaking his head. *Good God.*

He'd looked it up in the *PDR* for another case only the week before. It wasn't a drug you'd take casually. The stuff was a synthetic narcotic analgesic similar to codeine, with an anti-inflammatory agent thrown in. Alan could have recited the cautions: "sedation . . . drowsiness . . . impairment of mental and physical performance." With a half-life of 3.8 hours, a reading like that meant the drug level in the pilot's system was double the mean peak serum level. Before Sara set out, she'd dosed herself at least twice.

Sara Hawkins, he thought, staring out his window. Flying a plane all drugged up. *My God. What possessed you?*

In a week of shocks, here was another that made no sense.

He reread the blood analysis: why was she taking a drug like that—and even more, why didn't she have the good sense to let Dave fly the plane? Perhaps, for some reason, she couldn't let him know . . .

What kind of person was she, this Sara?

He began musing about the woman he'd never met. To marry Dave, he reflected, she had to be intelligent, probably athletic. And a good sport. Maybe a better sport than she ought to be, helping out whether she felt like it or not.

Or maybe none of the above. A darker scenario was possible—Sara Hawkins hooked on prescription drugs.

He shook his head. The coroner's report was incomplete, but he doubted he'd ever know more than he did now—or that Brody would, either. His boss deserved the truth, but it would take some soul-searching, finding the right moment to kick a man who was already down.

Just then reality broke into Wilcox's thoughts. The week had come full circle: Todd's lousy grades and Ellie convinced he'd been smoking pot; Sara Hawkins's astonishing toxicology report and he assuming . . . all kinds of things; Todd falsely accused—or so Alan believed—possibly his worst assumption of all. Perhaps Ellie was right: they should start with an acknowledgment of drug use and work backwards.

He made a mental note to find time next week, during Thanksgiving vacation, to lay it on the line with Todd. That is, if the pilots in the Western Region managed to stay out of trouble for a few days.

As Wilcox was getting ready to leave, his phone button flashed. "Wilcox," a jovial voice boomed, "I hear you're collecting gremlin gossip. I've got a good one for you. I was piloting this fly-by-wire craft—," the voice broke off with a laugh, "or it was piloting me—and just as we were about to land, the lights came on that the gear wasn't down, and hell, Alan, we were committed. We had no choice but to set her down, and know what? The wheels were right there, normal as normal . . ."

Chapter Eleven

Mark Brody looked like hell: haggard expression accentuated by a pronounced droop in his left eyelid; shirt and pants mismatched. "Alan," he said, "we need to take the Cessna's fuel pumps back to Mobile, Alabama, and have them checked out. Get a complete analysis. There are factors in that accident which haven't come to light."

Wilcox stared at him. *Oh, God, Mark . . . don't.* He said gently, "I don't think we'll find anything. My crew looked them over pretty well on the ground."

Brody's face tightened. "Not good enough. You didn't have the tools or the expertise. Only the factory can find the insidious problems." Tiredly, he pinched the bridge of his nose. "I know what you're thinking, Alan. But you understand why I have to get to the bottom of this. Nothing is ever as simple as it looks. I must know the truth."

The truth isn't what you want. "I'll help all I can. I'm sorry, Mark. I know it's been rough."

"Rough?" His boss smiled. "That's one word. I can think of ten others. Can you leave tomorrow?"

"Sure," said Wilcox. *And then you'll have to be told.*

Over the phone Mary Helen said, "Miles, there can't be any harm in coming by for dinner. I don't want to spend Thanksgiving by myself, and I can't imagine that you do, either. Afterwards I'll push you right out."

Kimball took a deep breath, a stall maneuver. The invitation felt all wrong, different from the quick restaurant supper they'd had together a week earlier. This would be her home; Thanksgiving was a family holiday. The whole thing had an intimate sound. He felt himself drawn toward an invisible line that somehow delineated the kind of man he was. On this side his values were secure. On the other . . .

"Well," he began, trying to assemble an answer that wouldn't make him look the fool.

"Look," said Mary Helen, "why don't you find out what the hospital does on Thanksgiving? Spend that part with Sondra. I'll work around it."

She made it sound reasonable. And then he saw the line as clearly as if someone had painted it for him and footprints the size of his shoes stepping over without effort.

He said with what he hoped was encouraging warmth, because he still wanted the option to talk to her, "I'm grateful for the invitation, Mary Helen. But I think I'll hang around the hospital. It'll be a long day for Sondra if I don't."

"Okay. But if you change your mind . . ."

As he drove to work he wondered if he hadn't overreacted to the point of being ridiculous. Was he really responding to some inner core of integrity—the self-image he'd carried for fifty-three years—or was he just a scared novice philanderer hiding behind morality like an overgrown Boy Scout?

Stirling's boardroom was not a happy place.

Lloyd Holloway sat at the end of the long oak table wearing a black suit that seemed less somber than merely drab. He'd clearly lost weight; the suit hung limp, as though occupied by little more than a coat hanger.

When he cleared his throat to speak, it did no good. His voice emerged strained and hoarse. *He's been shouting at someone*, Kimball thought. *Thank God, not me.*

"It all hit the fan today," Holloway began without preamble. "Our good friends in Congress are on our backs again. An hour ago the Pentagon served us with papers. We have a choice: agree to a ten-million-dollar fine or fight a lawsuit." His jaw thrust forward angrily. "They're out to break us. As if we were the first company that ever made a profit from the government. I'd like to know who the hell blew the whistle. It had to come from somewhere." He collected his thoughts. "As of a half hour ago, I notified our lawyers. Unfortunately, they consume money the way elephants eat fodder."

He tugged at his shirt, loosening his tie. "For the moment all corporate salaries are suspended. If Trans America Fleet decides to exercise their option we can survive the squeeze from the Pentagon. If not . . ."

The air in the room felt thick and stagnant, though Kimball wondered why, since nobody seemed to be breathing. Without thinking, he mumbled under his breath, "We all get the same Thanksgiving—cooked goose."

A few board members smiled.

Max Topping spoke up. "I did a little sweet-talking with Rawling Rivets, Lloyd, and they've agreed to ride with us and get their money when we get ours. And I'm talking to other suppliers who need our business and will probably accept the same arrangement." His lighter flared and he ran a finger through the flame. "Also, I want to say here and now that I'm happy to sacrifice my salary for the time being. Stirling has been a good working home."

Lloyd Holloway's tense features relaxed. "That's good of you, Max. We'll try to make this period as short as possible."

The reality of no paycheck hadn't reached Miles Kimball. Strangely aloof, he watched his colleagues, fascinated by myriad signs of tension: the controller who unconsciously raised his eyebrows, lifting and lowering them nonstop; the general manager folding and refolding a piece of notepaper and then rounding the edges until it resembled a pill bug; the VP for public relations nervously pulling down his shirt sleeves to keep them showing below his jacket.

And then he thought, *How in God's name am I going to pay my bills?* For a moment he lost track of reality and considered throwing himself on the job market, offering to do anything: pump gas, bag groceries, bus dishes, drive a taxicab. Only the realization that none of those jobs would even cover his mortgage brought his fanciful thoughts to a stop.

Lloyd Holloway stood. "Try not to let this spoil your Thanksgiving dinner. But if any of you are grace-sayers, you might offer a special prayer for Stirling."

Thanksgiving at St. Joseph's Hospital was a minimal affair. Though she'd improved somewhat the last week, Sondra didn't feel like eating, and after picking at her sweet potatoes and nothing else, she pushed her tray away and fell asleep.

Miles sat in the chair by her bed with despair backed into a corner of his mind. A corporate man all his life, he'd seen the financial creativity resorted to by other struggling companies. But few had ever had problems as large as Stirling's, nor had any threatened to drown while he hung on around their necks.

He looked over at his sleeping wife and realized how fast she was pulling out on him. Lou Gehrig's disease had always sounded like a friendly malady—until Sondra came down with it. He could hardly believe that only a month earlier all she'd had was unexplained weight loss and fatigue.

With a sense of having been dumped on by a garbage truck, he went out into the hall and called Mary Helen. "I need to get out of here. Have you got any pumpkin pie left?"

Mary Helen's home was a generic 1960s California ranch, abused by too much sunshine and the occasional movements of the tectonic plates. The driveway was marked by numerous fine cracks, like the broken capillaries around a drunk's nose. The blue clapboard siding had faded to a chalky, barely tinted white. Bleached wooden shingles formed a V in what passed for a protective overhang above the front door.

Miles felt he was slumming.

And then Mary Helen opened the door and held out her hand. Her beauty and warmth reached out to him and drew him into an aura that had nothing to do with fading paint. He said gratefully, "It's good to be here."

She glided around her pullman kitchen, setting out coffee cups and cutting pieces of pie and spooning whipped cream over pumpkin. He watched her, absorbed.

Savoring every mouthful, Miles felt his tension slipping away. The piquant taste of pumpkin. The cool cream. Mary Helen sitting nearby with her blouse open one button too many, giving him, at certain angles, a tantalizing glimpse of cleavage.

After the pie they talked, first about Sondra, then about her. She'd been married twice—widowed once—and had no children. For the last four years she'd lived alone, resentful that she saw so few of her old friends. "After Bill died, most of them disappeared. No more dinner parties, just lunches with occasional wives, like Sondra. I had the feeling I'd become a different species, because around me the women stopped bitching about their no-good husbands." She smiled. "They stopped mentioning husbands at all. Which made conversation pretty flat when you consider that's all we used to talk about." A shrug. "I don't fit anymore."

He nodded, trying to understand—yet not wanting to understand *too well,* lest it happen to him.

"My only family is a nephew who lives in San Diego. Right now Rudy's probably mad at me. I was hoping you'd come and didn't invite him for Thanksgiving."

Some distant conversation replayed itself. "Doesn't he work at Airtech?"

She smiled and laid her hand on his knee. "Yes. What a memory!"

He smiled back, acutely aware of the soft feel of her hand and her face too close and the curve of her lip around the protruding tooth. How much longer could he go without touching her?

He stood up. "I need a glass of water." On his way to the kitchen, he heard the doorbell. He whirled around guiltily, looking at her in alarm. "Were you expecting someone?"

Laughing at his panic, she opened the door. "Oh! Rudy!" she said, "we were just talking about you."

"Am I too late for Thanksgiving?" The voice was high-pitched and petulant. "I waited all morning for your call."

Miles stared at the man who limped into the living room: slight, curly-haired, prominent cheekbones. And then the man glanced at him briefly, and he thought, Where have I seen those enormous eyes?

The nephew turned to Mary Helen. "I finally went to a restaurant, but the turkey didn't taste like yours. When you eat alone, nothing does."

"Baby, I'm sorry." Mary Helen took his shoulders. "You said you'd be okay this Thanksgiving, remember?"

"I said I'd figure something out. You didn't invite me. Was I supposed to invite myself?"

"Come on, Rudy. I said I'm sorry." She turned to introduce them, mentioning that Miles worked for Stirling.

"Stirling?" Malec's expression changed subtly. "Don't I remember you from years ago—didn't we meet at a Stirling picnic once, when Bill was still alive?"

"It's possible."

Malec walked over with his hand out. "I was a teenager then. But I *do* remember you. How are you, sir?"

"Well—fine." Astonished at the sudden change in tone, Miles could think of nothing to add.

Malec seemed entranced. "You're in what department, Mr. Kimball?"

"Sales. And you?"

"Sales!" Malec cried. "That's where I've heard your name. From one of your counterparts down at Airtech!"

"That so?" Kimball was skeptical. "Stirling's sales aren't so hot right now. And largely due to Airtech."

"But our people respect you, nevertheless. Some way or other you've got yourself a reputation."

"I don't know about that." A smile. "Whatever they think I had, I wish I'd get it back. Stirling's in the doldrums. I'd like to think it's temporary . . ." He switched the subject. "Airtech obviously has smart management, future-oriented and—"

"And never mind the employees," Malec broke in, then caught himself. "Scratch that. They're leading the industry, that's true."

"But the employees—," Mary Helen prompted.

Malec hesitated. "Well . . . for us things aren't so hot. But I'm not complaining. I get my paychecks—and *most* of my money."

"Rudy, what on earth are you talking about?"

"It's a small thing." Malec shrugged. "We think they've altered the time clocks so a few minutes each day are taken off our cards. But we can't prove it. And it may be only our department. Also, they've set up a spy system among the employees. One of my friends threatened to go to the Labor Board, but his boss said, 'Do it and you'll never work in the industry again.' " His eyes were now full of anger. "If you complain, they put character slurs in your file. I happened to see my file accidentally. It said, 'Possibly a troublemaker. May have to be terminated.' "

"Rudy!" Mary Helen was aghast. "You've never mentioned—"

He looked at her hard. "I don't tell you everything. I need the job."

Kimball was astonished. "How long has this been going on?"

"Started a few months ago. When people quit they don't talk. Nobody wants to be blackballed."

"I'm surprised this hasn't leaked out. Made the papers, or 'Sixty Minutes.' It's hard to silence that many people!"

"It might not be the whole company," said Malec. "And it *will* get out one of these days. By then it may be too late for me." He smiled again. "Or possibly not—I learn fast. For one thing, I've learned to keep my mouth shut. For God's sake, don't either of you—"

"We won't say a thing!" Mary Helen said.

"Good. I'm trying to hang on . . . until someone else blows the whistle."

Malec lapsed into silence, then got up to rummage in the kitchen. Mary Helen followed, offering to fix him a plate of turkey.

Left alone, Kimball wondered about Malec—victimized but willing to put up with it. Hard to believe an industry giant like Airtech could get away with such shenanigans. Yet Malec's outrage seemed genuine.

With the two out in the kitchen, Kimball began to feel awkward and out of place. For the first time he noticed the plainness of the furniture and the long-outdated look of the gold shag carpet. *I don't belong here.*

He decided to get up gracefully and leave—until he realized his home was empty and he wanted to be there even less than here.

Ellie set the turkey on the table in their formal dining room and called everyone to dinner. *We have to eat now, even without Todd.*

It was their oldest son, Douglas, blond and serious behind his glasses, who expressed what she'd been thinking. "So today," he said, nodding toward the empty chair, "we have Harvey the Rabbit."

"Mom, where *is* he?" asked Jamie. "Didn't he call?"

"No," said Ellie, "but I didn't expect a call. I expected *him.*"

"There must be some other topic of conversation," said Alan, "besides Todd being a few minutes late for dinner."

Outwardly serene, Ellie began passing Jello salad and mashed potatoes. She doubted any physical harm had come to Todd. The truth, she suspected, would be subtle and much harder to deal with.

Todd came home as they were finishing dessert. Like a shadow he passed from the front door straight to his room, so quietly and fast that Ellie wondered for a split second if she'd really seen him.

Ellie stood up. "Alan, will you come here, please?"

Signaling him to follow her into the den, she turned and closed the door. "Alan, please go question Todd. Right now."

"On Thanksgiving, Ellie? You want us to have our big scene today? This minute? Why can't it wait until tomorrow?"

"It just can't. It must be done now. The timing is important. Something is wrong. This isn't a normal Todd, skipping Thanksgiving dinner."

He found himself smiling. "Ellie, I refuse to believe there's a bogeyman hiding behind every late appearance for dinner. Leave him alone. If he wants to eat, he'll come out."

She looked at him steadfastly, willing him to listen. "You're missing the point. Whether he eats or not doesn't matter. If you don't talk to him this minute and find out what kept him, we'll be losing the first round. It may be bigger than pot. He could be using serious drugs."

Before he could respond, his pager went off.

Ellie threw him a quick, exasperated look and walked out of the room.

Going to bed with Mary Helen proved to be easy.

To Miles's surprise, Rudy Malec had stayed less than an hour. After he left, Mary Helen served chardonnay, sitting close to Miles on the couch, letting her shoulders touch his. The wine numbed his brain and ricocheted through his body. Nothing mattered anymore except what was about to happen.

Before long she left briefly and came back into the living room wearing something he could almost see through, peach-colored, with just enough substance to make some areas of her shadowy and dark. The whatever-it-was she wore bonded with the wine like a chemical reaction. His response was almost automatic. He'd followed her back to the bedroom, dropping his inhibitions with his clothes.

Now as he sought her under the sheets, pushing away the filmy cloth so he could fondle her breasts, his hand recognized a difference. What he felt was softer and larger than normal. Normal, he thought with hastily denied guilt, being Sondra's breasts. *Even my hand knows this is the wrong woman.*

He refused to think any longer. What happened next passed in a blur of sensation uncomplicated by thought. He made love to Mary Helen with the same teenage urgency that had driven him in his first affair. Blindly. Keeping his thoughts submerged. Losing himself in moment-by-moment physical detail, swept away by rising, exhilarating tension.

"Speak to me, Miles," she commanded, but he was at a loss. Speaking meant thinking—and he was trying *not* to think.

What could he tell her? That she was synonymous with comfort . . . relief . . . escape? That she embodied release from torment, perhaps even momentary peace?

No, she wouldn't want to hear this. "You're beautiful," he murmured, but it felt forced.

Subliminally he heard her moan and knew from his years with Sondra what he should do next.

In the end he was rewarded with a rush of pleasure—and then sleep.

The sun came in through Mary Helen's bedroom window in long rays that looked to Miles like pointing, accusatory fingers. He sat up quickly in bed, mumbling that he was late visiting Sondra, even as he noted Mary Helen was as beautiful the morning after as he'd remembered from seven hours earlier. Her luscious blue eyes were rested and bright and needed no makeup.

"It's okay, Miles, Sondra will be okay." She took him in her arms and nestled his head against her breasts and stroked his hair back from his forehead. "Sondra is an extraordinary person. Generous and giving. She'd want you to be happy, I know it. How can you bring her comfort if you have none yourself? Think of our love as a well from which we're all drawing happiness, enough to sustain the three of us."

Love? he thought blankly.

She tried to push him out of bed. "Go buy her flowers, Miles, long-stemmed roses—"

He smiled. "I can get out of bed under my own steam." *What's going on here?*

"The roses will be symbolic to her. She needs to know that you still love her and nothing has changed. She's—"

"The roses will tell her everything's changed. She's never had any—not from me. We don't do symbolism. The last thing I gave her was a toaster, after the old one blew up." He smiled ironically. "We'd best keep Sondra out of this."

"You're too practical, Miles. Think romantic."

"Fine," he said, throwing his clothes on. "I'll think romantic. Now where can I find a razor?"

Chapter Twelve

Miles Kimball looked up to see Rudy Malec peering around his half-open door. No advance call, no notice from reception that he was down there, just suddenly a face at the door. Forcing a pleasant expression, he waved Malec inside. He didn't need the interruption.

The man smiled apologetically. "I can see you're busy, sir, I'll come back later." He was dressed in a blue sport jacket, white shirt, and what appeared to be an expensive blue paisley tie. And then Kimball noticed the blue jeans. And below, shoes that were literally falling apart. *The further south you look, the worse he gets.* Kimball bit back an impulse to laugh.

Instead, he stood up. "Now that you're here, tell me what's on your mind." Malec's hand was across the desk, his grip firm and confident. In the other hand he held a small cloth case.

"I happened to call Mary Helen," he began, "and she told me about your wife's illness. I know it isn't my business, but I got curious and went to the library. Just thought I'd offer a little hope, Mr. Kimball. Sometimes patients with ALS go into remissions that last for years." He shrugged. "For what it's worth."

"Well." Kimball was surprised. "Thank you. That's very kind."

"Also, I've done some asking around about you." Malec grinned. "You probably already know this, but people say you've got integrity . . . a sense of decency . . ." He broke off as though not wishing to make his recitation embarrassing.

Kimball smiled. "You've been busy."

Malec shrugged. "I had a reason. I'd be lying if I pretended I didn't. Mr. Kimball—," he seemed to be feeling his way, "sir, I'd like to work for you."

Caught off guard, Kimball stared at him. Through the window beyond Malec's head—the window that faced John Wayne Airport—he noticed abstractedly a distant plane angled steeply toward a landing strip. No problem out there, he thought, but a big problem right here at his desk. He said, "Won't you sit down, Rudy?"

Malec shook his head. "No, sir. I have to be on my way." Holding his little case, he hovered near the desk.

Kimball began slowly. "Any other time, Rudy, we might work it out. But not now. I'll give it to you straight." In a few words he spelled out Stirling's predicament, noting that all departments would soon be asked to trim personnel. "So you see . . ." With a dismissing gesture, he let his words drop off, expecting Malec to leave.

He didn't. He looked right at Kimball and said, "What if I did something to help? Something basic?"

"Such as?"

"Such as get you a contract from one of the major carriers. Wouldn't that solve your problems?"

Kimball smiled. "Sure. Most of them. But you can't. So thanks anyway." *Next he'll be offering to fix the ozone layer.* Again he waited for Malec to leave.

"I think I can do plenty. What if your biggest competitor was discredited? What if nobody wanted to buy their planes anymore? What would that do to your sales?"

Kimball started to laugh, then abruptly stopped. "Just what do you have in mind, Malec?"

Something changed in Malec's expression. A hardening. A fleeting look of hostility. "If I arranged . . . a shift in your situation, a shift for the better, would I get the job?"

Kimball stared at him and saw the blue eyes no longer pleasant, felt the presence of something different. Something ominous. And chilling. Like a scene remembered from a childhood horror story. It would be impossible to explain to anyone—hard even to imagine such eeriness in today's world, in one's own office.

In that split second he also realized Malec wouldn't leave without some kind of promise. *I've got to get rid of him. But I'll deny I ever said this.* "Okay, Rudy. You help us and we'll help you." He forced a smile. "Anything short of industrial sabotage."

To his relief the tension suddenly vanished, and Malec, smiling ingenuously as before, said, "Thanks, Mr. Kimball," and walked out, swinging himself along gracefully, still clutching his little case.

Kimball hoped he'd never see him again. *But I probably won't get that lucky.*

Back home in his computer room, Rudy Malec strolled among the hardware, thinking. With his breath coming faster, he looked down at a small, very old console—the one his father had made him steal. As he stood there he saw his father waiting for him on a street corner, a big, barrel-chested man, almost the twin of Nick Lewand. A sudden, uncontrollable rage burst out of him, and he slammed his fist into the framed picture of an airplane, shattering the glass and driving a shard into the flesh below his little finger. For long minutes he stared at the impaled finger. Then he deliberately broke off the glass, leaving the biggest piece inside.

That night Miles Kimball sat at his kitchen table idly wondering what he could fix himself to eat. Cooking seemed unimportant, somehow pointless, and he stared at a blank wall thinking about his life, feeling disaster coming at him from all sides. His failing job. The unsettling meeting with Rudy Malec. His few stocks dropping daily in value. His wife—probably dying. And now infidelity, which was the only part he could help.

No, not infidelity, he thought. Sin. Sooner or later you had to call it by its real name. SIN. With capital letters. Inconceivable now that he'd once considered entering the priesthood. He should go to confession and spill it all to Father Lindsey. Except he wanted to go on seeing her. In his whole shattered life, Mary Helen was the one thing he wanted to keep. She'd become solace, soft and comforting, where everything else was hard and thorny. So his confession would be hollow. When the priest told him to leave and sin no more, he would be hurrying away to sin again as soon as possible.

His stomach felt mule-kicked and full, though it had been hours since he'd eaten. How *would* he eat, he wondered, in another few months . . .

As Alan Wilcox pulled into his driveway Monday night, he didn't see the house or the neglected lawn, he saw instead the look on Ellie's face when he'd been called away, four days earlier, with the Thanksgiving dinner dishes still on the table and Todd still holed up in his bedroom. She'd said nothing when he had to leave, but her expression had been clear enough. *Goddam your job!*

He pulled his small suitcase out of the back. Maybe he *should* consider the job in Washington.

Later he was sitting on Todd's bed while his son slouched at his desk. "I got homework," Todd said sullenly, looking through the dark hair that fell over one eye. "I hope this isn't gonna take long."

"We'll see," said Alan, covering his surprise. Todd had always been willing to talk, anytime, anywhere. "What subject are you working on?"

"Chemistry. Mom got all over me about chemistry."

"And Spanish, too, I'll bet."

"I dropped Spanish."

"Oh." Obviously in his absence the family hadn't been sitting on "hold." "I'm surprised she didn't tell me."

"You were gone," Todd said. "So what do you want now?"

The kid wasn't going to make it easy. "How is school going? In general?"

"All right, I guess. I had too many classes for a while, but now I don't."

"And the swimming—it's okay too?"

"I liked the rough water swim we did last week."

"But swim team itself?"

Todd shrugged.

"Is that yes or no?"

"It's okay when I'm on the relays."

A bell went off in Alan's head. "You've always been on the free relay, Todd. And you've anchored the individual medley. You mean you're not on either one?"

The boy shrugged again. "Not this meet. Not with Anaheim."

"Why not?"

"Four other guys are faster than me, why else? I gotta study now."

"Hey—have you gotten slower or have they gotten faster?"

Suddenly Todd sat up straight. "What is this, some kind of third degree? Why are you hassling me? Is swim team such a big deal? I thought I was supposed to be swimming for *fun!*"

"You are," said Alan quietly. "But this sounds fishy. What's going on? How about giving me some straight answers?"

His son looked away, staring into another part of the room, refusing eye contact.

Alan thought wearily, *I'm too tired for this*. He sagged down on one elbow. He could think of nothing better than to ask the big question straight out. He took a deep breath. "Are you on something, Todd? Are you smoking marijuana?"

Without warning Todd jumped up and bolted for the door. "First *she* hassles me, now you. I'm sick of you both. I'm sick of this whole family!" He rounded the corner out of sight.

"Todd!" Alan stood up. He winced as the back door slammed ferociously, leaving behind an echo he could feel in his gut. He walked out slowly, feeling old.

Ellie appeared in the hall. "He won't talk to me either. Unless we do something fast, we'll lose control of him altogether."

"What do you suggest?"

"I don't know. That you take it seriously, for starters."

It was the last straw. His temper flared out of control. "Goddammit, Ellie, don't stand there playing Monday morning quarterback, second-guessing my motives. Where do you think I've been? If you want to give advice, dump the clichés!"

The minute the words were out, he knew he shouldn't have said them. Her eyes widened, her mouth dropped open, and she stared at him in hurt disbelief. Then she turned away in silence and seconds later the front door slammed as the back had earlier.

Alan wandered to the family room and dropped into his big easy chair, slumping in the seat. He and Ellie didn't often erupt like that. Interesting, he thought, that it took both of them being mad at Todd to ensure that they'd be mad at each other.

"I need three weeks off," Malec said to his boss, holding up his bandaged hand. "An accident. I had to have surgery. I've got the doctor's statement, if—"

"No problem." Nick Lewand was glad to give it to him.

The next morning, Malec was talking to the hiring officer at Navtronics, who was obviously new because Malec didn't recognize him from two years earlier. He was counting on that. "I used to work here," he said casually, "but I had to move back east. I was a chief programmer. You can look me up in your records." It was a bluff. The records would be okay only if they didn't include the part about his getting fed up and quitting.

The personnel officer was less than enthusiastic about considering an unknown. But he went to his personnel files, and sure enough, a Rudy Malec had once been on the technical staff. Ironically, he thought, the guy had walked in at a pretty good time; they were short of programmers right then.

After an hour's quizzing, and watching his potential employee work at one of the computers, the hiring officer ordered Malec a new identification badge.

Searching through some drawers at home that night, Malec found he still had the old modem telephone numbers. His heart began to race as it always did when a new challenge surfaced. He realized he didn't care that much about the job at Stirling; this was going to be fun. He'd already seen the shelves full of Airtech's manuals for the entire base program for the airplane—the control laws and the logic. It wouldn't be hard to send them home to his own computer. Once you had the password, you were into the system.

As Malec walked to his new station the next day, he glanced into the big trash bin in the corner. Just as he remembered: all the experimental "test" boards were still being tossed away.

Not for long, though. Not for long.

Chapter Thirteen

At thirty-one thousand feet, just north of Las Vegas with California in view, the left outboard engine on an Airtech 123 surged without warning, caught for a moment, surged again twice more, and died. Immediately the plane's nose yawed left toward the failed engine.

Inside the cockpit of Trans America Fleet's flight 67, the copilot started in his seat. "What the hell?" he blurted.

The pilot, who'd been on the public address system alerting passengers to the forthcoming view of Death Valley, stopped talking, snapped off the speaker, and simultaneously used his right pedal to correct the yaw.

The copilot stared at the left outboard engine gauges. Like cartoon characters on the CRT screen, various indicators rolled past in fast succession: the exhaust gas temperature gauge—the normal 600 degree temperature decreasing toward zero; the fuel flow indicator, headed toward zero; the N-1, showing fan speed, spooling down past 70 percent; the EPR—engine pressure ratio—headed rapidly toward "one"; the N-2—gas producer—somewhere below 45 percent.

The pilot saw too and wondered if the engine could be revived. With a muttered, "Son of a bitch . . ." he quickly disconnected the autopilot.

Reaching toward the panel over his head, the copilot tried to open the engine's flight start selectors to the flight position. No response. Sweating, he turned the cross-feed valves from closed to open, which would theoretically feed the failed engine from any tank.

No change at all. The engine was dead.

And then the right outboard surged once and stopped.

"We're runnin' out of fuel!" shouted the pilot. The two exchanged looks of disbelief and together turned toward the fuel totalizer gauge.

"No way!" cried the copilot. "I read twenty-eight thousand pounds—and even distribution, too."

"Screw what we see! The fuel's gone!" *Wake up, Idiot,* thought the pilot. Just then the two inboard engines pulsed with a last great effort and died together, exactly as the others had done.

For a split second the silence inside the plane was all-encompassing. Yet they felt it not as stillness, but more as a palpable, fear-producing presence. In the copilot's ears it was as though somebody had screamed. He thought irrelevantly, And it's the week before Christmas.

With his mind racing, the pilot reflexively unlocked the ram air turbine, which used wind as a source of power to operate the controls. He managed to slow the plane to two hundred knots, the speed at which he'd get the best lift over drag and the longest glide distance. But he was thinking, *I'm dead. We're all dead. This plane is a ballistic rock.*

Feeling the sudden calm of utter hopelessness, the pilot did what he could to fly his rock, hearing only remotely the voice of the copilot talking to Air Traffic Control in Palmdale, California. A lot of good shit-ass talking would do, he thought. The damned plane was sinking ominously, faster than he would have believed possible.

Suddenly his eye caught a shine, the sun reflecting off the dry lake bed some fifty miles away, and with a spark of hope he realized what it was: Edwards Air Force Base. And nearby, five miles of runway.

"We'll try for Edwards," he said to his copilot. "But don't count on making it."

The federal building in Lawndale, California, is top-heavy and reflects the sunlight—and because of its shiny, mirrored surface inspires jokes among its occupants, who call it "The Toaster." United in poking fun at their building, the various tenants have little else in common. Though the Federal Aviation Authority occupies floors three through six, and the National Transportation Safety Board's Los Angeles field office huddles in one corner of the first floor, in between are the IRS, the CIA, the Agriculture Department, the Drug Enforcement Administration, and Customs.

As the Airtech 123 clawed toward Edwards Air Force Base, the Com

Center on the sixth floor set up a party line that plugged Alan Wilcox into both the facility manager at Los Angeles Center and Edwards Air Force Base Operations.

Alan sat at his desk listening intently as Colonel Rayson, the base commander, relayed a continuing peril-by-peril description of the flight's final minutes. Having never participated in an accident as it was happening, Wilcox found it frustrating—no, agonizing—to hear the details while unable to affect the outcome.

"TAF 67 still descending, but fast," the colonel said. "With no engines, the pilot is controlling the plane by brute force. If they land intact it'll be a miracle." In spite of his attempt to remain nonsensationalist, Colonel Rayson's voice conveyed tremors of nervous excitement.

Wilcox could hear his own noisy breath as a moment of silence fell over the hookup.

And then Rayson spoke again. "The glide angle looks bad. I don't think they'll—"

He broke off, and Wilcox wanted to shout, For God's sake, WHAT!

A different voice came on—the Com Center. "Sorry, sir, we lost him . . . Oh, here he is . . ."

Rayson again. ". . . bad glide angle . . . dropping much too fast . . . Oh—he's pulling the nose up . . . made some kind of adjustment . . . think he's stretching it out . . . he may reach the runway . . . no, he's gonna land short . . . Oh, Christ!"

Wilcox's stomach tightened. Land short with no power. The implications were appalling.

Rayson. "He's reaching . . . my God, he may . . . the wheels . . . he's lining up . . . I don't know . . . I think he's setting down on . . . taking forever . . . It's . . . Yeah, the runway. He's on the runway. He's down! Rolling. Rolling nicely. Jesus, they made it!"

Only subliminally did Wilcox hear what happened next—the background voices, sounds of cheering, a general melee. In his stomach a knot suddenly uncurled, and muscles all over his body relaxed. He'd been in a vise and somebody'd loosened the threads. He could breathe again. A couple hundred people were still alive. He smiled. The rest would be routine.

"Colonel," he said, "you're no happier than I am."

"Gets you in the Christmas spirit, doesn't it?" Wilcox could hear laughter in the colonel's voice. "It's made our month." A dignified cough. "Well. This simplifies the picture, doesn't it?"

"Damn right," said Wilcox. "But we need a couple of things done. Have someone cut the power to all the recorders, so nothing gets taped over what's there. And after everyone's off, secure the plane and hold the pilots." He looked at his watch. "I'll be out on the LA sheriff's helicopter. Twenty, thirty minutes."

"Roger that," said the colonel. "All we have to do now is find out how a scheduled airliner happened to run out of fuel. But you'll probably figure that out right away."

"Sure," said Wilcox lightly. "With the pilots available, I'll just *ask*."

But it wouldn't be simple at all, he thought, as he dialed the number for the Los Angeles sheriff. The more straightforward something *looked,* the less obvious it usually was.

The sheriff's helicopter took Wilcox from the TRW building across the street directly to the plane, now sitting in the ramp area at Edwards Air Force Base—near Base Operations, where it had been towed in.

Wilcox ducked under the copter's slowing rotors and gave the area a quick scan. Immediately he recognized what was clearly a new generation of McDonnell Douglas and Boeing craft lined up on the ramp near the Airtech 123, though he did a double take at how Douglas was testing its new Ultra-high bypass engine: the plane was outfitted with a new engine under one wing and an old under the other.

In the distance he could see the four buildings of the B-2 Flight Test Facility, and next door the Air Force Test Pilot School—all painted brown, like the desert. The complex facility had expanded markedly since he'd been there last, some four years earlier. Rarely did Wilcox conduct investigations at military installations; military craft did not fall under NTSB jurisdiction, though the civilian group would lend its expertise if asked.

In a few notable instances they *had* been asked: when a Titan rocket blew up at Vandenberg Air Force Base and when the *Challenger* went down off Cape Canaveral. The NASA scientists investigating the Shuttle, with obvious expertise in other areas, knew little about reconstructing accidents, thus had neglected such fundamental steps as washing off the ocean water to stop the corrosion around the fracture faces.

Before he entered the Airtech, Wilcox circled it, noting the plane appeared undamaged. Nobody could have tinkered with anything inside; the area was guarded by two Black Beret Air Police holding automatic weapons—the kind of men you speak to politely, he thought.

Displaying his badge, he climbed up into the tail and retrieved the "black box"—the cockpit voice recorder—and the flight data recorder, each bright orange and about the size of a two-foot-long shoe box. Later he'd send them out on another plane to the NTSB in Washington, D.C., the only place they could be read.

As he deplaned, he was greeted by Colonel Rayson. Surprisingly tall and thin, with a long sharp nose that gave him a hawkish appearance, Rayson topped Wilcox by three inches.

"You got here fast, Wilcox." They shook hands. "We've asked the pilots to hang around until you arrived, which they weren't keen on doing," adding with the hint of a smile, "I suspect they wanted to get home and clean up their clothes. That was one helluva hot landing."

"Anybody hurt?" Wilcox asked, as the colonel led him toward the Base Operations building, a two-story structure in the usual shade of brown.

"A few bruises, nothing else. But we have a lot of emotional passengers—and the predictable few who haven't the sense to be glad they're alive." He smiled grimly. "Naturally, a couple are trying to reach their attorneys." Taking Wilcox's elbow, he guided him up the outside stairs.

"We haven't a lot of room in here," the colonel apologized. "It's not often we have to accommodate a whole planeload of people."

And indeed, Wilcox saw at once, the facility was overrun. Passengers were everywhere—in the halls, in the VIP lounge, overflowing the restaurant and snack bar, stepping over carryons.

Just inside the lobby, Rayson pointed proudly to a glass-enclosed case. "Those are models of every plane that's ever been tested at Edwards. Now we'll need a 123!" The colonel led him upstairs to the airfield operations officer's private office.

Two pilots and five flight attendants sat on chairs and couches, talking. As they entered, the pilots stood, and Wilcox thanked them all for waiting.

The taller of the pilots, Jim Kelly, with the large-shouldered, pugnacious look of an ex–football player, said sharply, "We weren't exactly given a choice. You'd think we hijacked the plane."

Wilcox knew then what he was faced with—a belligerent, defensive pilot, guarding his behind. He said quietly, "This is standard operating procedure. But let me say first, against bad odds you landed safely, and that's what counts. A lot of people downstairs just got their life-passes renewed, and I can assure you, they're grateful. We all are. And that's the understatement of the day." He smiled. "This won't take long, and it's more efficient to get your story while you still remember all the details."

Howard Monroe, Kelly's opposite in body type—slight and under six feet—said dryly, "I can't imagine this event slipping our memories. Ever. In twenty years I'll still recall every detail."

The colonel excused himself and Wilcox took a chair. "Now," he said, "tell me what happened. From the beginning." Pulling a tape recorder from his briefcase, he set it unobtrusively on a table, hoping the airmen would forget it was there.

To the pilots, the trip had been routine. They'd taken over in Chicago, though the flight had originated in Puerto Rico. Inbound to O'Hare Airport the prior pilots had logged 59,000 pounds of fuel on board, and the dispatcher had ordered the fueling crew to load the wings with 101,000 additional pounds. They'd seen the crew at work and were given a fuel slip that agreed with the manifest.

There'd been no indication of trouble until just north of Las Vegas, when the left outboard surged and died.

"Did you look at the fuel totalizer gauge?" Wilcox asked.

"Not right then," Monroe admitted. "I was pretty busy trying to get the engine restarted."

"And I was correcting the yaw," said Kelly. "But you can be damned sure we saw the gauge once the right outboard quit."

Wilcox nodded. "Okay, we'll get to that gauge in a minute. Describe the symptoms in the engine."

Monroe glanced at Kelly for the answer, and Kelly seemed surprised at the question. "You know the scenario, Wilcox—the big surge. The way an engine always reacts to fuel starvation."

"You ever had this happen before?"

"Not live," said Kelly. "But they did it to us on the simulator. And we get an engine fuel-out on all our refresher runs. Those are realistic as hell."

"And the engine gauges backed up our impression of what was happening," Monroe added, and repeated what he remembered of the readings on the CRT display.

"So then the right outboard went and—" Wilcox prompted.

Just then the colonel came back. "The FAA people are here, and the director of safety for Trans America Fleet. And I got a call from the chief pilot from domicile. What'll I do with everybody?"

The mob, Wilcox thought, *gathering already.* He'd never quite accepted the fact that besides being an investigator with his own set of chores, he was a kind of program director as well, responsible for the activities, if not the happiness, of all the official people who collected at the site of an accident.

"Have them wait out in the hall. We're almost through." He turned back to Kelly, who, he'd noticed, answered most of the questions. "So the right outboard engine quit, and then—"

"And then," Kelly went on, "we both saw that the fuel totalizer gauge showed plenty of fuel—twenty-eight thousand pounds, in fact. And the tank quantity indicators were reading even distribution among the tanks. We never got any low-fuel warnings. So we're asking each other what the hell's going on, because here we are with two engines gone and both spooling down toward zero. About then the two inboards went and—" He shrugged. "I can't remember whether I was praying or pissing my pants."

"Probably both," said Monroe, with a smile. He turned to Wilcox. "You guys are all pilots. You ever flown one that lost its entire load of fuel? Zippo, like that?"

"No," said Wilcox, affably. "And for *that* experience, I'll pass." He paused and looked at his notes, trying to think of the right words for the difficult part of the interview. A couple of details in the story didn't fit, and it made him uncomfortable that he would have to bore in on the discrepancies, in effect suggesting that the pilots had erred—or worse, were liars.

In the background, he could hear the flight attendants talking and was glad for small sounds that partially filled the silence. "Well." He looked up. "You can see we've got a problem here. Are you both quite sure there were no warning beeps? No flashing lights?"

The two shook their heads.

"And you saw the fuel totalizer gauge clearly?"

Kelly said, "You're damned right."

"In the excitement of engines flaming out unexpectedly, it wouldn't be too unusual to *think* a gauge read something it didn't. Under extreme stress your mind can play tricks on you."

Kelly stirred and his face reddened. "Not *my* mind! What do you think we were cussing about at thirty-one thousand feet? Here was the goddamned gauge telling us there was plenty of fuel, and all around us engines are conking out. We did *not* get it wrong! That crap-eating gauge has a problem, Wilcox. Go read it, you'll see. It'll show that ship still has twenty-eight thousand pounds of fuel aboard!" He pulled a handkerchief from his pocket and mopped his forehead.

Monroe nodded his concurrence. "We both saw it the same way. Besides, wouldn't mental tricks work just the opposite? I mean, the engines are quitting on us, so we *expect* the gauges to agree. Only they didn't." He shrugged, outwardly calm. But one foot, crossed over the other, swung nervously up and down.

Wilcox said, "You're right, you'd expect the gauges to conform to what's happening. So we're left with a mystery." He took a deep breath. "It's not my intention to make this difficult for you two. From what I've observed, you don't deserve a hard time—you deserve a medal. That whole gang of people is still alive, thanks to some incredible flying. In fact, we'll have to look closer at how you performed, what you actually did up there. It's not easy to make a dead-stick landing of a jet come out the way this one did. You probably know, it's only happened once before—in Canada."

Kelly shrugged. "Can't say I was thinking about that. We had a stake in it, too."

Monroe turned to the other pilot and touched his shoulder. "Did I ever tell you thanks, Jim?"

Kelly said gruffly, "Forget it."

Alan Wilcox stood and shook both their hands. "The colonel has given me your phone numbers. Here's my card. Call me if you remember anything else. Otherwise I may catch you again in a few weeks. For now, go home and enjoy Christmas." He grinned as he turned to leave. "But you've probably already gotten the best present you're going to get."

Chapter Fourteen

Trailed by two investigators from the FAA, the director of safety from
Trans America Fleet, and the base commander, Alan Wilcox headed
back toward the plane. And then it occurred to him he didn't need
this entourage, so he asked the two FAA men if they'd mind driving
to the Air Traffic Control Center at Palmdale, twenty-two miles away,
to begin gathering ATC tapes. And he sent the officer from Trans America
Fleet—an affable man who was overweight and too soft for being in
his mid-forties—to search for a technician with a power cart.

Watching them all leave, the colonel said, "This inspection of the
plane . . . ah . . . got any idea, Wilcox, how much longer it's going to take?"
Adding quickly, "Not that you can't have all the time you need—"

No hurry, thought Wilcox, *as long as you get that hulk off our property.*
And relieve him of the responsibility. "I'll do it as fast as I can. Shouldn't
take more than two or three hours." The colonel's relief was so ill
disguised, Wilcox wanted to laugh. *You were afraid I'd turn this into
a national project.*

The colonel left and Alan stood in front of the Airtech thinking about
the job ahead. He'd had a riddle laid on him by the two pilots. That
they were sincere and believed what they'd seen on the gauges, he
had no doubt. He could usually tell when someone was lying. And,
God knows, no pilot would knowingly take a chance with his fuel.
But here was the 123, on the ground, with all observers agreed that
the engines hadn't been operating. Dead-stick landings created strong
impressions among those who watched.

So how could the cockpit crew keep insisting the fuel gauges showed twenty-eight thousand pounds?

Bruce Cavalier, TAF's director of safety, came back and edged up to Wilcox. "Your power cart's coming. I hope to God it tells us something. We can't afford this kind of mystery. I just gave away one helluva lot of free airplane rides to the passengers." Then, anxiously, "You won't be keeping the plane long, will you? It's costing us a bundle every hour it sits here. My boss said—"

"Let me guess," replied Wilcox with raised eyebrows. "He said, 'Give that NTSB guy a kick in the pants and get him going. Even if you have to use a screwdriver yourself.' "

Cavalier was startled, then amused.

"I've heard what bosses say."

The power cart arrived, and under the watchful eyes of Cavalier, a mechanic plugged it into the plane. With the power on, Wilcox climbed into the cockpit and read the fuel gauges.

The fuel totalizer gauge read zero. Zilch.

For long seconds Wilcox stared at the digital readout in consternation. No fuel at all. The message was there as plain as if someone were speaking to him: the Airtech crew had misread the gauges. Somehow screwed up.

It made no sense. What had they been thinking? Why had they ignored the low-fuel-level warning systems?

It was so ridiculously simple he suddenly wondered if some other part of the system had gone wrong. Perhaps the fuel was there but for some reason failed to reach the engines. Okay then, he had to find out for himself the status of the damned fuel. Using the radio, he called the tower and asked for an Air Force mechanic to come out and physically "stick the tanks."

In the wing at the low point of each fuel tank was an access panel that the airman unscrewed. He found the manual fuel stick and pulled it down. "Fifty-two pounds," he called out—an amount that wouldn't get to the engine pickups. "Ya' might say, empty."

Wilcox stood by, watching. He rubbed a hand across his forehead. Square one, he thought. You start with one piece of empirical evidence, one absolute. Whatever else he learned, the absence of fuel was a given. It helped that not everything was subject to debate.

He fingered his tape recorder and noted the only two facts he had: fuel totalizer gauge reads zero; tanks stick out empty. And then he stopped and stared up at the plane, feeling it mock him. Okay, hulk, what's with you?

"So—is that it?" asked Cavalier.

"No," he said, "but I'm going to do you a favor. I'll borrow fuel from the Air Force, and we'll fill this craft in hundred-gallon increments and watch the gauges. When that's done, you can have your airplane back. I'll release it for a ferry flight back to your maintenance base. LAX, right?"

"That's right," said Cavalier, clearly pleased at developments.

"But there's a catch," said Wilcox, holding up a finger. "This is all conditional on your personally overseeing the taking out of the fuel level transducers and the computer boxes and putting them on the test bench when you get there. I'll be over tomorrow while you're running the tests."

"Right," said Cavalier. "It'll be done. The minute I get there."

Wilcox believed him. He liked the man.

"You can be sure," said Cavalier, "we want to know what's going on as much as you do." He reached out to shake Wilcox's hand. "Well. We'll be flying out soon, then. It happens I brought a crew with me— just in case. I'll go get them." Moving as fast as his pudgy legs would take him, Bruce Cavalier disappeared in one of the hangars.

As requested, the fuel truck rolled up and filled the plane in increments, with the crew waiting and interested. But all the gauges behaved normally and the low-level warnings came on at the predicted moments.

Nothing made sense.

An hour later a jubilant Bruce Cavalier watched as his crew taxied the plane away.

At 11:00 P.M., Alan Wilcox wanted a cup of coffee. Badly. He wanted it hot and strong, a small sop for the fact that dinner had been a microwaved burrito from an ATC vending machine. He looked around his small room at the Edwards BOQ as though expecting something to materialize. Nothing did.

Out into the hall and down some stairs he went on a mission of search-and-indulge. But the kitchen was closed and the halls were devoid of any kind of vending machine.

Feeling the full weight of his fatigue, he returned to his small room and rummaged in his pack for the instant coffee he carried with him for just such emergencies. Always prepared, he thought wryly, but he could have bet the hot water wasn't hot.

It wasn't. The just-better-than-lukewarm tap water left half the crystals undissolved.

So I drink damp crystals, he thought, and sit here functioning while everyone else sleeps. God, I ought to be home with Ellie. Why didn't I remember to call Todd?

At midnight, his job suddenly had a desirability rating on par with ditch-digging.

He pulled out his tape recorder and settled into the room's one chair—dark green and at least as tired-looking as he felt—and mentally reviewed his day:

After examining the Airtech 123, Wilcox had driven a borrowed car to Palmdale to the Air Traffic Control Center, a kind of grassy oasis near the desertlike Palmdale Airfield. The building itself was a windowless, nonsymmetrical four-story structure painted red and gray. Because of the varying heights of its roofline, it appeared to have been built in stages—which in fact was the case. Great microwave dish antennae sat atop its roof, intermingled with the more conventional stick antennae, which together gave the building a Martian look.

Inside, more than sixty controllers sat in a single enormous room, each with his own trio of oversize CRT display consoles—one on each side and another overhead.

Wilcox had always felt awed by the place. There was an atmosphere about it that he had difficulty explaining even to himself—a sense of intense concentration flowing into the air from sixty people all exquisitely on edge and tuned to the possibility of peril. And yet it was quiet, with the multitude of voices absorbed by an acoustical system that damped them all to a great hush.

Each time Wilcox saw the place he was struck by it anew, freshly conscious of the fact that in this room hung the destinies of all the travelers in some million miles of airspace. Every pilot who flew a plane west of the Colorado River was at some point advised by someone in that building.

Wilcox's first job had been to find the facility manager and request the various tapes gathered by the FAA men: the control tapes that recorded the conversations between pilots and controllers, and the National Track Analysis Program, which was a four-inch stack of folded computer sheets—twenty-four inches wide and eighteen inches high—that was a replay of the radar data recorded for a given plane at a specified time and place, all at five-minute intervals.

He sat down at a playback system to listen to the TAF 67 control tapes, making a copy of the voices on his own cassette recorder and scribbling notes on the time sequence, which appeared as a digital readout in a small window.

And that's when he heard the copilot asking in a taut voice for emergency vehicles to stand by in case they crashed during their dead-stick landing.

He took a deep breath. He never heard such conversations without experiencing a sense of profound humility at eavesdropping on the last words of someone's life. And he felt pride, too, in the flying profession—in pilots who knew they were about to die, yet still functioned with an outward appearance of calm and in full possession of their dignity.

When he brought the tapes back to the Edwards BOQ and began telling his recorder the events of the day, he knew the investigation had just begun.

So far he'd learned nothing.

Ellie Wilcox got up for the second time that night and looked in Todd's bedroom. The same tennis shoes and blue jeans were scattered on the floor and the bed was rumpled the way he'd left it—and no person was in it. No boy. Nobody. In the silence of night the room seemed emptier than empty.

She went back to bed and lay awake with her mind in turmoil. Sleep was as far away as it could get.

Todd! Where *are* you?

At last, anxious to the point of desperation, she looked up the phone number of the BOQ at Edwards Air Force Base and, feeling justified, she dialed.

Just before the ringing began, she quickly hung up. No, not at three in the morning. Besides, out at Edwards, what could Alan do?

Nothing. And tomorrow he'd be home.

But would Todd?

Rudy Malec sat in his computer room with his chin in his hand, absently aware that his hip hurt more than usual. *You screwed up,* he thought. *You messed up your own job.* The knowledge depressed him profoundly. The plane wasn't supposed to run *out* of fuel, just land mysteriously short of fuel. How had he miscalculated so badly?

Seeking solace, he turned on one of his computers and, using his mouse, drew crude pictures of Hank and Lewand, except he turned them into children. Beastly children.

For a moment he stopped, feeling a rush of impressions sweep over him. Childhood impressions. No, younger than childhood. *I'm in a crib. Cold. So cold. Sobbing. Something over my mouth. Trying to cry. Can't cry now. Can't cry . . .*

His eyes overflowed and rage poured out of him. He scribbled lines through his beastly children, burning with hatred, hatred so intense it seared along his limbs and filled his gut. His head boiled and filled with fury until he thought it might explode. He might die! He saw demons and devils and unearthly symbols.

"I'LL HAVE TO KILL THEM!" he cried aloud, scrubbing away the tears in his eyes.

Physically ill now, he tried to force back his images. He sat in his chair, shaking. Sobbing. Begging the devil to help him.

The anger passed. In time his mind was calm again. No, more than calm—still and cold. He felt no passion at all, just remoteness. Infinite detachment.

He stood and, limping across the room, dragged a stool from a closet and set it next to a tall bookcase. When he'd maneuvered the big atlas off a high shelf onto a chair, he opened it to the Atlantic Ocean. *Put this in my record, Lewand.* With his finger holding the place, he turned to the back for a table on ocean depths.

He'd have to keep working at Navtronics awhile longer.

Chapter Fifteen

The late shift at Airtech Aviation, always less popular than days, was seldom run at full quota. And a different atmosphere prevailed during the late night hours, as though everyone who worked after midnight did so because the plant was an extended family, a substitute for home. Bosses bossed with a looser hand and employees took liberties. Extra freedom was one of the perks of being on the night shift.

Even while he was on leave, the rigger was able to limp into Flight Operations to find the Fleet Utilization Report for Trans America Fleet. He'd known for some time that Airtech had gotten the contracts to maintain their own planes.

The report was posted on the schedule board. With his finger tracing down the list, he located the next Airtech 323 due in for a "C" check, glad to see it would be going into San Francisco International Airport. Not too far away, he thought. A lot closer than the last one.

Back in his apartment, he reserved a flight out in an hour. Then he got his new badge out of a drawer and studied it intently. "Jerald Johnson" was printed across the bottom—an easy name to remember. He squinted down at the picture. He should have angled his eyes so they didn't look so big.

"Alan, I had to call you. Todd didn't come home last night."

Weary from too little sleep, Alan blinked and tried to assimilate what Ellie had said. "You mean he stayed out all night?"

"I mean he isn't home *yet*."

"Oh boy." He rubbed the corners of his eyes, which suddenly burned, then leaned forward in his office chair. "When did you see him last?"

"Yesterday, after dinner. He said he was going to a show and he'd be back about eleven, and I didn't think much about it. But at midnight he still wasn't here." Alan could hear the distress in her voice when she told him how she'd stayed up all night, checking Todd's room periodically because she was sure he'd sneak in late, and then how stunned she was when he never showed up at all.

"Have you called the police?"

"No," she said. "I doubt if he's in that kind of trouble. I've called his friends—those I know. But I don't know them all, I can see that. Yesterday he spent an hour on the phone, keeping his voice low. At the time it didn't seem significant. Oh, Alan—," he could hear her sigh, "I don't feel like Christmas at all."

"Hang on, Ellie." Rotating his tired shoulders to ease the ache, he said, "I'll make this a half day and leave right away. Courage, Babe. Todd will probably beat me home."

"Maybe," she answered.

He stood up and scanned his desk, asking himself what he needed to take home over the weekend. It came to him that his life was out of control. When his phone line flickered again, he almost walked away from it.

But didn't. It was one of his friends who worked out of the Kansas City field office. "Wilcox," the man said, "I heard you were handling the dead-stick landing at Edwards. Just thought you'd want to know there's been a close call in Boston. An Airtech 323 landed at Logan on fumes. It wasn't a total flameout because they suspected something and had the good sense not to try to make Kansas City. One of the pilots just didn't believe the numbers when he looked at the fuel slip in Gatwick. So the incident won't get much attention. But I thought you'd want to know."

He did want to know.

Before he left the office, Alan took out his private file and added the incident to the two already there.

When Todd walked in the door that afternoon, Ellie and Alan were waiting. Seeing him in one piece brought all of Ellie's anger to the surface, and she realized she was trembling. She grabbed her son's shoulder. "Where have you BEEN?"

While Ellie held on, glaring, Alan studied his son's face for tell-tale signs of marijuana—red-rimmed eyes, a dazed expression.

But Todd looked back at them with sullen resentment and Alan saw nothing.

"Tell me!" Ellie demanded again.

Todd muttered, "Didn't my friend's mom call you?" He jerked himself free and tried to walk past them.

Ellie stopped him with an outstretched arm. "*Nobody* called us, we haven't heard one word, and you've been gone since last night."

"What's the big deal? I slept at a friend's—"

"It's a *very* big deal," Ellie cried, "when you leave after dinner and don't show up until the next afternoon. Don't give me that 'no big deal' stuff."

"You had us going around here," Wilcox said.

Todd's expression turned hard. "So I stayed all night at someone's house and nobody happened to call. So now you're treating me like a baby. Why don't you—"

"We're treating you like a baby because that's how you're acting. Irresponsible." Ellie's hands went to her hips. "You'd better tell me exactly who this friend is."

"Jeff!" Todd spat out. "He lives in Santa Ana! We went to a movie and got back late. So I stayed all night. Cripes, I didn't think you'd make it a federal case."

Ellie looked at her watch. "That was fourteen hours ago. Did you sleep fourteen hours?"

"I told you. Jeff's mom was supposed to call."

"Ellie, he *might* be telling the truth," Alan said.

"I don't think so. And I've never met this Jeff. Give me his phone number, please, I intend to call his parents."

"Go ahead," said Todd with a shrug. "But you won't find anyone home. They left town for Christmas. They dropped me off on the way."

"How convenient," said Ellie. "Give me the phone number anyway." She reached across the kitchen counter for a scrap of paper and a pen and stood waiting.

Todd drew up short, all his hostility returned. He gave Ellie a venomous look, so nakedly resentful it caught Alan off guard. He'd never seen his easygoing Todd so ready to explode.

Alan reached for his son's shoulder to calm him down, but Todd pulled away, wild-eyed and furious. "You don't trust me for one day, do you? You or her. Not for one minute! I have to be here all the time, I can't get one inch away or you both go crazy. Well, this place sucks! You'd think I'd committed some kind of crime!"

With that he bolted, and from the far corner of the house they heard a door slam.

Ellie and Alan looked at each other in silence.

After a few seconds, Alan spoke. "He's got this 'poor me' act perfected, down to the last gesture."

"Doesn't he!" agreed Ellie, wrapping her arms around herself as though she were cold. "Think about it, Alan—we didn't accuse him of anything. And more than that, he never gave me that phone number."

Later Alan tried to talk to his son one-on-one, but Todd was fidgety and remote and shut him off so effectively Alan knew he was being stonewalled.

He didn't stay in Todd's room long.

Afterwards he and Ellie sat in the family room looking out at a mist that swirled across the tops of the city lights. "Well, Ellie, I'm open to suggestions." He tried to keep the emotion out of his voice, but he knew his frustration crept in around every syllable.

You can't have it all, he thought. Nobody gets everything—which he'd never fully believed until now.

"We set limits," Ellie said firmly. "We insist on knowing where he is at all times and who he's with, and we ask for phone numbers and check up on him."

Alan groaned. "I'm not sure I'm up to being a jailer."

She gave him a sharp look. "Don't worry. You're not around the jail that much."

He met her eyes angrily. "Careful, Ellie. If Todd gets the two of us snarling at each other, it won't matter whether he's on drugs or not. We still lose."

She looked away. The room grew silent. Then she said stiffly and in a small voice, "I'm sorry. I guess that was my way of crying for help—the Ellie Wilcox, guaranteed no-success approach. You see, Alan," she gave him a wry smile, "it turns out I'm not much of a jailer either."

Stu, from the coroner's office in Tahoe City, decided to preface his written report with a phone call. Unusual cases like this didn't come in every day. "Alan . . . you know the female who went down near Tahoe about six weeks ago?"

"You mean Hawkins?" Wilcox was still having trouble referring to any of them impersonally.

"Yes. That one. Well, I got interested in something I saw on the first exam. Evidence of infection, a virulent vaginal infection." As Stu described what he'd seen after a deeper examination, Wilcox shook his head. The Sara Hawkins story had just taken a twist he'd never have predicted—and most of his assumptions had been wrong.

The coroner was still speaking. ". . . the doctor who did that procedure should limit his practice to monkeys. Frankly, I don't see how she functioned. She must have been hurting like hell."

"I appreciate the call, Stu."

So that explained the heavy dose of Vicodin.

Though he'd already dictated the probable cause of the accident— the pilot's failure to turn back in the face of an unexpected frontal system—for Wilcox, that phone call answered his last questions about Sara Hawkins.

He laid his notes on the desk. *I'll have to tell Brody. But I'd rather take a whipping.*

With difficulty he went back to dictating his report on the dead-stick landing at Edwards Air Force Base. He'd worked on the case continuously in the three days since the incident, going over the bench reports on the fuel systems, talking once more to the crusty captain of the plane, examining his collection of tapes for the fourth time.

Nothing made sense.

Every one of the fuel systems tested out perfectly. As far as he could see, they'd been operative the whole trip. Yet one bit of physical evidence supported the pilots' contention that *something* wasn't working right. The Bureau in Washington had sent him cassettes duplicating the cockpit voice recorder. Surprisingly, they showed no evidence that the cockpit crew had been alerted by the low-fuel warning systems. No beeps could be heard on the recorder and no voice mentioned the presence of warning lights.

Frowning, Wilcox turned off his hand-held recorder and tipped back in his chair, putting his feet on the papers strewn across his desk. He wasn't about to leave the report inconclusive. *It's my stubbornness,* he thought, *the feeling that not knowing is the same as defeat.*

The reasons for an accident might be obscure, but they existed somewhere—as surely as a new puzzle contained all the pieces. He'd just decided to have the secretary type what little he had when Brody appeared in his doorway.

"I know it's almost Christmas, Alan," Brody began, "but I need a favor. Consider it my Christmas present."

Wilcox waited, wondering what was coming.

"I want you to take the locking pins for the seat rails—the pilot seats—back to Wichita."

"For what plane?" There'd been a rash of accidents in the last two weeks; Wilcox wasn't sure what he was talking about.

"The 421-C," Brody said shortly. "Sara's plane. I imagined by now you'd have thought of it yourself."

Wilcox looked away. *You're becoming obsessed.*

"Well?"

"Mark, I don't think you'll find what you're looking for." *I never figured this would be easy.* "The cause of the accident wasn't the plane. But it *has* been determined."

"Not by me!" said Brody. "Not to my satisfaction. You think my niece screwed up. Well I know her, Alan, and she didn't. Something failed. Something on that goddam Mickey Mouse airplane failed and killed her. The only daughter I've ever—," he broke off and cleared his throat.

Wilcox looked up and saw his boss's eyes shining with tears. *Oh, Lord.* "Mark, why don't you come on in? There are a couple of things you should know."

His boss stared at him, stiff and wary, but didn't budge from the doorway.

So we do it like this. "I'd like nothing better than to blame the plane, believe me. I'd look harder, if it would make a difference. But it won't— the lab and coroner reports tell the story."

"Which were?"

"The first concerned additional fractures. You know the pattern— ulnas, tibias, fibulas. No doubt about who was the pilot. Then toxicology revealed Vicodin. She'd taken a lot of it, Mark, probably a maximum dose. I've got the blood serum figures if you want them."

Shaking his head negatively, Brody came into the room at last and pulled the door closed behind him. "What else?" His lips were thin and tight, his expression resolute; he'd take his pain without an anesthetic.

"The last report explained the pain killer. She had a vaginal infection, Mark, and—"

"How could *that* matter?"

"Let me finish. The coroner felt he needed to look further, so he did. He found she'd been pregnant, perhaps only a week earlier. Her uterus showed signs of an abortion, but a bad one, with fetal material left behind." He tried not to hear Brody's soft groan. "Whoever did it was worse than incompetent. The coroner guessed she was full of toxins and hurting like hell."

"Jesus God!" Brody's face was twisted and he wasn't looking at Wilcox—or anything else in the room.

It would take minutes before the implications sank in. Wilcox tried to make it easier. "It happens to decent people, Mark. Getting in trouble outside the home, panicking, running for help in the wrong places. She—"

"You didn't know Sara. She was better than decent."

"I wish I'd met her," Wilcox said, and meant it. "She had to be a fine person—or another fine person wouldn't care so much." Idly he studied a paper on his desk, respecting Mark's need for privacy, however minimal. *He'll hold this against me—it's inevitable.* Through the tense silence he felt his boss's agony as acutely as if it were his own.

Sensing movement, he looked up. Brody had taken a step closer to the desk and was looking at him with an unreadable expression. Brody said tightly, "You're a professional, Alan. My first reaction to all this was, Let's cut the damned crap. My second was, You've done the hardest job I ever saw a man do." He reached for the doorknob, unsmiling. "Thanks for telling me the truth."

"You're welcome," said Wilcox, watching him leave. *I was right. This will hurt our relationship.*

With heavy feelings that extended past Brody to Dave Hawkins and Sara, he inserted the notes he'd taken on the abortion into the closed file and slammed the heavy file drawer. So long, you two, he thought sadly. *Vaya con Dios.*

They happened to meet in the executive men's room of Stirling Industries. Max Topping said casually, "You've always come through for us, Miles. Making any headway with Trans America Fleet?" He thrust his hands under the faucet.

Kimball zipped his trousers. "Nothing. We're nowhere."

"Trouble is," said Max, "Airtech's got some wizard in PR promoting automation like it's foolproof. A wonderful new toy. We need a wizard of our own."

"That's me," said Kimball dryly, "boning up on spells." Then for no good reason the chilling moment with Rudy Malec came back to him and he added with a careless smile, "How about sabotage?" The minute the words were out he regretted them.

Topping stopped washing and stared at him.

"That was a joke." *My mother always said my tongue would get me in trouble.*

Topping said, "Don't even whisper such an idea. It's abhorrent. The human lives involved . . ."

"Come on, Max." Kimball forced a smile. "Where's your sense of humor? I haven't the mechanical expertise to foul up a bicycle."

With a wrenching motion Topping turned off the faucet. "Some topics are not appropriate for humor."

An hour later, Lloyd Holloway opened the board meeting by reading aloud from the Irvine *Tribune*. "An aircraft industry source has raised questions about Airtech Aviation 323's reliability."

Kimball listened in disbelief. And then he caught Max Topping looking at him across the table. *My God, does he think I had something to do with this?*

Holloway folded the paper carefully and set it in front of him. "The article came out in this afternoon's edition. Somebody just handed it to me. I hope TAF's going to do some rethinking about their contracts." He looked off into space. "If we can get proof of TAF interest, I may be able to get the bank to support us another few months. The minute they extend our letter of credit, we get our salaries back. With interest." He allowed himself a smile. "All I'm asking of everyone is to hang on a little longer. Get yourselves through Christmas, and then we'll help Miles go to work on Trans America Fleet."

Kimball thought, *What Christmas? I just sold the last of my stock.*

Wilcox said, "Wait a minute, I'd like to get this on tape."

The pilot had called, as pilots sometimes did, asking if Wilcox was still looking for information on the dead-stick landing, and did he want additional insight on the captain, Jim Kelly.

"Of course," Wilcox had said. "Whatever you tell me will be confidential."

Now he turned on his recorder and listened to the pilot's words with growing fascination.

"I used to know him well," the pilot began. "We flew together in Canada. Kelly's what I'd call rammy. He's aggressive and intimidating. Very competitive. He doesn't mind breaking the rules to get things done, and he's always looking for a way to jump to the front of the line. With Jim, everything has to be done now, his way and fast." There was a moment's hesitation. "I'm not happy to be talking about him, but I heard you're having trouble finding out what went wrong. I got to wondering . . . well, if Jim *knew* he was low on fuel . . ."

"You mean it might have been pilot error?" Wilcox asked.

"Something like that. On one of our runs, Vancouver to LA, a gauge malfunctioned and I wanted to declare a mechanical and divert to Seattle. But he said, 'The hell with it, we'll work around the gauge, I'm bringing this flight in on time.' He didn't report the malfunction until afterwards. I decided right then I'd never fly with him again if I could help it."

After they hung up, Wilcox sat for long minutes, thinking. How often he'd heard similar descriptions of pilots who got into trouble, as though their personalities had set them on a course that made disaster inevitable. He'd come to believe that some men literally chose the way they'd die.

The disturbing report on Jim Kelly began to have a profound effect on his view of the accident. He could no longer rule out pilot error as a possible cause.

San Francisco had worked out all right, thought "Oliver Jones," but Los Angeles was going to be better. He knew what he was doing now. By watching other mechanics, he'd learned that you had to "sell" the paperwork to the inspector, who looked over what you'd done and then "bought off" the job, which meant both the mechanical repairs and the accompanying paperwork were considered finished.

After that, you could slip back in and do anything you wanted.

Airports, he thought, *are too fucking easy.*

Chapter Sixteen

On Christmas Eve, Miles Kimball rolled into Mary Helen's arms intent on oblivion. It was time to shut down the overloaded circuits, reach for a little comfort. He began kissing her lips and throat.

"You're as hot-blooded as any young man," Mary Helen whispered.

Reality came rushing back. "My God, I hope not," he murmured. *At my age, I don't have the time.*

Groping for her bottom, he found himself fighting laughter. *She's taller than Sondra. I can't get used to her rear not being where it's supposed to be.*

A minute later she rolled over and said, "What are you *doing,* Miles?" and he wondered if she really expected him to explain. Laughter threatened to engulf him. *What* are *the norms in this bed?* It came to him that every coupling is different . . . that different people feel different under your fingers, and they expect different kinds of conversation, too. And learning it all could take years.

She said, "Miles . . . ouch!" and he said, "Oh . . . I'm sorry," and actually laughed out loud. *Apparently I'm not a gifted philanderer.*

"What are you laughing about? I don't see anything funny."

"It isn't you, Mary Helen. Trust me, it's not you."

"There's no one else here."

"Well, you're right about that. At the moment that seems to be true." He paused; the whole thing seemed absurd. "But someone else could still show up."

"*Will* you be serious! Do you make jokes about everything?"

"Only the things that strike me as funny. The problem is, I don't know your body very well. Or maybe it doesn't know me. But part of this isn't . . . working." *Why am I trying to explain?*

"I'll make it work," she said grimly, and began to play with him. Her fingers and lips were soft. Her words were titillating. Her naked body was exciting. He stopped trying to analyze. In moments he was lost, wholly absorbed. Best of all, he'd stopped thinking.

When they rolled apart, the sated, relaxed state of his body enveloped his mind as well. It was good to feel good; he deserved it.

Mary Helen murmured sleepily, "Happy Christmas Eve, darling," and turned away, curling up to sleep.

Christmas Eve!

He woke up fully. Lying in bed awake and alert, he thought of other Eves—the mock ceremonies with Sondra when they opened their nonsense gifts: one year a hand-knitted wool condom for him; another, a pair of crotchless panties for her. She'd held them up, laughing. "In case there's an accident, nice girls don't leave the house in dirty underwear. Can you imagine someone finding these?"

At eleven they had homemade Christmas bread and a jar of jam saved from summer and then, at her insistence, midnight mass.

All his agony came back. He slipped out to the kitchen. *The affair hasn't helped as much as I thought.*

His rummaging for instant decaffeinated coffee must have roused her, for he whirled to find Mary Helen leaning against the divider, watching him. "You all right, Miles?"

"I was looking for decaf." He didn't feel like unloading on her.

"Something's wrong, isn't it?"

"Sure," he said lightly. "I can't find anything in your cupboards," which, he admitted to himself, were a mess. Distorted cereal boxes jammed by a gorilla's hand into too little space, packages of noodles crushed against jars of mayonnaise. The cupboards represented a quality in her he didn't want to think about.

"I may not have any, but I'll fix something else."

Soon she brought him a salty hot bouillon, and what happened next was exactly what he'd meant to avoid. Leaning against him, she coaxed out the whole miserable story of Stirling's travail and the fact that the sinking company was dragging him down with it. The confession brought him no relief, merely reminded him that his own problems were largely insoluble.

When he stopped talking he heard the shrill yelping of a neighborhood dog, eerier than the howl of a wolf. He shivered and wished he were back in his own house.

Mary Helen smiled. "That damn dog only barks after 2:00 A.M. I think that's when they put him out."

So it's Christmas, he thought, glancing at her unlit Christmas tree; it seemed to mock him, a strange, dark shape growing incongruously upward to butt against the ceiling.

She took his hand and held it in both of hers. "Will you accept a mystery present in place of a real one?"

"Sure." He forced a smile.

"You'll get it soon. Now let's go back to bed."

Alan Wilcox patted his wife's ankle under the covers. She was running her foot up and down his back, giving him a lazy massage. He said, "Remember when the kids used to roust us out of bed before six on Christmas morning? I must have liked it better than I thought—I actually *miss* being tortured at dawn."

She ran her toe down his spine, smiling. "Spoken by the adult who did *not* spend the wee hours of Christmas searching behind dusty furniture for the stocking stuffers. What was six A.M. to you?" She sighed. "You know what I liked best about those years? You! Men are incredibly sexy when they're all soft over a child. God, Alan—you used to turn me on."

He grabbed her foot. "*Used to,* Ellie?"

She grinned. "What else about you could possibly be considered sexy?"

"I don't know. All these years I imagined it was the way I combed my hair."

She touched his thick black hair, cut to military length. "You don't comb your hair. It's too short."

"I'm told I have a classical baritone voice."

"I wouldn't know. You never sing."

"Massive pectorals, then?"

She giggled.

"That's about it," he said. "I've covered the list." He studied her thoughtfully. "We could always make another child."

"Of course!" she cried. "Why didn't I think of it? Just promise you'll be here when it's born."

He groaned. "There you go again, being unreasonable."

*   *   *

Miles woke after ten, stunned by the knowledge he was going to be late visiting Sondra on, of all days, Christmas!

He raced away from Mary Helen's, vowing he wouldn't when she suggested as he left, "Come right back, won't you?"

Will she try to orchestrate my every move?

When he got to St. Joseph's Hospital, Sondra was looking at something on television, but he could tell by how quickly she turned she'd been watching the door.

He'd remembered to grab the present he'd been carrying in the trunk of his car, a soft, blue nylon bedjacket, wrapped in silver-and-blue paper.

When he handed it to her, tears rolled down her cheeks, and she shook her head with a wobbly motion. "No . . . nothin' for you," she said.

"Forget it, Sondra. *You're* my present. Just being here to spend the day with." He meant it. It was the only honorable emotion he'd felt in weeks.

A glimmer of her old warmth flickered across her features. She tried to reach her hand out to him but didn't quite make it because her muscles trembled so much. "Miles . . . you look . . . t-tired."

Suppressed guilt made him jump and quickly deny being tired. No, he wasn't tired. He was doing fine.

She smiled sadly. "Take care . . . yourse'f. You . . . are won'ful p-person . . ." He leaned closer to hear as her breath gave out and her words faded away. "You're all I have."

Oh God, he thought. Why had she said that? How much guilt could a man carry?

He tried not to answer. But somehow her innocence irritated him . . . that she could be so dense, that her belief in his goodness was so grotesquely misplaced. Why didn't she read the clues that were right in front of her? She was his wife; she ought to see how tarnished he'd become. How could she fail to notice? Angrier by the minute at her lack of perception, he couldn't leave it alone. "I'm *not* wonderful. And I'm not all you've got! No one person is ever all anybody has. That's asking too much!"

She lay against the pillow staring at him like a stranger. He knew with awful certainty he'd said the worst possible words at exactly the worst time.

*   *   *

Rudy Malec drove north listening intently to his radio, fuming to himself that the news was all about Christmas-in-places-he-didn't-care-about and nothing else.

But his irritation was on the surface. Deeper, more pervasive worries mingled with the others—that maybe he didn't understand computers as well as he thought. What would he say to Kimball when he saw him an hour from now?

I won't say anything to him. Let him guess.

What was left of Christmas was going to be crappy—sucking up to Kimball for a whole afternoon.

"Todd drank three glasses of wine at dinner," Ellie remarked as Alan helped her scrape and load the dinner dishes. "I wonder where he went?" She craned her neck toward the dining room, where Jamie and Doug were gathering the last of the dessert plates and water glasses. "You seen Todd?" she asked as her two oldest appeared with armloads of china.

They looked at each other blankly. In his room, they guessed.

"For an hour? Didn't we sit at the table for nearly an hour? He got up, but . . . did he ever come back? I don't think he did." She looked around anxiously. "Why isn't he helping?"

Alan, drying one of the serving dishes, snapped a dish towel at her rear end. "Come on, Ellie—Todd's having wine at Christmas and not pitching in to clean up are normal teenage behaviors. No reason to call out the Marines."

She said unsmiling, "Something's funny. Todd always helps."

He put the towel down. "I'll drag him out here so you can see he's the same old kid—make positive identification."

Before he got there, Alan saw that Todd's door was closed. He knocked and, hearing nothing, opened it fast, suddenly irritated—by what, he didn't know.

The room was empty. And cold. He looked around quickly, sensing an ominousness about the place that was more than just the absence of his son. Something was wrong.

And then he spotted movement, one of the curtains blowing, and he went to the window to close it. He pulled the curtain aside. The bottom half of the window was pushed up, and where there was normally a screen—nothing. Baffled, he leaned through the hole. Where the hell had it gone?

He looked down and saw all too well—the screen was outside, lying in the bushes. Todd had literally escaped.

Chapter Seventeen

Over Bryce Canyon, Utah, the copilot of TAF's flight 81 had finally been served his food. Capt. Tim Baylor pushed his seat back a comfortable distance from the console and examined his friend's tray. As a concession to Christmas, someone had stuck a red cocktail cherry and a green dinner mint in the au gratin potatoes, and Baylor found himself smiling. Sniffing the thin vapors that rose from the turkey and wine gravy, he said, "Eat up fast, I want mine."

His copilot looked up with a grin. "What's the hurry? All you'll get is clear air turbulence."

Baylor nodded, acknowledging the cockpit version of Murphy's Law: things always go wrong when the captain gets fed.

Back in the cabin's main section, the population was sparse. Most people didn't want to fly on Christmas Day, so the plane had empty seats in every row. Even so, flight attendant Alice Singer had said "Merry Christmas" more times that day than she expected to say for the rest of her life.

For the past half hour she'd been selling after-dinner drinks from her cart. She'd gotten within three rows of the back galley without doing much business, but one of her more aggressive male passengers wanted company. At any rate, he was bombarding her with questions, obviously trying to keep her near his seat—also trying to work up some postflight action. His questions were getting increasingly personal. She decided to humor him. He couldn't exactly rape her right there in the aisle.

"No, I'm not married," she said with a smile, "my German shepherd doesn't think anyone's good enough—"

She never finished. The plane suddenly rolled on its side, and the nose pitched down. Alice Singer went weightless and slowly rose toward the ceiling. She screamed as a strong hand fastened itself on her leg and pulled her back down.

Up in the cockpit, the captain pushed wet turkey off his face and grabbed the controls. Outside his window the horizon whirled sideways, like a camera's-eye view from an acrobatic plane. He gritted his teeth and tried to pull the nose up. He knew what was coming next.

Just behind the fore restrooms, two women passengers and a small boy felt their heads lightly touch the ceiling. Almost immediately the plane started pulling g-forces, and their directions reversed. One woman slammed into a seated passenger, separating the passenger's shoulder before she came to rest on the man's lap. The second woman struck a dinner tray and broke it loose on her way to the aisle floor, where she landed with her ankle twisted at right angles beneath her. The boy dove into one of the seat backs and wrenched his neck.

Overhead, storage bins sprang open and pieces of luggage hurtled through the cabin like missiles. A salesman's sample case struck an elderly passenger on the chin and knocked her out.

Screams filled the cabin and a man's voice shouted, "Jesus!" as a child hurtled at him from across the aisle.

And then the plane pulled up, and into the shocked and sudden silence came a single hysterical sob.

We're all pretending, Ellie thought, the whole family. Like invited guests they sat primly in the living room, as though that Christmas were no different from any other, talking about subjects they already knew too well or didn't know at all . . . trying to overlook the fact that Todd had chosen to escape their company by going out a window.

During every lull in the conversation somebody glanced toward the front door.

"You called Jeff . . . " Alan murmured.

She smiled ironically. "I never got Jeff's phone number."

Doug said, "Mom, you should have *made* him give it. You'd never let us get away with this!"

Feeling truly helpless and outwitted, Ellie glanced at her two oldest children. *I never thought I'd be defending myself to them.* She said,

"When I'd think of it, Todd wasn't here. When he was here, he'd divert me into discussing something else."

Jamie said furiously, "Don't feel guilty, Mom, he's a sneak. A couple days ago when you were at work I came by, and you should have seen the creep who was out in the kitchen. A loadie if there ever was one. I pulled Todd away and asked why a guy like that was raiding our fridge. You know what he said? 'Bug off!' " She made a face. "Todd's changed. I can't stand him anymore."

Wilcox said, "If you see any more such friends, Jamie, feel free to run them off."

We've failed, Ellie thought, absently taking in the Christmas cards she'd draped in loops over the doorways, the well-used red knitted stockings hanging over the hearth, each with one or more of its tiny bells missing, the somewhat bruised crèche that sat on the coffee table— these were the threads of tradition that tied them together. Yet as much as she'd tried to weave the family into an impregnable unit, one of them had broken off and drifted away. By his own choice, he was out there now with the predators. *And here we are and we can't help.*

"I shouldn't have let him have the wine," she mused aloud.

Doug said, "We've always had wine at Christmas," and Alan added, "For God's sake, Ellie, don't blame yourself."

The doorbell rang and they all jumped.

"I'll go," said Alan.

They might as well all have gone. Ellie jumped up the minute she heard a deep, masculine voice talking to Alan. Behind her came Doug and Jamie.

The scene in the front hall was worse than she feared. Todd was slumped sullenly against the wall, and next to him stood a county sheriff. Ellie's quick impression of "The Law"—boots, badge, nightstick, holstered gun—seemed to be the fulfillment of nights of dread. The sheriff's hand was against Todd's back, a subtle reminder of who was in charge. "I would have taken him straight to juvenile detention, Alan," the sheriff said, "if he hadn't been your son. He and his friend were at a Seven-Eleven trying to buy beer."

Wilcox gave him a questioning look.

"I wish that was all," said the sheriff. "Unfortunately, when we flashed our lights into the car we saw drug paraphernalia, so we searched further. They had some cocaine. Not a lot, but enough so they'll have to appear in court."

"He had no business lookin' in Jeff's car!" Todd burst out. "We bought it for someone else."

Above his head, the officer gave Alan a look of skepticism. He pulled a pad from his pocket and began writing. "I'm giving you custody, Alan, as long as you promise to have him appear in court on this date."

Ellie's stomach lurched and she felt physically ill. Aware of the older children hovering behind her, she wished fervently they weren't witnessing Todd's humiliation.

Nobody spoke as the sheriff finished writing.

Into the thick, depressing silence came a new sound: Alan's pager.

No, Ellie thought, *you're not going to leave. You damn well better not leave.*

Alan turned and gave her a rueful smile; she guessed he didn't want this either. But she couldn't respond. Feeling utterly cold, she turned away.

Alan said, "Please wait, Sheriff. I'll be back in a minute."

Kimball hadn't meant to return Christmas Day, but he did—only because Sondra, hurt and silent, had stopped trying to be company.

Mary Helen opened the door, beaming her surprise. But then behind her Miles saw Rudy Malec sitting on the couch with his ear pressed to a small radio. *I knew I shouldn't have come.*

Immediately Malec was on his feet, hand extended. "Mr. Kimball! I was hoping you'd be here."

"Is that so?" It was all he could think to say.

"Been trying to catch the news. You'll excuse me . . ." He fumbled for his instrument, which seemed to be trying to get away. "Sit down, sir. Sit down." Radio to his ear again, he waved vaguely at a chair.

Above Malec's head, Mary Helen signaled that they'd escape to her bedroom.

Kimball pretended not to understand. *This ménage à trois wasn't what I had in mind.* He began edging toward the door. "I'll give you two back your Christmas."

"Oh no, Miles. Wait!" She held up her hand. "We *want* you to stay, we—"

At that moment Malec heard something and turned up the volume, listening intently.

The announcement filled the room: ". . . bulletin just in. A commercial plane apparently dropped more than five thousand feet. It is now proceeding to the nearest airport, believed to be Phoenix, Arizona, with its injured passengers. We'll bring you an update after it lands."

Malec quickly snapped off the radio. "Well, sir. You said you wanted Airtech neutralized. It seems to be neutralizing itself."

Kimball's backward motion stopped. He said carefully, "I'm afraid I don't recall saying that."

"But that day in your office—"

"Think back, Rudy. I was quite aware of what I was saying. I wouldn't want to be quoted making such a statement."

Mary Helen looked shocked. Malec's blue eyes opened wider and an unreadable expression crossed his face.

Kimball reached for the doorknob, his mind whirling. *What's he up to? What the hell is going on out there?* "Sorry, Mary Helen, it's been a long day. No need to walk me to my car."

He'd driven about a mile before he realized the radio hadn't said anything about the plane's being an Airtech.

Chapter Eighteen

Alan Wilcox waited on the phone, torn by inner conflict. God, the look in Ellie's eyes! Now, of all times, he ought to be there. Just once he ought to ask, "Mark, can you replace me on this one?"

Nobody outside the NTSB would understand why he couldn't.

He fidgeted while the Com Center at the Federal Building in Lawndale began the process of connecting him to the Air Traffic Control Center, Albuquerque, New Mexico. In the background he could hear Ellie talking to the sheriff, and some inner voice told him he was running out on her—that, job or not, he ought to stick around so she wouldn't have to deal with Todd's humiliation like a single parent.

Yet the duty rotation made this accident his and he wouldn't ask to swap. It was like being a Marine; you took the assignment knowing that in everything except life or death your job would always come first.

"You ready, Wilcox?" a voice asked, and he said, "I'm here." Bad luck, he thought. Crummy. Ellie deserved better.

"Okay, Albuquerque. What's the flight location?"

Did I subconsciously choose this job because it allowed me an easy escape from family problems?

"They've passed Bryce Canyon, Utah. We have an in-flight upset with some injuries on board. The emergency seems to be over. We're diverting the flight to Phoenix, Sky Harbor Airport. How soon can you get there?"

Wilcox looked at his watch. "I'll hop a flight out of John Wayne. A couple of hours if I'm lucky."

"They'll be waiting. That plane's not going anywhere." He caught a note of urgency on the other end. "If you hurry you may get here before the passengers have all dispersed."

Maybe, he thought. If he *really* hurried.

A number of calls later—after he'd talked to Bruce Cavalier, the director of safety for Trans America Fleet, who grumbled about being called out on Christmas Day—and to Operations at John Wayne for a jump seat ride to Phoenix—he stood at his own front door with his small suitcase in hand.

Ellie was still talking to the sheriff, but Todd had disappeared. Ellie glanced at Alan and then at the bag in his hand.

"You're going," she said.

"I have no choice." He read her expression perfectly: she was trying not to blame him but blaming him nevertheless.

"When will you be back?"

"It'll be a quick trip. Two days, probably." He turned to the sheriff. "Is everything under control?"

The man shrugged. "That depends on your son. I laid it right out to him, talked as tough as I dared—like I'd want someone to do if it was my kid. He may be scared. For now. But I'll tell you, Wilcox. When these kids start sliding, it takes something pretty major to turn them around. What I said may not be enough."

Alan could sense Ellie looking at him, silently begging him to get involved. And he could likewise sense his time slipping away relentlessly. A couple more lost minutes and he'd miss the only plane that could get him to Phoenix within the next four hours. He felt as torn as it was possible to be.

He stuck out his hand to the sheriff. "Thanks for your help. I'll call you from Phoenix. I've got a bunch of questions, but no time to ask them now. And Ellie, I'll call you in a few hours. Bye, sweetheart."

He kissed her. And wondered as he ran toward his car if it was possible that a woman's inner coldness could be mirrored by the cool skin of her face.

It couldn't be the crew's fault this time, Wilcox thought as he finished interviewing the two pilots. "We told our story to Flight Operations," said Tim Baylor, the captain, "and now we're telling it to you, and pretty soon it's going to sound like a recorded message. But we've honest-to-god got nothing to add. We were just sitting there fat, dumb, and happy when it happened. I've had some glitches with these fly-by-wires, but nothing like this." He reached up and absently touched his furry upper lip. "It's damned aggravating when your first warning is a mustache full of gravy."

The copilot nodded his agreement. "His dinner pasted itself to the cockpit door. Turns out the gravy was kind of gluey."

In danger of laughing, Wilcox tried to suppress the image. "How long before things came back to normal?"

"If you're talking *perceived time,* oh . . . about an hour. Actual time, maybe half a minute."

Wilcox stood up. "I've already pulled the cockpit voice recorder and flight data recorder, and they're on a plane to Washington. We're lucky TAF has a hub maintenance base right here in Phoenix. We'll be going over the flight control system, including the computers. We'll let you know what we find out. If you don't hear, call my office." He pulled out his business cards.

Tim Baylor studied the card absently. "I'm thinking of switching aircraft type—something closer to the Wright brothers, where the pilot is still boss. The hell with this committee of computers."

As Wilcox walked them through Operations, where they'd soon catch another plane to Los Angeles, he said sympathetically, "Computers remind me of animated cartoons. When you see the final product, it's hard to remember an artist created them eighth-inch by eighth-inch . . . or microchip by microchip. In both cases the damn things seem to get away from their creators."

Baylor said, "I used to think automation was great. I had this idea that a smart engineer could multiply his own brain geometrically and predictably. I never thought of the hitch. When computers go haywire, you can't ask them what went wrong."

"Yeah, who is it? I'm busy," said Rudy Malec before whoever called could say anything. He pulled away from his computer, holding the phone impatiently as he looked back at what he'd been doing.

"It's me."

"Oh," he said. "Hi."

"Have you ever had a scandal at Airtech?"

"Sure. A couple of different ones."

"Do you remember the details?"

"What do you think? I keep track of them right here." He pulled the phone over to one of his computers and typed furiously. "I've got a document that has all that stuff." He laughed. "It cuts some of the bigwigs down to size."

For the next ten minutes he fielded questions, for what reason he couldn't fathom, until he'd told all he knew about the worst scandal, when the jerks screwed up and tried to cover themselves before the FAA found out. At the end he promised to sneak into the executive offices and swipe some interoffice memos. It wouldn't be hard, he thought, after the call was over. There were times of day when security was a joke.

Bruce Cavalier, director of safety for Trans America Fleet, called out, "I've brought more black boxes," as he crossed the room in Operations where Wilcox sat talking quietly into his recorder. From Edwards Air Force Base, Wilcox remembered Cavalier as fairly overweight, but in the interim, it appeared, he'd put on still more pounds. The man's stomach seemed to roll along with a motion of its own.

Fat but powerful, Wilcox thought, watching him approach. His was one of the few autonomous positions in the company; safety directors of most airlines reported directly to the chairman of the board.

Cavalier sat down heavily two chairs away. "Our maintenance people tell me you watched them check out the flight control system and computers. What did you find?"

"Nothing." Wilcox turned off his recorder with a sigh. "Nothing anyplace. Just like the mystery at Edwards. We get something bizarre and all we find is nothing."

Cavalier leaned toward him across the empty seat. "TAF had another incident in Florida. A plane landed on vapors."

"I heard."

"So I don't like what's happening, Wilcox."

"Nor I," he said, wondering if he and Cavalier might be thinking alike. "You talked to the pilots, Bruce. Are we both getting the same story?"

The fat man's eyes became slits as he grinned. "Do I go first, or do you?"

For the purposes of investigation, I rank you, Wilcox thought. He smiled. "They said they were eating dinner and expected nothing. And their story corroborates the verbal readout from the lab in Washington. The plane rolled left 140 degrees—"

"Almost inverted," Cavalier broke in.

"And did a split S. The peak g-loads were 4.1 positive. All that with no reported turbulence. Now what did they say to you?"

Cavalier smiled. "They said there was food all over the goddam cockpit. But the rest was the same."

Alone in the plane at midnight, Alan Wilcox had the feeling he'd gone to the Inn and been refused. Where was Christmas? The fire in the fireplace? Ellie curled up on the far end of the couch? His three kids rummaging in the kitchen for leftovers? The last of the day's Christmas programs fading on television as though reluctant to let the season go?

He'd called Ellie and she'd been brief. "We're fine," she said. "We miss you." It was what she always said. But he detected a difference. Resentment, probably. Or was it only his own feelings projected onto her?

Trying to shrug off the impression that he was the victim instead of Ellie, he began moving through the cabin of the plane, documenting survival factors—all the failures of storage bins, seat backs, and restraint systems.

He found the overhead bin from which the salesman's doorknob sample case must have flown out. Knowing which way the plane rolled and where the unconscious grandmother sat, it was pretty clear where the case had come from.

Cursing silently, he knew he'd soon be recommending—again—that airlines not allow weighty luggage to be stored in the overhead racks. Like all NTSB investigators, he believed that cabin storage should be restricted to coats and purses—items that did not become missiles under g-loads.

An hour later he sat in the cockpit, and in the eerie lights from its instruments dictated his summary of what had happened. "One A.M.," he began. "December 26, . . ." He broke off, wondering what Brody would say if he included what he was *really* thinking: This is Christmas; I am looking at the glowing lights from a variety of impersonal instruments and they have become my altar. This cockpit is my church, these dials are my masters, the words they speak are the thoughts I live with, this place is my sanctuary and the focus of my life. I am not a father or husband or friend. I am a communer with instruments.

It's Christmas, he thought. *I am alone and crazy.*

He started over. "One A.M., December 26. Trans America Fleet flight 81 experienced an in-flight upset . . ."

At the end he said, "Preliminary suspected cause of accident: Faulty design in software."

He leaned his head back against the captain's headrest and rubbed his eyes. He wasn't just alone; he was profoundly alone.

Worse still, he didn't know why he was here. Beyond doing his job, he thought. *I haven't the first idea why these planes are coming unglued.*

Chapter Nineteen

Mary Helen reached for Kimball's hand and began playing with his fingers. "The office was like an empty gymnasium today—all echoes. Nobody looks at houses two days after Christmas. I'm not sure why we were open."

He waited, knowing she'd started the conversation with a mission. *This is about Christmas night. And why I left and stayed away until now.*

She sighed. "I've missed you, Miles. It feels wrong, being apart." She waited. "Sondra must be worse."

He nodded.

"But maybe you *do* think about me . . ."

"I think about you, Mary Helen. More than I should."

"Christmas night what were you thinking?"

Ah, he thought. She got there. But how do you tell someone the night had gone sour in numerous subtle ways? "Mary Helen, I was tired."

She looked at him expectantly. In the silence of her living room small sounds reminded him that this wasn't his house. Her refrigerator came on, inordinately loud and grinding, as if the motor were burning out. And the damned neighborhood dog began to bark—nowhere near 2:00 A.M.

She said, "What's *really* bothering you . . . besides Sondra?"

He glanced at her sideways, then away. Everything, he thought. Her controlling personality. That nephew, who disturbed him in ways he couldn't define. Malec was like a piece of slightly tainted meat: the odor wasn't bad until you got up close. In some ways the nephew rubbed off on her, though Miles wished it were otherwise.

"Guilt," he said, because that was true, too. "A sense of sinning. I was raised a Catholic, a few Hail Marys away from the priesthood. I'm not good at this."

"You were Catholic a month ago." Her voice dropped. "Oh, Miles, you bring me more happiness in bed than—"

"Robert Redford?" he asked with a smile.

"Why do you always resort to cracks?" She turned and touched his chin. "When you're unhappy it drives me crazy. I *must* help. I seem to love people most when they need me. Like Rudy." She paused. "He's so lonely. He had a terrible childhood. If you just understood him better . . ."

His lips closed tight. *I don't want to understand him.*

She was looking at her hands. "I lived two streets away when he was tiny. His mother was my older sister, but I hated her. She was never kind to anyone. From the beginning she wouldn't let Rudy cry, she clamped her hand over his mouth and kept it there until he stopped. She even went shopping and left him by himself. I used to find him, the poor little thing, so cold and wet his feet were blue and you could have wrung his diaper into a bucket. She came back pretending she'd only been gone a minute."

When Miles looked at her calmly, she said, "I can see you don't care." But *she* cared, and even now she could see the skinny baby lying in his crib alone in the house, whimpering disconsolately . . . hungry, his diaper filthy . . . and she remembered how he acted when she picked him up. He'd stop crying, but he wouldn't look at her, wouldn't smile, as though he were indifferent to her being there. But she knew better. He couldn't *afford* to care. It broke her heart.

Miles asked, "What about his father?" and she looked up, having almost forgotten he was there. "A blowhard," she said. "But he took Rudy on an airplane trip once. Rudy was only three-and-a-half. When he got home he was a changed boy. Then a week later his father moved out."

She couldn't share any more with Miles. She'd never told anyone because it made her feel guilty that she hadn't taken Rudy away from her sister, gotten a court order or whatever it took. Instead she'd brought him home to visit. After the airplane trip he strutted around her house saying with baby bravado, "My Daddy's comin' back and get me."

And he'd look at her as if challenging her to disagree. But he ran down after a while like a dying record, until the words were said automatically, without conviction. Eventually he slipped back into indifference.

The rest was a nightmare: Beatings. Rudy tearing up the house; his mother locking him in the closet with the dirty clothes. The bad hip from a dislocation caused by too many hours spent crouching among the shoes.

"Whatever happened to his mother?" Miles asked.

"Died of an infection when Rudy was nine. I don't know if her boyfriend cared. None of *us* did."

"And then—"

"I took him. But my husband didn't like him. The first time the man ever saw him, Rudy was on the bike I'd given him for Christmas, trying to run over a little girl. I knew it was just a boy thing—he didn't mean to hurt her—but it didn't leave a good impression." She paused. "I shouldn't be telling you this, I want you to care about him."

"Well . . . I'm sorry for him. And I care about *you*."

Her frown said he was hopeless. She wanted all the people she liked to like each other, he thought. But they never would. You couldn't collect people in one pot and stir them together and have them come out with something in common, like stew.

His mind drifted back to Malec and his comments after the inflight upset. A horrible thought occurred to him. "Is your nephew . . . intelligent?"

"Not intelligent—brilliant. He knows absolutely everything about airplanes, he's buried himself in technical manuals since he was a kid. And he's a whiz at computers. About the only thing his dad ever did for him was show up when Rudy was thirteen and get the kid his own computer—with what money, I never figured out."

She brushed back the hair that had crept into her face. "Kinda too bad, really. You can't make love to a computer. After work he's always alone."

Thinking, thought Miles. *My God, was it possible?* Implications rushed at him faster than he could take them in. He stood up. "I need to ask Rudy a question. May I have his phone number?"

And then he was in her bedroom by himself, carefully formulating words as he dialed San Diego.

But Malec wasn't home.

*   *   *

Alan Wilcox gave up his room near the Phoenix airport and went home. Driven by stray nudgings from his conscience—and loneliness, dammit—he talked his way onto a dawn flight for Los Angeles.

The jump seat was a silent seat; at that hour nobody wanted to talk. Instead of watching the instrument panel, he reran all he'd learned about the in-flight upset, drawing comparisons to the dead-stick landing. The two incidents had little in common. Or did they? How much in common were two puzzles with the critical piece missing?

They landed in Los Angeles at 5:30 A.M. Another occasion when he silently cursed the fact that John Wayne Airport in Orange County felt obliged to placate nearby homeowners by keeping definite hours—which didn't include jets in the middle of the night.

Driving home in a rental car, he wondered how much good would be accomplished by arriving dead tired on a Tuesday. Except he was beginning to think every day at home counted. He had to take charge of Todd, tired or not. He wondered vaguely when the two of them were supposed to show up in juvenile court.

An hour and a half later he crawled into bed beside Ellie. As he fell asleep, fitted to her like a spoon, the feel of her hips, the warm sleepy smell of her, brought him the first peace he'd experienced in days.

The president of Trans America Fleet—housed in an eleven-story building five miles from the international airport in Los Angeles—gave only cursory attention to his mail until the interoffice memo caught his eye. A small orange paper somewhat larger than a Post-it note, it had been stapled to the envelope's flap by his secretary. When he turned the envelope over, he could find no indication of the sender. Only that the envelope had been postmarked with a zip code he guessed was some place south of Los Angeles.

Howard Paterno, Jr., called in his friend and vice president, Bill Christensen, whose office was across the hall. He held out the orange paper. "What do you make of this, Bill?"

Christensen frowned. "An interoffice memo from Airtech. What are we doing with this?"

"Read it."

Christensen did—aloud.

Dick, if only one plane came up with clearance fit bolts instead of interference fit, I wouldn't get too excited. Chalk it up to the crew having a bad day.

*   *   *

Christensen shrugged. "I'm in public relations, Howard. This doesn't mean much to me."

"Interference fit," said Paterno, "meant something quite specific to me in my engineering days. When you want a bolt to fit so tight it can't work its way out, you make the hole slightly smaller than the circumference of the bolt. And then you pound it in, so there's no chance of its coming loose. A clearance fit allows the bolt to slide in with no problem—which of course is easier to accomplish but not such a tight bonding."

"So how did we get this bit of information?"

Paterno smiled. "It came in a plain brown wrapper. Hell, Bill, I don't know. But I think I'll hang on to it."

Max Topping didn't like what he was about to do. After rapping softly on Holloway's door, he almost backed out and let the whole thing go. But then his CEO called, "Come in!" and Topping was stuck.

Holloway stood up, smiling. "What's up, Max?"

"Lloyd," Max began, "I'm not sure how to broach this—I've always detested backstabbing, but . . ." he cleared his throat, "have you talked to Miles Kimball lately?"

Holloway looked surprised. "No more than usual. The man's under a lot of strain. Why?"

"I think he's about to crack. Last week I made a point of drawing him out. Lloyd, his comments were irresponsible. I'm wondering if he shouldn't be given . . . a vacation."

"Comments?" Holloway asked. "What kind of comments?"

"An offhand joke about industrial sabotage. But I don't think he was joking."

Holloway snorted. "Kimball's *always* had a loose tongue. The rest of us just ignore it." He sat down again, signaling the end of the meeting. "I'm sorry if he offended you, Max. He irritates me sometimes, too. But not enough to do anything about it. Thank you for coming in."

As Topping turned to go, Holloway said, "As you know, Max, I'm results-oriented. And Kimball gets results."

Topping left, wishing he could bite off his tongue. Holloway had completely missed the point. Not only had he, Max, done the company no good, he'd done himself a great deal of harm.

*   *   *

Todd and his father drove back from the session at juvenile court without talking. Because Wilcox was so well connected with the court system, the judge, recognizing him instantly, had given Todd a stern warning and sent him home. As a father, Alan had heard the judge's words with vast relief.

Now, as a dispassionate observer, he took a sideways look at his son, sitting calm and cool in the passenger seat, and wondered if he'd been scared enough. Or even scared at all. Todd had an air of insouciance that suggested the whole event had left him unscathed. At the moment, thought Alan, scathed was what he should be.

Ellie met them at the front door. "I see they let him come home."

Alan said, "This time," and glared at Todd, who, with a smirk and a careless toss of his head, began to walk off.

It was too much. Seeing red, Alan grabbed his son's sleeve. "Look here, you don't seem to be properly impressed, but you came *this close*," demonstrating with thumb and forefinger, "to going to jail. We're not going to tolerate this happening again. We don't do drugs in this family."

"That wasn't my cocaine," Todd answered defiantly.

"Whose cocaine was it, then?"

Todd turned his face away.

"He'll never tell you," Ellie said. "They consider ratting worse than murder."

Alan reached out and turned the boy's face. "Listen to me. When some kid gets you in the worst trouble of your life, you'd *better* tell us who it is."

Sullen and silent, Todd simply glared at him.

"So that's it? You're not talking?"

No answer.

Anger surged again, turning Alan's face fiery red. He'd never wanted so much to physically lay hands on his kid, to shake him, to throw him around until he confessed. His fists clenched and words burst out of him in a rising tide of fury. "Let me tell you something, Todd Wilcox. If it ever comes to our attention again that you're fooling with drugs, you're out of this house. For good! You've had your fling with the law. It damn well better be the last." Leaving his words echoing across the room, he stalked out.

He wasn't out the door before he knew he'd made a tactical error.

Soon afterwards Ellie confirmed it. "What good did *that* do?" She stood in the doorway of their bedroom with her hands on her hips and her eyes afire, and when he glared back she stepped inside and closed the door behind her.

"You handled him all wrong. Blowing up shows weakness. And then he's in control."

He answered her with steely anger. "Forgive me, but I'm human. I come home early and my first assignment is juvenile court. And then here's Todd defiantly refusing to answer our questions—as though he's untouchable and we're his groveling subjects. Somehow I find that abhorrent."

"You don't *ask* questions," she said, "because when he doesn't answer, he's got you. You try to keep the superior position, you insist, you never plead. You—"

"Ellie, I'm not the only one he's making a monkey of."

She stopped short.

"Do *you* always know where he is? What he's up to?"

She said fiercely, "I'm telling you the rules, Alan. I *know* what you're supposed to do." She sat down on the bed and her shoulders sagged. She fell silent.

He began taking off his shirt.

After a while she said, "I guess I'm telling you so one of us gets them down pat. So one of us can put them into practice." She smiled wanly. "I hereby make you my deputy, Alan. You wear the badge. You enforce the laws."

He smiled.

"And rule number 83 is, don't make threats you can't keep. We won't throw him out of the house, you know."

He sat down beside her, dropping his arm over her shoulders. "That's right, Ellie, we won't—as long as he's still fifteen. For the moment he's got us. But I'm older than he is. And smarter. I didn't play on the college chess team for nothing."

Chapter Twenty

Airtech Aviation in San Diego sprawls along the I-5 adjacent to Lindbergh Field, separated from the airport by a small field of stubbly grass. Building after building—pale gray aluminum with rounded tops like overgrown army Quonset huts—spread from the freeway to the harbor. In the center of the compound, one structure looms taller than the rest—Building 17, where final assembly for the Airtech 323 demands four stories of height.

Adjacent to Building 17 are the two-story executive offices, outlined incongruously with flagstone walks. Small, light green pittosporum shrubs and a few compact olive trees distinguish the offices of the top layers of management from those below.

As Alan Wilcox made his way down a long hall toward the conference room, he braced for his meeting with the four Airtech engineers: Senior Safety Engineer Ed Randall, the design engineers for flight instrumentation and flight controls, plus the senior software designer. Before he entered the room he knew what he'd see: four silent, unsmiling faces. The experts would speak only when spoken to.

Though Randall had agreed over the phone to bring the documentation Wilcox required, he'd wound up the call by asking tightly, "Will that be all?"

Wilcox could hear the limits implied in the question: tell me what you want to discuss and that's what we'll talk about. He knew perfectly what the man was thinking: *We have to cooperate, we have no choice. But we've done nothing wrong, and by God he's not going to make a case that we've screwed up.*

The conference room, carpeted in dark green, had light green walls on which hung artists' renderings of red-and-gray Airtech planes. Piled on the rectangular table were system-design schematics and mounds of computer fanfolds—a change from the blueprints of a few years ago, Wilcox reflected.

The four men stood as he entered, and one of them put out his hand. "I'm Ed Randall, senior safety engineer." He wore dark-rimmed glasses, and his thin hair was combed straight back and slicked down with something that molded the hair into numerous separate strands. His expression was stiff and formal—anything but welcoming. It was clear he was there by obligation, not choice.

"Where do we begin?" asked Randall, as they all sat down.

"We'll start with an overview of the flight control system, since that failure was the most recent incident."

Randall nodded toward a man whose strong, aristocratic nose and formidable chin gave him a rugged appearance in spite of his being entirely bald. Frank Farraday picked up a design schematic and began to talk.

Wilcox sat back in his chair listening quietly, hoping he'd hear some detail from Farraday that might be at odds with what he already knew. Since the military had long been the largest users of fly-by-wire aircraft, he'd spent the last week talking to engineers in the Air Force and Marines. In the evenings he'd read technical manuals, enlarging on what had once been scanty knowledge of the details of computerization.

In a resonant voice, Farraday talked about the function and overall design of the Airtech control system as applied to the 323. As Farraday explained how the various systems interrelated, Wilcox could see the engineer was skirting important information. *He thinks I don't know the difference.*

Wilcox stopped him, and with feigned perplexity asked, "Would you mind exploring that last point in greater detail? And slower?"

Across Farraday's features passed a fleeting look of exasperation. But he grabbed a breath and started over, speaking as though to a child. *That's better,* Wilcox thought. The session was going the way he intended.

As Farraday began to run down, Wilcox asked innocently, "What about the failure scenarios? If this thing fails," he stabbed at the flow charts, "how would it manifest itself?"

"As you may know," Farraday said with exaggerated patience, "each computer is running a diagnostic check on itself at all times, so any failure would be self-corrected. But if one of the computers happens, for whatever reason, to become disabled, it shuts itself down, and the other two keep functioning. With triple redundancy, it's virtually impossible to have a simultaneous failure."

Wilcox nodded. "Unfortunately, over Bryce Canyon, your aircraft experienced what appeared to be a momentary but total failure of the control systems." He detailed the incident, realizing he was telling them nothing; every man at the table knew the story intimately. In the last week they'd probably been involved in little else.

The senior software designer, Bennett Bergman, scholarly and thin, said quietly, "We've looked into that incident thoroughly. One could get a few systems failures that might cause erroneous readings, but with triple redundancy . . ." he looked to the others for supporting nods, "we can't find any evidence that the computers caused the problem. In fact, the only way you could get such bizarre results would be to have somebody misprogram *all three computers*." He turned palms up in a tragicomic gesture, and everybody smiled. The idea was ludicrous.

Wilcox knew he'd played his dumb-country-lawyer role well. They honestly believed he didn't know much of anything, and they'd all become relaxed, assuming he would soon be off their backs.

Bergman went on, "We've got the core dumps from the affected computers," he pointed to stacks of fanfold paper. "We've run it all through a comparator program, comparing the original program with the readout from the affected computers. They all came out the same."

After Bergman finished, Wilcox looked around the table, frowning. "Is it possible—just theoretically—for the machines to be programmed with instructions that were later replaced?"

The four men looked incredulous and nobody answered.

Wilcox let it drop. "Did you reload the computers with new software? How do we know this is the original stuff?"

"It is," said two voices at once.

"Well . . . let's explore," he said. "Could we insert one anomaly in the program instructions? Something that doesn't quite match?" Knowing he had his own copy of the original dumps—and seeing by the expressions on their faces that they suddenly realized what he had—he felt the atmosphere subtly change. There was a shifting of postures, a tightening of expressions. All four sat up straighter.

Wilcox thought, *Everyone knows you don't tell the Board a lie*. "How about letting me see a copy of the originals?"

Bennett Bergman cast a quick look at the others, and when no one spoke he said, "Well, there has been an anomaly. But it's small. Nothing important. As to operating the plane, it would have no significance."

"Show me."

"Well. Sure." He said it softly, and when he stood, so did the others. No one looked at anyone else. Instead, all four headed quickly for the door, and when two tried to get through simultaneously and collided, they backed off in unison. Straight-faced, the same two started forward again.

Nobody laughed.

In the computer room, Wilcox saw what he would have called Creation, twenty-first-century style. With seven VAX computers the size of motel refrigerators, the place gave him a sense of human brainpower extended to its limits. Here, in one place, was machinery that could duplicate—in minutes—the lifetime's computational output of all five men in the room.

Wilcox wondered fleetingly what Galileo or Leonardo da Vinci might have accomplished with such tools ... and realized how little twentieth-century men had been able to enlarge on what the two had envisioned.

While the group watched, Bennett Bergman ran the plane's control system program through software testers—the simulators—which in essence was a computer-directed display that would portray the flight of an airplane, except that most of the flight would occur at an accelerated pace.

"You see?" said Bergman, as images rushed by on the television-sized display screen. "It's working okay—even with the anomaly."

Wilcox asked, "What about EMP—electromagnetic pulse?" He had learned long ago that any kind of magnetic energy, as from radar or a nuclear bomb, would erase every computer that wasn't hardened.

Bergman said, "We thought of that in the design. Everything is suitably shielded—which of course we did after the Blackhawks."

Ah, the Blackhawks, thought Wilcox. An outstanding example of fly-by-wire failures. There'd been a whole rash of unexplained helicopter crashes, mostly in Europe. An army chopper would be cruising along and suddenly something bizarre would happen and the aircraft would plummet. As one bystander offered, "It just thumped into the ground!" It was only after the most intensive investigation that the cause was discovered: every one of the helicopters had been flying near radio antennae.

Wilcox said, "Let's intentionally fail two of these computers—scramble them with a magnet—and see what happens."

The four engineers glanced at each other momentarily. Wilcox could feel their shift in attitude, could almost hear what they were thinking: *This guy isn't stupid. He's dropping the hammer on us. We'd better come clean.*

Ed Randall spoke up. "You're going to see how the triple redundancy works, I promise you," and after Bergman set up the experiment, they all watched the system on the screen running its checks. In moments Wilcox saw "System Failure, Memory Fault," and one of the computers dropped off-line, but the other two kept functioning.

"You see?" said Bergman again, as the second computer shut down, "the last one is still performing okay. Any way we monkey with this system, it's going to work. So that one small anomaly can't be the problem." He searched Wilcox's face. "We've given this problem a bunch of hours. I mean intense hours. And now you've seen what we've seen." After a minute he added, "We've tested for a failure in the wiring. And we've studied the control surface actuators. Everywhere we looked, our systems functioned the way they should."

He lifted his shoulders in a gesture of resignation. "We've nothing to hide, Wilcox. What else can we tell you?" Scanning the faces of his colleagues, he turned back to Wilcox as though with a consensus. "There's only one answer left. It has to be the pilots."

Miles Kimball found the small story in the back pages as he sat by Sondra's hospital bed. "AIRTECH AVIATION FINGERS PILOTS." He read on. "Baffled by two recent in-flight failures, the president of Airtech Aviation declared at a news conference today that the mishaps could not be traced to any aircraft failure."

Kimball laid the paper down and went in search of a phone. He found himself grinning like a kid. "Mary Helen, are you alone?"

"Of course. Why?"

"Last time we were together, I was thinking some pretty uncharitable thoughts about your nephew. May I come over and apologize?"

Her laughter was inviting. "Sure, honey. I'd love it. When?"

"Any time he's not there."

Chapter Twenty-one

"How's Sondra?" Mary Helen's face was full of sympathy as she closed the front door behind him, explaining she hadn't seen her friend lately. Taking Kimball's hand, she led him to the couch.

"The same," he said.

"It's so terrible. But at least she doesn't know how bad she is."

He looked at her sharply. "Where did you get that idea?"

"Well—"

"She knows," he said grimly. "She knows everything that's happening. She responds. Sometimes it's only a whisper, but these are adult, grown-up, understanding words she whispers."

"Does she know about . . . us?"

Startled, he said, "God no."

"Maybe we should tell her."

"Mary Helen, this is not some kind of club we all belong to. You and Rudy and Sondra and me—everybody with a membership because you and I . . ."

"Sondra would want to know you're okay."

"That's the last thing she'd want to know." He pulled back, looking at her worriedly. Was she thinking of going to the hospital . . . ? No. No. *She's not that duplicitous.*

"You don't have to worry, Miles. I won't do anything rash. Except maybe try to seduce you." She looked up at him cautiously—her face open, her blue eyes and peach cheeks inviting. Innocent. And trusting. Decent. No, she wouldn't tell Sondra.

He pulled her in close. He needed her, suddenly. Needed a lover's anesthesia and the warmth and lassitude afterwards when he lay in her arms feeling so much better. At the moment he didn't care that "better" never lasted long.

Howard Paterno, Jr., was in no mood for jokes. The evaluating committee at Trans America Fleet, having almost made up its mind about the purchase of a hundred and fifty planes, was waffling. As president, he'd looked in on the meeting the day Phil Swenson said he had suspicions he wanted to investigate. When quizzed, Swenson responded angrily, "What kind of sloppiness have we got in this group? Don't you read the reports from our director of safety?"

The meeting became chaotic. Nobody liked being called sloppy. Worse, a committee hung up by doubt didn't function efficiently.

Now this. Frowning, he studied the second Airtech interoffice memo he'd received that week:

> Okay, Dick, what now? Clearance fit bolts on *thirty-four* planes
> is a whole different game. Firing a five-man crew is only a start.
> What do we do next?

He fingered the note thoughtfully, turning it over once more to look for clues. Although sure it was the handiwork of a crackpot, Paterno realized it raised the same kind of doubt that was hamstringing his committee.

Who should see the memo? he wondered, and thinking of Bill Christensen, he reached toward the intercom.

Then he changed his mind.

Abruptly angry, feeling somebody was trying to manipulate him, he crumpled the note and threw it in the wastebasket. *Anonymous letters should always be ignored.* His Presbyterian minister had said it years ago, when he'd served, briefly, as a deacon and somebody had written a vicious anonymous letter to the church excoriating the assistant pastor. The assistant had tried valiantly to accept the minister's view of anonymity, but couldn't, and to everyone's regret he'd resigned.

Somebody's trying to scare us. That's all it was.

It was hot. Unseasonably hot for Las Vegas in winter, thought First Officer Howard Monroe. Probably over a hundred on the runway, which shimmered with rising vapors that seemed more light rays than gas.

The captain, Sidney "Sledge" Sardoff, adjusted his shoulder harness. "Last stop Los Angeles. Then four days off, just time enough to slap a new roof on the house."

"You doing it yourself, Sledge?"

"Sure. Not about to get my house screwed up by a bunch of incompetents."

That figured, thought Monroe. He didn't get the nickname Sledge for being a lovable wimp. He wondered why he always drew the aggressive captains—like Sledge Sardoff and Jim Kelly—aggressive-assertives, according to the Cockpit Resource Management Team from the FAA. They'd offered Monroe a slot in an experimental assertiveness training program—presumably so he'd speak up when he thought the captain was wrong, but more likely a veiled hint that he didn't belong in a cockpit.

He hadn't decided whether to take it; he wasn't sure he could change that much. He wasn't even sure he *wanted* to. As a boy he'd wondered what people saw in rough, domineering men like his father, and here he was, apparently fated to be copilot to a whole series of them—to have his life saved, even, by Jim Kelly's rock-hard decisions when their plane ran out of fuel.

But he wasn't Jim Kelly. Nor ever could be.

"Weather's great," said Sledge.

"Hot," said Monroe.

"Yeah. So plan on a long takeoff roll. Balanced field length is 12,500 feet." In Sardoff's mind the words meant the number of feet required to accelerate to V1, abort takeoff, and stop. "Damn runway's bare minimum—only a hundred thirty-six extra feet." Sardoff peered out his window. "Jesus, nothing but desert . . . why skimp on *cement!*"

Monroe glanced down at the speeds he'd pulled out of the charts and taped to his console. "Our V1 speed is 142 knots . . . rotation 147 knots . . . V2, 155.

The captain nodded.

Monroe, flying that leg, guided the ship into line while Sardoff called out the checklist. At the end Sardoff said, "After V1, climb straight out to six thousand feet."

Monroe heard him, but didn't answer. He was busy making a right turn onto the takeoff runway, looking out over a nose that was so damned long it appeared to be sticking into sagebrush.

They sat in first position, waiting. When the tower said they were cleared, Monroe released the brakes and brought the throttles up, adding power.

For almost fifteen seconds the plane seemed unresponsive. Even quiet. Watching the gauges slowly spooling up, Howard Monroe waited. Slow motion, he thought, always slow motion.

Sardoff reached over and adjusted the power levers to match, and the airplane began to roll. At that moment they finally heard the low, faraway sound of the engines.

The sound grew. The plane rolled faster.

Resting his hands lightly on the throttles, because he was the only one who could order an abort, the captain called out, "Eighty knots. Power stabilized."

Below the copilot's window—far below—the runway moved faster.

"A hundred knots," called the captain, eyes darting from inside to outside and in again, visually measuring the acceleration profile of the plane.

Monroe knew what he was thinking. *We're running out of runway.* From sixty-eight feet up, runways never looked adequate.

The captain's voice started again, "V—" and broke off as the master caution horns started. A blinking red light appeared on the CRT.

Stunned, Monroe saw the captain yank the throttles back to idle, heard him yell, "I've got it!" Sardoff's hand grabbed for a tiny steering wheel near his left knee, and with both feet pressing forward on the rudder pedals, he steered the nosewheel and simultaneously tried to brake the plane.

For the second time in his life Monroe felt he'd soon be dying.

The end of the runway raced toward them. The plane began to slow. But not enough, Monroe thought. Not enough.

With sweat gathering on his face and inside his shirt, Monroe saw the captain pull up on the two reversing throttles near the throttles, listened for the rush of sound that accompanied engine reversal, waited for the feel of power holding them back.

And then the master caution horn blared once more, and red lights flashed on the monitor. "Anti-skid failure. Anti-skid failure." The lights flashed over and over.

Jesus God, thought Monroe.

"Son of a bitch!" shouted Sardoff. Without the anti-skid device there'd be no sensors in the wheels, no way of releasing a small amount of brake pressure in any wheel that slowed more than the others.

The wheels locked up; 180,000 pounds of airplane skidded sideways, threatened to leave the runway.

Monroe tried not to hear what came next. Explosions. Tires blowing. The end of the runway passed under the nose.

The plane slowed.

The nosewheel went off the pavement and dropped into sand. With a grinding thump, the plane stopped.

That's my last flight, thought Monroe.

In one of the terminal windows overlooking runway 25, a face smiled as fire engines raced down the pavement to put out the flaming tires. The man muttered to himself, "Doing better. Kept that one exactly where I wanted it."

Chapter Twenty-two

The caller from the Regional Com Center apologized immediately. "Sorry Alan, we dialed you by mistake. Forgot Las Vegas isn't your territory anymore."

"No problem," said Wilcox. "What's up?"

"An aborted takeoff out at McCarran Airport. No injuries, but we've got a bent-up plane."

"Oh?" said Wilcox. "What's the make?"

"Airtech 123."

He might have known.

"Started a short hop to Los Angeles," the man continued, "but got only as far as the end of the runway. And I do mean the *end* of the runway. The nosewheel went off the cement and dropped into sagebrush, which bent the nose assembly upward, which in turn punctured a hole in the bulkhead of the forward baggage compartment."

Substantial damage, thought Alan. Someone would have to do a report, but not necessarily look at the plane. What they called a "little hole, big airplane." "Any idea why the abort?"

"Nobody seems to know. The pilots are screaming about warning lights going off for no reason."

"Computer failure?"

"Anyone's guess. *Something* failed, but I couldn't say what."

"Look," said Wilcox, "don't call Seattle. I'll handle it."

So, he thought afterwards, pushing his chair back. Another odd one. Not in his territory, but he wanted to look at it. He wanted to hear the pilots saying, as he knew they would, that there'd been some kind of freak occurrence. To them, unexplainable. To him, no longer a coincidence.

Knowing he was overstepping his bounds, Wilcox called the Safety Board field office in Seattle, asking to take the Las Vegas incident.

Currently two men short, the Seattle field office chief made no attempt to hide his pleasure. "If you want the job, Wilcox, it's yours."

That left only one remaining obstacle.

It was only as Wilcox walked down the hall toward Mark Brody's office that he realized he ought to have a few arguments ready—something to counteract the obvious fact that the Western Region was already well supplied with its own accidents. His boss wasn't going to like this.

"Come in," said Brody when Wilcox's face appeared in the crack of a partly opened door.

"You got a couple minutes?" Wilcox asked, smiling disarmingly.

"Sure," said Brody.

Wilcox sat down in the chair near his boss's desk. Unable to come up with a graceful lead-in, he said without preamble, "I signed up to take an accident in Las Vegas."

"Vegas?" Raised eyebrows. "Any special reason?"

"Because I think I'm onto something. And the Vegas incident is part of it."

"I'm not sure what you're talking about," said Brody.

"It's some kind of pattern, a bunch of incidents cropping up one after another, all similar, but not identical." He chose his words carefully. "There might be a connecting cause."

"Like what?" Brody moved forward on his chair.

"I don't know. It's only a hunch. But I'm beginning to think there's something going on at Airtech's factory—maybe even a deliberate something to foul up the planes." He wouldn't use the word he was thinking. It was too unreasonable.

Brody shook his head. "That isn't possible. You'll have to develop another theory."

"It's the only theory that works."

Brody smiled. "Come on, Alan, you know what the airframe factories are like. Supervised to death—one out of five workers an inspector. You might get the occasional weirdo in a factory, but he'd never last long, not with all those watching eyes. One or two missteps and somebody would notice and he'd be gone."

"I'm not convinced."

Brody's eyebrows went up. "Do you know something I don't?"

"No. It's more a gut-level feeling."

"Look, Alan—," Brody extended a hand toward his colleague, "I respect you. I admire your work. I even admire your hunches. But not this one. In the history of aviation there's never been a case of repeated vandalism against a line of aircraft. Against *one airplane*, sure —for insurance reasons, or a personal vendetta against another individual. Or a terrorist act, like the Pan Am flight over Locherbie. But this . . . Wilcox, if you're going to bet on a horse, pick one that's in the race."

He'd known Brody would feel that way. Wilcox rubbed his hand across his forehead, chagrined. He shouldn't have broached the idea with so little to go on.

He guessed the meeting was over and stood. Then the importance hit him again; he had to stick to his guns. "Do I have your permission to go to Las Vegas?"

Brody didn't answer immediately. After some thought he asked, "What about that in-flight upset over Phoenix? How far have you gotten?"

"As far as I could go. All the reports from Washington came back inconclusive. The boxes verified *what* happened, but not *why*. The pilots are sticking with their story. Down at Airtech, the engineers claim perfectly functioning computers, and from what I saw I couldn't disagree. Naturally Airtech is blaming the pilots."

"Naturally."

"Right now there's nothing more to do."

"And you've whittled down your backlog of other investigations?"

"Not much," said Wilcox.

"Yet you want to run off and work in some other guy's territory."

"Because I think it's relevant." *Sorry, Brody. I have to hang tough on this.*

Brody shook his head. "Taking on Vegas would be unreasonable. I have to say no." And then abruptly, "There's something else I want you to do. The Cessna radios need to be taken back to Olathe, Kansas. Within the week."

Inwardly Wilcox groaned. *I didn't convince you at all.*

Brody wouldn't look at him. "Try to arrange it ASAP. I've already spoken to the company. They're expecting you." With that, his boss picked up a document on his desk. Dismissed.

He's embarrassed, Wilcox thought as he headed down the hall. *He knows this isn't rational.*

A half hour later he was in his own office dialing Seattle when a shadow crossed the open doorway.

Brody said, "Hold up, Alan."

Wilcox paused.

"Go ahead," Brody said gruffly, "take the Vegas job if you want it. You're good enough—I'll trust you on this. The radios can wait 'til you get back."

Wilcox thanked him. *We've each got our obsessions.*

Over the phone Wilcox learned that the warning system failure and the anti-skid failures had occurred together, right at 138 knots, just before V1—as though some conniving mind recognized the worst possible moment, in that gray area of abort–no abort. He couldn't believe it was accidental.

Before securing his jump seat to Las Vegas, he called his friend Tom Peterson, a computer expert in Washington's Bureau of Technology. Working out of the Operational Factors Division, Peterson was being considered to head his own division, thanks to the Board's awareness of the ever-expanding role of computers.

"Tom," said Wilcox, after the formalities were dispensed with, "is it possible to program some kind of anomaly into a software program so it does a couple of unexpected things, and at the same time program a future directive into the system that would erase the earlier commands and leave no trace? Like a self-destructing order?"

"It's possible," said Tom.

"And when you examined the computer board later you'd never know the anomaly had been there."

"Right." Tom laughed. "What are you up to, Alan—trying to plan the perfect crime?"

"No," said Alan. "Just wondering if someone already has."

Wilcox was at home collecting his overnight case when the reporter caught up with him. The man standing at his door wasted no words.

"Alan, the *Times* has learned there's been a string of incidents with Airtech planes in the last few months. What's going on?" The slim, alert-looking newsman held a pencil poised over a pad.

"A string, Doug?" Wilcox smiled and began walking down the path. "Hardly. But you already know the exact number, don't you?"

"Sure." Doug Donahue grinned. "Four. I wondered if you did. Don't you think that's a lot?"

Though Wilcox had known the reporter for years, he stopped and proceeded cautiously. "We're aware of what's happening. Incidents that make the news are not always reliable indicators of a problem. There are turn-backs every day that aren't picked up by the media. I wish I could tell you more, but until the Board makes a determination . . ."

Donahue stopped scribbling. "Okay, you're not talking." He folded up his pad and put the pencil in his pocket. "But I'm curious about something—as a citizen now, not a reporter. Why hasn't the FAA grounded those planes? Why is the public still flying Airtechs?"

Wilcox set his suitcase near the car. *Donahue's never let me down.* "Can we talk off the record?"

"Strictly. I just want to know."

"Those were four relatively small 'incidents' as far as the NTSB is concerned. Except on a slow news day, they'd escape the notice of the national press. So the public hasn't noticed, either. As for grounding, the regulatory agencies are spring-loaded *not* to find problems."

Donahue shook his head in disbelief.

Wilcox continued, "The hardest thing in the world is to get the FAA to ground an entire fleet of aircraft—or even restrict them. A move like that would reflect on their own certification process. As for these incidents you're looking into . . . the FAA's daily report of accidents and incidents in the U.S. lists *pages*—literally—of incidents like these. The public would be aghast if they knew . . . if they even suspected all the engine failures, low-fuel incidents, rejected takeoffs, and turbulence upsets. Which ones people hear about is all a matter of competing news. So you see, Doug, air safety is touted as greater than it is. But we never stop trying. Don't get me wrong about that." *And these four incidents are not the norm. But I can't tell you everything.*

"Thanks for your candor, Alan. Frankly, I'm astounded."

Wilcox had said a great deal more than he'd intended. "If this reaches print, I'll have to deny it."

"It won't," said Donahue, "but it should."

Chapter Twenty-three

"Steve!" said Wilcox as he slid into the jump seat behind the pilot, "what are you doing flying for American?"

The pilot swung around, giving him a broad, youthful smile. "Hey, Wilcox! San Francisco, right? The autopilot disconnect in the fog?"

"Right," said Wilcox.

"That trip is one reason I'm here, as a matter of fact. Plus more money. What's your mission?"

Briefly, Wilcox told him in the lull before takeoff.

After the plane reached cruising altitude, Steve gave control to his copilot and looked back. His open expression and light blond hair marked him more California tennis player than airline captain. "Trans America didn't lose me right away—not until after that Airtech ran out of fuel over Edwards. One of my best friends happened to be the copilot: Howard Monroe. He didn't say a whole lot, but I got superstitious about TAF."

A nod. "I interviewed Monroe after that incident." *And I think I'm interviewing him again.*

"So what's the story?" asked Steve. "I hear another Airtech did a whoop-de-do over Phoenix."

"That's right."

"Something major going on? Why so many incidents with one manufacturer?"

Wilcox shrugged. It always happened, he thought—the grilling that went with the jump seat. "This isn't unusual," he said, explaining only as much as he had to. He disliked being devious with pilots. But his confessions to Donahue had been enough for one day.

"Well, if you ask me," said the captain, "TAF has a problem. They ought to dump those Airtechs."

Wilcox nodded, trying to appear noncommittal. So the pilots were noticing, too. He'd have to make another trip down to the airframe factory. Soon.

Howard Monroe was clearly shaken by his latest experience. "This is twice something weird has happened to one of my planes. They say the third time's the charm, but there isn't going to be a third time. I'm quitting."

They sat in the pilot's lounge at McCarran Airport, though Howard Monroe's slight body could hardly be described as "sitting." Every few seconds he moved, and periodically he appeared ready to leap from his chair.

Wilcox could understand how he felt.

Sidney Sardoff, on the other hand, didn't seem unduly disturbed. "Hell, we came through it, Howard. We're sitting here talking through our everyday bodies. That's the bottom line."

"What do *you* think set off the master annunciator horn?" Wilcox asked, addressing them both.

Sardoff shrugged. "I've got no opinion. Everything was working, far as I could tell. I was calling out the knots, minding my own business, and the plane was rolling exactly on cue and then—hell, who knows what set it off?"

Howard grimaced. "It was the loudest damn noise I ever heard. When you're not expecting it, it's like a blast from a train. And then we get it again for the anti-skid devices. I feel like I've been shot at." He looked right at Wilcox. "What do *you* think happened?"

"I wish I knew," said Wilcox. "I wish to hell I knew."

Wilcox came home the same day. His examination of the plane's nose had confirmed what he'd been told. The passengers were lucky their captain had reacted so fast.

Without stopping to dress down, Wilcox rushed into his house and called his friend Tom Peterson in Washington, hoping he'd be working late. He was.

Wilcox got right to the point. "The black boxes and circuit boards are on their way. How about taking a look at those computer boards, Tom? See if you can find something subtle that nobody else sees. If what I think is true, those boards could be key to a whole lot of incidents."

"Glad to, Alan."

"Oh, and Tom—don't tell anyone I suspect tampering. In case I'm wrong I don't want to get laughed out of my job."

"Sure enough. But I'm one of the few people who believe something like this could actually happen."

Kimball learned about the Las Vegas incident from Topping as they were both leaving for the day. "Thought you might fill me in on some of the details, Miles." Max held the outside door open and with his free hand gave Kimball a friendly push.

"All I know, Max, is what you just told me."

They paused outside. "This is getting to be more than coincidence, wouldn't you say?"

Kimball nodded. "Agreed. I wouldn't want to be Airtech." He looked up and saw Topping's expression. And then it dawned on him. *Good God, he thinks I'm implicated.*

Gnawing questions plagued Kimball all evening. At last he found the phone number he'd jammed into a drawer and began dialing.

Malec's answering voice vibrated with hostility; somehow Miles wasn't surprised.

"Rudy, it's Kimball here. Sorry to bother you at home. I have a question. Do you happen to know anything about Airtech's three recent in-flight incidents?"

Malec laughed. "I wondered when you'd ask."

"You mean you actually . . . *did something* . . ."

Another laugh, high-pitched and mirthless. Kimball found the sound chilling. "You wanted me to help your company," said Malec. "Said you'd give me a job. Well, that's what I'm doing, making Airtech—"

"NOT SABOTAGE! JESUS, MARY, AND JOSEPH!" Miles's shouted words appalled him; he was out of control. With an effort he said tightly, "Listen, Malec, I *never* suggested fouling up planes. Not for one second. That's murder!" His voice turned low and deadly. "*You're sick!* And you're bucking for the electric chair. If you don't stop I'm calling the FAA. Is that clear? I mean, *very* clear?"

"Sure. Be my guest. But you're in it as thick as I am."

"Why you bastard . . ." *He's making a monkey of me.* Sweat began to form under Kimball's arms. He said scathingly, "Slaughter by airplane isn't something I'm going to debate. Consider yourself warned."

The phone was on its way to the cradle when he heard shouting. "WAIT! LISTEN!"

Reluctantly he did.

"Thought you'd want to hear this." A different voice came on. To his horror, he recognized it as his own. "You help us and we'll help you. Industrial sabotage."

So that was what he had in that little cloth case. And the tape was spliced so cleverly the gap couldn't be detected. He felt as if he'd peered through a peephole into hell.

"So, Mr. Kimball." Malec was cheerful again. "When you sell TAF, I get the job. Right?"

My God, does he have this on tape, too? Kimball slammed down the phone.

The room closed in on him. His breath came in gasps. He ought to call someone. Do something about that maniac. Notify the FBI. Or the FAA. He looked around wildly. Anyone.

But he couldn't: he was paralyzed by fear. What if those organizations actually believed Malec? What if they saw this as a conspiracy, with himself the connecting link? God knows, he had enough motive.

Finding a chair, he heard a litany begin in his head: I believe in the Holy Ghost. The holy Catholic church. The communion of Saints. The forgiveness of sins. The life everlasting.

I have just lost my life everlasting.

Amen.

Rudy Malec smiled as he hung up. Dismissing Kimball, he lay back on his bed, thinking about what he'd just seen on his computer screen. "I can do it!" he thought, and while he lay with his eyes closed he imagined himself on a ship watching a plane scream past him into the waves. It wasn't enough. Survivors surfaced in large numbers, shouting, holding up their arms. With a machine gun he mowed them down, but only some, watching the others paddle frantically away. Their fear reached up to him, excited him. He could feel an erection coming on.

For once he had absolute power.

Chapter Twenty-four

"Ellie!" Alan hadn't expected to see her walking into the house on a Wednesday afternoon. With only a brief impression that she looked great in some kind of colorful flowered dress, he stood up and brought her into his arms. Under his fingers he felt a slippery silkiness and beneath that her soft, yielding body. He slid his hands down over her hips. God, it felt good to be holding his wife. Why did he ever leave this place?

"How long are you going to be home, Alan?"

He didn't want to say.

"Not long, then." Back in their bedroom, she watched from the doorway as he tossed his jacket onto the bed and stripped off his tie. "Where to this time?"

"San Diego. I'll drive down tonight." He hoped there'd be no more questions; this trip was essentially his own. He wasn't expected back in the office until tomorrow, which meant he could stretch it until *late* tomorrow.

She said, "Can you possibly be home by five on Friday? Todd is swimming in a meet with Newport Harbor and he'd like us both there."

"I'll try. So he's back on relays, I take it."

"Depends on his times today and tomorrow. But he's working hard—so he says." She smiled. "I'm feeling better about Todd. He seems almost normal. Maybe he's figured out the only place he can escape me is the swimming pool."

He crooked a finger at her. "Come here, Ellie." Pulling her down beside him on the bed, he said, "You're quite a woman; Todd and I are lucky. Have you got a minute?"

"You're back. What can I do for you?" Bennett Bergman pushed his glasses against his face, not smiling. Looking even more academic and studious than the first time—his glasses seemed somehow more prominent—Bergman clearly wasn't glad to be playing host once more to the NTSB, and especially not glad to have him nosing around in Airtech's files.

Wilcox expected as much. The engineers had already done what they felt was required. Further investigation would be interpreted as meddling.

Wilcox said, "I won't need you with me this time—unless that's what you want. I'd just like access to the personnel records on everyone involved with software design. After that I'd like to see specific software and programs for the control systems of the A-123, and have available a programmer who can run programs and answer questions."

Bergman said stiffly, "If you want questions answered, you'll have to ask me."

"Fine. I'll try not to take too long."

Bergman nodded. That was what he hoped, too.

By four that afternoon Wilcox had made only a poor start.

Computerization of aircraft was infinitely complicated and generated more records and more computer printouts than anyone could possibly go through in one day. So he'd started with the personnel records, which contained nothing significant—no disgruntled employees, no sudden firings—and later pored over schematics and computer fanfolds, trying to grapple with what was essentially a foreign language called C.

For a while Bergman hovered nearby. Then he left, making it clear he was on call, that any programs Wilcox might want to see also had to be run by him. Wilcox understood Bergman's role perfectly. He was acting as watchdog.

By four-thirty, Wilcox knew he had to return the next day and left a message with his office accordingly.

They started at eight the next morning, a replay of the day before: Wilcox studying, Bergman hovering. Wilcox hoped he'd get around to actually running some of the control systems programs.

At ten-fifteen his pager sounded. The man trying to reach him was Mark Brody.

"Can you make it up here by noon?" Brody asked tersely.

"Not possibly. Unless I abandon my car."

"By one, then?"

"Closer to one-thirty."

"All right, get on the freeway right away. I'll go out to lunch and be back in my office, waiting, at one-thirty."

Wilcox hoped Brody was handing him an important assignment. But instinctively he knew that wasn't the case.

The ambulance, with Kimball riding in back, took Sondra to the Sunny Day Convalescent Center, where she could be monitored without the excessive cost of a hospital. Dr. Hurley had said to Kimball outside Sondra's hearing, "We can't do enough for her to justify the expense." Then he'd put his hand on Kimball's shoulder and said with genuine regret that the course of the disease couldn't be predicted—nor, unfortunately, altered. "Making her comfortable is the only realistic goal."

A death sentence, thought Kimball bitterly, as he looked over at Sondra, lying face up and quite still on the ambulance bed. Her forehead was strapped down so she wouldn't fall. The doctor's advice had been a shock, though he'd known the worst almost from the beginning. It was just that nobody had said it to him in so many words.

"Bart Smith" looked down at his badge as he walked through the maintenance station at Denver's Stapleton Airport. Even upside down he could tell that the profile shot was better than usual.

Somebody stopped him. "You must be the new mechanic they hired this morning. An expert at circuitry, eh?"

"Sure am." He smiled genially.

"I'm supposed to take you to that Airtech 323."

"Right." He covered his limp well as they walked together. It was all working out better than he'd hoped.

The Airtech interoffice memo read,

Dick, come see me. We've got to discuss this thoroughly . . . re FAA Airworthiness Directive . . . have we got billions to lose?

*   *   *

At Trans America Fleet, Howard Paterno, Jr., dropped the note into
the basket, this time without crumbling it, wondering if he might decide
to retrieve it later. If the notes happened to be authentic, the implications were staggering.

But they probably weren't.

Mark Brody was angry. "I gave you permission to go to Las Vegas, Alan, but I did not authorize another trip down to Airtech."

Wilcox nodded, surprised that his trip had become an issue. He noticed Brody had not asked him to sit down. "Mark, I'm sure what I'm
looking for is down at the factory and no place else. Every time I run
into a stone wall, I come to the same conclusion—our problem origi-
nates at Airtech."

"*Your* problem," Brody said. "The so-called factory problem is yours,
Alan. Unfortunately this morning it became mine. Our director of the
Bureau of Field Operations called me at eight this morning, trying
to be diplomatic, but reporting he just took a lot of flak from the president of Airtech Aviation. Every time an NTSB man visits an airframe manufacturer, the word gets out and the company gets bad
publicity. Donovan Smith claims if this keeps up you're going to cost
Airtech millions."

"Oh, for crying out loud!" Wilcox was exasperated. "Nobody saw
me go in to that building."

"Not true." Brody picked up a newspaper from his desk and pointed
to a small article. "This may be sandwiched between better stories,
but somebody did see you, Alan."

Wilcox read the brief account for himself and looked up, holding
on to his patience. "This is about the *first* time I went there—totally
unrelated to today's trip."

Brody said, "Listen, Alan," and pointed to the seat in front of his
desk. "I heard some mighty uncomplimentary epithets about you today. Airtech said they cooperated fully the first time, but with this
second visit you've been labeled "overzealous, unbalanced"—not the
kind of image we want for the NTSB. Part of our effectiveness lies
in a reputation for fairness and diplomacy. We've never been considered a strong-arm branch of the government." He gave Wilcox a searching
look, as though expecting a rebuttal.

"It'll do nothing but hurt us," he added, "if one of our members runs wild on a personal vendetta."

What about your *vendetta?* Wilcox bit back his anger. "Hardly personal, Mark." But he knew how it looked to everyone else. It boiled down to his having reasonable cause or not. Without some kind of corroborating evidence, he supposed he might appear overzealous.

Brody said, "Unfortunately, politics and clout are a part of the aircraft industry we have to live with. Airtech's message was to get you out and keep you out. I said that was getting into *my* jurisdiction. But I will ask you to stay away from that place unless you've got a very good reason to be there."

Wilcox said tightly, "I'm sorry you took the heat. One of these days I'll have proof." He stood up.

"One last thing," Brody added, "Airtech called the FAA, too, it seems. Since the FAA certified those planes, they don't want anyone looking for trouble where none exists."

Alan whirled around, incredulous. *"The FAA called you too?"*

Brody smiled apologetically. "That information came by way of Washington. With Donovan Smith we're looking at a wheelbarrow full of clout."

"Good God," groaned Wilcox.

His legs felt stiff and unworkable as he walked back to his own office, and in the pit of his stomach a churning had started, harbinger of a digestive upset. He plopped into his old leather chair, wondering if he needed this job . . . wondering, even, if his hunches had for once gone awry. Four aircraft with unexplained computer problems did not a conspiracy make.

Picking up the file on the Las Vegas takeoff abort, he read the statements from the pilots, trying to imagine what might have caused the alarms to go off. But only three words came to mind. Unexplained. Unreasonable. Mysterious.

One of the pilots, scared twice, was quitting.

The inner voice he'd always relied on spoke to him again. *It's sabotage.*

He recognized the idea with a start. Yes, that was it—the concept that had been mulling in his brain for weeks in a fuzzy, amorphous state without ever becoming a definite word. Until now, too unreasonable, even for him.

But nobody else would buy it. Without proof of some kind, the thought would never get further than his own head. He could run around screaming sabotage to the wind, and the wind would blow it right back, because Airtech Aviation, the FAA, the Washington Bureau, and his boss were all lined up against him.

Aware that he was late, Wilcox drove straight to Newport Harbor High School, running toward the outdoor pool at seven-twenty, just as screams rose from hundreds of voices.

He pushed into the crowd and saw a relay race in progress and the time clock hanging on the gymnasium wall, alive with a giant, slowly moving black finger.

He tapped a swimmer on the shoulder. "Which relay?"

"Freestyle," said the girl. "Last one."

Todd. Where was he?

In a frenzy of searching, Alan studied the faces of the boys lined up behind the block. No Todd. Oh, boy, bad news. And then he looked down in the water and saw Todd resting at the finish line, already finished. He'd been the lead-off swimmer.

Another failure, Alan thought. He hadn't just missed one of Todd's events; he'd missed the whole damned meet.

Typical of their lives, he thought grimly on the way home. He and Ellie and Todd had all gone to the meet separately and now, with Todd on the school bus, they were all going home separately—the American way.

When Wilcox got home, he found Ellie in the kitchen stirring a pot of homemade soup. The kitchen was full of an appetizing vegetable aroma. Sniffing appreciatively, he put his arm around her. "Where's Todd?"

He could feel her stiffen. "In back."

"It was a rotten day at work. I fully intended to make his meet."

"I'm sorry about your bad day."

"Todd's taking it hard, huh?"

She shrugged. "He knows what you do. He should be used to this kind of thing."

He let out a long, slow breath. "Okay. I deserve that."

"Don't talk to *me*, Alan. Talk to him."

Back in their bedroom wing, he opened his son's door and looked around briefly. Then he checked the bathrooms. Nothing. Through a bathroom window he saw that the basketball area was deserted.

When he got back to the kitchen, Ellie asked, "What did he say?"

"Nothing. I couldn't find him."

Instantly alert, she swung around. "Did you look out the window—to see if the screen's off?"

"Was I supposed to? Is this a prison check?"

"Dammit, Alan . . . I can't believe this." She was running, tearing pell-mell down the hall with her hair flying.

More slowly he followed, knowing with dull certainty what she'd find.

Wild-eyed, turned almost hysterical in the space of a minute, she cried, "The screen's in the bushes, Alan. He's gone!"

Chapter Twenty-five

"I can't handle TV with Todd missing," Ellie said quietly. "Please turn it off."

Alan pointed his control at the screen and watched the picture fade away, wishing absently that the heavy feeling in his gut would disappear as easily. "You sure you reached all his friends?"

"Yes." She gave him a look of hopelessness. "You don't understand. In his world it's a moving conveyor belt of new friends. Every time we forbid one, another slides into place without leaving a gap. Kids like Todd literally sniff out other users."

A funny image, he thought, but neither laughed.

"Where's he getting the money?"

Ellie shrugged. "Not from me." And then, "I've finally made up my mind, Alan. Right after Jamie's wedding he'll have to go into a program."

He stood up and walked to the window, looking down over a city of mocking lights.

"The program will cost ten thousand dollars," she said sadly, "more than we're spending for the wedding. Imagine, ten thousand dollars . . . and we may not get the old Todd back. He could just—"

They heard a noise in the back of the house and turned to look at each other. "You go," she said. "I'm afraid I might kill him."

He fought back a smile. This was the Ellie who up to now had preached calm and reason and firmness and staying in control. He jumped to his feet and strode rapidly down the hall.

When Alan opened the bedroom door, he saw a leg coming in over the windowsill, then a hand. Todd's face soon appeared, disheveled and, when he saw his father, belligerent. He finished extracting himself from the window and stood in the center of the room, defiant as a cornered skunk.

In one furious step, Alan reached him and grabbed his shoulder and spun him hard against the bed. He slid off. Grappling clumsily with his son's legs, Alan maneuvered the boy back on the bed, and for good measure gave him an angry push against the mattress. "Now stay there! If we have to, we'll nail shut the goddam window!"

From his prone position, Todd spat back, "What do you care what I do? You're never around. You don't even come to my swim meets!"

Alan's hands fell to his sides. A wave of guilt swept across him and left him speechless.

"That's malarkey!" Ellie said it from the doorway, glaring at Todd with her hands on her hips and her face a mask of white anger. "What you do is *your* fault! The drugs you take are *your* drugs! DAD IS NOT RESPONSIBLE! *You are!*"

Alan saw her turn away, watched her straight, stiff shoulders disappear from view, and knew again exactly why he'd married her.

On Monday Mark Brody called Wilcox into his office. He held up a memo just faxed from the Washington Bureau. "A couple of slots have opened up for field investigators to spend a week studying what's been done in Locherbie. They've asked you to take one. You'll go to Washington for a briefing, then fly over and help with what's left of the investigation. I'm assuming you'll take it."

And that way I'll drop my vendetta. It was easy to see how this had come about.

Yet a change of scene for one week wouldn't be all bad, he thought, and for a moment Wilcox saw himself involved in one of the biggest, most challenging—and most tragic—disasters in aircraft history. Then he thought of Todd. "I can't do it, Mark, I've got a kid in trouble. But look—Jim Higgins in the Washington office is crazy about Scotland . . ."

A few days later Alan Wilcox held the daily that told him Jim Higgins was dead.

*   *   *

He read the daily over and over; he couldn't seem to stop looking at it. As he learned more over the course of the next six hours, he pondered the event single-mindedly, almost hypnotically . . . the mid-Atlantic . . . a disappearance without warning . . . the absence of any trace . . . as though it were the only event in his life.

Which in a way, it was. Because the downing of that plane became a trigger point, the moment when Wilcox understood perfectly what had happened and what he had to do.

The accident wasn't accidental. It was a conspiracy. Sabotage. Murder.

Whatever anyone else learned about the event didn't matter. They'd never see the disappearance as he did, as part of a larger, more sinister scheme.

For starters, unless extraordinary measures were taken, the plane would never be found. Whoever had arranged for its going down had also ensured *where* it went down—which to him was the final, incontrovertible proof.

That plane, the conspiracy, the making sure it didn't happen again, had become his burden—though it neither exhilarated him nor gave him any sense of power. Instead he felt weighted down and, yes, sad.

How could it be otherwise . . . when he was in it alone?

"Mark," he began. It was late afternoon a day later when he walked into his boss's office unabashed, so strong was his sense of purpose. "Mark, we've got to find that plane."

Brody looked up sympathetically. "I know how you feel about losing Jim Higgins."

"That isn't it, that's not why I'm here." Knowing it probably would do no good, he nevertheless selected his words carefully, on the outside chance that Mark Brody would understand. "That plane going down like it did over the ocean . . . don't you see, it's part of a pattern, it's another mysterious event that may never be solved . . . one more knot in the string. And they're going to keep coming, Mark, because somebody's out to get Airtech planes. They've been after them now for the last three months."

"I think the problem lies elsewhere, Alan, but let's talk later. It's late, and I've got something to finish."

Holding his ground, Wilcox regarded Brody steadily. "Why do you think all the Airtech incidents have no probable causes? How do you explain all the dead ends?"

Brody drew in an exasperated breath. "No one knows better than you that the causes of accidents are subtle—and sometimes take months to determine. Maybe you just haven't looked hard enough."

"That's not true." He didn't want to argue uselessly, defend himself where he needed no defense. "Okay, then, you don't believe me. But dammit, Mark, the answer is lying somewhere on the bottom of the Atlantic. *That's* the wreck we have to find, that's the one that's key." He added grimly, "When someone brings that plane up, you'll see."

"You know, Alan, sometimes you *are* obsessive." Brody put down his pen. "This is the only major, catastrophic event of the lot, and there'll be plenty of investigation of this one, I assure you. But not by you or me."

Wilcox turned away, seething, and walked back to his office. *I'm the only one who can tell them anything. But nobody's going to let me.*

Ships of all nationalities searched the last reported position of the plane. As airliners flew across the ocean, pilots kept their eyes open for floating debris. But all proved useless.

Trans America Fleet flight 160 had disappeared.

After a week Wilcox heard from his Washington sources that the investigation was "on the shelf." Which meant everyone had written it off.

Except him.

That was when Alan Wilcox went into his office, closed the door, and tried to think like a saboteur.

Where would I put that plane?
How would I get it there?
What would I have to know?
What would be my motive?

Alan got out ocean floor maps and studied them. In Goode's *World Atlas* he read about the Atlantic Ocean: "Where the plates meet certain continental areas or island chains, they plunge downward to replenish inner-earth materials and form trenches of profound depth." *Trenches of profound depth. That's where I'd aim the plane.*

How deep was deep? he wondered, and discovered that the Atlantic Ocean, in places, pitched downward to slightly over 30,000 feet— too deep for the most sophisticated deep-submergence vehicles, whose range was above 20,000 feet. A plane in one of those trenches would be lost forever.

And to get it there? *I'd do what I've been doing all along—misprogram the computers that ran the automatic flight control system.*

The knowledge requirement would be staggering. The saboteur would have to understand both the plane's navigational system and attitude reference platforms—the aircraft's spatial orientation over the earth and in three-dimensional space. He would have to understand routing, destination codes, flight levels (aircraft altitudes), geographic longitude and latitude fixes, and the Atlantic "tracks"—the assigned pathways along which high-altitude aircraft travel between North America and Europe. Without a thorough grounding in both computer and aircraft technology, the sabotage would be impossible.

For the first time, Wilcox wondered if the man was a pilot—and realized he was thinking it must be a man, and probably only one. Somehow he couldn't imagine that a *team effort* would be so diabolical—or so brilliant. Which ruled out industrial sabotage by a competitor. No airframe manufacturer, however desperate, would risk being caught in such a demonic scheme.

As Wilcox finished his review, he began to wonder if the bizarre occurrences might have been coincidental after all. Because even with everything the man would have to know, what would be his reason? *The fact is, I have no motive.*

In the end, that became the most baffling aspect of all.

Just as Alan Wilcox decided his quest was both far-fetched and hopeless—how could he possibly accomplish what the Safety Board in Washington, D.C., had failed to do?—he heard a news story that gave him hope. After a mission that took years, a determined woman had found the buried Temple of Aphrodite, abandoned since the seventh century A.D. In the face of official disbelief that the "lost" city of Knidos was where she said it was, the woman had managed to enlist enough help to bring the ancient city to light.

Wilcox began to reason anew. Suppose the plane had strayed off course? Unexpected high-altitude winds could have subtly altered the plane's computerized routing so it did *not* land in one of the trenches, but settled instead on one of the shallower continental shelves.

What if the plane *could* be found?

He began making calls—first seeking meteorological data from the National Oceanographic and Atmospheric Administration, whose archives were housed in North Carolina. He learned that on the day the plane disappeared there had indeed been headwinds of unusual velocity.

Next he got through to Mark Upton, an old pilot buddy who was now a senior man at the CIA in Langley, Virginia. He asked Upton to look at data from the KR2 spy satellites to see if the satellites had recorded any trace of the plane. Upton declined. "I'm sorry, Alan, it's impossible. We can't help at all. This material is classified and just too sensitive."

He should have known.

His last call, to the Air Force Safety Center at Norton Air Force Base in Riverside, California, was for Phillip Teal, whom he'd known for years. "Phil, how about searching some week-old records made by the AWACS to see if you can find flight 160?"

"How much info can you give me, Alan?"

Wilcox supplied his friend with all the data he had: flight 160's place of departure, its assigned track, and the transponder code with its last known position. He knew, of course, he wasn't the first to ask.

Only minutes later, Teal called back. "Sorry, Alan. Someone here has already looked along that track, at Washington's request. There's nothing."

Wilcox was ready. "Look, I know it's asking a lot, but I want you to go through everything you have for that date on the North Atlantic."

"You want me to do *what?*"

"Phil . . . I need this favor." *All right, dammit, I have to beg.* "I have some scenarios in mind. Call it a hunch. But not what anyone else is thinking."

"Well . . ." Teal wouldn't refuse, but he wouldn't like it, either. "You'll have to give me a night to do this."

"Fine. And I'll owe you."

"You will," Teal growled. "My next vacation, I'm staying at your house."

As he signed off, Wilcox knew he'd need some luck for the search to prove fruitful. Coverage by the AWACS of any given point of airspace was sporadic at best; each AWACS' range was only four hundred miles.

Luck, hell. If Teal found anything it would be a miracle.

When the return call came next morning, Wilcox knew by Teal's tone of voice that he had his miracle. "Wilcox, I don't know what tea leaves you're consulting, but your hunch paid off. One of the AWACS happened to be coming back from London, so we got a number of hits— the two most significant being at just under thirty-eight thousand feet, the other at twenty-five thousand. The plane was obviously on its way down. One interesting fact, though. Flight 160 was nowhere near its assigned track."

Wilcox felt his pulse quicken. *Now we're getting somewhere.* He said, "How about keeping this information under wraps for the moment?"

After they hung up he knew he should share the news with the Washington Bureau. Well, he would in time. But for now it was his baby because no one else wanted it—and because there wasn't one other person who'd buy the scenario as he saw it.

A few hours later he received, by courier, an aeronautical chart marked with a string of X's, which indicated positions, times, and altitudes of the plane.

By comparing the aeronautical map with the map of ocean depths, Wilcox began to believe that nature might have foiled the devil's Grand Plan.

Without telling him why, Wilcox went to Mark Brody and asked for two weeks' leave—until after his daughter's wedding, he said. Judging by Brody's quick acquiescence, his boss was glad to get him out of the office.

From his room on the sixth floor of the Omni Hotel in Norfolk, Virginia, Wilcox had a superb view. He stood at the picture window looking down at the sparkling Elizabeth River, which seemed to be more metropolis than waterway. Anchored some dozen yards offshore was the German ship *Deutschland,* and across the river were two cruisers tied up at Navy repair docks. On the opposite bank, only a few hundred yards away, he could see the city of Portsmouth. It was a bright morning, with sunshine glinting off the canopies of the outdoor restaurants that lined the river and formed part of a marketplace called Waterside.

It felt like vacation. Only he wasn't there for pleasure. He was there because he'd made a dangerous decision to ignore accepted NTSB procedure and go off on his own trajectory, like a meteor breaking away on a spectacular, life-ending path. He stared down at the river. He could still change his plane reservations and nobody would know he'd been there. He could opt for safety, hoping he'd eventually find his evidence through channels.

At the cost of how many lives?

Before he dressed, Wilcox called headquarters for the Atlantic Fleet and asked for the name of the chief of staff, learning he was a rear admiral named Franklin.

Showered and shaved, he called back soon afterward and asked to speak to Admiral Franklin, and was transferred, as he expected, to the man's flag secretary, who identified herself as Lieutenant Boggs.

"This is Alan Wilcox from the National Transportation Safety Board. It's urgent that I make an appointment to see Admiral Franklin. Today if possible."

"And this is about . . .?" The lieutenant had a brisk, no-nonsense voice, which suggested he would get no appointment. Wilcox guessed that Boggs was another in the sizable minority of people who'd never heard of the Board.

"It's about the recent disappearance of Trans America flight 160 in the Atlantic. If you'll tell Admiral Franklin I'm from the NTSB, I'm sure he'll agree to see me."

He was right. A few minutes later the lieutenant was saying, "Can you come in at one o'clock?"

"Yes, of course. And thank you very much."

The Naval Operations Base, approximately six miles from downtown Norfolk, was a sprawling complex of brick and steel buildings, aircraft runways, and open fields. The admiral himself was housed in a three-story brick building shaped like an E—unmistakably military, Alan thought as he entered the reception area. The first objects he saw were mounted, two-foot-long brass shell casings retrieved from bygone guns, and a grouping of large nautical knots in fancy white rope.

Directed up a flight of stairs carpeted in blue-gray, he found the admiral's suite on the second floor. Entering the outer office was like coming into a roomful of people: faces stared at him from every wall, photos of prior chiefs of staff dating back to 1917.

After a cursory look at his badge, the secretary pointed. "Admiral Franklin's waiting in there."

Wilcox opened the door.

Nothing he'd seen so far equalled the dignity of the inner office. Wilcox was flooded with impressions of what it meant to be chief of staff in one of the most powerful navies in the world: you got dark wood paneling, a big couch, leather chairs, polished wood coffee table, a framed aerial view of Norfolk Naval Base. And, brought with you enclosed in a glass case, a commissioning pennant from a previous command and framed photographs of all the vessels you'd served on.

Power. Prestige. Tradition. They were all represented.

Admiral Franklin rose to greet him. A tall, thickly built man, his erect posture bespoke an assumption of lifetime respect. His white hair was cut short and his dark navy jacket seemed more calibrated than tailored. He came around the desk to shake hands, and Wilcox saw, to his surprise, that the admiral's shoes, though polished, were worn— as though his rank stopped at the ankles. He suspected the shoes had been retained for office wear because they were comfortable.

"So how can we help you with flight 160?" Franklin began. "I saw it on the news, of course. Terrible tragedy. No sign of the plane, eh?"

"None," said Wilcox, unfolding a large oceanographic map. "May I?" and at the admiral's nod, he spread it across the orderly desk, explaining that air and sea searches had proved fruitless. "But we've been able to narrow the area of disappearance to somewhere around here," tracing over a large circle drawn in mid-Atlantic. "Since we've reason to believe the accident might have been criminally caused, I'm here to ask if your sonar buoy system would lend its underwater sonar to the search. I understand the system is quite comprehensive and capable of detecting sounds anywhere in the Atlantic."

The admiral's eyebrows went up. "You're keeping better track of us than the Russians."

Wilcox smiled. "We're wondering, too, in the event that you recorded a big splash, if one of your deep submergence vehicles, like the *Turtle* or *Seacliff*, would go and search the area. It happened on March 18. You keep records of those things . . . ."

The admiral smiled back. "Indeed we do." He punched a button on his telephone console, and began to scribble on a sheet of paper. When the lieutenant appeared, he said, "See what you can find out about this. Call Captain Jones. Have him do a search of records generated by the sonar buoy network. We're looking for the downed Airtech that disappeared mid-Atlantic, tell him."

Franklin tilted back his leather chair and regarded Wilcox through narrowed eyes. "And if we find there *has* been a big splash . . . and our sonar picks up an underwater something that might be a plane . . ."

"We're hoping you'll go down in one of the vehicles and identify it. And then help us retrieve the black boxes—which are orange, by the way."

The admiral brought his chair back abruptly. "That's a tall order. At twenty thousand feet, even large objects aren't easy to identify. We get sonar bouncing off underwater debris all the time, and most of it remains unclassified." He played with two ballpoint pens, laying them at angles to each other. "But just say we get lucky and decide we've found your plane . . . getting the black boxes adds new layers of difficulty. You don't just go down and grab things off the bottom of the ocean. You got any idea, Wilcox, how complicated this all is?"

"I have," he said, and thought of the *Titanic,* whose locating took repeated attempts over three years.

"This project better be awfully damned important."

"Well, of course I think it is, or I wouldn't have come." The minute he'd said it, he knew he'd made a mistake. *I think it's important* gave the absolutely correct impression that the project was his instead of the Board's. He hoped to God the admiral hadn't noticed.

He had. The admiral squinted at him for what seemed minutes, and then picked up his phone. While Wilcox stared back at him in agony, the admiral said, "Get me the National Transportation Safety Board in Washington, D.C." To Wilcox he said, with his hand over the receiver, "I'd better see how much effort they want us to expend."

Wilcox could do nothing but sit and wait. Driven to stand up and walk out the door, he crossed his knees instead and forced himself to appear relaxed and unconcerned. It was the best acting job of his life.

"I see," said the admiral after a brief conversation. "That's very interesting. Thank you."

He hung up and looked at Wilcox with veiled contempt. Veiled because even *he* could not be absolutely sure, Wilcox realized, that the request wasn't coming through some oblique channel not known to the whole Board.

"The Safety Board has no record of this request," the admiral said coldly.

Wilcox nodded his agreement. "I was afraid this might happen. The man who gave the authorization is out of town at the moment. Of course you'd have to be cautious. Well . . ." He stood up. "I'll leave you the oceanographic map, and when you hear again from the board, you can decide how to proceed. Thank you for your time, sir."

He wondered if the admiral would shake his hand in parting—and guessed correctly that he'd cover himself.

Just before Wilcox left the room, he turned with a last thought, "When the Navy retrieves those boxes, it'll be an important coup."

Admiral Franklin waited until Wilcox appeared on the walkway outside his window. Then he picked up his phone. "Get me Admiral Stewart."

Chapter Twenty-six

"Stew," said Admiral Franklin, "something important happened this afternoon that gave me an idea. I think I've figured out a way to improve our relations with Congress."

Twenty minutes after his conversation with the Commander of the Atlantic Fleet, Admiral Franklin was on the phone to the Chief of Naval Operations in Washington, D.C., Adm. William Stevens. "Bill," he began, trading on a friendship that dated back to their years together in Annapolis, "McClay Stewart and I think we've found ourselves a chance to score points with Congress. You remember the plane that went down in the Atlantic about a week ago . . . well, it seems the National Transportation Safety Board hasn't been able to find it. One of their investigators came to me asking if we'd help.

"I sent him away when I suspected he came without Board sanction. But after he left I learned that the sonar buoy network recorded a big splash that day. It happens the man left me his map, and the two pieces of information dovetailed.

"I got to thinking about it later. If we managed to locate that plane, it would be a plum for the Navy. God knows, we could use some help with our public image. We might even get Congress to give us some of our money back."

Stevens said, "Are you asking permission, Jim? If this has to be official, I'd say no. We can't justify it as a priority. Unofficially, however, who knows what stray plane you might see on the sonar when you're out there looking for Russian subs."

"And if I find the plane, do I have your permission to dive for the boxes?"

"If you find that plane, you'll be *forced* to bring up the boxes."

"Thanks, Bill. I thought we'd see this alike."

"You're welcome. You got any more ideas, just call. I'm looking for more out of Congress than a little money, though; we've got to get our fifteenth carrier back."

A wasted trip, thought Wilcox, looking at Mark Brody's terse note, which had arrived at home while he was gone. No, more than wasted. He was in deep, deep trouble.

It wasn't pleasant stopping by the office; he'd never seen Brody so angry. Brody looked up sharply. "What in the hell did you think you were doing, taking on the Navy's chief of staff without a word to anybody? Have you gone crazy, Wilcox? How much trouble are you trying to bring down on yourself? Not to mention the Board!"

Wilcox knew there was no point in trying to justify what he'd done. Better than anyone he understood how far he'd strayed from accepted Board procedures. Realizing he could be suspended or fired, he stood in front of his boss's desk and waited; he was at Brody's mercy.

"You know, Alan, if you'd been a general screwup all these years, I'd have you out the door. You'd be gone. Today. It's only because of fourteen years of excellent work that I can save your butt. I'm telling headquarters you've had personal problems and aren't yourself. But you'll get a letter of reprimand, I promise you." He nodded toward the door. "That will be all."

Wilcox had to say something. "Can you answer one question?"

Brody waited. His lips were tight, but he listened.

"Do you think the Board would have gotten the Navy to search officially?"

"No."

"Thanks." He turned to leave. Behind him he heard Brody say acidly, "And they're not going to search for you, either."

People are going to die, Wilcox thought on the way home. Innocent people. People he could save with a little more information. But he'd never find the saboteur if he lost his job—and his badge. From now on he'd have to maneuver carefully, within the standard methods of the Board.

If that was possible.

*   *   *

Ellie looked as if she'd been angry for days. When Alan arrived home she took him straight to their bedroom and closed the door. "Todd stole money out of my purse."

He had his back to her, ready to set down his briefcase. The words spun him around, still gripping the handle. "Good God, what next?" He wondered distantly how he was going to process so many blows in one day. "When, Ellie?"

"A couple of days ago, I think. While you were gone. I was ready to pay my lunch tab and found I had only two dollars plus change—not tens and twenties like I thought. But you know my memory for money. It took a couple of days to reconstruct what I'd cashed at the bank and everything I'd bought since. Sure enough, forty dollars was unaccounted for."

"Have you spoken to Todd?"

"Of course. He denies it. He's absolutely unshakable, arguing I must have bought something I can't remember."

"But we don't have absolute proof."

Her eyes became a bright pillar of flame rising abruptly out of a few embers. "*I* have proof. Weren't you listening? I'm absolutely sure that money is missing. But maybe you don't care . . ."

This was a new Ellie, hard and bitter. He felt himself responding in kind. "Hold it, Ellie! Wait one minute . . ."

She went right on. "Another thing. You've been paying no attention to Jamie's wedding, none at all, which, in case you've forgotten, happens in one and a half weeks. When I talk about it you listen glassy-eyed, but your mind is ten thousand miles away."

"Goddammit, Ellie. There's some kind of conspiracy out there, and—"

She didn't hear him. "Mentally you've been out of the country for weeks now, and it's getting worse every day. Every time an Airtech plane has a problem, you go into a fugue and nobody can get at you." Her eyes brimmed with tears. "This isn't marriage, Alan. It's nothing."

He stopped trying to reason with her and waited instead for her to finish. Some part of him noted with cold, dispassionate logic that she'd failed him at least as much as he'd failed her. In the last three months she'd never asked about *his* problems, never learned that he was backed up against a wall fighting everybody.

He looked at her again, and for no good reason suddenly felt sorry for her. Mad as he was, he tried to see things from her perspective;

she'd never had a kid on drugs before. He responded calmly. "Be fair, Ellie. With Todd I've been in on every messy detail."

"Okay. You have. But I'm telling you right now, if that kid steals from me again, I'm calling the police."

"You really *want* to sink him, don't you?"

She said, "It's stop him now or stop him in jail. One of us has to lay it out to him. Will you do it or shall I?" She fixed him with an icy, hard stare.

"You're in a telling-off mode, Ellie. Be my guest."

Miles Kimball stared at the ringing phone; it was midnight. *It's him. I know it.* Suddenly he was filled with revulsion. Eyes riveted, he tried to collect himself. *For God's sake, it's only a phone.* He picked it up, dimly hearing the long-forgotten voice of his father: *Weak men fear; strong men hate.*

A high-pitched, excitable voice began without preamble. "You got any idea who's out there investigating?"

"No. And I haven't the slightest interest in the subject, either. Haven't you got a clock?" He could feel his jaw getting tight.

"*I'm* interested," Malec said.

"This is not my affair. I warned you—"

"So I'm warned. Am I supposed to be peeing my pants?"

"The FBI will be looking into this," he lied.

The creep actually laughed. "Then why is the NTSB working so hard on the case—if they already know? Why is Alan Wilcox busting his butt these days? Don't you try to find out *anything?* He's the best. Think of the honor, Mr. Kimball. For us they had to call out the best."

Us?

It was fear after all that made Kimball's anger so irrational. His face flooded with heat and his jaw tightened until it threatened to break his teeth. His heart pounded in his chest. Some part of him wondered if one of his veins would explode—if you could die from too much rage. He heard a great slam and knew it was the receiver striking the cradle. But he had no awareness of doing it.

A vice president, thought Malec with elation, *and a big name on the National Transportation Safety Board. And Nick Lewand.*

He was brilliant. He was controlling them all!

*   *   *

Airtech. They'd want to see him even less than before, Wilcox thought grimly, speeding down the I-5 to San Diego. Yet he was sure the answer lay somewhere in the plant. If not in computer program design, then in the personnel files. It occurred to him it would be like trying to find a certain leaf in a square mile of forest. And he didn't even know what species of leaf he was looking for!

He parked in the visitors' parking lot. Without an appointment, he wasn't sure how he'd get access to the buildings, much less the files, but he was counting on diminished vigilance from the night shift.

He was right. In the brightly lit visitors' reception area, the guard took a quick look at his badge, looked into his face once, and scanned the badge again indifferently. "You need a guide?" he asked.

His first reaction was no. Then he reversed himself as he realized a guide would make him less conspicuous. "Please," he said. From that moment he knew his effectiveness would be governed by whoever showed up.

The whoever turned out to be a woman. Chubby, cheerful, obviously happy for a change of jobs. She said, "I used to be a newspaper reporter, so they figured I had a good memory and trained me to conduct tours. I like doing this. Where do you want to start?"

"The personnel files," he said. It was all working out better than he'd hoped.

Personnel, she thought, swallowing hard. *Rudy Malec.* The memory was still hideous. But she led him to a group of offices manned by an elderly, tired-looking woman whose brown slacks hung in equally tired folds. "He's from the National Transportation Safety Board," she explained, and the other woman nodded, not interested.

Sandy Wallis pointed to a room filled with file cabinets. "Which end of the alphabet do you want?"

He looked around and could think of no answer. A field of gray covered every wall and extended from floor to ceiling. They would contain thousands of names. No, tens of thousands. "How many people work here?" he asked, covering his dismay.

"Twenty-three thousand," she chirped.

Twenty-three thousand, a small city. He should have known. He'd been swept away by a naive hope that he might accomplish something—gone off without his brains. He looked around again. Combing through that mass of material would take dozens of people—and weeks of time.

Stalling while he tried to decide on his next move, he asked, "What kinds of projects do you work on?"

"Fleet Utilization Reports. Know what those are?"

"Yes."

"They're boring. Just recording a lot of statistics. But I guess they've got to keep track of who's doing what to which airplane."

"And you get the results back after the work is done . . ." he said, as an idea began to form.

"Sure. We get them back all signed off, with the mechanics' names, and what they did, and what parts went on the plane."

He gave her a rueful smile and shrugged. "The files here are more numerous than I thought." *By about a thousand percent,* he decided. "I'm afraid I don't have time to do much good. Instead, I'd like to have a look at your utilization reports."

"But those aren't Airtech employees—I mean they don't work at the factory. They're out at the airports."

"That'll be fine."

She shrugged. "I don't know what you're looking for, but . . ." When he offered no explanation, she said, "We'll have to go through Building 23 to another area," and led him back through a cavernous structure full of partly assembled fuselages. As they passed one of the great hulks, where men stood on an elevated platform near the cockpit, he had the feeling somebody was watching him.

He turned to see.

But no, they were all busy. *I must be getting paranoid.*

After a while she left him alone and returned to her own office. Given a large flat table to work on, he spread the reports out and began searching, grateful that here, at least, the material had boundaries.

He'd brought the dates of the incidents and the aircraft identifying numbers, so it was a simple matter to eliminate some aircraft and trace the checkup orders on others.

The first important discovery he made was that all five of the problem planes had come in to one maintenance station or another for a routine "C" check. Which, as a matter of logic, was not saying that all "C" check planes had mishaps, only that all suspicious planes had undergone recent checks. Statistically, though, five "C" checks and five problems did not mean much.

Next he began examining the completed reports for mechanics' signatures, discovering immediately that the various signatures were random and did not show any kind of pattern.

Since the anomalies all originated with the control systems, he concentrated his search in that area, ignoring the rest. By 3:00 A.M. he'd located repairs to the computerized systems of all five planes. With a growing sense of excitement, he studied the signatures of the mechanics involved, looking back and forth among them as he compared both airports and names.

His excitement faded. Nothing tied together. The five had all been checked at different airports, and no two names matched.

He was at a dead end.

Discouraged and exhausted, he slumped on his chair. He'd come to Airtech for nothing. The night shift was nearly finished. He ought to leave.

He found Sandy and asked where he could get coffee.

Later, drinking tasteless instant, he thought of something else. Picking up the sheets once again, he studied the records of other planes that showed repairs to their control systems, gathering the signatures and writing them down. These he compared with the five problem planes.

As he worked, a hubbub began in the plant, workers preparing to leave, others beginning to drift in. Sandy stopped by his table. "Will you be all right? I have to go home now."

"Sure."

"I can find you another escort."

"It's okay. I don't need one."

"Well, just in case . . ." she said, and left before he could stop her.

And then he was lost in his work. To his astonishment he saw that whereas the random planes showed some signatures appearing over and over, the five affected craft were signed off by a different mechanic in every case. Five planes, five different "new" names on the records.

And the new names didn't appear on any other craft . . .

He was onto something. Something big.

A hand touched his shoulder. "What are you doing here?" Unfriendly eyes swept over him, took in the sheets spread out on the table.

It was Bennett Bergman. He knew he'd stayed too long.

Chapter Twenty-seven

"Dammit, Alan, I never thought I'd have to say this in so many words. Get out of that plant and don't go back!" Mark Brody's voice rumbled through the phone and Wilcox cursed under his breath and tried to block out what he knew was coming.

"You're going to bring down the whole NTSB the way you're acting, and us with it! Listen, you wanted two weeks' leave—take the time and get off this damned case. Have you forgotten your daughter's getting married?"

Bergman had done this to him, Wilcox thought, Bennett Bergman, the senior software designer, who had turned paranoid over the investigation. "Mark," he said tightly, "however this looks to you, there's something going on down here. But I can't fight you, so I'll stop looking for now. Eventually I'll have to come back." He wondered what Bergman was trying to hide.

"Is this a flatout refusal?"

"No. No, it isn't. By the time I come again, you won't have any objections, I assure you."

He left, as he'd been ordered to do. When he returned later, he knew exactly where he'd start.

The man may not be in the factory now, *but he was there once.*

"I've picked a hospital for Todd," Ellie announced. "It will cost us almost eleven thousand dollars, it's—"

"*Eleven thousand dollars!* What happened to ten?"

"This is where the psychiatrists' kids go."

He couldn't help smiling. "Naturally they'd have a designer drug program."

She said coldly, "Be sarcastic all you want, we'll send him where they get results."

He could see her sense of humor was gone; her mouth was twisted and hard. Pulling open the oven door, she jerked away from a blast of steam.

He wanted to talk to her but decided it was futile.

To his surprise, she turned and looked at him sadly. "I'm sorry, Alan. I don't recognize myself, speaking to you like this. You must be under pressure too." Her shoulders slumped. "You tried to tell me something the other day, but I was too distracted to let you. About your job, I think. Do you remember?"

He shrugged. Now that she was ready to listen, he resented having to tell her—as though they could converse only on *her* timetable. Fighting his irritation, he began telling her about the Airtech disasters and his gut feelings about causation. To his surprise, she listened.

"Sabotage!" she cried in the middle of it. "Oh, Alan!"

"For me it's a bigger crisis every day. It's become the central fact of my life." Somehow he couldn't bring himself to tell her no one else on the Board agreed.

She said slowly, "No wonder. At times, lately, you've been like one of those shells we used to pick up on the beach. The shell was there, but the clam was gone. Oh, Alan. I'm so sorry." Her expression said she meant it.

"Look," he said, "I guess I didn't pay much attention to Jamie's wedding because nothing bad was happening. But Todd . . ." he cleared his throat, "for Todd's sake I should apply for the director's job in Washington. To get him out of town." Embarrassed at his own hypocrisy, he added, "I probably wouldn't get it. Not now."

"Why would you take a job you don't want?" She turned to glare at him. "Todd may hit bottom, but he's not dragging us with him."

He felt as if he'd been pulled back from the edge of a crevasse. He sat down at the kitchen table. "Exactly where are we with Jamie's wedding?"

For the next hour she sat beside him and laid out the plans, telling him what she'd done.

He stood up. "Come here, Ellie." She felt good in his arms, warm and yielding. Close to her ear, he whispered, "It's going to be a very good wedding—because Jamie's got such an incredible mother."

"Evil done in a noble cause is still evil." Where had he heard that quote? Kimball didn't know; he only knew he had to do *something*. Once more he called Malec.

"Listen, Rudy," he said, "I'll pay you to stop. Let me send you a cashier's check and this whole nightmare will be over."

"How much?"

He had no choice but to start low. "A thousand dollars." Even that would be hard to come by.

The creep hooted.

"How about my watch? It's a Rolex." Another downside to bribery: it was demeaning.

Malec didn't answer.

"The watch cost seven thousand dollars," he growled, "take it or leave it."

More silence. *Oh Jesus, he doesn't have a price.*

And then, "I'm glad you made the offer, Mr. Kimball, it has a good, solid sound. I like knowing we're full partners now, together all the way."

Kimball's stomach lurched. He ran to the bathroom. *How could I forget the tape recorder?*

Alan Wilcox found the astonishing quote in *Aviation Week*. Responding to badgering from the media over the mid-Atlantic disappearance and other Airtech incidents, the FAA had called a press conference. To Wilcox's amazement, the deputy director for regulatory affairs said, "We don't have an airplane problem, we have a human factors problem."

He slammed the magazine down on the coffee table and stood up angrily. Trust the FAA to put blame in all the wrong places.

Hands behind his back, he stood at his picture window and looked down over the county, remembering what had happened after the DC-10 crash-landed at Sioux City. A similar statement had been made then: "We don't have an airplane problem, we have an engine problem."

But he knew better. From the moment it was decided to route all controls through the tail adjacent to an engine, the DC-10s were saddled with a design flaw. If that engine ever exploded—as it finally did—shrapnel was bound to sever the hydraulic lines of all three systems. Over Sioux City the plane literally bled to death.

The problem was, the FAA had its DERs—designated engineering representatives—inside all major manufacturing plants for the express purpose of helping the manufacturer certify planes. But because those individuals were on the payroll of the manufacturer, not the FAA, it was tantamount to letting the foxes guard the chicken coop. Once again, he thought, the FAA was trying to cover itself.

He sat down again and idly thumbed through the magazine. Unfortunately, the FAA had been given a dual role by Congress—to both *regulate* and *promote* the aircraft industry, which clearly couldn't be done. The United States was the only nation in the world to assign its regulatory body conflicting roles. He wished the FAA were patterned after the British Civil Aviation Authority. Never concerned with "How do we downplay this?" the Brits could solve their aviation problems immediately.

Feeling grim, Wilcox tried to finish his article. But his mind kept playing with an ominous truth: as long as the regulatory bodies in the U.S. were even partly political, they would never function exactly as they should. *I've got enough ideas to write a book. I wish I had time.*

Lloyd Holloway smiled tightly as he stood up at Stirling's executive meeting. "We got our letter of intent signed by TAF last night. This morning the bank agreed to renew our line of credit. As of this moment, all salaries are restored. Each of you will receive a ten percent bonus."

A controlled, dignified cheer rose from the conference table.

Max Topping frowned. "Tough break for Airtech. I wouldn't want to be in their shoes."

Holloway threw him a surprised look. "Our own shoes are not exactly comfortable, Max. Just because Congress isn't pursuing that eighty-million-dollar fine doesn't mean it will disappear. It depends on the chairman of the committee—and *his* troubles with the ethics committee. I've got our lobbyist back there reminding him that we can poke around in his affairs as easily as he can mess with ours."

"A little blackmail," said a voice.

Miles Kimball looked around to see who'd spoken and saw Topping at the far end of the table eyeing him with an inscrutable expression. Suddenly the room seemed hotter.

Holloway continued. "Before any of you pass judgment on recent events in this company, remember that our survival is in the public's best interest. The jobs we provide, the reliable aircraft we build, cannot be regarded lightly." Challenging them to disagree, he looked at each man in turn. When nobody spoke, he asked for a report from the vice president for quality control.

Miles Kimball heard none of it. The revulsion and fear he'd felt the two times he'd called Malec engulfed him again, as they had many times since. He knew he'd capitulated. The last call had been a turning point in his life, the moment he knew absolutely that he'd surrendered the last vestige of his personal morality.

He knew he'd never turn in Malec now. The impulse to do so had burned out, leaving only the shame.

Ironic, he thought. Now that he was getting his salary back he didn't particularly want it. Every dollar would be ill-gotten gain.

"I think that's all for today," Holloway said.

As a group the men pushed back their chairs—all except Topping. He sat nearest the door, watching each board member file by. When Kimball reached him, Topping leaned forward. In a quiet voice he asked, "How does your food taste?"

Henry Sweetser didn't like what he saw outside his cockpit window. Solid gray. No visibility. A lot of vapor swirling against the glass. They were leveling off at ten thousand feet on the profile descent into Minneapolis–St. Paul International, and the stuff showed no sign of letup. Moments earlier he'd listened to the recorded weather from Automatic Terminal Information Service: two-hundred-foot ceiling and half a mile visibility, meaning their approach would be to minimums. He hoped something would change.

Something did. It began to snow.

Sweetser glanced at his captain, Jim Kelly, a pugnacious, hard-nosed man who hadn't exactly made the trip a party. When you flew with Kelly, you knew you were going to get your ego tromped on.

Kelly scowled at the windshield. "This is going to take someone with plenty of weather experience."

Meaning you instead of me, thought Sweetser. He said, "Descent checklist complete, Captain. Gear down and final approach checklist to go."

Kelly grunted and Sweetser tuned the radio to the Minneapolis approach control frequency. He listened for a moment and heard nothing. Odd. He said, "Minneapolis approach, Fleet 83 is with you level at ten."

And then a man's voice came on. "Fleet 83, good afternoon. You're number one for the airport with lots of traffic behind you. I need your best speed to the outer marker. Descend and maintain three thousand five hundred feet, heading 320 for radar vectors to runway 4 ILS— instrument landing system—approach. Will you accept a seven-mile turn onto final?"

Best speed, thought Sweetser. A gentleman's agreement that meant "I won't tell if you exceed the 250-knot speed limit below ten thousand feet." Great for making up time on a clear day, he thought, but not in weather like this. He knew why the controller had asked: as lead plane they'd be like the lead car in a freeway jam—if that car slowed, there was a decelerating effect on all the cars that followed, so the last car would be almost at a stop. With airplanes it couldn't be allowed to happen. He said, "You want me to tell him we need more distance for the turn-on, Captain?"

Kelly turned to stare at him. "We've got a chance to block in on time, Sweetser. Number one in the pattern with no speed restriction and you want to ask for a delay? Be real."

Sweetser threw a quick look out his side window at the swirling gray blanket. He fought his rising anger. He and Kelly had flown together a month, and the trip to Minneapolis would be their last assignment as a team. Their last ever, he hoped. Early in the month he'd tried to be charitable and pass off Kelly's attitude as supreme confidence. But the man had gotten to him, rattled his chain more every trip. A few minutes earlier, when Kelly disconnected the autopilot at the beginning of the profile descent and announced with a grin he was going to hand fly the approach—in those conditions!—Sweetser decided Kelly wasn't just confident, he was an arrogant ass.

An impatient voice spoke into the cockpit. "Fleet 83, Minneapolis approach. How 'bout the early turn-on?"

Making no move to pick up the microphone, Sweetser turned and looked right at Kelly.

Kelly yanked the microphone off its cradle and jabbed the transmit button. "Fleet 83'll be happy to help you."

"Fleet 83, Minneapolis approach. Thank you, sir. Fly heading 360 now. Break." And then he was speaking to someone else. "Northwest 344, approach."

A second voice came on. "Northwest 344 is with you level at ten slowing to 250 knots."

"Northwest 344, approach. Descend and maintain five thousand feet, fly heading 310 degrees for vectors to the ILS runway 4 approach. Will you accept an early turn-on?"

"Approach, Northwest 344 wants a little more distance, please."

Sweetser listened to the exchange and at that moment wished fervently he worked for Northwest.

Looking down at his instrument panel, he saw the radio magnetic indicator needle approaching the 35-degree position, and the DME indicator—distance measuring equipment—showing 7.5 miles out. They were about to cross the final approach course at a 35-degree angle descending at over two thousand feet per minute at better than 270 knots—and they hadn't even begun the final approach checklist!

He began to sweat.

The controller's voice came back. "Fleet 83, approach. Sorry I let you go past the final approach course. Turn right heading 075, intercept the localizer. You're cleared for runway 4 ILS. Can you make it from there?"

Kelly punched the transmit button. "Fleet 83'll do it all right. Thanks."

Sweetser sat bolt upright. *The hell we will.*

"Fleet 83, contact tower now. Good day."

Quickly Sweetser tuned the radio to the tower frequency and said, "Tower, Fleet 83 is with you."

"Fleet 83, Minneapolis tower. Cleared to land runway 4. An aircraft just reported runway braking action poor with patches of ice."

Great, thought Sweetser.

Suddenly the aircraft banked violently to the right, then to the left. The first officer instinctively grabbed his armrests as Kelly yanked at the control stick, trying to capture the fast-moving ILS guidance needles on his navigation display. Simultaneously, he deployed the spoilers, all the while struggling to trim the aircraft.

Sweet Jesus, Sweetser thought, watching the ILS needles swipe back and forth across the indicator face. The needles were a cross-hair presentation—keep the vertical and horizontal needles in the center of the bull's-eye and the airplane was on the glide path to the obscured runway; let the needles wander and you were asking for it.

As Kelly literally manhandled the sidestick controls, the plane rocked back and forth like a ball in a washing machine.

At that moment the captain reached over and yanked the throttles to idle—forbidden so close to the ground. Once the engines decelerated, fifteen seconds were needed to reinstate emergency power.

Sweetser wanted to shout at his captain, to shake him, to alert the idiot to their peril. The plane wasn't stabilized, and wouldn't be in time. Without the autopilot, the damned fool was trying to do too many things too fast.

They passed the outer marker, an electronic transmitter five miles from the runway, and the ILS needles showed they were high and left of course—with airspeed still at 250 knots. Moving fast. Much too fast to begin lowering the landing flaps. They should have been down to 146 knots.

Sweetser glanced at the instrument panel. The airspeed showed 210 knots. Kelly called out, "Flaps five, and give me the gear!"

"You going to get this thing stabilized?" Sweetser's hands raced over the levers controlling flaps and landing gear.

No response. Instead Kelly said, "Flaps twenty-five!"

With the flap lever at the twenty-five-degree position and the gear down, the aircraft began to slow at a faster rate. But the copilot knew the downside only too well: every flap change necessitated a retrimming of the plane for stability. And Kelly wasn't keeping up.

The DME showed two miles to the runway, and the airplane was still too high and too fast. A shiver of naked fear went down Sweetser's spine; he remembered NTSB accident reports that read just like this approach. *Don't let the bastard kill me now,* he thought, and suddenly he yelled, "LET'S GO AROUND!"

"Hell no!" shouted Kelly, "I'm not getting in line again . . . we'd have to go back to Chicago! Flaps forty."

Good God, thought Sweetser, no final checklist, nothing going right. At that moment he could have strangled Jim Kelly.

As Sweetser's hands moved furiously over levers and switches and his mouth recited airspeeds and altitudes, the plane bucked and heaved like a car on a wavy country road.

The pilot fought the controls furiously, and they came punching out of the clouds at two hundred feet into blowing snow. Below them, the runway raced past, the point of touchdown already gone.

Again Sweetser grabbed the armrests. He could feel sweat trickling down his arms.

A hundred and twenty feet up. Twenty knots over speed. The plane skimmed above the ground like a goddamned Frisbee. Sweetser tightened his seat belt and shoulder harness. They were going to crash. It was inevitable.

Kelly forced the sidestick forward, then all the way back again, trying to jam the craft onto the runway.

At last the wheels banged down hard, rose again, and came down a second time with a teeth-jarring crunch.

Just above the throttle, Kelly grabbed for the thrust reversers, simultaneously cramming the brakes with both feet.

Nothing happened. The brakes were inoperative.

The plane continued to roll, slowed only ineffectually by the reverse thrust of the engines. With the runway a virtual ice rink, the aircraft careened wildly from side to side.

Inside the cockpit the master annunciator horn blared and a red warning display flashed, "Anti-skid failure! Anti-skid failure!"

Sweetser's hysterical laughter was swallowed up by the horn. *Who cares about anti-skid when we have no brakes?* He guessed they had only two thousand feet of paving left. Without brakes even the normal ten thousand feet of runway wouldn't be enough.

At eighty knots, the plane skated off the end of the runway and mowed down the approach lights. A metal pole holding one of the lights ripped through the right wing like a can opener.

On an access road ahead, an old man driving his car cautiously down the slick pavement happened at that moment to look up. To his astonishment he realized something big was coming at him through the snow—something that made no sense. He blinked and looked again. Suddenly he understood. He was about to be run down by an airplane!

With all the strength in his feeble legs he stomped on the brakes and his car skidded sideways, its forward progress stopped. Behind him another car skidded too, and plowed into his trunk. And then a third crashed into the second and came to rest against the driver's door.

The plane slewed across the road and missed them all.

Deep in a muddy field, Trans America flight 83 settled into a grinding, labored stop.

The old man's astonishment turned to horror as he saw an expanding yellow glow under the right wing—a glow that metamorphosed into flames, which began to lick at the fuselage.

Chapter Twenty-eight

Alan Wilcox stopped shaving and stood motionless in the bathroom. "A bulletin just in from Minneapolis," blared the radio. "Trans America Fleet's flight 83, coming in for a landing, skidded across an icy runway this morning and burst into flames as it came to rest in a field. TAF reports three fatalities and forty-nine people taken to local hospitals. Neither the pilot nor copilot were injured, claiming that the brakes failed and—"

Alan snapped the radio off and began shaving at a faster pace. Off duty or not, he had to go to Minneapolis and take a look.

Minutes later he was dressing while he organized the trip in his mind: Minneapolis by late Wednesday afternoon, one day to look at the plane and ask questions, return to Orange County about noon Friday in time for Jamie's rehearsal dinner. Yes, it would work.

After a scribbled note to Ellie, who'd already left for work, he picked up the phone to call the airport—and stopped short. Todd was on the line.

With mixed emotions, he eavesdropped. He'd never done that before, and it was hard convincing himself this was for Todd's own good. But he listened nevertheless.

Todd said, "Did you hear something, Boomer?"

"Naw. It's your imagination." A laugh. "What are you, getting paranoid?"

Nevertheless, Todd's voice dropped to a whisper. "Listen, Boomer, I don't have enough money. And I can't get it by Friday night."

"What about your Mom's purse?"

"She counts her money now."

"Oh." And then, "Maybe your dad has money."

"I'd never rip it off *him*."

"Why not?"

"Oh . . . you know."

"Well, these guys won't take skis—if you still had any." Laughter from both ends.

Todd said, "What about your cassette tape player?"

Boomer responded with irritation, "They said *cash*."

"Maybe we better wait." Todd sounded anxious. "I can hold off a couple more days."

"Until what?"

"I don't know. Maybe I'll earn it."

"Are you nuts, we can't earn money. They don't pay us to swim." Boomer laughed. "But who's swimming any more?"

"*I* am, Boomer. Hey, Dad's in the house somewhere. I gotta go." Without saying good-bye, Todd hung up.

Quietly Alan replaced the receiver and sat down heavily on the bed. His sense of urgency had vanished like steam, replaced by a bewildering jumble of emotions that immobilized him.

Todd. My son, Todd. Whom I've known since he was a baby. My son the drug addict.

Slumped on the edge of the bed with his head in his hands, he mentally replayed the words of two kids gone astray and felt helpless and doomed—as if he knew there was a mountain out there somewhere, a mountain he couldn't find and couldn't get away from, but could only fly into. The pain was personal and deep, where it couldn't be reached.

My son . . . my own son . . . the baby who never cried, whose first steps were a family event, whose first word was "Daddy"—for which at the time he took some kind of foolish credit, but uttered more likely because it was easy to say.

Todd . . . whose innocent, small-boy bragging about his father once prompted a stranger to say, "Your daddy must be superman."

Todd. Whom I've watched and guarded all these years.

God, did all parents feel like this? Did the father of a murderer waiting on death row . . . did he, too, grieve for the long-gone child, the baby he'd once held . . . did he think back to the nesting years when innocence was a shield and the child could never be blamed? Did parents of perverts and thieves and rapists . . . did they also cry for their babies?

And when . . . at what moment . . . did parents decide they could step in and save their children—or decide they couldn't and let them go? Was it age ten . . . or eleven . . . or fifteen? When in a child's life did badness become fixed and late was *too* late?

He stood up, knowing what he had to do. All these months he'd been fighting to uncover a saboteur—and at home Todd was becoming a distortion. A decaying kid with values already warped by drugs.

The saboteur and the drug addict—they were both his burden, and neither could wait.

He finished dressing, quickly but carefully. Yes, fifteen was the age. If he didn't stop Todd now, this week, he'd be one of the fathers he wondered about—visiting his son in prison.

Howard Paterno, Jr., waited impatiently for the final report on the anonymous orange sheets collected on his desk—ostensibly copies of interoffice memos from Airtech, though his chief engineer didn't think so.

A buzz came from his telephone console, and he grabbed for the receiver. "Howard—Larry here. About that problem with the thirty-four Airtech planes. It happened, all right. A couple months' production when the tail sections were theoretically attached with interference fit bolts—except X ray proved they weren't. I got the whole story from someone over there who knows."

"You're kidding!" Paterno was incredulous. "I guess we made the right—"

"But wait," said his informant. "The FAA issued airworthiness directives and by now they've all been fixed. The mistake won't affect us."

"You're sure . . ."

The other man laughed. "Quite sure, Howard. It happened eleven years ago."

Afterwards, Paterno felt like a fool for having taken them seriously. He crossed the office to his couch and sat down heavily. His evaluating committee had already decided to switch their recommendation to Stirling Aircraft—on the basis of Airtech problems that had nothing to do with those memos.

Thank God I didn't run all over the building with those damned things. His minister had been right about the value of anonymous letters, he reflected.

On the other hand . . . who'd gone to all the trouble to send them?

Dressed in suit and tie, Alan stood in Todd's room facing him down. "You're going with me because I *said* you're going. You're getting on that plane in forty-five minutes and we're flying to Minneapolis."

"But *why?* Why do you wanta haul me off to Minneapolis? There's nothing to do there."

"*Do* isn't the point. Nothing we've said so far is the point. You're just going. Now get dressed."

"I *am* dressed."

"Not good enough. Take off those jeans and put on a pair of good slacks. And one of your white shirts. And a sweater." And a tie? he wondered. No, a tie wouldn't be necessary.

Todd didn't move.

Alan took the boy's shoulders and stared straight into his kid's brown eyes. "*I said get dressed.* NOW!"

Todd stared back. For seconds they remained two statues frozen in silent combat. Wilcox tightened his grip on the thin shoulders and squeezed, feeling his fingers cram flesh against bone. He bore down until his muscles were ready to explode.

Todd's lips came together in a hard line and he averted his eyes, bearing the pain as long as he could. Eventually he shouted, "CUT IT OUT!" and jerked away, fumbling toward the closet.

Ten minutes later they left.

The two said almost nothing on the way to the airport, and Todd hung back sullenly while Alan stood in line for tickets, learning to his dismay that coach was sold out. "Then two first-class," he said.

At the ticket counter the woman's fingers danced across a calculator. "That'll be two thousand, six hundred, sixty-four dollars. How do you want to pay for this?"

Wincing mentally, Alan handed her his credit card. Twenty-six hundred dollars! How long had it been since he "rode the cushions"—except on vacations with Ellie? Years. Fourteen at least.

When had he ever shelled out money for first class?

Never. *Will it really make my point?*

*   *   *

The flight attendant handed them embossed paper napkins and smiled solicitously. "What would you like to drink?"

"Orange juice," said Alan. He glanced at Todd.

The boy shrugged. "I dunno. Coke, I guess."

She brought the drinks and handed them fancy mixed nuts in heavy foil, which Alan fingered thoughtfully. How did one swallow two-thousand-dollar nuts?

Uncommunicative, they drank drinks and crunched nuts while the plane roared down the runway, rotated, and lifted off. So much power, thought Wilcox. Always awesome, but never to be taken for granted.

While the plane climbed toward cruising altitude, Wilcox wondered how he was going to broach what needed to be said.

Todd didn't help. Shoulders averted, he looked out the window. *Why did I give him the window?*

Eventually Alan leaned toward his son. "Do you know why we're here?"

"No." A flat answer.

"We're here to talk."

Silence.

"Stop looking out the window."

"And look at you?"

"Yes. Or at least stop giving me your back."

No response.

Wilcox put a hand on the kid's shoulder—a threatening hand—and his son turned enough so he was facing the seat ahead of him.

"Now," he said, "if you want to break in at any time, feel free. But until you do, I'm going to say what's on my mind. I brought you along on this trip because what I have to say can't wait until I get back. You're in danger, Todd. In danger of snuffing out your life. You're already into heavy drugs—"

"You don't know that."

"I do know that."

"How?"

"It doesn't matter how. I know. By heavy drugs I mean cocaine, which is one of the worst. Maybe *the* worst. Ask anybody who works in rehabilitation. Smart, creative, accomplishing people get on cocaine and their lives go down the sewer. Patrick Bissell, one of the most promising ballet dancers of all time—possibly as good as

Baryshnikov—tried to stop using and couldn't. His last injection killed him. Two basketball players—one of them was Len Bias—died without using much at all. You don't know what you're playing with. You think it's a lark. A little entertainment at night. It isn't. Cocaine is a loaded gun pointed right at your head."

Flaring. "You have no proof that I'm—"

"Todd, let's get one thing straight. I have all the proof anyone needs. I *know* what you're doing. So start with a given. *You've been using cocaine.* And you are going to stop."

Todd turned away, leaning his forehead against the window and his chin in his hands.

A boy's chin, Alan thought, attached to a man's forehead, in that peculiar configuration of a growing male. He waited, knowing instinctively he had to be silent so his words could percolate down through the layers of Todd's resistance.

After a while a small voice spoke, so softly Wilcox had to listen hard. "I've *tried* to stop."

It worked, Alan thought jubilantly. *My bluff worked. Now I know.* He wanted to yell his victory to the whole plane. All the money he'd spent on the trip had already paid off.

And then he grew sober again; all he'd gained was momentary honesty.

It would be nice, he thought, trying to let go of his tension, if knowledge was all he needed, if Todd's admission solved anything. He found himself pressing his forehead between his fingers, trying to figure out how to be a parent. Which no one ever taught you, as though it was the one job anyone could accomplish without help.

How *did* parents deal with their kids' addictions?

Oh, he knew how adults were handled—by letting them sink into a morass of their own making, by encouraging them to "hit bottom." When friends, money, home, car—even freedom—were gone, some adults relinquished their drugs.

And some didn't.

Juveniles were different. He guessed they had to be physically stopped.

Proceeding on instinct, because that was all he had to work with—and because instinct had always served him well—he said, "Todd, there will be no more drugs while you're in our house. I won't let you have them. No child of mine will destroy himself. So this is what we're going to do."

For emphasis, he enumerated on his fingers. "One. You're going to be tested every week. Two. Any week you fail the test, you will have to stay in all weekend and—"

"I'm NOT a criminal!" Todd shouted.

"No," said Alan fiercely. "You're my son."

Todd turned his face away.

With a bad feeling in his gut, Wilcox steeled himself to go on. "And three. Until you've been drug-free for a month, every time you go out your friends will have to come to our house first and introduce themselves. And we'll be asking where you plan to go and what you're going to do. And checking up on you."

Todd's lip curled. "My friends will *never* do that!"

"Fine," said Alan. "Get new friends."

After a silence. "What will you do if I don't do all that stuff?"

Abhorring threats, Wilcox said evenly, "In that case, you'll become a ward of the court and live at the Youth Guidance Center, where the rules are enforced for those who can't obey them at home."

"I hate you," Todd said unemotionally.

Alan didn't respond. But the words hurt. God, what kids could do to you.

The stewardess brought a miniature white tablecloth for each of their trays and set it with silverware and a skid-resistant plate that gave off meaty vapors from the steak and baked potato.

They ate in silence.

After a while Todd said, "What if I drink beer but don't do cocaine? Beer isn't bad."

"For you beer is bad."

Todd stiffened and his words were a snarl. "What do you mean, beer is bad? Huh? You drink it. Mom drinks it. You're just being stupid. Everyone drinks beer."

"*Everyone* doesn't go on to something worse. We're not using beer to lead us to the drug of choice." He looked at his son hard. "Your mother and I are not fifteen."

"You're crazy," said Todd, and turned away, slumping down in his seat.

They stopped talking and Wilcox leaned back, trying to concentrate on the vibration of the engines purring through their seat backs. Insistent. Relentless. And in spite of everything, comforting.

He looked over at Todd. The boy was either asleep or faking it.

Alan adjusted his seat for comfort and spent the next hour and a half thinking. Eventually he arrived at a decision, but it came only after endless internal arguments and such intense soul-searching he wondered if he was turning martyr.

When Todd awoke, he reverted to looking out the window, shutting his father out. A half hour out of Minneapolis, he said tentatively, "What if I quit the cocaine? Would I still have to drag my friends to the house?"

Wilcox smiled. "Once you're drug-free, no. But you may be surprised, Todd. Your friends might like us."

"Maybe," said Todd.

"There'll be another change soon," said Alan. "Once I figure out this problem with Airtech, I'm going to quit my job. I'll do something with normal hours, like . . . oh, I don't know yet . . . something."

Todd looked at him, amazed. "You'd do that?"

"Yes," he said. But it felt like punishment—a self-imposed exile from a familiar and beloved country. As a best-worst moment in his life, Wilcox could think of no equal.

Chapter Twenty-nine

Max Topping heard the news in disbelief. Another one at Minneapolis . . . Airtech again. He could no longer stand by and do nothing.

His eyes turned to the picture on his desk—his father in his Army
colonel's uniform accepting a medal from the president for his surprise attack on a German convoy, for daring to take on Rommel's best.
"The Toppings do what's necessary," was all his dad had said to the
press. But Max had heard the phrase, or variations thereof, more than
once before that interview.

His thoughts drifted back to fifth grade and the day he'd stared at
the teacher as she scribbled facts on the board about Rommel and Africa
—facts he knew to be false. He'd muttered from his desk, "Miss Goose"—
her name was Swan—"hasn't a clue. She must be deaf and blind."

She'd heard *that,* all right, and reported to his father.

"He'll make it up to you, Miss Swan," his dad said. "He's a Topping. He'll be over this afternoon to clean your house."

Chagrined, Max had appeared as advertised, and during the clean-
ing some ten-year-old sense of reparation had taken over, and he'd
not only vacuumed and scrubbed her floors, he'd gone on and cleaned
her bathroom as well, working so diligently she'd watched from the
doorway amazed. But even then he couldn't seem to stop, and when
he began sweeping the garage, attacking it with a ferocity that surprised even himself, she finally took his arm. "Max," she said, "you've
done enough."

It was the start of a lifelong self-image about the Toppings in general, and his sense of duty in particular.

Now, downstairs in Stirling's accident department, he found the directory he was looking for. It included the names and home phone numbers of all the local NTSB men. The closest was a man named Wilcox.

Back upstairs he called the man's home number. "Hello, this is Max Topping . . ."

"Put these on," Wilcox said. He tossed his son an old blue jumpsuit and a well-used baseball cap bearing the gold letters NTSB on blue cloth. As they left the hotel room, he handed Todd a blue windbreaker with the same gold letters across the back and the safety board seal in front. He looked his son up and down. "Not a perfect fit, but . . ." he shrugged. "You've got the height, just not the pounds. Try to hang back and not attract attention. With luck, they'll leave you alone." What he wanted to say was, When we get there—hide.

Todd's eyes opened wide. "I've never seen an accident before. Is it . . . a big mess?"

Wilcox laid his hand briefly on the boy's shoulder. "Tell me later what you think."

At the site of the accident, the battered plane listed incongruously to one side, partly submerged in a muddy field. Though the fuselage was intact, scorch marks darkened most of its lower half. Around it, the wet field was alive with people: policemen, county sheriffs, Airtech engineers, representatives of the FBI, the FAA, and Trans America Fleet, salvage crews, and three investigators from the NTSB. As he and his son walked through the cordoned-off area without question, Wilcox saw immediately that what might have been bedlam was instead an orderly, efficient scene of intense activity. The NTSB was nothing if not organized.

The minute he came through the ropes, an Airtech engineer came up and asked a procedural question about a part he'd pulled off the landing gear. Wilcox said, "Wait here, I'll find the right man." Trailed by Todd, he headed toward Bruce Cavalier of Trans America Fleet. Before they got there, a man whose jacket was stamped "FAA" stopped Wilcox with another question.

Wilcox forgot all about Todd.

With hardly a breather, he spent the next hour near the damaged plane, automatically slipping into the role he'd played so often. Overseer. Orchestrator. On-site expert. Even as he solved one problem, somebody was at his elbow with another. Only briefly did he manage to grab a few quiet words with Joseph Palm, his old friend from Chicago, who was in charge. Wilcox said, "Joe, I'm here on the QT this time."

Joe smiled wearily. "QT or not, we can use the help."

"Mind if I ask the pilots a few questions?"

"You want to lend a hand with that, too? Sure." Joe, graying, with fine wrinkles across his face, glanced over at the tall boy standing nearby. "Who is that kid?"

"My son."

Joe's expression changed subtly. Bringing someone along on an investigation was against regulations, and they both knew it. "He's on the QT also," added Wilcox unnecessarily.

"I see."

"Trust me, Joe. The whole thing—my being here, his being here—it's all important."

Distant thunder interrupted them. Wilcox looked up. The sky seemed to be lowering, getting darker even as they talked.

Joe growled, "I assume you'll get him out of here soon."

"That's right," said Wilcox.

"As to the pilots—they were kept overnight in a hotel. They're supposed to be meeting me in a private room in—" he looked down at his watch, "about an hour. I'll have to do the official interview, of course. But you can have them first."

Wilcox smiled. "Call me when you want to collect on this one."

Soon afterwards, Wilcox caught Todd's eye and signaled him away from the wreck. They'd only started to leave when Todd stopped and his head jerked sideways. Just as suddenly he began walking again, quickly.

Wilcox turned to where Todd had been looking. A member of the coroner's team was lifting a charred body out of a patch of weeds— somebody young, somebody whose damaged muscles pulled him up into a fighter's crouch. The coroner lowered the body to a yellow bag.

Todd looked once again and no more.

Together they went out through the restricted area and across cement and grass toward the terminal. After a while Todd spoke. "It wasn't anything like I expected."

"How's that?"

"I thought you'd be . . . picking up bodies."

"The coroner does that, under our supervision."

"When do you collect the purses, and stuff like that?"

Wilcox said gently, "Purses don't cause accidents." He glanced over at Todd with a smile. "I guess I haven't talked to you much about this." Had he ever told him anything about the job?

Todd said, "I always knew what you did, but I didn't picture it like that. I thought you'd be putting tags on bodies and poking around in the wreckage with big tongs, or something. And picking up pieces of the plane and looking at them."

"We do that later, after the salvage crew moves the wreckage to a warehouse." He stopped. How much would his son really want to know? He began, "At the warehouse we lay out the parts of the plane close to their original positions, and then we go over them piece by piece. It takes time, it's—"

Todd's face was alive with interest. "How can you tell one piece from another? When they're such a mess?"

"Practice, son, practice. Small clues. You see a rounded edge or a certain shape, and you figure out where it goes. That's when the hard part starts. We go over all the important fragments and study them in detail. We can tell by the way something is bent or crushed where it was at the moment of impact."

"You *can?*" Todd's eyes were riveted on his face. "How would you know, Dad, whether the flaps were up or down when they're burned— when they're just a bunch of junk?"

Wilcox smiled. "The junk leaves clues. We might recover the flap handle and take it all apart. There'd probably be enough left to show us, for instance, a line of damage along two parts that normally correspond. So we'd know whether the two parts were aligned when they hit. And we'd have the flight data recorder giving us flap information. And eyewitnesses. Before we were through, we'd *know* about the flaps."

"And other things? You'd be able to tell about the brakes? And the landing gear?" Listening intently, Todd had slowed to a crawl.

Wilcox nodded. "One way or another, we can figure out how every single system was functioning when it hit. But we tend to concentrate on the areas that are suspect." He touched his son's shoulder. "It's a fascinating job, Todd, like working the world's most complicated puzzle. Except we do it for a purpose. To save lives."

In a low voice, Todd said, "Awesome." He took one last look backward as Wilcox held open the terminal door.

Inside, Todd asked, "Do you always tell all those people what to do?"

Wilcox grinned. "That's the good part. NTSB means, When I say it, you do it. Pretty nice, huh?"

"Yeah," said Todd, and laughed. "When I say it, nobody does it."

In the back of the building they started down a corridor that was empty. Looking around, Wilcox made a decision. He stopped walking and turned to his son. "Todd, there's something you should know. This isn't an ordinary investigation I'm doing. We've got a problem here we've never had before. Somebody is deliberately sabotaging airplanes. A criminal. Probably insane. *That's* why—"

"Are you kidding, Dad? You're tracking down a crazy man?"

"I think so. And I have to find him because I'm the only one who's looking." He sighed. "So you see why I've been working so hard. And why I have to keep this job a little longer."

"I hope you find the guy. And I hope he ends up like that burned-up kid."

So he is getting involved, thought Wilcox. Well, it was a start.

Wilcox and Todd found the small room Joseph Palm had indicated, but to Wilcox's surprise, only one of the pilots was there. He sat by himself, reading unconcernedly.

As he'd been told to do, Todd found an unobtrusive chair in a corner and sat down. Wilcox said in a loud voice, "I'm Alan Wilcox from the NTSB."

The man looked up and nodded but made no move to stand.

Suddenly Wilcox recognized him. "Aren't you Jim Kelly? Didn't we meet at Edwards Air Force Base?"

"That's right." Kelly didn't smile or extend a hand. Instead his eyes were two points of defiance with a single message that was clearer than clear: You just *dare* lay this on me . . . He seemed larger and more burly than Wilcox remembered. His shoulders were massive, as though in the intervening months he'd added pounds to what had already been an ample build. Wilcox wondered if he lifted weights.

"Where's your first officer?" Wilcox asked.

Kelly shrugged. "I expect he'll get here."

"Trouble in the cockpit?"

"When a plane loses its brakes, it's trouble everywhere."

That wasn't what Wilcox meant. But what Kelly meant was clear enough; he intended to say what he intended to say and nothing else. The interview wasn't going to be fun.

Wilcox glanced at the door. "I think we should wait for your first officer. How long do you think he'll be?"

"I'm afraid only he knows."

They sat in tense silence while Wilcox wondered what to do next. Ordinarily pilots were interviewed as a team, but nothing about the situation was proving ordinary. Wilcox said, "Well. I suppose I can ask a few preliminary questions. You say the brakes failed. Anything else?"

"Yeah. The anti-skid system failed too—but so what when you've got no brakes? On an icy runway that's all the disaster factors you need."

Wilcox heard a sound and turned around. A slim, very erect man with the presence of a screen star strode into the room. He came directly to Wilcox and put out his hand. "Henry Sweetser. It seems the hotel could scare up only one cab every fifteen minutes." As Wilcox introduced himself, Sweetser sat down. Without looking at Kelly, he asked, "What's been said so far?"

"Very little," Wilcox said. "Kelly mentioned failures of the brakes and anti-skid system."

Sweetser nodded his agreement. "That's true." Under his breath he added, "But that's not all that failed."

Kelly sat up straighter. "The *brakes* were the cause of this accident, Sweetser."

"The brakes were part of it," Sweetser said coldly, "but not the biggest part."

Wilcox looked from one to the other, wondering how to proceed. He said, "There seems to be some disagreement here. We'll start with you, Jim. What other factors do you see being at fault?"

"None," said Kelly. "It was all bad conditions—snow and poor braking conditions on the runway—plus the goddam brakes failing. We'd have been okay if we'd been able to stop. As it was, when I applied the brakes there was no response. I mean zero. We slid and slid and eventually we plowed off the—"

"Not eventually," Sweetser broke in, "damn near immediately. We'd used up more than half the runway before we ever put the wheels down. Before *he* put the wheels down."

"There was plenty of runway left."

Sweetser said pointedly, "There wasn't, and you know it. You were so busy trimming the plane, it's a wonder we ever got *near* the runway." He looked at Wilcox. "Way back, when we still had time, I told him to go around."

Kelly stiffened and turned red. "Don't give me that shit! This was a brake failure, that's all it was."

Henry Sweetser jumped up, his composure suddenly gone. "Look, Kelly, I'm not getting shafted for this. I yelled at you to go around and you were so goddamned pigheaded you said we'd have to go back to Chicago to get in line. So don't be telling Wilcox here the damned brakes were the whole cause. *You* were as much to blame as any brakes."

"You're a goddamned liar!" Kelly shouted.

Sweetser rushed at Kelly's chair. "You jackass! Until I flew with you, I had a perfect record, twenty-five years with no incidents, and now I've got a goddamned accident on my record because I happened to be flying with a baboon who thinks he knows it all. And you took the auto-land off when you shoulda left it on, when we might have had some *brains* running that plane! So why don't you tell—"

Kelly jumped to his feet. "You wanta settle this here and now? You want to use fists, you friggin' patsy—"

Wilcox rushed to get between them. Using both hands, he physically pushed them apart. "Calm down!"

Behind him, Sweetser shouted, "Don't feed Wilcox your stinking lies, Kelly. *You're* fifty percent of that accident, or more!"

"Stop!" Wilcox shouted. "Both of you shut up!" He swung toward Sweetser. "Now sit down! We're getting nowhere. And you, Kelly. Sit down and keep still!" He let his voice die away as the two angry men took their seats. Glaring at each in turn, Wilcox dared them to misbehave.

And then he glanced at Todd. The boy was sitting on the edge of his chair, riveted.

Wilcox said, "This behavior is uncalled for and unproductive. I'll forget this ever happened, but you better give me straight answers. Both of you. And one at a time. From now on, *I'm* running this meeting, *I'm* deciding who's going to talk, and you—both of you—will speak when spoken to. And only then." He took a deep breath. "Now— Kelly. What was your altitude when you started final approach?"

*   *   *

"Gee, Dad—that was awesome." Todd looked up at his father as they walked toward the gate for Todd's plane home. "Those guys were ready to kill each other, they—"

"That wasn't a typical pilot interview."

"I thought they were going to slug it out right there." Todd grinned. "The skinny guy tried to reach around you and punch out the big one. He was *so mad*. But you didn't let him."

"It wouldn't have solved anything. Or answered any questions. All that fight proved was the two pilots didn't like each other. Nothing else. The real issues—"

"Yeah?" Todd interrupted. "I think it proved who was boss around there. You were."

Wilcox laughed. "Just hold that thought, son."

Together they waited in line at the terminal. Outside the windows, Wilcox could see the heavy cloud layer becoming more ominous.

Todd said, "I wish you were going back with me."

"I wish so, too." He meant it. And wondered momentarily if he wasn't taking a chance, staying on. "I've got to finish inspecting the plane, Todd. But I'll leave first thing in the morning." He punched his son's arm. "Hey, we had fun last night, eh?" After calling Ellie—who couldn't hide her anger that they'd left three days before the wedding—they'd gone out for pizza and then a show. Todd was good company, making surprising, often wry observations about the people around them. More than once he made his father laugh.

A loudspeaker called Todd's plane. Todd dug into his pocket, fumbling for his ticket. He turned around. "Dad, I've definitely decided—I'm going to kick the cocaine. But I still think you're wrong about beer."

"I'm as right about one as the other," Wilcox said. And then, "I love you, Todd." Awkwardly, because they hadn't done it often in recent years, the two hugged.

As Todd started down the tunnel, Alan called out, "See you at home on Friday. Tomorrow before noon."

Todd got out of line and ran back. "Dad . . . uh . . . well, thanks for the trip. I hope it didn't break you—I mean, going first class."

Wilcox smiled. "It did. But if I'm going broke, I might as well go broke in style."

He watched the tall, slender figure of his son until the boy disappeared where the loading ramp made a bend.

You're worth it, Todd. Whatever I have to do is okay.

Heading out toward the field again, he felt a surge of pride in his boy that warmed him to the point of being unreasonable. It made no sense that this separate person could make you care so much just by existing. Because he happened to be there.

He guessed being a parent wasn't supposed to make a lot of sense.

Chapter Thirty

I've got to say good-bye to her in person; it's the decent thing to do.
Miles had made up his mind after weeks of stalling. He'd called Mary
Helen only once in that time, using Sondra as his excuse. Well, she
was a reason—but hardly the only one.

Though he rang her doorbell early on a weekday, Mary Helen wasn't
home. Stumped momentarily, Kimball decided to go ahead and retrieve
his possessions.

In her bedroom was a change of clothes and an extra shirt; in the
bathroom, his spare razor. And her scale. He stood on it and blanched.
In four months he'd lost over twenty pounds, which explained why
his pants had lately been fitting like flour sacks. He looked in the
mirror. His skin was grayish and his hair seemed thinner . . . but no
wonder, he kept finding strands on his pillow.

He was tired, too. Exhausted. He supposed it was the mental conflict—his agony over Malec, and Mary Helen as well. His wanting
her and not wanting her at the same time.

Except for that nephew, he might still be seeing her, though he wasn't
sure. Only deep into their relationship had he realized she watched
everything he did, listened to everything he said, and then tried to arrange and control the smallest details of his life. But subtly, always
subtly and in a nice way, so at first he'd scarcely noticed. He knew
now why her first husband had left her.

He combed his hair and found loose hairs in the comb. As he dropped them into the wastebasket, the word *Airtech* on a discarded piece of paper caught his eye.

He read the orange interoffice memo in some surprise. What was Mary Helen doing with an incriminating paper like that? He supposed it had something to do with Malec, the thought of whom sent his stomach into fresh churning and bigger knots. *I've got to get out of here.*

The doorbell rang. He jerked upright, not sure whether to answer it or not.

Before he got to the living room, he heard the door opening and moved a little faster. Suddenly he felt like a burglar.

To his horror, it was Malec himself, already inside and holding Mary Helen's hide-a-key.

Kimball stared at him.

"I'm sick," said Malec, and indeed, his eyes were half closed and his face looked feverish.

Good. Kimball regarded him with contempt. *Do me a favor and die.* He watched the nephew drop onto the couch, clutching his head and slumping against the cushions. Kimball found himself studying the man, mesmerized as though by a venomous snake, yet intrigued in some strange way that Malec was actually rather normal-looking, that he didn't have the ghoulish aspects he'd envisioned over the past weeks. He remembered now the youthful enthusiasm that had bubbled out, uncontrolled, when Malec spoke of his computers, and his occasional, childlike deference . . . No, he wasn't *always* weird.

Except for that strange, high-pitched voice.

Odd, he thought, how one's perceptions could shift back and forth. On the street Malec would be taken as ordinary, just another curly-headed man with a slight limp. Nobody would turn to look at him twice.

Maybe I can talk some sense into the man. Looming over the couch, he said vehemently, "You can't go on messing up airplanes, Rudy. The government is too smart for you. There are agencies. Bureaus. Dozens of men out there with sophisticated instrumentation. As sure as I'm standing here they'll catch you. And then you'll be—"

Malec looked up, his blue eyes now fully open. "I'll be nothing. Most of those men are stupid. Alan Wilcox isn't, but he hasn't a clue. Wilcox could figure it out if he knew where to look."

"Like where, Rudy?"

The other straightened, his eyes wild in the flushed face. "Think I'm gonna tell you?"

Kimball backed away. "Sure. We're partners, remember? You and I—" He stopped, aghast at what he'd said, and looked around desperately for the cloth-covered case. And saw Malec watching him.

"You don't know whether I brought it or not. Guess."

Kimball couldn't.

Malec waved him off. "It's not you and me anymore, Mr. Kimball. It's me and Wilcox. Just the two of us. The match is between us and you're out of it." His eyelids slowly lowered.

Kimball stood rooted, his thoughts reeling. This would be the last time he'd ever be in the same room with Rudy Malec, he was sure of it. *There must be some way to stop him.*

When Malec spoke again he seemed delirious. "Nobody's ever figured out any of the things I've done . . . the girl's parents never found me, either."

"What girl, Rudy?" *Keep him talking. Think.*

He was rambling to himself. "She was five . . . but real strong. I held her under until she stopped moving. Her yellow hair . . . it floated around, and bubbles popped out her mouth. Stuff came out her nose, too. White stuff. When I went back next day she was bloated. I pulled her out . . . hid her in old refrigerator . . . around all the time, but they never asked . . . a little boy couldn't be smart enough. I was laughing . . ." He opened his eyes dreamily. "Probably two hundred bodies out there in that trench, all bloated." He tried to smile. "And I did it."

Good God, he expects me to applaud. Kimball wanted to ask where? In what trench? but couldn't. Malec's story had made him physically ill. He began backing toward the door.

"Where you going, Mr. Kimball?" Malec pulled himself upright. "Hey, Mr. Kimball, listen to me! I haven't told you about the deep Atlantic trench. MR. KIMBALL!"

The door closed behind him. *He's monstrous.* Miles would never go back.

Malec watched Kimball leave with shock so profound it made him gasp. *He walked out on me.* For a moment he sat there, trembling. *He thinks I'm nothing.*

Rage followed immediately. He jumped off the couch and slammed his fist into a lamp, sending it hurtling to the floor.

Sick as he was, he left Mary Helen's and went home. He began planning his next move, the biggest, smartest feat yet. The Grand Finale. After it happened, they'd know who it was. Him. Rudy Malec. *The whole world will know. People will listen when I talk.*

Until late Thursday afternoon, Wilcox worked with Joe Palm, looking over the plane's control systems, especially those that affected the brakes. As expected, they found nothing. "Maybe Washington will give us a clue when they examine the computer boards," said Palm.

"Possibly," Wilcox said.

"You got any ideas?"

Wilcox shook his head. "None." His mysterious-saboteur theory wouldn't go over any better with Palm than it did with everyone else.

Palm said offhandedly, "It makes you wonder. The plane just finished one of its 'C' checks."

"It did? Where?"

"Right here. In Minneapolis."

"Interesting," said Wilcox. Together, they walked back across the field toward the terminal. The wind was gusting and snowflakes appeared sporadically, blowing in confused circles like tiny feathers. Palm glanced at the sky. "Strange weather for April. Snow two days ago, and now again today. No wonder the Scandahoovians settled here."

"Yeah," said Wilcox, but his mind was elsewhere. The day's last plane to Los Angeles would leave in one hour. With snow threatening, he ought to be on it.

But this would be his last chance to look over those maintenance reports.

In a rush now, he said good-bye to Palm, and as soon as his colleague was out of sight, he diverted in another direction, hoping the "C" check records were still in Minneapolis.

They were.

Sitting in a tiny office at one end of the maintenance hangar, he pored over sheets of paper, studying signatures, searching for clues. Suddenly aware of the passage of time, he looked at his watch and sucked in his breath guiltily. It had already been an hour and a half; the plane to Los Angeles was gone. Friday morning would have to suffice.

For the next hour he lost himself in paperwork.

And then he found something. On his second go-around he noticed one of the signatures for an exchange of computer boards was partially overwritten, as though the signer had started to write a name and changed his mind and written something else. It was hard to see on casual examination, which was why he'd missed it earlier.

He held the paper up, looking at it with a light behind it, at the same time trying to minimize his own fingerprints.

Sure enough, he could read certain letters: an *R* something, a *D*, then another letter, and what he thought was an *M* and an *A* to start the last name before the writer realized his mistake and stopped. The overwriting, in pen, had been firm and intentionally obscuring. The top name seemed to be Bart Smith, the same number of letters as whatever was underneath.

Using the authority of his badge, Wilcox took possession of the maintenance sheet, wrapped it carefully in borrowed cellophane, and put it in his briefcase. One of the crime labs in Los Angeles would decipher the written-over words. He hoped to God they could get fingerprints as well.

Friday morning at dawn, awakened by his travel alarm, Wilcox went to the window. His heart sank. He saw nothing but white, endless snow boiling out of the sky in a tumultuous swirl that could only be described as a blizzard.

Knowing before he asked what the answer would be, he phoned the terminal. As he'd guessed, the situation was hopeless; no planes were coming in or going out. He was stranded.

With a dull sense of remorse, he knew he'd given the job too much. To get that one signature he'd sacrificed Jamie and Ellie. He sat down heavily on the bed, envisioning them both at the rehearsal dinner, feigning festivity, simmering with resentment. He'd seen it before.

Unwillingly he conjured up the image of a young girl thrown onto a pyre to appease some nameless god. Oh, he knew what the god was, all right. But none of them would understand. Nor would he expect them to.

He went into the bathroom to shave, for once appalled by the affable, calm look of his own face. *You fool.*

Because it was too early to call California, he went downstairs for breakfast, and at ten took a chance that Ellie would be up.

"Ellie—"

"Where are you?"

"In Minneapolis. It's snowing. Honey, it's snowing so hard no planes are going out. I'm—"

She interrupted him. "And I'm taking your phone calls and getting harassed. On top of the wedding and everything else, a Mr. Topping has called four times and doesn't believe you're still out of town. He acts like I'm lying."

Wilcox groaned. "Ellie, I'm sorry. Did he say what he wants?"

"No. And he won't leave his phone number, either. He says he'll keep calling until you get back. Whenever *that* is. Obviously you'll miss the rehearsal dinner. If you miss the wedding too, Mark Brody will walk Jamie down the aisle."

How could he apologize? Did words exist that could make up for his not being there the night before his daughter's wedding?

He doubted it. Yet he said, "Ellie, yesterday late, I got a clue that's vital to unraveling this conspiracy. It's—"

She cut him off. In the coldest of tones she said, "Mark wants to talk to you. I'll tell him you're at the Holiday Inn. You *will* try to make it for the wedding itself. Tomorrow?" She didn't wait for an answer. When he tried to say something, all he heard was a dial tone.

The snow continued unabated, and the airport remained closed. Wilcox spent the day reading and watching television.

At four his time, the phone rang and Mark Brody began without preamble, "The results just came in from that computer board you sent to Washington after the Las Vegas incident. Tom Peterson wanted me to tell you the computer chips checked out normal—no aberrations."

"Oh," said Wilcox. There seemed to be no other response.

"One other thing. The Bureau of Field Operations is coming down on your case. The director got wind that you showed up on this accident in Minneapolis—which you didn't tell *me* about, by the way. He called and gave me the business about you, and what the hell was I supposed to say? When I didn't even know you'd gone?"

"Mark, I—"

"Goddam it, Wilcox, you're making me look bad, and I'm beginning to think, Screw you, why should I go on covering your butt like this? For almost a month I've gone along with your bizarre behavior— ever since the dump over the Atlantic. But I'm finished, I'm not going to cover you any longer. Are you crazy, Alan? Have you flipped out?"

That's what I once wondered about you. "No, Mark. I haven't. You can believe this or not as you like, but I'm finally on to something. I've got here—"

His boss broke in, "All the physical evidence says you've got nothing. Every goddam thing you've sent to Washington came back negative."

"I've got a signature—"

"What's a signature?"

"Listen to me, Mark, for one minute. I found a signature on one of the 'C' checks that was written over twice. Somebody started to write a different name and changed his mind. It's very significant."

"And that's *all* you've got. If you're going to lay a whole string of events—this whole damned so-called conspiracy—on one miswritten signature, you really *are* losing it. What you've got is survivor's guilt syndrome about Higgins—nothing else. Now listen! I haven't even gotten to the real purpose of this call, Alan. You've not only blown any chance at the director's job, they're talking of transferring you to Anchorage."

"Anchorage!" Wilcox sat up straighter, immediately furious. Brody might as well have said Siberia. Anchorage was the outer fringes, tantamount to banishment. You went to Anchorage when your effectiveness was gone. "That is the goddamnedest threat I've ever heard— hard to believe it's coming from you. I *thought* we were friends, Mark, but I'm obviously wrong. If I weren't so bloody well convinced about this conspiracy, I'd hang it all up. Tell you to shove your job." His face was red and he was trembling with rage.

"Watch yourself, Alan." Brody's voice was cold. "Anchorage wasn't my idea."

"Why tell me, then?"

"Because you've got to know, that's why." More kindly, "I know it's a lot to throw at you all at once. If you give up this obsession, I may be able to talk them out of the transfer. Meanwhile, try to get here before the damned wedding, will you? Jamie's going to take it hard if *I* walk her down the aisle."

"You bet I'll try." *Oh, will I try.* Brody's walking his daughter down the aisle was the last thing on earth he wanted. He could hardly refrain from slamming down the phone.

There's no place to hide, Miles Kimball thought dully, as he passed a newsstand on his way to lunch. The Minneapolis accident was big headlines. Two more people had died, bringing the total to five. The investigators were coming up with nothing, as they'd done ever since he first met Malec. *They won't find "nothing" forever.*

And what about the big one, he wondered for the first time—the plane that went down over the Atlantic? Did the maniac cause that, too? Trenches . . . had he heard Malec say Atlantic trenches?

Something had happened to him after that event, he realized now—a blanking out of the episode as though it had never happened. Denial. To the already guilt-ridden, some events were too terrible to contemplate.

That night Kimball went to the Sunny Day Center and with his first glance at Sondra knew it was going to be the worst night of his life.

Chapter Thirty-one

Sondra's eyes were only half open as Miles entered the room. She tried to open them all the way but couldn't, and with a terrible shock he saw Death on her face, as though the word were chalked across her forehead.

At the top of a bed cranked partway up, her head lolled, and under the sheet near her chest was a thick, unnatural curve.

He went to her and tenderly kissed her on the cheek, shocked again by the cool dryness of her skin. Curious about the hump under the sheet, he lifted it and looked. Sondra's chest was encased in a large, round green dome that rose and fell rhythmically. He realized it was helping her breathe.

She whispered, "Hi!"

"Hi," he said, hardly able to breathe himself.

Laboriously she smiled, hunching her shoulders with effort. She said softly, "It won't . . . be long . . ."

"No, Sondra . . . no." Shaking his head in denial, he lifted her gently and put his arm under her shoulders. And noticed she was so tiny, weighed so little. "Honey, we've still got—" he broke off, not finishing, because it struck him that you don't lie in the face of death. *If I can't be honest with her now—then when?*

Without a hint of sadness she whispered, "I . . . woun't want . . . years." She gasped and fell silent.

Suddenly he wanted to tell her everything, to confess about Mary Helen while she was still conscious—and realized before he spoke it was he who would be helped, not her, he who'd be seeking absolution for his crime. He could only be punished sufficiently by not telling her. *Even your priest can't help. You will do lifelong penance for this.*

For a long time, until his body ached from the awkward position, he perched on the edge of her mattress holding her. Eventually his spine and shoulders gave out, so he drew up a chair close to her bed and sat silently holding her hand. And gave way to tears. Which was all right because she wasn't looking.

She seemed to sleep.

When her eyes opened again, she motioned him to come closer. "You . . . your girlfren . . . it's okay."

His eyes gaped open. But he forced himself not to draw back, not to register his shock. My God, how much did she know?

"You . . . luv me . . . Miles." She forced a smile, and scrabbled for air and a few more words, "so . . . 'ts okay."

"Oh, Sondra. I do love you, I do love you," he cried over and over, weeping openly now, because she meant so much to him and when she was gone he'd have no one left. His hands were on her face, reaching past the respirator, stroking her hair, stroking the cool skin. Patting her. Fondling her. Pouring out his love because he sensed they had such a short time.

Her skin. It seemed somehow colder, and after a while he drew back and looked at her.

Her eyes were closed. The respirator moved up and down, but he surmised it worked for no purpose. He put his fingers to her lips. Air moved, but was it hers?

Desperate, he grappled for her hand and found it limp.

Sondra was gone.

The Minneapolis airport opened again just past noon on Saturday. At twelve-forty-five, Wilcox was sitting in a plane bound for Orange County. At home it was almost eleven in the morning, and the wedding would begin at twelve-thirty.

Wilcox wouldn't be there before three-fifteen.

Waiting for takeoff, he sat in his first-class seat trying to read a magazine whose words had no meaning, while his mind detoured back to his noon call to Ellie and the bitterness in her voice. "I knew you wouldn't make it, Alan. I'm not surprised at all." Then she wouldn't let him speak, but calmly ended the conversation with, "I have to go now, Jamie needs me."

It was worse than the ugliest marital fight he could imagine.

The four hours aloft were brutal; Alan couldn't relax, couldn't stop reaching mentally for home. The minute the plane landed in Orange County, he ran across the terminal and across two parking lots, then in brief circles looking for his car. With his foot pushing on the gas pedal, he seemed to be running still.

At ten past three he pulled up in front of the Westin South Coast Plaza Hotel, threw his keys at an attendant, and raced to the Garden Court where the reception was being held.

The outdoor courtyard was empty.

He looked around in bewilderment. The fountain bubbled merrily, and from the archway and trees hung a riot of blue and white balloons tied with ribbons. Dirty dishes sat on scattered tables. He rushed to the maid who was gathering them up. "Where is everybody?"

"No Englesh," she said, smiling apologetically.

At three-twenty the party should still be going.

He ran again. Not caring that the receptionist at the front desk was busy with customers, he almost shouted. "Where's the Wilcox wedding party?"

The woman looked up and saw his expression. "Are you—?"

"I'm the bride's father. Where are they?"

"The party ended about forty minutes ago." Her hands dropped to her sides in a gesture that begged him not to ask more.

"Why? Why did it end?" He felt ragged, out of control.

"It's . . . you'll have to call your wife. She'll tell you."

"Tell me WHAT? What in hell is going on?"

She drew back. "Please, Mr. Wilcox, try to be calm. I really don't know much. Call your wife."

"Is my daughter all right?"

"Yes. Yes. Your daughter is fine."

"Then what?"

"It's something about your son."

In the nearest phone booth, Alan punched in his telephone number and listened as the phone rang and rang, an accompaniment to the pounding of his heart. No one answered.

He stood in the lobby of the Westin at a loss. *Todd. It must be Todd.*

Not knowing what else to do, he went home.

Nobody was there. Frantic, he raced from one room to another. Everywhere he saw evidence of a wedding: Jamie's froth of a wedding dress discarded in a bedroom, a pyramid of wedding gifts in the living room, Ellie's street clothes piled on their bed. The house was an ancient mastodon frozen cataclysmically in the arctic with buttercups still in its stomach.

At last Wilcox thought to call Mark Brody.

He found his family on the second floor of St. Joseph's Hospital sitting in a small lobby off one of the main halls. His first impression was of people incongruously dressed. Ellie still wore her long, rose-colored mother-of-the-bride dress, but Jamie, the bride, was in blue jeans.

As a group they did a double take. Jamie cried, "Dad!" and everyone stood—everyone but Ellie. They formed a circle around him and waited for what he would say.

He took his daughter in his arms, and over her shoulder he saw the anger on Ellie's face. "Jamie . . ." He heard his own hoarse voice saying, "Baby, I'm sorry." There was more to say, apologies without end, but somehow the words stuck in his throat.

At a loss, he sat down. "How is he, Ellie?"

She shook her head. "He's still in surgery." She sat hunched on a small couch, staring at the floor. While he watched she dropped her head in her hand and quietly began to weep.

At that Jamie burst into tears, and her new husband, Brent Fischer, in formal pants and a T-shirt, put his arm around her.

Alan turned to his oldest son, oddly garbed in parts of a tuxedo. Like the mastodon, thought Wilcox remotely, he'd been caught with his buttercups. "Tell me what happened, Doug. Mark Brody didn't say much."

"We don't know exactly," Doug began. Lines of worry creased his forehead and aged him; he wasn't a twenty-year-old kid any longer. "The bartender at the reception came to Mom and told her Todd had had quite a few beers, he thought she should know. She tried to find him and couldn't, so she asked me to look for him. When I couldn't spot him anywhere near the Garden Court, I went out to the front of the hotel and saw the getaway car was gone. With all the streamers and old shoes and everything.

"I couldn't believe Todd would take it, but he did. The police found the car smashed up on the 55 freeway, not far from St. Jo's."

Alan groaned. "What . . . how bad are his injuries?"

"They didn't tell us exactly. He'd already left the emergency room. His neck, someone said. And one of his legs. Nobody's been out to talk to us yet."

My son. My son. In the pit of Wilcox's stomach the upheaval already under way became calamitous, and he left the group at a run. A few yards down the hall he found the men's room just in time.

When he returned, Dr. Berkman, still in surgical greens, was talking to the family. Pulling off his cap, Berkman gave Wilcox a tired nod. "He won't be paralyzed. The paramedics did a good job getting him into a neck brace before he came to and made the displacement worse." Alan glanced at Ellie, who'd been listening raptly and now began to nod with tears in her eyes. He put his hand on her shoulder. "I'm sorry, the rest isn't as good. He may lose his left foot."

Ellie gasped.

Alan felt he'd been walking a tightrope. Safe until now. And then the rope broke.

Dr. Berkman went on. "The foot was crushed when the engine broke loose. So many bones were damaged, we—"

"Oh no!" Ellie broke in, shaking her head. "Dear God." Turning away, she walked to a corner chair and sat down. No sound came from the corner, to Wilcox more ominous than tears. His two children stared at the doctor, horrified.

Alan drew in a breath. "Is there any chance on the foot? Any chance at all?"

"We'll know in a few days. It isn't life-threatening. And we'll save it if we can. If we can't, he can be fitted with a prosthesis in new, lightweight plastic. Young men like Todd can do almost anything . . ."

Don't say any more, thought Wilcox, blotting him out. *Don't tell us about prostheses . . . about Todd with an artificial foot.*

Dr. Berkman must have finished his spiel. Alan wasn't even sure. All he knew was, the doctor was leaving.

The doctor was gone, and Alan and Ellie sat in the small room, but not together. When he joined Ellie on the couch, she moved to a chair. Doug, Jamie, and Brent had returned to the house. She said bitterly, "It was a good wedding. And a good party, for as long as it lasted."

"Ellie, I didn't choose this."

"He wouldn't have gotten drunk if you'd been there."

"You don't know that. Neither do I."

She turned on him furiously. "How could *I* keep track of Todd and all the guests and make sure things were running smoothly? How *could* I?"

She, who was never weepy, began to cry again, sobbing, becoming almost hysterical while Alan looked on, not knowing how to comfort her—or even if she'd let him.

Suddenly he didn't care whether she'd let him. He pulled a chair beside hers and reached across and took her in his arms, holding her, murmuring to her, rocking her. "Ellie. Ellie. Shh. It's okay. Todd's going to live, that's the important thing. He'll be okay in time. I love you, Ellie. Shh. Shhh." *I love you more than I thought it possible to love a woman.* Only dimly did he note that she never relaxed, never yielded to him in any way. Holding her was like gripping a board.

They saw Todd asleep, pale, with his head encircled by a metal ring whose four pins seemed mercilessly driven into his skull. His left foot, wrapped in bandages, was elevated by an ankle pulley. His nose was swollen and his chin abraded. Through the swollen nose he snored.

Ellie looked at him without speaking. After a while she said, "Snoring can sound—redeeming."

Later, sitting stiffly on the living room couch at home, Ellie gestured toward the newlyweds. "Go ahead and go, you two. Todd won't miss you."

Jamie and Brent exchanged doubtful glances.

"We do have a phone . . . you can call us."

When the two still looked uncertain, she said, "You think I want two more people hanging around to be fed?"

Alan saw them to the door, mustering a smile. "Todd would gladly sacrifice your company for a Kapalua T-shirt."

Between Alan and Ellie nothing was resolved. Ellie, no longer pointedly cold, nevertheless had little to say. In silence she made Alan a sandwich for dinner, and without comment wandered into the family room and tucked her legs under her to watch television. To Wilcox the house felt like Anchorage.

He dropped into his own big easy chair. "Turn off the television, Ellie."

"Why?" She wouldn't look at him.

"We need to talk."

"I don't think so, Alan. You expressed yourself very well by missing the wedding. Your values, what's *really* important to you is crystal clear. There's nothing more to be said." She switched channels.

"Damn it! TURN OFF THE TELEVISION!"

"Oh! You're shouting now?"

"This isn't like you! Being totally unreasonable. Bitchy."

She sighed. "Maybe I'm tired. Maybe this isn't me, I don't know. Maybe we just don't understand each other. Last week I thought I knew you, and then I found I didn't." She turned down the sound.

"It won't help to go on punishing me, you won't gain anything. I meant to be at the wedding, dammit, I tried—"

"Not hard enough."

"It was a blizzard. Nobody was going anywhere."

"That wasn't the day you blew it." She turned to him with the venom back in her eyes. "You know, I was thinking of divorcing you. I decided I'd walk out right after the wedding. And I still would, if I had the energy."

His own anger rose to meet hers. "Okay, you've said your piece. Now you'd better listen. This isn't some personal lark I've been on, it's not a cat-and-mouse chase with a lot of curious clues that will turn out to be amusing some day. There's someone out there who's been bringing down planes, a madman, and right now, this very minute, he's probably planning to sabotage another. He's already killed a planeload of people. Three hundred human beings, Ellie! If I don't find out who's doing it, there's going to be another disaster, another whole planeload strewn across the landscape. I couldn't ignore all those lives."

She wasn't moved. Rearranging herself casually on the couch, she said, "What's new? You've *always* been in the lives-saving business. What about *our* lives? Mine and the kids'?" She looked at him sideways. "You know, Mark doesn't believe all that stuff. He thinks you're the madman. He said there's no evidence at all to support your theories. He told me last night they've had some of the other field men double-checking behind you, and there's nothing. Absolutely nothing."

"So—Mark has more credibility than I do . . . and how long have you known me?"

"I didn't say that."

"In effect you did." He clenched his fists. "In light of the last two days, I guess it's expectable that your compassion would go. Even your humanity."

"Not fair, Alan. Not fair." She sighed. "I didn't want to tell you this—not today—not after Todd—but it won't matter much longer what you think about . . . the madman. They're going to fire you. Mark's going to ask for your badge."

He turned white. He could actually feel the blood draining out of his face, leaving him so weak he felt paralyzed. While the clock ticked in the front hall and outside a mockingbird fired up, he sat without moving, his disbelief registered in a jaw that hung slack.

He closed his mouth. *I must have the badge.*

Later they went to bed in silence. As though she'd handpicked this latest calamity, he wanted no part of their marriage, or her. She willed it, he thought. She wanted Mark to fire him. He couldn't shake the notion that his own wife, Ellie Wilcox, had kicked the props out from under him.

Before she rolled away from him in bed, she said, "An Admiral Franklin called you from Norfolk. He wants you to call him back."

Big deal, thought Alan. Big goddam deal.

A short time later her breathing changed, so he was sure she'd fallen asleep. In every marriage, he thought grimly, someone stays awake full of fury and someone else blithely falls asleep.

An hour later he was still awake when the phone rang. Shocked by its shrillness in their quiet bedroom, he jumped up automatically to shield Ellie. Reflexes . . . a lifetime's commitment to protecting each other. That's what you got for twenty-five years of marriage. Sometimes, it seemed, that's *all* you got.

He pulled the phone out into the hall where she couldn't hear and softly closed the door.

"Yes?" he said. And received the third shock of the day.

Chapter Thirty-two

He'd never heard the voice before. Excitable. High-pitched. A man's voice, not backed up with much testosterone. "Is this the Alan Wilcox who works for the National Transportation Safety Board?"

Wilcox stiffened. The caller was strangely eager, somehow disturbing. He asked warily, "Who is this?"

"You wouldn't know if I told you. Besides, that would ruin the challenge." The man laughed—brief mirthless laughter.

"What challenge? Who is this?" Wilcox asked again, more sharply. In the quiet of night the voice had the power to make his skin crawl.

"That's just a detail, Wilcox. I'm letting you hear my voice so you'll know I'm real."

It's him, thought Wilcox, trying to stay calm. *He couldn't resist.* He felt both exhilaration and a horrible foreboding, already knowing what the message would be. "I'm glad you called," he said, buying time. "That was wise of you." Did his own voice waver a little?

"Thanks. You've known about me, haven't you? You've known all along I'm smart?"

"Of course," Wilcox said evenly. "Right from the beginning." *Good God, he's infantile.* "But you'll have to tell me who you are. How can I appreciate someone if I don't know his name?"

More laughter. "You're smart, too, Wilcox. It's obvious. I really admire you."

Wilcox thought, *This is ludicrous—all these damned compliments.* "You want to know why I called?"

No. The dread began again, and he steeled himself. The conversation was infused with overtones of death; it had vibrated with death and insanity from the moment the man began to speak. He felt as if all normal standards had disappeared from the earth.

Silently he held the phone, too sickened to answer.

"You do want to know," said the man. "Tomorrow there's going to be a big one on takeoff. Watch for it."

"Where?" he asked. "What time?"

"Come on, Wilcox, figure it out. I'll just tell you one more thing. It's in eight hours. Eight hours from now we'll both know who's the winner here, you or me. Okay?" With a last peal of laughter, his informant hung up.

Eight hours. For a moment Wilcox felt dazed. His heart pounded mercilessly and he stood in the hall gripping the phone like a lifeline. Somehow he'd never imagined he'd be speaking to a killer. A psychopath. Without a voice the man had remained anonymous, an idea more than bones-and-flesh reality. Suddenly Wilcox preferred him that way—formless, untouchable.

Matching wits with a known adversary, elements of hate and malice would color his efforts. He could already feel it starting.

He put down the phone and went out to the kitchen. Exactly 11:00 P.M.

Tomorrow, he thought. Good God, I'm not ready, there's too much left to do. Too many clues still untracked. And Todd . . . What will I do about Todd?

He considered waking Ellie—and couldn't rob her of more sleep. Instead he wrote her a note, repeating the gist of what the sick voice had said, begging her to understand. "Ellie, I love you and Todd with all my heart. I wouldn't leave now . . . you know me well enough to know I'd stay right here if it was anything less than this." He propped the note against the phone out in the hall.

In five minutes he was dressed and his badge was in his pocket. With the help of a full moon, he drove eighty miles an hour toward Hawthorne.

Somebody has to know, Malec thought. Somebody. Whether Wilcox had gotten the whole picture or not, he couldn't tell. He should have spoken plainer, stopped playing games. He paced the corridor outside the men's room in Building 23, wishing he'd done it differently. Eventually he stopped and dialed again. This time he'd use the exact words and be sure the man understood.

He let the phone ring awhile. Only this time nobody answered.

Ellie heard the distant ringing as part of a dream. She fought the sound, incorporating it into a fragmented scene that played itself out in the wild Technicolor of her subconscious.

The sound wouldn't stop. Awaking, she reached for the phone—realizing at last that it was someplace else.

Eventually she found it in the hall, but by then the ringing had stopped.

She stood there, perplexed. What was the phone doing so far from their bed? And where was Alan?

And then she saw the note. Feeling groggy from a sleeping pill, she took it back to the bedroom and switched on the light.

Sitting on the edge of the bed, she read it once and then again. So it had finally happened. Alan had found his man and he was real.

Her heart went out to Alan—wherever he was, out there in the middle of the night chasing his saboteur, an honest-to-god person at last. Somebody with a body, a voice, a way to make threats. Somebody tangible. Why hadn't she taken Alan seriously?

Flooded with waves of guilt, she stood up and walked to her bureau and picked up her husband's picture. For long moments she gazed at his unsmiling face, so serious, so ridiculously intense. *My God! I deserted him!* She could hardly believe it—she, Ellie, who'd always thought of herself as the understanding wife, brimming over with patience.

When it really counted, she hadn't been understanding at all.

Odd, she thought. She'd believed him until the wedding, and then she'd stopped. As though his letting her down on that one occasion had changed everything. From that moment she'd listened only to his detractors—to Brody, who was supposed to be his friend. Some friend, she thought bitterly.

Only guessing he might be there, she dialed Alan's office. She let the phone ring and ring. Ten, fifteen, twenty times.

Nothing. God knows where he'd gone.

Chagrined that she'd been so disloyal, she hung up carelessly and stomped back to bed.

She never heard the staccato beeps that signal a phone off the hook.

*   *   *

Beside himself, Miles Kimball parked in front of Mary Helen's house. Had she, or had she not, told Sondra about them . . . he had to know. *Sondra. Sondra. Were you just guessing?*

Moving like an automaton, used up by grief, he knocked, and when Mary Helen didn't answer, he scribbled a note on the back of a bank deposit slip, slid it into the crack of her door, and got back in his car. But his mind was focused inward, so full of agony he scarcely saw the road—or signs or anything else. It was a wonder he saw the flashing red lights behind him.

Dazed, he found himself stopped and looking into a flashlight—then fumbling for his driver's license and registration.

The flashlight moved to one side and a stern face appeared. "Have you been drinking?"

"No, Officer. Nothing."

"Are you on some kind of medication?" The policeman peered at him, searching his face.

"No. Please tell me why I was stopped."

"You were all over the road. First one lane, then the other."

Dully. "I wasn't aware. I—my wife just died."

"I see." A nod. The man's voice was kinder now. "I'm sorry, sir. Do you live far from here?"

"Just a few blocks."

"Try to keep the car on the road, then." He switched off his light. "Take care."

Kimball pulled into traffic. *Take care of what? Me? Her? She's already taken care of.*

Rudy Malec decided to make one more phone call. But he dialed with resentment burning his gut. Telling Kimball was only slightly better than telling no one.

Though he caught the phone's last ring, Miles wished immediately he hadn't. It was that high, raspy voice again, all too familiar, but now with undertones of fury. "Mr. Kimball, this time you'd better listen. DON'T HANG UP. Watch for Trans America Fleet, flight 255, taking off in seven and a half hours. When it happens, *you'll know I'm a genius.* You'll never walk out on me again." He sounded on the verge of collapse.

"You should see a psychiatrist . . ."

"The devil is with me, Mr. Kimball. Why would I need a shrink?"

Afterward Miles felt it was *he* who'd communed with the devil. He went to the bathroom and stared into the mirror. *Your life is a shambles anyway. Make the call.*

As Kimball fumbled the message to whoever answered the phone, he sensed that his semihysterical voice was making him sound screwier than Rudy Malec. Worse still, he'd forgotten part of it. All he remembered was the seven and a half hours and the Trans America Fleet. He hoped to God it would be enough.

The regional duty officer at the Com Center in Hawthorne looked at his watch and jotted down the time. Twelve-ten. Then he casually made a note of the message, the third such vague threat against an airline that evening. Before morning there'd doubtless be more, multiplied in all the Com Centers around the country. For some reason the weirdos always surfaced under a full moon.

He took a break. In a couple of minutes he'd have to respond by making phone calls.

Rudy Malec scribbled Miles Kimball's name and phone number on a requisition sheet and taped it to his locker. Sooner or later somebody would come looking, and what he wanted them to look at, besides himself, was the man who'd had the gall to walk away when he was talking.

The blank subpoena forms were buried deep in Mark Brody's desk. Scrounging among Mark's papers, Wilcox found something that contained his boss's signature, and with painstaking effort signed several forms in a close approximation of Brody's handwriting.

As he headed out the front door, the office phone began to ring. For the briefest moment he paused with his hand on the doorknob. No. There wasn't time. As he rushed down the hall he heard it still ringing, ever more dimly. Somebody was awfully damned persistent.

By twelve-fifteen he was back in the car again, heading south toward San Diego at insane speeds.

I shouldn't have done it. My career is over.

*   *   *

Mary Helen got in at twelve-twenty, astonished and pleased to find Miles's message. *Oh, honey, I'm on my way.*

Minutes later she was at his door. "You're coming back to me!" she cried the minute she saw him. Before he could stop her, she was in the living room.

"I'm not coming back, Mary Helen." This was going to be worse than he thought. "The note asked you to call. Why didn't you?"

"Oh, Miles, that's so . . . impersonal." Smiling, she settled into his favorite chair.

He stared at her. *Don't get comfortable.* "All I want is an answer. Did you or did you not tell Sondra about us?"

For a moment she seemed perplexed, and then, pulling her blue sweater off and dropping it on the leather arm, she said, "Well, no. I just went in one day and said you and I had become close friends. I thought she'd be pleased to know. I said you'd shared so many wonderful things—"

"That was *telling* her!" he exploded. "Do you think she was stupid? Did you imagine her brain had stopped functioning? Didn't you listen to *anything* I said, that Sondra's mind was as good at the end as it was in the beginning, that she—," he couldn't finish. Instead, to his chagrin, his chest began heaving and the sobs he thought safely trapped inside broke free. He heard his own voice making animal sounds he couldn't control.

With a ferocious act of will he started for his own front door.

Mary Helen intercepted him and tried to put her arm around his waist, making it impossible for him to leave.

"Don't touch me!" he said, low and threatening.

She pulled away, looking up at him with innocence and bewilderment and the beginnings of tears.

He wasn't fooled anymore. It was an act. A deliberate, calculated maneuver, as spiteful in its intent as any act of Malec's. And dishonest as well.

Furious, he opened the door.

She followed. "Miles! Miles! You need me."

"I need to get away. I'm going to San Diego." His mind raced. "To the airport. To Airtech. Here are your house keys." He pulled them from his pocket and tossed them past her onto the rug.

"Wait!" she cried, standing in his doorway. "Do you know how much I've done for you? Did I ever tell you I saved Stirling—just me?"

"What are you talking about?"

"Come back inside, Miles."

His eyes narrowed. "Tell me from here."

She began explaining without thinking. "I wrote memos and sent them to Trans America Fleet, I let them know the Airtech planes had problems, I—"

"So it was *you*," he said in soft, white-hot anger. "You, Mary Helen. Just like your nephew!" The wrath he felt for Malec transferred to her. His fists clenched and his biceps tightened with murderous, nearly uncontrollable desire. *I could kill her,* he thought. *Right now I could kill this woman.* He could almost feel her throat inside his hands, see her eyes bulge, gangland style. The impulse grew and blinded him. He moved toward her.

And instead controlled himself and fled to his car.

The regional duty officer looked up the phone number for Trans America Fleet's director of safety, and while the phone rang he rifled through his memos for any special admonitions relating to TAF. Ah! He found one.

Bruce Cavalier's sleepy voice said, "What's up?" and the officer told him, adding, "Please hang on. I'm going to patch you in to Alan Wilcox."

Wilcox's line rang busy. The duty officer had no recourse but to call his boss, Mark Brody—not his first choice at one in the morning. But Wilcox, he recalled now, had sounded pretty adamant when he asked to be alerted to all threats relating to Airtech or Trans America Fleet.

It took only minutes for the duty officer to reach Brody, explain the nature of the threat, and patch him in to Bruce Cavalier.

Brody began, "This seems pretty routine to me, Bruce, the usual crackpot stuff. I'm not sure how seriously we have to take it."

Cavalier responded sharply. "With what's been happening to our Airtech planes, we're taking *everything* seriously. Alan Wilcox said—"

Before he could stop himself, Brody said, "We'll have to leave him out of it. Now . . . once we've alerted all Airtech flights departing within the next twelve hours, we—"

"Is there some problem with Alan Wilcox?"

Brody hesitated, preferring not to share his personnel problems with anyone outside the Board. The situation was particularly awkward in a case like this, where Wilcox had been working so closely with Cavalier. "Let's say we're beginning to doubt Wilcox's judgment in some matters."

"As in, for instance, the incidents with Trans America Fleet, I gather."

"Well, yes."

"He has theories you don't agree with?"

"Not just me, Bruce. There's been no corroboration anywhere. So we'll have to discount him in this discussion. He's got an obsession about Airtech planes that goes way beyond reason—probably because he's been working too hard. Which is one of the ironies. Until recently—until flight 160 disappeared—Wilcox was one of our best investigators."

Cavalier said stiffly, "He may still be. He called up one day and told me those theories, and I'll tell you, to us he makes sense. What's happening to our Airtech fleet isn't random stuff, it has to be deliberate, some kind of obscene plan. Wilcox told me he's had to do a lot of investigating without Board sanction because he can't get anyone to listen."

"You think we haven't listened to him? By the hour?"

"Listen, maybe yes. Take him seriously, apparently not. Over here we're beginning to wonder if the NTSB is more worried about airframe politics than public safety."

Brody's blood pressure suddenly shot up. He said hotly, "I resent that accusation, Bruce. I find it reckless and ill considered. No one knows better than you that we cut through *every kind* of politics to get at the truth. If I thought Wilcox was behaving normally I'd give him all the support in the world, which you know full well."

"So what's normal? In the context of what's been going on, his behavior seems damn near restrained."

"Bruce!" Brody said sharply, "you're out of your territory! Wilcox has been running amok, breaking every damn rule in the book! When the methods turn bizarre, the theories behind them become suspect. We *can't* disregard his abnormal behavior."

Cavalier said, "All right, then. We each know where we stand. But in the event he's right, Mark, we've got a time problem. That eight hours is sliding away fast."

"Here's what I propose—"

Before he could finish, the duty officer broke in. "I've had an urgent call from Washington—the director of the Bureau of Accident Investigation wants me to put together a conference call in one hour

with both of you and the Laboratory Services at the Bureau of Technology. If you'll both hang up and stand by, I'll be getting back to you."

Max Topping had awakened in the middle of the night knowing what
he had to do. *If I can't reach Wilcox, I'll have to stop Kimball myself.*

Two punches on the man's doorbell produced no answer. The third
had to wake him. He surveyed the richly carved door, waiting impatiently for his saboteur.

He was rewarded. He heard the rattle of a chain and the door opened
fast. To his astonishment a woman stood there smiling seductively,
looking right at him.

His mouth fell open. She was naked.

Before he saw very much, she gasped and swung away, all in one
motion.

"Oh shit!" he said to her retreating behind. He had a momentary
glimpse of dimpled flesh—very white, very full—disappearing around
a corner. His surprise, mingled with the intensity of his mission, ren-
dered the view meaningless; her rear might as well have been carved
in marble.

But now he had a problem: should he leave or stay?

When she didn't return, he rang the doorbell again and shouted into
the empty room, "Where's Kimball?"

Eventually she returned wearing a man's shirt.

"Haven't you had enough?" she said, glaring at him. "What do you
want?" With a quick swipe, she tried to push him off the stoop. "He's
not here."

Topping stuck an expensive leather shoe in the door. "I'll leave when
you tell me where he is."

"None of your damned business." She looked down at his shoe,
frowning.

With that his patience vanished, and he grabbed her shoulders and
shook her. He couldn't seem to stop. "WISE UP, LADY! GET SMART!"
He dropped his hands. "Whoever you are, you don't *know* this Kimball.
He's not what you think. He's got a private, sinister life, and if you've
got any brains you'll take yourself out of here. He's dangerous! Now
WHERE IS HE?" Suddenly aware he might have miscalculated, he
said slowly, "Or maybe you're part of the conspiracy?" He looked her
up and down, eyes narrowing. "I wouldn't cover for him if I were you."
The threat was as dark as he knew how to make it.

The fight went out of her. "He's in San Diego," she said, with no energy in her voice. "Somewhere. That is, if he gets there. I didn't believe him. I thought he'd be right back."

"Thank you," said Topping.

For the next hour Wilcox drove like the lead car at Indianapolis, watching constantly in his rearview mirror for the inevitable flashing red lights. If some policeman stopped him his badge would be all he needed—and he might even get a police escort the rest of the way. God knows, he could use the help. But naturally when you *wanted* a policeman, there was never one around.

He needed to think—not easy the way he was driving, but suddenly essential.

The overwritten signature. That was the key. He'd studied it again on the plane home and decided it was definitely a name that started with *R,* space, *D* and contained four letters. The last name, beginning *Ma,* could be almost anything. He wondered if there might be hundreds of *Ma's* in the employee records at Airtech.

His mind wandered and he tried to conjure up a name and face to go with the voice he'd heard. *I'm no longer dealing with a phantom.* Too bad he hadn't thought to have a police tap installed on his home phone. And then he smiled grimly. Brody would have had him committed for *that.*

As he resumed his inner dialogue, he realized he was still operating on the assumption that the saboteur worked at Airtech, or had once worked there; how else would he have such familiarity with Airtech planes?

Yet he could see two reasons why the sabotage itself must have taken place elsewhere. With every fifth person at Airtech an inspector, it was inconceivable that a lone saboteur could infiltrate production. His second and strongest reason was the number of affected craft that had failed after a "C" check—all of which took place at airports.

Maintenance at airports is where the whole system breaks down.

He'd given a lot of thought to the strange variety of signatures signing off the affected airplanes—and no others. It had to be significant.

Only when he was halfway to San Diego did Wilcox remember that it didn't matter whether he lost his job over today's escapade or not: he'd already made an honor-bound commitment to Todd.

*   *   *

Miles couldn't decide what to do next. He'd blurted a destination—several destinations—mindlessly, trying to escape from Mary Helen. One of them was Airtech: shows how the subconscious operates. Now he sat in an all-night restaurant, still shaken, toying with a cup of black coffee and a bowl of tepid soup. Murder. He'd come *that close*. It terrified him now to think that one moment of uncontrollable rage could have sent him to prison, a common criminal . . . when all these years he'd been Miles Kimball, one of the good guys. Respected VP. Upstanding citizen. But who was he? He found himself smiling—an ironical, bitter smile. *We don't know who we are till we're tested.*

He saw himself in court trying to explain: "I'm an ordinary, decent man, *not* a murderer! I loved my wife, I'm religious, I've never done anything violent in my life . . ." *Of course, Mr. Kimball. Can you explain the beating—tell us how she happened to get herself strangled?*

When he decided he'd been there long enough, he paid his bill and went out to his car and drove aimlessly down the dark streets of Santa Ana. Without Sondra he had no destination. A faintly lit number on a storefront jogged his memory: 255. *Flight* 255. Ah! Now he remembered.

But what did it matter, unless . . . unless . . .

It came to him at that moment, a possibility—a way to do penance and save his soul.

He found a phone and called Trans America Fleet's night reservation number. To his surprise, the plane was leaving out of San Diego. *So I have to go there after all.* There was still plenty of time.

He turned his car around and headed south.

Even in downtown San Diego, traffic on the I-5 was light at two in the morning. As Wilcox slowed to turn into the factory, he thought again about Todd, wondering how good an orthopedic surgeon had to be to save a crushed foot. They should probably find a specialist.

He and Ellie would have to start looking—tomorrow, when the crisis was over.

Chapter Thirty-three

The rigger was going out as Alan Wilcox was coming in.

The rigger stopped, surprised, and watched at a distance as the other man showed his badge. Hard-pressed to suppress a smile, he waited near the door, allowing himself to linger only until Wilcox straightened to put his leather folder back in his pocket. Then, alert as a deer to Wilcox's every movement, he ducked his head and limped out of the plant.

Outside, he stepped off the lighted walkway and into the shadows of a building, where he unclipped his Airtech ID from his shirt and pulled a different one out of his pocket. Moving as fast as he could, Al Smith swung himself toward Aircraft Maintenance at Lindbergh Field.

Mark Brody wondered where Alan had gone. Loath to bother Ellie after such a traumatic day, he debated about calling on the phone she would answer—their private, unlisted line—until he decided his duty to keep track of Wilcox transcended Ellie's need to sleep.

To his surprise, Ellie answered immediately.

"Ellie, I'd never have awakened you if it wasn't—"

"I wasn't asleep," she said flatly.

"Oh. Do you happen to know where Alan is?"

"No. Do you?"

He was taken aback at her coldness. "Is something wrong?"

"Yes," she said, "there's plenty wrong. Alan left me a note that the

230

saboteur called him in the middle of the night. The *saboteur*, Mark, do you hear what I'm saying?"

"Yes."

"Well, the man exists, he's a fact, and Alan's out somewhere, trying to find him." She paused. "Do you know what that makes us, Mark?"

He thought he knew, but he waited.

"Bastards. Both of us. Fair-weather friends. We didn't believe Alan himself—who's always had integrity coming out of his ears, who's selfless to a fault. Oh no. We had to wait for proof. Well that puts us in the category of acquaintances. A friend, a *real friend,* is someone who takes you on faith."

He shifted uncomfortably in his chair. "I'm sorry, Ellie. I had to go with the evidence."

"No! You're wrong. You had to go with the man."

It occurred to him right then he was losing valuable time. "Will you feel better if I tell you I've just decided to find him—to help?"

"I don't know," she said. "He's had so little help already he probably wouldn't recognize it."

"You're tired, Ellie. Go back to sleep."

"Sure, Mark, sure." And then wearily, "Do what you can, huh?"

Taking an educated guess, Brody rang the night officer at Airtech Aviation. "This is Mark Brody, Los Angeles chief of the National Transportation Safety Board. If an Alan Wilcox from the NTSB shows up, please hold him in the outer office, I need to talk to him. Notify me at once. I will be down shortly by helicopter."

The night officer thought it a peculiar message. What was this Wilcox— an impostor? But he said he would, and went back to reading *Penthouse* magazine, indulging himself twenty extra minutes to finish the article. It was only as he strolled to the front entrance later that it occurred to him Wilcox might already be there. He asked the guard, "You seen anyone come in from the Safety Board?"

"Sure. About half an hour ago."

The night officer grimaced. "Oh boy. You got any idea how we might intercept him?"

The guard shrugged, not interested. "Without a guide? You've gotta be kidding. He could be anywhere."

"Well, look," said the officer, "notify a few key people to grab him. Or the Safety Board is gonna have my ass."

The guard's interest perked up. "Yeah? What's going on?"

"It's only a hunch. But I suspect this guy Wilcox is a fraud—maybe a spy from another company, or wanted by the FBI. We've gotta nail him, quick. I get the idea he wasn't supposed to have access at all."

The guard grinned. "Fancy him sneaking in at night. Well. This shift is getting interesting." He began dialing numbers inside the plant.

The regional duty officer told Mark Brody and Bruce Cavalier to stand by while he patched in the last two lines—the Bureau of Accident Investigation and Laboratory Services at the Bureau of Technology, both in Washington, D.C.

Angus Schrafft, from Accident Investigation, spoke first. "Sorry to get everybody up at such an ungodly hour, but we've just received vital information on the Trans America flight 160 that went down over the Atlantic."

Across the country, two listeners made small, audible responses.

"Admiral Franklin, from the headquarters of the Atlantic Fleet in Norfolk, Virginia, has been in touch with me this past week about a possible sonar buoy location of the Airtech plane, but we've kept the news quiet because we didn't want the press hounding the Navy for information. Not until they brought up the boxes."

"You've got the *boxes?*" Brody asked.

"That's right. The Navy brought them up about noon yesterday and flew them to Washington. We've been listening to the recorders and analyzing data all night. It turns out—," he seemed to be choosing his words, "it appears we've got a hero on the Safety Board. Maybe two heroes. We've never heard anything like it."

Brody could hear Cavalier sucking in his breath.

"It seems Jim Higgins spoke into the microphone as the plane was going down. As he was dying. Literally. We could hear screaming wind in the background, so this wouldn't have been easy. Yet his voice was quite calm as he told us everything that was happening, described all the incredible events, even remembered something that preceded the catastrophe. What Jim Higgins said, in effect, was the plane was sabotaged."

"My God!" Cavalier exploded. "Just what we thought."

"Let me read you Higgins's transcript." Schrafft began speaking matter-of-factly.

This is Jim Higgins. We've got something bizarre going on. The plane is now pitched eighty degrees toward the ocean, all the screens are blank, and I calculate we've got about two minutes before we hit. Before everything shut down, our navigation display showed we were right on track, yet the INS showed us a hundred miles off course. When we did a sudden roll to the left and went inverted, the pilots tried to disconnect the auto-flight system, but it wouldn't disconnect. They had no control of the plane whatever, and I suspect the computers were somehow programmed to prevent pilot input. I can't confirm this, but blame might lie with a man I saw at the loading tunnel. His behavior was suspicious. He's about five feet nine, with curly hair, a limp, and extraordinarily large eyes, probably blue. I'd look for him. *Au revoir.*

An intense silence followed the reading.

To his surprise, Brody found he had tears in his eyes.

"We had some trouble dealing with that recording," said Schrafft, "as you might imagine. And now here is Andy Brompton from Laboratory Services."

Brompton cleared his throat. "Our information from the digital flight data recorder is even more startling. Throughout the flight we see one of the computers constantly querying the others about position and ordering changes in course that are inconsistent with the normal flight track. The odd computer was given overriding navigational control. Yet there seem to be instructions incorporated into the program that dictated erroneous cockpit displays—that is, the display was at variance with actual aircraft location. According to one line of instruction, the craft was programmed to go down, as near as we can calculate, into one of the deep Atlantic trenches."

"I presume that was not the case," said Brody, "or even the Navy couldn't have recovered the plane."

"That's right," said Brompton, "but only thanks to some unexpected and very strong headwinds."

Cavalier asked, "How was the sabotage accomplished?"

"We show all the spoilers going up at once, then the left side going down. The plane went inverted. It seems the flight surfaces were literally commanded to dump the craft."

"Whoever did this," said Cavalier, "did not intend that these boxes would ever be found."

"Exactly," said Schrafft; "You're right," agreed Brompton.

Schrafft continued, "He especially did not anticipate that Jim Higgins

would be on that flight—or that a man in the process of dying could
be so courageous."

For a second there was silence on all the lines.

Then Cavalier said, "You mentioned two heroes. Who is the other?"

Schrafft answered, "Admiral Franklin believes Alan Wilcox is also
a hero. Perhaps he is."

"Oh my God!" Brody stiffened in his chair and realized he'd shouted.
"I have to go," he said quickly. "Wilcox is down in San Diego right
now. He received a threat, he's on to someone. He believes another
plane is about to be sabotaged. I'm afraid I discounted the idea—a
bad mistake. I'm signing off."

Schrafft said, "Brody . . . if it helps, you had plenty of company.
You'd better go."

Fifteen minutes later Mark Brody was on a Los Angeles sheriff's
helicopter headed for Airtech Aviation.

Where in San Diego? Topping wondered as he turned his car onto
the I-5, south. He patted the handcuffs he'd thought to tape to his body
under his shirt. Realistically, looking for Kimball in a city would be
like trying to find a faulty rivet on a fully assembled 747. A fool's
errand; where would you begin to search?

Yet he kept driving. His eyes closed momentarily. It was like the
irrational afternoon he'd spent at his teacher's house long ago, scrubbing everything in sight. Driven in some inexplicable way, as he was
now. *He* understood what he was doing, but no one else would.

In fact, nobody he'd ever met saw duty as he saw it—or the value
of discipline, self-sacrifice, and following through. Even his father,
who'd started him on this course, had not followed through sufficiently.
Topping felt his cheeks grow hot with embarrassment at the memory,
and he gripped the wheel tighter. Rommel should have died right then
and there. *That* was following through.

After Wilcox had threaded his way through various cavernous buildings, trying not to appear lost but lost nonetheless, he looked up and
saw coming toward him down a long walkway between fuselages
the same woman who had led him through once before. Her eyes widened
in recognition. "You're—Wilcox?"

"Yes." He smiled. "And you're Sandy Wallis."

She didn't smile back. "You'll have to come with me."

"Oh?" he said. "Where?"

"They want you in the front office. Right away."

"What for? What's this about?" Unconsciously he sized up the mammoth room for ways to escape, realizing on another level that such a move would get him nowhere.

"I have orders. They don't want you in the plant."

"Orders from whom?"

"Somebody phoned the night officer, he said—"

Brody, thought Wilcox. And then he looked at his watch: 4:00 A.M. They were wasting precious time. He said, "That was a crackpot call, I can prove it. I have a subpoena here, signed by Brody himself. I must see the personnel records. Now."

Wallis looked torn. She said, "But I have orders—"

"Look," he said, "you take me to the personnel room so I can start searching while you're bringing the night officer to me. Leave someone guarding me if you want. But please hurry."

When she still looked doubtful, he whipped out his leather folder and held it open. "This badge designates me a representative of the United States government. I am here officially to prevent a major airplane catastrophe. If that plane goes down because you kept me standing here arguing. . . . Now where is that room with all the files?"

A few minutes later, he was standing on a high ladder, leaning against the top rung as he searched rapidly through the *M*'s.

Topping's sense of mission grew with every mile he drove. *I've got to save Airtech from Kimball.* It had occurred to him suddenly the place to search was the factory itself. He'd be wasting his time anyplace else.

His intensity translated to the pedal and the car picked up speed until he was doing close to eighty-five. He felt more alive than he'd felt in years, energized by the knowledge that he was needed. *If I stop that man, it will do the world good—a helluva lot more good than wiping out a few Germans.*

"Ah," said the night officer, rushing into the room. "It's him." Behind him came Sandy Wallis, panting and distraught. The officer made for the ladder and grabbed one of the legs and shook it, as though trying to dislodge Wilcox from a tree.

The ladder wobbled precariously, and Wilcox shouted down, "What in hell are you doing?" His hands were between two heavy files, and he considered dropping one on the man's head. "Let go of that goddam ladder," he bellowed, "if you know what's good for you."

"Come down," shouted the man, staring upward with dark, angry eyes. His black mustache quivered as he spoke.

"I'll come down when I'm done. You've got a saboteur working out of this plant, and I'm going to find him. Now get your hands off that ladder."

"We've got orders to move you out."

"And I've got orders to keep working." He pointed. "There! On the table! If you don't believe the subpoena, call my boss, Mark Brody. His name's on the bottom."

"Brody called *me!*"

"The man who called you was *not* Brody. It was someone else, God knows who. Go verify, you'll see."

"Stay here, Sandy," the man ordered, and left. Wilcox hoped fervently the man would take some time finding the number. With renewed haste, he searched through one file after another.

And then he found what he was looking for: a thick file with notations from various bosses. The man had been working there at least two years. "Well. Rudy Malec," he muttered aloud.

Sandy Wallis's head swiveled and she stared up at him. "Is *that* who you're after? I know him. He's crazy."

Chapter Thirty-four

The Trans America Fleet maintenance hangar at Lindbergh Field was big enough to accommodate three large jets in its three bays. Sixty feet tall and open to the airport runways along one side, it encompassed just under four acres—acres of endless red tool kits on wheels, elevated tail stands forty feet tall that rolled on tracks, and a half dozen mobile air compressors. Walkways outlined in yellow were painted on the concrete floor and the ceiling was a complicated mix of steel girders, overhead cranes for changing engines, and piping for the fire extinguisher systems. At the moment only a single Airtech 323 occupied one of the bays.

Knowing how badly they needed mechanics, Al Smith reported hours late for his moonlighting job in Maintenance. Let them fire me, he thought. After today it wouldn't matter. He was carrying a large brown paper bag and feeling well again, in fact almost unbearably high—partly because of no sleep but more because he was exhilarated by what he was about to do. He'd outsmarted them all. There was Wilcox running around the Airtech plant like the FBI—without a clue—and Kimball . . . His high faded somewhat. *You'll see what I can do, Mr. Kimball.*

He looked around as he entered the hangar from the street side and saw someone working up in the cockpit of the big Airtech, while two men stood outside on one of the tail stands, talking. A bunch of incompetents, he thought, who could use a screwdriver but not much else. He wanted to shout his accomplishments to the lot of them and watch their expressions, see the jealousy narrowing their eyes. But he'd wait. It wasn't them he cared about; it was Wilcox, Kimball, the people at Airtech—Nick Lewand. He stood just inside the hangar planning how he'd break it to Lewand when they met after the big crash. I did it, Lewand, you flea brain. I brought down the whole goddam plane. And you thought I couldn't pull anything over on you.

He stood there thinking until someone asked, "You going to go to work, or what?"

"In a minute," he said. "Give me a minute."

He went back inside and found a small bathroom, where he opened his bag and took out two ROM—read-only memory—boards. Both were about six inches square by half an inch thick, and he turned them over in his hands fondly. You could carry enough in a brown paper bag to sabotage half a dozen airliners, he thought. And the boards didn't weigh much—about the same as your lunch.

He knew he'd done the job exactly right, though nobody could tell by visual examination. They were just small boards with some tiny cylindrical "pills" on top, which were the resistors and capacitors, but mostly a lot of thumbnail-sized rectangular black chips—the integrated circuits—which resembled centipedes with their black legs poked through the board and soldered on the other side.

The two boards looked exactly like the two he would swap them for—nothing anybody could see that was different. And when someone examined his software later, after the crash, they'd never know what went wrong, because the defect, a self-perpetuating computer virus, did not appear in the human-readable source code. He smiled. The defect, of course, had been erased.

Handling his two boards gently, as if they were alive and delicate, he slipped them back into the brown paper bag and rolled it down from the top. He felt as if he'd just said good-bye to them. *His* offspring. The final issue of his inventive mind.

Malec went back through a hallway and out to the hangar itself and walked up to the big Airtech plane. He imagined it with its spoilers rising just before rotation. And then he saw the ensuing crash, with flames swirling like a tornado, and then the worldwide headlines.

And he saw an admiring crowd, smiling but keeping their distance, a mass of people all worshiping *him*. And all at once he was among them, but for some reason he felt no anger, only the gentlest kind of warmth.

He shook his head and the faces disappeared. Later he wondered vaguely what he'd find to do after today.

As Alan Wilcox climbed down the ladder, he said to Sandy Wallis, "What do you know about this man?"

"Nothing," she said. "Exactly nothing. Everything he told me about himself was a lie." It was all she dared say.

Disappointed, Wilcox was painfully aware of time getting away, of unknown sabotage already in progress. It was past five in the morning. Less than two hours left, he thought desperately. And so much proof still to nail down. As he gathered his papers and added them to the file in his hands, he considered racing to the airport to alert Trans America Fleet to the danger. But how could they respond? He didn't know the flight number or even what state the plane would leave from—only the time. It wasn't enough.

With the Rudy Malec file almost burning his fingers, he said to Sandy Wallis, who stood blocking the doorway, "I'll be taking these papers to the local crime lab."

"I can't let you go."

"I'm sorry, you *will* let me go," and because she wouldn't budge, he lifted her by the shoulders, moved her out of his way, and stalked out. He could hear her gasp as he left.

On his way to San Diego, Miles Kimball wondered if anyone besides himself and Rudy Malec knew the flight number of the plane that was going down. He decided they probably didn't.

Longing to propitiate his God in whatever way he could, he pulled off the freeway near the town of La Jolla, and after a short search located a phone behind a gas station. He dialed the FAA's number and the operator said, "That will be eighty-five cents, please," so he fished in his pocket for change and found himself twenty cents short.

"Look, operator, this is an emergency," he shouted, and a voice came on, "Eighty-five cents, please. That will be eighty-five cents." He was shouting at a recording.

He slammed the phone down and looked around. The gas station and the few surrounding stores were deserted. There was no way he could possibly get the other twenty cents, not at five-fifteen in the morning.

Like being refused at the confessional, he thought, a grim irony.

The ultimate turn-away. *With my luck they wouldn't have believed me.*
Slowly he continued on.

The plant supervisor and the night officer descended on the file room
together. Sandy Wallis still stood there, shocked.

"You let him go!" shouted the supervisor.

"Where is he?" yelled the night officer.

"Don't blame me!" she shrieked. "How am I supposed to stop a two-
hundred-pound man?"

The two gave her no sympathy, only glared down at her in contempt.
She decided right then she wouldn't tell them anything.

Without giving the appearance of running, it was hard for Wilcox
to move as fast as he wanted through the plant. Out through the exit
of that building, in through another massive assembly room, and out
yet another door, he sailed along on lengthened strides. He'd reached
the executive offices, largely empty at five in the morning. He spoke
to the only person in sight, an immense man who sat behind an equally
immense desk. "Where is the computer design center?" he asked.

The man suddenly rose and lurched toward him, reaching out an
enormous hand.

Wilcox backpedaled toward the door.

"You're Wilcox!" the man shouted, coming around his desk but
hampered by his enormous girth.

Wilcox spun around, got the glass door open, and ran through fast,
pushing it hard behind him. A grunt, a shout, then thunderous foot-
steps followed him down the walkway. Sure he could outrun the man,
Wilcox sprinted to the end of one of the mammoth buildings and across
an open space to another.

After that he heard nothing. But he knew he couldn't safely return
to Airtech. Instead, slowing to a trot, he headed to his car. He spun
out of the parking lot, driving at a reckless pace toward the offices of
the San Diego sheriff.

Max Topping was into the building and started down an aisle before the Airtech guard caught up with him. "Hey! Where do you think
you're going?"

Topping stopped in surprise. "I'm looking for a supervisor, to report a problem. The building looked open, and—"

The guard had him by the shoulder, spinning him around. "Out! Unless you've got a badge. This may be the middle of the night, but we ain't asleep."

"Sorry." *You were asleep. I just didn't get in fast enough.*

The watch commander at the sheriff's office gave Wilcox a welcoming grin. "Hey, Wilcox! Welcome to the Playland of the South. What are you doing in San Diego? What's up, did we lose one in the bay we didn't hear about?"

Sheriff's Captain Wannamaker always seemed glad to see him. Not a handsome man, his sparse hair was colorless and receding, his nose somewhat bulbous, his tall frame overburdened with sagging flesh. But his blue eyes conveyed so much intelligence and warmth, Wilcox had long found Wannamaker's office one of his favorite stopping places.

Wilcox said hurriedly, "We haven't lost anything yet, but we've got a threat we're taking seriously. Phil, I've got to call up a bunch of favors. I need them now."

"Shoot."

Wilcox opened his file. "We think we've got an airplane saboteur about to pull off something major," looking at his watch, "in exactly one hour and forty minutes. All I've got on the man right now is a name and his place of employment, and something else that might link him to a prior crime." He pulled out the maintenance record from Minneapolis, still wrapped in plastic, and held it out.

"I suspect we've got fingerprints here that may match some on file with Airtech Aviation. If that's the case, it's damning evidence. Get Sacramento to fax an image of the man's face and his thumbprint down here from his driver's license. I presume they'll do that in the middle of the night. Also, I need past addresses. And someone to run a check on his current address and see if he's there. If he is, bring him back here. I've got his phone number from this file, so I'm heading to the phone company to subpoena his calls. Can you let me have a car, and can we do this code three?"

"You've got it," said Wannamaker.

Mark Brody jumped down from the still-running helicopter and, head lowered, dashed into the reception room of the executive offices of Airtech. After showing his badge, he described Alan Wilcox and asked if the man had been in the plant.

The fat man said, "You bet he was in the plant. I just chased him off."

"Off?" said Brody, dismayed. "Off to where?"

The fat man laughed. "He was running so fast, none of us are gonna know where. I was tailing right behind him, though, spooking him pretty good until—"

"Look," already Brody was impatient with this slob, "did he talk to anyone? Did anyone else see him? I have to know. Fast."

The behemoth lumbered to his feet. Brody couldn't imagine him running a step. *Move!* he thought. *Faster.*

"The night officer's the one who alerted me. We'll go see him."

It was getting light as Miles Kimball pulled up to Lindbergh Field. Scanning the big overhead signs that directed him to the various airline terminals, he veered right when he saw Trans America Fleet.

Flight 255, he discovered as he stood looking up at the monitor a few minutes later, was scheduled to depart for Chicago at 7:00 A.M. But there was no one behind the desk at TAF, and the whole terminal was largely deserted.

Kimball located a bench and sat down to take stock. Despair washed over him and he dropped his head, staring at a beetle that crawled along the floor. The bug seemed to have more going for it than he did. Without a wife—without Sondra—there'd be no one who understood him, no one who'd laugh at his wacky irreverence, who'd be genuinely thrilled over a new toaster, who'd reach for him and tug him into bed. Without Sondra he'd lost all the bright mornings and the muted, comforting evenings—a mug of tea, the hot brown smell of homebaked bread. Without Sondra, he wouldn't live well again. But he might have lived in dignity. Except for Malec.

It was Malec who'd despoiled him as a human being, Malec who'd turned him inside out, like a shirt in the laundry, and revealed that his seams had never been any good. Because of Malec, he'd lost his eternal soul.

It was useless now to confess to a priest. But he had a vague concept of an abstract justice that existed apart from everything men did. He intended to become part of it—by getting on the doomed plane.

Mark Brody could have punched out the fat man who lumbered through the buildings of the plant like a ship rocking at anchor. It was only after they burned up minutes that they caught up with the night officer, who told them Wilcox was no longer on the premises.

"But he ran off with one of our goddam files," said the officer, his black mustache quivering.

"It's okay," said Brody, "he'll need them. We'll get the files back to you later. Does anyone *else* know where he went?"

A young woman appeared from nowhere. "*I* know where he went," she said, throwing the night officer a contemptuous smile. "*I* heard him say he was going to the nearest crime lab."

"That's exactly what I needed, Miss. Exactly. Thank you very much." Out of the corner of his eye, he saw the woman give the finger to the night officer—who, with his back turned, didn't see her.

Outside the main gate he waited for the cab the man promised to call.

Alan Wilcox found the telephone company almost deserted. The front office was manned by a sleepy-looking young girl who obviously had no interest in why he was there at six in the morning.

He leaned against the counter and held out the subpoena and a slip of paper bearing the name Rudy Malec. "I need this man's phone records for the past six months."

"What's that?" she said, pointing to the subpoena.

He tried to explain.

"I can't get you any phone numbers no matter what you've got." She'd been standing briefly, but now she sat down again.

"Get your supervisor!" He looked at his watch. Only one hour left. It was about sixty out, but he was sweating and his shirt was stuck to his back.

"She's not to be bothered unless it's an emergency."

"This *is* an emergency."

"You look like an ordinary person to me."

Wilcox leaned over the counter as far as he could get. "Look ma'am," he said, speaking very slowly and very carefully, "here is my badge. I am with the—," he thought fast, "I am with the United States Presidential Police Force. This is my picture, right on the badge. Now *go get your supervisor!*"

"Oh," she said, and scurried away.

The supervisor needed only a glance at the subpoena before she brought Wilcox the records he wanted.

It took fewer than three minutes to see that one phone number accounted for dozens of hours of Malec's phone time during a particular two-month period that ran between December of the prior year and January of the current year.

When Wilcox asked the supervisor to find the subscriber for that number, she supplied it immediately. It belonged to a company, she said. A company called Navtronics.

Navtronics, he thought, as she waited. *So our saboteur didn't operate in-house at all. He did what he did through the autopilot manufacturer.*

"Thank you," he said when the woman handed him photocopies. "You've helped a lot."

Rudy Malec finished installing his ROM boards in the plane's E&E—electronic and electrical—compartment, which was in the nose of the craft right under the cockpit. He climbed down a ladder clutching his brown paper bag. Threading his way among the tool carts, he crossed the hangar and found a trash bin in one corner. The sack looked like nothing more than trash from his sandwiches. He dropped it casually into the big receptacle.

When no one was looking, he left the protected area of the hangar and crossed a large cement pad, and then the end of two runways, and strolled toward a tiny patch of open field between the airport and Airtech Aviation. There he sat down to watch and wait.

A few minutes before six, Miles Kimball decided to make one last call to the FAA. The bug he'd been watching had abruptly flown away, and that small, defiant act had prodded him anew. It occurred to him he still had a viable choice: instead of being on the plane, he could stop it.

"It's me again," he said to the man who picked up the phone at the Com Center. "You know that plane I told you about last night? The one that may have a problem? I've thought of the flight number. It's Trans America Fleet, flight 255, leaving out of San Diego this morning."

"Hold on," said the man at the switchboard. "What was your name?"

Kimball panicked. "I had nothing to do with it, you don't need my name." In a sweat he slammed down the phone and hurried to the far end of the terminal, lest somehow, by some mysterious means, the FAA could trace the call to him.

*　　*　　*

"Alan!" Mark Brody shouted as Wilcox ran into the sheriff's station. "It's about time!"

Wilcox stopped on the spot and stared at his boss. Brody was the last man in the world he expected to see there, and the shock turned him cold. Instantly he knew that all his sleuthing, all the horrendous effort of months was finished. In forty-five minutes a planeload of people would die. With Brody there to stop him, he was powerless to act. Stunned, he envisioned another Locherbie, another *Hindenburg*.

Brody said, "Snap out of it, Wilcox, we've got work to do."

"I'm not sure what you mean."

Brody waved an arm in the direction of Sheriff Wannamaker. "Your fingerprints check out, Alan. The man who signed off that work in Minneapolis is the same person who works at Airtech. I would guess he's also the man who committed the rest of the sabotage."

Sabotage. Brody had actually used the word he'd been thinking for months.

"You've done a damned fine job, Alan." Brody smiled. "And before you start climbing all over me, Ellie did it for you. She pinned my ears back."

"Would you care to expand on that?" Wilcox felt a spark of joy begin to glow somewhere inside.

"Can't," said Brody. "Not right now. There's no time." His tense expression returned. "While we waited for you, we called Airtech and found out this man Malec still works there, in fact he was seen there this evening. Right now we've got to split up. They'll take you in the squad car over to Airtech to search for Malec. I'll stay here and wait for his picture to be faxed in from Sacramento. Soon as I get it, we'll—"

Brody's pager sounded.

Brody waved Wilcox off. "Get going. We'll see you there."

A thousand questions pounded through Wilcox's tired brain as his driver sped down the freeway toward Airtech with lights flashing and sirens screaming. He forced his thoughts aside. For now he had only one mission: grab Rudy Malec.

Max Topping glared at the man guarding the obscure entrance. "Okay, you caught me trying to sneak in. How many outside entrances do you have in this place?"

"Three."

So I've tried them all. And walked miles—too many miles to start over. He said harshly, "You've got a saboteur in this plant. You'll have to let me in, I'm the only one who knows the man's identity."

The guard laughed. "Well, that's certainly an original line. First time I've heard it."

"Do I get in? And talk to someone in charge? Or does he foul up another plane while we stand here talking?"

"Look, fella, you've got no ID and no legitimate business, far as I can see. If you really believe this saboteur stuff, come back and show me something. Then we'll talk." He stood with his legs apart and his body blocking the entrance. His hand slid downward toward a hol-stered gun.

Topping saw the subtle movement and backed away. *I'll have to go to the airport, it seems. To make a phone call if nothing else.* Turning slowly so he wouldn't rile the guard, he began walking toward the grass that separated them from Lindbergh Field.

Alan Wilcox decided it would be simpler to try a different entrance to the plant. At twenty after six, just as he was showing his NTSB badge to a different guard and trying to explain the urgency of his mission, the guard said, "You're the second guy in the last minute and a half talking about sabotage."

Wilcox did a double take. "Who was the other?"

The guard pointed. "See that bozo heading toward the airport? Him."

Wilcox whirled and shouted, "Stop!"

Instead of stopping, Topping began to run.

Chapter Thirty-five

Wilcox lost seconds getting his feet moving at any kind of speed.

Ahead of him, across a field that separated the building he was leaving from another straight ahead, the man had gotten an incredible head start. He wasn't young, but he was running like an athlete, and Wilcox wondered distantly what it took to stay in that kind of shape. With a sense of despair, he knew he was losing ground with every second that passed.

For the first time since he'd begun running marathons, Topping saw an external benefit to his life-style. As he outran whoever was chasing him, he had a heady sense of achievement, of tangible reward for years of roadwork. He ran without effort, skimming over the ground so lightly it was almost as if he weren't trying at all. If need be, he could run to the Mexican border. Too bad it wasn't necessary.

When he reached the next building, he slipped around the corner and found an outside fire escape that led to a small platform two stories up.

With a burst of energy he leaped to the high bottom rung, hoisted himself up and, monkeylike, climbed the stairs to the platform.

To his surprise, he found a big metal cylinder of some sort in the corner of the platform. Thin as he was, he knew it would hide him very well.

And it did. Whoever was chasing him ran by and never saw him at all.

*   *   *

The picture of Rudy Malec came in on the fax machine just as Wilcox disappeared in the squad car.

Instead of waiting for his return call to go through to the Com Center, Brody decided to answer his page later. He hung up the phone to study the picture. "Not a bad-looking guy," he remarked. "Big eyes. Looks normal to me."

Phil Wannamaker nodded.

Then Brody glanced at his watch and blanched. "You got your car ready?"

The watch commander said he did.

"Let's go. We'd better use lights and sirens."

At 6:30 A.M., Miles Kimball thought it safe to return to TAF's counter to buy his ticket. As he handed the woman behind the counter his credit card, she punched numbers into her computer and shook her head. "I'm sorry, sir. We're all sold out. In fact we're overbooked." Looking up, she smiled. "There must be something big going on in Chicago."

Whatever it was, thought Kimball, nobody from here would get there. Worse, a malevolent fate had dealt him another blow. *And I won't be on the plane.*

At a loss, he wandered out of the building to the street. Far beyond the runways, he saw the buildings of Airtech spread across acres of land. *Rudy Malec is over there somewhere.* His hands tightened into fists.

Wilcox kept running, sure that the man he needed to talk to had disappeared in the direction of the big maintenance hangars he could see at a distance. When he rounded the intervening building, at first he saw no one. Then he realized there *was* someone out there in a small grassy area, though how the man had gotten so far away, he couldn't imagine.

Coaxing his legs to go faster, Wilcox covered the remaining distance in less time than he'd have thought possible.

And then he realized his quarry wasn't running at all. Nor was he dressed like the man he'd been chasing. Whoever it was, this person was wearing an orange jacket and standing quite still.

Brody intercepted the Airtech supervisor just as the day shift came on.

Nick Lewand knew Rudy Malec well. "You always know the misfits," he said. "He's strangely unpopular. We keep him on, though, because at times he's brilliant. Lately I've been watching him closely. Something's going on with that guy, but I haven't figured out what."

Brody said, "I have to know whether my associate, Alan Wilcox, is in the building—can you find out in a hurry, please? We have a crisis here."

After calling all three entrances, Lewand said, "One of the guards tells me Wilcox started in and changed his mind. Instead he disappeared out the door, chasing somebody away from the building. I doubt if the guy he was after was Malec. He didn't look familiar to our guard."

The slender man stood in a skimpy patch of grass, watching Wilcox with an odd look of intensity, almost recognition—though he was a complete stranger to Wilcox.

Panting, Wilcox managed to gasp, "Did you see someone running this way?" He glanced at the man's ID. It said, "Al Smith." He was surprised at how clearly the large eyes showed up in the picture.

Smith gave him a curious look. In a strangely eager voice, he asked, "Are you sure you know who you're chasing?"

Subliminally, Wilcox thought he'd heard that voice somewhere. "What do you mean?"

A pause. "Nothing. Just making conversation." He seemed disappointed. "I did see someone running near the factory. But it could have been you."

And then the man was watching him again, as though waiting for words that weren't forthcoming. He had an air of expectation—of challenge. Wilcox found the blue eyes with the intense, unwavering stare unnerving. He was about to leave when the fellow edged closer, looked up into his face and said, "I'm glad you came." Then he laughed softly. And he kept his eyes on Wilcox's face, as if inciting him to some unspoken duel.

Involuntarily, Wilcox pulled back. There was something so unsavory about the man—even menacing—that Wilcox braced himself. He had no time for such nonsense. "Later," he said, and giving Smith no further opening, he ran back the way he'd come.

A sense of doom descended on him as he sprinted toward the factory, a terrible awareness that his time was almost gone. He could no longer look at his watch.

As he headed back to Airtech, he turned briefly and saw an enormous jet leave the maintenance hangar and roll slowly toward the loading gates. Suddenly he had a hunch, the way he'd sensed everything else, that this was the doomed plane. But he couldn't prove it. Without proof, he was powerless to take the only definitive action an investigator could take—which was to seize the plane.

Malec sat down on the grass. *He flunked out. He's not as brilliant as I thought.* Expecting a rush of triumph, of jubilation, he was surprised when he experienced neither.

He stared out across the runways feeling strangely hollow, as though everything he expected was already over. To comfort himself he looked into his own mind, trying to conjure up his admiring crowd. Yearning for smiles, for warmth, he sensed only a cloudy void and indifference that stretched to the horizon. *I'm alone,* he thought.

He wrapped his arms around himself and rocked back and forth in the grass. As he rocked, he pretended it had happened before, that he'd once been rocked in the hazy days of his babyhood.

It wasn't true. He knew it wasn't true. But he had been in a plane, once . . . A terrible longing grew inside him, swelling so enormously he could hardly breathe. He thought he might die. His mind leaped to save him. *My daddy's comin' back and get me.*

Kimball began to walk faster. *I should try to find Malec.* Knowing his chances were hardly better than zero, he went around the building and spotted a mechanic's gate ajar. Opening to the runways, it was the most direct route to Airtech. To his surprise, he was able to slip through unnoticed. Walking fast and purposefully, he crossed the cement in the direction of the plant. Nobody tried to stop him. *Unbelievable. Anybody could get out here with the planes.*

Driven by ever greater urgency, he broke into a slow trot. Glad no one could see him—he must look as awkward and out-of-shape as he felt—he lifted his chin and pushed himself to move faster. Airtech was farther away than he'd thought.

At a distance, he saw something bright orange in a patch of grass. A person? Coming closer, he realized it was indeed a person. "You!" he cried, staring down at Malec in revulsion. "My God, it's you!"

"Yeah it's me, Mr. Kimball. Surprised?"

"What are you doing out here?"

"Waiting. For the biggest extravaganza this airport's ever going to have." He looked up. "And now you'll be in on the big happenings yourself." He pointed toward Airtech. "I left your name and phone number at my locker."

"You *what?*"

"I decided you ought to have some publicity too—since you've been in this from the beginning." His grin was taunting. "Partners, right? When this is over, you ought to help with expenses—pay me back for some of the airplane tickets, all the IDs—"

Kimball didn't let him finish. Before he knew it, he was on the ground shoving Malec's face into the grass. All the rage and fear of the past few months poured out of him, as though a dike had burst bringing a flood of emotion. Hands on the man's head, he pushed and jammed, shutting out the sound of that infuriating voice. His mind emptied of all save rage. In those few moments he couldn't see, couldn't reason. He could only feel.

A strangling sound, the gargle of death. The gagging penetrated his mind the way images couldn't, brought him a mental flash and then a burst of reality. *My God! What am I doing?*

Abruptly he stopped. *I could have killed him.* He pulled his hands away fast, letting Malec gasp for air, letting him blink and rub the dirt out of his face. He stared at Malec with fear and revulsion as he might a black widow spider, trembling because of what he'd almost done. Yet despising himself. *I should have finished the job.*

Malec coughed, and his words were a whisper. "Couldn't do it, could you?" Gulping air, he strained to be heard, "I always knew you were gutless. You don't have the balls to screw a—"

Kimball didn't hear the rest. Across the grass, coming fast, he saw Topping, and then his colleague was there, standing behind the orange-jacketed figure but looking straight at *him.* Except this was a different Topping, no longer controlled and pleasant. His short hair was uncombed. His shirt was half-buttoned and tieless. And there was a Green Beret's set to his jaw.

"Good God, Max, what are you doing here?"

Topping ignored Malec, who sat where he was, looking up in fascination. "You're coming with me, Miles, you're turning yourself in. To the FBI." Slowly he began edging around Malec, holding his gaze and creeping closer, as though stalking a skitterish colt.

Kimball watched in astonishment. "Max. Max. Think what you're doing, this is me, Miles. Stop this stuff, you're making an ass of yourself. Stop and let's talk."

"We're through with talk," Topping said, holding out a bridging hand. "Don't even *think* about running."

Kimball stared at the hand, mesmerized.

Moving closer. "You've been sabotaging planes—"

"That was me!" Suddenly Malec leapt to his feet. "Don't give him credit, you moron, what does *he* know about computers? I'm the one— Rudy Malec!" He laughed triumphantly. "So people are really noticing, huh? Wait 'til you see what happens next!"

Topping's mouth dropped open. Then he collected himself. "Bullshit. I've been watching Kimball—"

Malec grabbed Topping's shirt. "Mr. Kimball's a flea brain! He doesn't know squat. *I* infiltrated Navtronics, *I* got the old computer boards, *I* designed erasable viruses. And not one fucking person . . ." he paused as Topping wrenched the hand off his shirt, "*nobody* figured out how— not him, not Lewand, not Wilcox. Maybe *you* should try putting two hundred and seventy people into a deep Atlantic trench, Mr. Smart Ass! See how easy it is!"

Topping's eyes glittered.

Kimball said, "As you can see, he's proud of it, Max. Being that kind of genius." He watched Malec puff up with pride. "Unfortunately, he's subhuman. A psycho. He should have been removed from society long ago." He laughed harshly. "I had my chance just now. I—"

"And you didn't," said Malec, smiling. "Because you're weak."

"But *I'm not*." In one quick motion Topping secured Malec's arms, pressing one against his own body, twisting the other behind Malec's back. "Hold him!" he ordered, and tightened his grip while Kimball grabbed the twisted arm. From under his shirt Topping produced the handcuffs and quickly snapped them in place.

Bound as he was, Malec could move only awkwardly. "Look!" he cried suddenly, "that's the plane!"

Still gripping their prisoner, the others turned.

Malec nodded toward the field. "In a couple minutes it's gonna take off and make me famous. You watch. It'll rise fast, pass through two hundred knots, and climb to six hundred feet. But that's it. That's as high as it gets."

The two men stared at him.

He seemed not to notice. "The altitude was the tricky part, targeting the six hundred feet. But I did it! That's when one of the on-board computers will take over and half the surfaces will change configuration. The plane will do a slow, graceful roll until it's upside down." He smiled. "The passengers will scream and wet their pants because it'll happen in slow motion and they'll *know*. You ever seen a plane's nose pull down through the horizon until it's pointed straight at the ground? Still with maximum thrust?"

Nobody answered.

"Hey, it'll be a trip! A jet powered full-out, but headed *down*. The people won't just be killed, they'll be mangled. Torn into tiny pieces. A coupla teeth here, an ear there—the press will go nuts. And that goes for the computer boards, too. Parts of the plane will be on their way to China. Nothing left but a big, black smoking hole in the ground."

"My God," breathed Kimball.

"I'll be a household name," Malec gloated. "All over the world I'll make headlines."

"If you do," said Topping, "you'll never see them." Outwardly calm, his self-control in place, he wrapped an arm around Malec's throat and began to squeeze. *Even the man on the street would strangle him now.* He tightened his arm.

Awkward because of the cuffs, Malec raked the arm with his nails. His legs thrashed. His body wriggled and his face contorted in rage. His mouth worked, seeking air. From under the curly hair dirt tumbled out.

Kimball turned away. Unable to look, he wished he could blot out as well the hideous sounds of choking, of wretched gurgling. He began walking. He heard a kind of snap. He walked faster, now almost running. The last thing he heard was silence.

And then he started listening for the plane.

After a while the bastard didn't move anymore. Topping opened his arm and Malec slithered to the ground. Topping looked down at him without regret. *Somebody had to do it.* Composed and detached, Topping pocketed the man's badge and flipped him over on his face. Nobody should have to see that evil expression.

He turned and began running toward the airport. There must be someone he could tell. A phone he could use. Some way to deliver a message. And then he stopped, horrified. It was already too late.

*   *   *

Unable to find Wilcox, Mark Brody called the Com Center back, on the outside chance the page had something to do with the current sabotage.

It did. For the first time Brody learned that the doomed plane was TAF flight 255—due to depart the airport within minutes.

Just as he hung up, Alan Wilcox burst into the office. "I found someone who knows about the sabotage!" Alan shouted, "I saw him briefly, but he got away!"

"Forget that!" Brody yelled back at him, though they were standing only feet apart. He was already dialing the tower frantically. "I just learned it's flight 255, leaving from this airport—," he turned back as someone answered.

"Emergency," Brody shouted into the phone, "Alert flight 255. This is Mark Brody, NTSB. The flight is in extreme danger. Stop flight 255!" He paused, looking incredulous. "What? You want to *see* my badge? You orangutan imbecile! Okay, okay. I'll be there. But you better warn the pilots! Fast!" He slammed the phone down.

Together Brody and Wilcox ran outside, tearing back the way Wilcox had just come, racing toward the nearest runway. As they got closer, they saw the plane's door sealed and the stairs being wheeled away.

Across two runways they hurtled, and then across a large turnaround and refueling area, and then up to a locked door, where they pounded for admittance.

It seemed minutes before anyone came.

As a gate guard tentatively opened the door, Wilcox looked back. At a distance he saw everything he'd staked his badge on happening before his eyes as though he'd made no effort at all. The great Airtech 323 was gathering speed on the long ribbon of cement, boiling down the straightaway like the sleek bird it was, reaching, pouring on power, straining toward flight.

Suddenly, for no perceptible reason, all the spoilers went up on the left side of the plane.

Chapter Thirty-six

The plane had used up more than three thousand feet of the nine-thousand-foot runway and was still accelerating when the excited, high-pitched voice of the controller came into Tim Baylor's head-phones. "Fleet two-five-five. Abort! There's a threat against the aircraft!"

Henry Sweetser heard it, too, and instantly tensed. *Goddammit, not again!*

Baylor reacted instantly. *I'm taking this one on the ground.* Just past V1, he yanked the throttles back, hoping to God he could stop in time. But he couldn't. He knew with absolute certainty the plane would race ahead until he plunged off the runway. With all his strength he pressed on the rudder pedals. His calves knotted and his hands turned clammy. He swore vehemently.

Miraculously, the plane slowed. But not enough. Damn it to hell, not enough.

In the coach section of Trans America Fleet's flight 255, just back of the wings on the left side, a TAF pilot on vacation broke off a conversation with his wife to turn and watch the takeoff—which he did habitually, as though he were never entirely off duty.

Outside his window, hangars and buildings raced by while Lawrence Minette sat in that alert state of semitension that was somewhere be-tween ho-hum and oh-my-god. Suddenly Minette's eyes widened. Out on the wings, the spoilers came up at the very instant the pilot turned on maximum power.

For a split second, feeling the plane's struggle for speed, he dismissed the image as false, as a kind of mirage devolving from some quirk of his eyesight. He couldn't be seeing what he saw. It was impossible.

Minette's heart began to pound. It was true; the plane was configured for landing. The spoilers were definitely *up*. Stunned and uncertain about what he should do, he waved at the female flight attendant, who sat in a jump seat facing him beyond the first class section.

The attendant remained blank, oblivious to his waving.

He had to do *something*. While the plane's engines struggled against the barrier of excessive wind resistance, he undid his seat belt and hurled himself over his wife and down the aisle toward the cockpit.

The flight attendant saw him coming and screamed, "Sir! Sir! Take your seat!"

"The spoilers are up! The spoilers are up!" Minette's voice was a bellow and his arm waved in the direction of the wings. "Tell the pilot! The spoilers are up!"

The flight attendant jumped up to force him into a seat, struggling with the berserk passenger who pushed her down, trying to force his way into the cockpit.

A half minute later, flight attendant Mary Simpson and passenger Lawrence Minette, flung against the door of the cockpit, would be the first two people to die on flight 255.

Brody reached the counter first. In one motion he whipped his badge from his pocket and waved it furiously at the female ticket agent. Though she was on the phone, he shouted, "Call the tower! Stop the plane!" Wilcox, too, waved his badge.

The TAF ticket agent, white-faced, hung up and said in some distress, "The tower has already notified the pilot, sir. They said—"

Brody and Wilcox didn't wait. Back at the door to the outside boarding area, they pushed past the guard and ran toward the runway. A quarter mile away, the big jet accelerated away from them, started its rotation for the briefest moment and came back down again, tires smoking as the nosewheel smashed against the pavement.

While they watched, each lost in chilling, unspoken fears, the plane slewed to one side of the cement and then the other, its speed only partially diminished as the end of the runway approached. Beyond the pavement, a grassy field with approach lights and an elevated ILS waited to swallow up the runaway plane.

Sending up a plume of sparks, the jumbo Airtech plunged through a fence and across the grass, until at last it came to a shuddering halt. Immediately fire spewed out around the wings, and Wilcox and Brody, gasping for breath, once more began to run.

For Wilcox, the next few minutes became a blur of frenzied activity—catching passengers as they hurtled down the chutes, pushing them away and shouting "RUN! RUN!" swinging back to grab other catapulting bodies, jerking at arms and legs and yelling into faces.

A wind came up momentarily and blew the flames sideways, so the air cooled. Five passengers at once, and then six more, hurtled down the chutes, and then a rush of passengers poured out in a literal flood. One of them, a teenager, was pushed, or misjumped, and tumbled over the edge and fell a room's height to the ground. Out of the corner of his eye, Wilcox saw the youth pick himself up and hip-hop away.

The wind died and as the flames surged again toward the fuselage the heat became more intense. Wilcox smelled singed hair and wondered if it was the hair on his own arms.

He reached for a child and saw the top of the chute curl up in flame and disappear, dropping at the high end so the little boy fell six feet. Before he could act, flames crept along the ground and enveloped the child, but he could still see him down inside, and he dashed into the center and grabbed up the screaming boy, then turned from the plane and ran, beating at flames as he went.

Heat followed, and he wondered if he himself were on fire, but he couldn't stop running.

Halfway to the Airtech factory, he caught up with the rest of the passengers. Brody saw him coming. "Duck!" he shouted, "EVERY-BODY DOWN!"

Wilcox dropped to the ground, still carrying the child, and placed one arm over the boy and another over his own head.

Tensed and curled up, he waited.

The world exploded. Under his body the ground shook, and overhead, sparks and debris swirled upward in a blazing holocaust and rained down all around them.

People jumped up, flailing at burning embers, and were pushed down again by others, who beat out flaming clothes. Through the cries and confusion, Wilcox saw there were heroes everywhere.

At last the worst of the firefall died down and people backed farther away, watching mesmerized as fire engines poured foam on the burning plane.

Wilcox was still clutching the child when a woman ran up crying, "Peter! Oh, Peter!" and grabbed him away, saying nothing at all to Wilcox. Somehow her behavior didn't seem out of place or even strange.

To Wilcox, nothing that had happened that day was real.

Soon medics swarmed over the area, talking to dazed passengers, taking a few people away on stretchers.

Brody said, "We'd better find a phone and make a report."

"Let's go back to Airtech," Wilcox said. "The airport will be overrun."

Walking slowly for what seemed the first time that day, Wilcox felt his energy drain away so he could no longer stand straight. Every muscle was limp, and the sag was in his emotions as well; he could hardly react when Brody drew up short and said, "Jesus, what's this?"

Dispirited, Wilcox came up and looked down at the orange-jacketed body lying face down in the grass. "He's dead!" he said with new energy. "How in the hell . . ." He bent down for a closer look. "I spoke to him. Earlier, I talked to this man. He was . . ." Something came back to him then, an expression on the man's face, a look of arrogance, of triumph . . . a challenging, half-crazed look of confrontation that Wilcox seemed to understand better now than he had earlier.

Brody was watching him expectantly.

Wilcox said, "I think he's our saboteur."

Brody nodded. "I know he is. I saw his picture." He looked at Alan and smiled. "But I would have believed you without it."

Three hundred ten of three hundred twenty-one passengers aboard TAF flight 255 lived, including the pilot and copilot. Among the survivors were a Bennett Bergman and his wife, Millie. Having seen the spoilers for themselves, they were trying desperately to reach an investigator named Wilcox.

The press swooped in for the story, learning quickly from survivors that Mark Brody and Alan Wilcox had remained at the escape chutes pulling people off until the last possible second. The press wanted to declare them heroes, but Brody refused to take any credit. "The passengers who lived can thank Alan Wilcox," he said. "Of everyone remotely connected with this event, only Wilcox understood what was going to happen and acted on it. Without him, there would have been no warning sent to the tower—and probably no survivors."

The statement given, he looked around for Wilcox so he could drive his friend home. But Wilcox was gone.

Having been awake continuously for twenty-nine hours, Wilcox was too dazed to be rational. Blinking steadily to keep his eyes open, he drove the two hours to Santa Ana with a single thought running through his mind: *The spoilers went up too soon. He screwed up. Even a genius screws up.* It became a litany because his mind refused to focus on anything else.

When at last he pushed open his front door, Ellie was waiting for him. To his surprise, she drew him into her arms wordlessly, holding him against her and rubbing his back. In a rush of fatigue, his knees turned rubbery and his vision clouded and streaked. Yet he yearned to remain there for as long as she would have him.

Something was bothering him, though; he finally remembered what it was. "Todd . . . find a specialist for Todd . . ." He was too tired for further words.

Taking his hand, she led him to the bedroom, and when he flopped down aimlessly, unable to do much about his clothes, she pulled off his shoes and pants, wrenched the blankets out from under him and tucked them around his shoulders. He supposed she'd pull the drapes and shut the door, but he didn't stay awake long enough to find out if she actually did.

Miles Kimball drove home again knowing he would pay the ultimate price for his affair and for keeping silent about Rudy Malec: he would have to go on living. He wasn't a murderer, it seemed. Just a philanderer. And weak. Embarrassingly weak. He was pulling into the driveway when it occurred to him the note was still on Rudy Malec's locker. He stomped on the brake, hard, and sat there thinking . . . about what would happen, about the questions they could ask, about getting the story off his chest, at last. With Malec gone, the evil was out of his life, leaving only a self-consuming conscience; now he knew penance would find him, track him down, come knocking at his door. Somehow the thought made him smile and his old irreverence was back. *The devil made me do it, he thought. I'll tell them I've been under a spell, communing with Satan. They don't need to know I've made love to Satan's aunt.*

When Alan awoke it was almost dark. He opened his eyes tentatively, aware of a bewildering mix of feelings. Now that he'd been vindicated, where was the elation? The rejoicing? Why, when he'd never before doubted his instincts or wavered from his convictions, did he now suspect he'd spent himself foolishly?

Eyes fully open, he tried to take stock.

Exoneration had come, but at a price; lives had been saved, but they'd cost him. His son might have to get used to an artificial foot. After twenty-five exceptional years, his marriage had eroded, becoming ragged and frayed like a flag that has flapped too long in the wind. He wasn't sure he and Ellie would ever get back to where they'd been— that he would ever quite believe in her essential fairness, or she would ever quite trust him not to shut her out.

When at last his feet were on the floor, every muscle ached. He wondered vaguely how many people he'd literally thrown off the exit chutes. His arms said it had to be hundreds.

He pulled on his pants, wishing he could put aside his pessimism. It lay on him like dank earth, warning that his job was still at risk and his marriage more so. When would he feel the satisfaction that is supposed to come after one is finally justified?

Possibly never.

For now he felt nothing very much. Just tired.

He ran fingers through his hair. Only then did he think of the specialist. Had he ever mentioned it to Ellie?

It was time he saw his son; he began moving a little faster. When he reached the family room, Ellie was making him a sandwich. She held it out to him. "Eat this, honey. If we hurry, we can just make visiting hours. Todd doesn't believe you want to see him."

The doorbell rang just as Wilcox reached for the doorknob. He jerked the door open and pulled back, surprised. In the light from his porch he saw a man holding a large camera at face level. Before he could speak, a flashbulb blinded him.

When his vision cleared, Wilcox saw a van at the curb with antennae sprouting from its roof and another vehicle just pulling up.

"Alan Wilcox," a voice called out of the darkness, "did you know the president of the United States is going to call you?"

"No," said Alan, pushing his way past someone carrying a mini-cam. He found himself bathed in a sudden flood of light. "What's all this?"

The man followed them down the walkway and so did the lights. "Your boss, Mark Brody, has called you a world-class investigator. What do you have to say?"

Wilcox was opening the car door for Ellie. Turning, he grinned at the reporter. "Well, I'm not going to argue with him."

Without success he tried to open the car door on his side, hampered by a second reporter grabbing his arm. "Do you feel like a hero, Mr. Wilcox?"

"No," he said, wrenching his arm free and at last sliding into the car. "Let me close this, please. That word doesn't apply. Investigating accidents is what I do. Now if you'll let us go—"

"Mr. Wilcox! Mr. Wilcox!" A second camera had suddenly appeared next to his window. "Did you know they've found a strangled body and a murderer—both near the scene of the accident? What is your reaction?"

Wilcox shook his head. *I'm not through with this yet.* He said, "I'll have to react for you later." Resigned, he stuck his head out the window. "Come back tomorrow at ten and I'll give you a statement." But it wouldn't be much, he thought as he backed carefully down the driveway, not with Board policy being what it was. Minimal, factual, and open-ended was what they'd get. He hoped, by the time the Board issued its conclusions, there'd be a few members of the press still interested.

Todd was lying in a cranked-up bed with his shoulders against a mound of pillows and his bandaged foot in a sling. His head was still locked into a halo with four silver rods reaching down into a thick jacket. He looked up at them uncertainly. "Hello, Dad. I thought you wouldn't . . . I guess I pretty much screwed up."

"You pretty much did." Alan looked down at Todd, wondering what part of him he dared touch. The shoulders were buried in cloth; the head had a ring around it; one of the legs was off limits. He considered the nearest hand. *Should I hold it or shake it?*

He smiled. "You look as fragile as an egg."

Todd laughed. "I'm glad you're not mad."

"No. I'm not mad." *What am I? Disheartened, I guess.* "How do you feel? Do you hurt anywhere?"

"Just my left foot, but they give me shots. I'm sorry about . . . well, everything. I guess the car's totaled."

"It probably is."

"I didn't mean to wreck the car."

"I don't imagine you did." *But how about yourself?* Wilcox turned and walked to the window. *Why can't I say what should be said? You've*

made a mess of things, Todd, your body will never be normal, you'll
be a cripple for life, and I'm not sure you've learned a lesson even
now. Just because you've got an artificial foot doesn't mean you won't
drink.

"Dad . . ."

He turned around.

"A foot doctor came in this morning and took more X rays. He asked
if I'd ever seen the basketball player who's got an artificial leg. I knew
what he meant. He didn't have to . . ." his voice wavered "hedge around
like that."

Wilcox glanced at Ellie. She was brushing at her eyes, but smiling
determinedly. A strained silence settled over the room. *He's not dead,*
thought Wilcox. *Better plastic than dead.*

Todd was speaking again. "When the doctor came back this afternoon, I asked if he knew the guy who won a rough water swim with
an artificial foot. He said he didn't—who? I said I'd give him a year
to figure it out."

The call from Brody came to Todd's room some time later. "It's
for you, Dad."

Brody got right to the point. "I know you're with your family, Alan.
But a member of the five-man board called just now and asked me to
relay a message. I promised I'd try to reach you. The members have
asked you to consider filling a forthcoming vacancy on the executive
board. They want me to persuade you it's for the good of the country—to give the NTSB the kind of positive image it needs. Something
about additional funding from Congress."

Wilcox said, "I promised my son I'd give up this line of work,
I—" Peripherally aware of motion, he turned and saw Todd waving
his hand. Unable to shake his head, the boy mouthed words: No, Dad!
No!

Alan smiled. "I seem to be getting a message. I think Todd wants
me to stay on." He glanced at Ellie. She nodded affirmatively.

"I'll tell you what, Mark. I'm inclined to go on doing what I've
done all along—because I think I do it well. But tell the Board to give
me a week. Who knows what I'll decide?"

On the way home Ellie said, "All along, I think Todd understood
your job better than I did. But he didn't want to admit it. He needed
an excuse for his drugs."

She fell silent as he began negotiating the curves to their house. Then she said, "I tried to call you in the middle of the night, when I saw your note. I—"

"Tried to call me where?"

"The office."

"Ah." He nodded. "It was you. I had no time to—"

She cut him off. "I let you down, Alan. After Jamie's wedding my feelings got in the way and I couldn't imagine living with you anymore. I was a fool."

Absently she smoothed her skirt and dropped her hands in her lap. "Last night I was thinking, Good Lord, what's changed? He's *always* done whatever was most important at the moment, whether I understood the reasons or not. Whether anyone understood. The wedding was just another example." She smiled sadly. "God, what a wife I've been!"

"Oh, come on, Ellie."

"I was angry. Furious. I watched your friends blasting you out of the water and did . . . nothing."

"Sure you did. You hit me over the head with the life preserver!"

She turned to him. "Be serious, Alan. If it's any help, I *respect* you. Sometimes, I think, respect is more important to a marriage than love."

"Is that what you think?" He let her words simmer a bit. He supposed it was a compliment. But not exactly what he'd been looking for. He reached over and took her hand. "When we get home, babe, we'll have the house to ourselves. We can respect each other out of our minds."

She smiled.

As they pulled into the driveway his pager went off.

For the briefest moment he and Ellie looked at each other in dismay. And then, spontaneously, they began to laugh. "Did you hear something?" he asked.

"No," said Ellie. "Did you?"